I0772358

The War Between Us

The War Between Us

Fearless Sons of Erin and the Time Traveler Series

2

TARA NOLAN

THIS IS FOR THE
WARRIORS WHO WILL
RISK IT ALL FOR THEIR
PEOPLE.

Author's Note

The War Between Us contains dark content that may be triggering to some. You can find a list of possible triggers at the end of the book. It is not intended for those younger than 18 years of age.

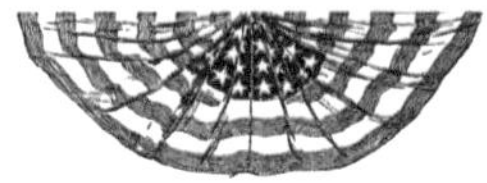

A glossary of language translations provided at the end of the story.

CHAPTER ONE

Emilia

December 1861 ~ Boston

The fire crackled as I stood before it, arms wrapped around my middle as if I could hold myself together. Nervous didn't come close to what I felt at that moment.

By now, eleven states had seceded from the Union, making up the Confederacy and causing Lincoln to call for 75,000 troops in the spring, and when that proved not enough, another 500,000 a few months later. With July came the Union's defeat at the Battle of Manasses. A quick punch in the face to let us know this war wouldn't be won so quickly.

And what a shit show it was when Congress announced they would fight to preserve the Union rather than end slavery.

Tempers flared, to say the least.

Of course, Shay and I knew this. We knew that there was more to come. More bloodshed. More pain. More death. It wasn't a surprise when they wanted to recruit more men for a war that was supposed to end in three months. It didn't even surprise me that Thomas had enlisted as soon as his shoulder healed.

No. What took me by surprise was my family's history, my mother's death, and what I planned to do about it. I couldn't find her murderer; my father already killed him. I refused to take revenge on his family. I would not become the monster I sought to destroy.

I sighed. I'd been over it a thousand times, and I knew what I had planned was the path I needed to take. There was no turning back.

A sudden, loud knock on the bakery door startled Shay and me, pulling us out of the trance we had fallen into around the crackling fireplace.

Turning slowly, I tensed as I prepared to see him, my heart racing with anticipation.

Rose threw a rag over her shoulder and gestured for her daughter Mira to unlock the door.

I rolled my lips between my teeth, my nerves getting the best of me even as my heart swelled as I took in sweet George, who had helped look for Shay when she went missing upon entering the nineteenth century. He leaned in one of the chairs by the hearth, waiting with a patience I had yet to achieve. And then his wife, Rose—the bull-headed, no-nonsense, loving woman I grew to respect—tidying up the already clean shelves.

Most may have known them as the owners of the bakery, one of the few black family-owned businesses on that street, a considerable feat in that century, I learned. But to us, they were our rescuers. They took us in at the most challenging time of our lives, giving us a place to live and food in our bellies. I could never repay the kindness they bestowed upon us, but I'd spend the rest of my days trying.

I frowned as Mira wrung her hands all the way to the door. Though naturally timid, one would think she'd be comfortable in her home.

I guessed the blasted war could be blamed for that as well, sparing no one from its crushing grip.

I let out a sigh, heavy with two months of waiting. Each day dragged on, filled with doubts, fear, and the anticipation of departure, permeating the air as the winter chill seeped into my bones.

It hadn't always been that way. At first, time flew by quickly with the excitement of action. Then December came along, and they mustered Boston's 28th Massachusetts Regiment to train at Camp Cameron, and time slowed, darkening my world with anxiety as heavy as the snow-laden clouds.

The end of my time with my loved ones drew near, and though the days crawled with quiet dread, they were few in between. The bitter reality that this war could rob me of the opportunity to see them again fell on my shoulders like a shroud of regret, even as I knew I had to fight—a propulsion of duty I would willfully bear again.

Every man prepared supplies, their hearts no doubt as heavy as mine while they said farewells to their loved ones. It didn't matter if they rallied to join the war. Saying goodbye would be the hardship we all had to carry.

War may have been a bitch, but we heeled accordingly.

Now, the door swung open on rusty hinges, letting in a fierce, cold wind, and the man I loved with my entire soul. Despite the cold, a warm shiver ran down my spine.

My breath caught in my throat as Thomas took off his indigo hat, his eyes flashing a darker green as he stared at me. Clean-shaven for the first time since I met him, I marveled at his newly defined face and shuffled my feet, self-conscious as my eyes roamed over how well his coat fit his broad chest, it pulling just slightly on the gold buttons adorning it. I swallowed and looked away, tugging on my baggy clothes in discomfort.

"Ye look good, gypsy."

I scowled, glaring at my sky-blue pants that hid all of my curves. It was a blessing to lose weight since joining the nineteenth century. It would help keep up my disguise, but that didn't mean I wanted *Thomas* to see me as a man.

I nodded, avoiding everyone's gaze and my irrational thoughts.

"Lass," he said, suddenly in front of me, tilting my chin up as his thumb brushed my cheek, sending shivers down my spine. "What is it? Ye aren't having second thoughts, are ye?"

"No." To my surprise, my lips began to turn up into a smile.

"I can't believe you're doing this," Shay said for the millionth time, bracing herself on the table as she struggled to stand and came over to me. Her pregnant belly looked like it was ready to pop. She was due within the next month. I avoided the pain in my chest at having to miss the birth. *She'll be okay.* Shay was one of the strongest people I knew. There would be no complications.

"You know I have to do it," I said, grabbing her hand, thankful that I had my best friend travel with me back to the nineteenth century. "For

Mammina. For you." I eyed her stomach, seething at what those men had done to her. A part of me wondered if they would have done it to any woman or if they singled her out because of her race.

She scoffed. "We already know how the war ends, Mill." She whispered it so nobody but me and Thomas could hear. Rose and George kept busy with the inventory to let me say goodbye, pretending they weren't listening. "You don't have to prove yourself to me."

"For Mammina, then. My family was enslaved, Shay." I shook my head in disbelief at the injustice dealt to the Romany people. Why wasn't this discussed more in school? Why did I have to travel to another century to learn this from my biological father? Who, mind you, had to reveal my mother's history for me to find out. "I have to fight for them."

"But pretending to be an Irishman?" She raised her eyebrows, face alight with humor as she eyed my tan skin and womanhood hidden beneath my clothing.

I suppressed a grin even as the memory of enlisting returned. I was scared as hell, trembling in my boots with my newly shaved head. At first, Thomas was furious, threatening to lock me up. Michael thought I'd lost my mind. And Shay put her head in her hands, a look of understanding washing over her, as if she'd just remembered that women fought in the war disguised as men.

I signed the papers and took my father's name—Eamonn O'Connor. *I could have been Thomas' long-lost cousin, for all these people knew.* I had shaved three years off my age and gave them my height, eye color, and complexion. Remembering that Thomas once told me he was from Lansdowne, Ireland, I also wrote it down.

When it came time for my physical exam, I nearly threw up out of anxiety. The doctors were ordered to give thorough physicals, asking the men to strip down. However, Thomas had told me they didn't follow those guidelines, wanting to evaluate and produce soldiers as quickly as possible. But how was I to know I wouldn't get the doctor who followed the rule book to a T?

So, when it was my time to stand in front of the doctor, I shook with trepidation, praying that he would let me keep my clothes on.

When there was no threat of him exposing my womanhood, I let out a breath of relief, not knowing what I would have done.

The doctor, a small but formidable man, tapped the man before me on the chest a few times and made him hop around on one foot before sending him on his way. I mentally reminded myself not to mess with the binding around my breasts, not wanting to draw the medical examiner's attention to it.

With his attention on me, the doctor verified I had all my fingers to pull a trigger.

"Walk for me," he commanded. Feeling foolish, I took a few steps. After that spectacular examination, he deemed my feet sturdy enough to support me.

He grabbed my hands. Feeling my soft palms, he raised a cynical brow. "And what type of work have these hands done?"

"Whatever blows me way, sir," I said it in my best Irish accent as he had me flex my fingers. I narrowed my eyes in what I hoped passed for annoyance and shrugged. "Mainly singing at whatever place will have me."

His thick brows knitted together. "You sing?"

"Aye."

Lips pursed, he checked something off his list before grabbing my chin and inspecting my lack of facial hair. "How old are you, boy?"

"Eighteen, sir." It was the youngest age I could use to enlist. I didn't want to take any chance of them turning me away.

"Open," he said, sticking his finger in my mouth to check my teeth. I cursed myself for getting braces as a kid. My teeth were too white and straight for this time. Too pretty to be used as tools to rip open cartridges.

"Are you considered Black Irish, per chance?" he asked.

I shrugged, grateful for the out he just gave me. "It runs in me family. Me mother's side. Strong Italian blood, that one." At least the Italian part was genuine. He didn't need to know it was from my Papà's side, but I couldn't reveal that and take the O'Connor name.

He only nodded, jotting something down in his notes, and with a quick flick of his hand, told me to go before signing the papers and turning towards the next man. There was a line out the door, and he had no time to waste.

I stumbled out, thanking him as I tried to stop shaking. Thomas straightened up from the side of the building where he'd been leaning, waiting for me. He'd enlisted only a few days prior and prepared me for what to expect.

"Ye are out of your mind," he said as we walked down the street. "I suppose I can't talk ye out of it, lass?" He watched the people go by, avoiding my gaze. "I don't know what I'll do if something happens to ye."

I went to grab his arm but let my hand fall back to my side. We were in public, and I couldn't forget my disguise. "I could say the same thing about you, soldier."

His eyes caught mine.

Thomas may not have been thrilled about it, but I, a newly enlisted soldier in the 28th Regiment of Massachusetts, was filled with an unexpected surge of pride as I clutched my enlistment paper. I was about to embark on a mission that surpassed any of my previous endeavors, even my time-traveling. I was about to fight for a cause that would put an end to slavery, preserve the Union, and jumpstart the Reconstruction Era.

Well, I couldn't shoulder all that responsibility, but I would fight for the people's injustice and the necessary changes in the country.

This is for you, Mammina.

"Mill?" Shay asked, pulling me out of the memory. Everyone was staring at me now, waiting for me to answer.

What did she say? I thought about it a second. *Oh, right. Pretending to be an Irishman.* I gave her a cheeky grin and shrugged. "What can I say? I have a thing for Irishmen."

Thomas let his head fall back, exasperated, as Shay and I grinned. Suddenly, an overwhelming sadness filled me, and I embraced my friend awkwardly, trying not to bump her belly. I would miss these moments.

"Are you sure you're going to be okay?" I asked.

"Get out of here." She shoved me towards the door. "And come back in one piece so you can meet your little niece or nephew."

That had me bouncing on my toes with excitement. "Maybe both," I said, earning me a glare that had me laughing. My friend had enough to deal with, and twins wouldn't be added to the mix.

Hopefully.

I grabbed my bag, pulled it over my shoulders, and fastened the canteen to my side. After another quick go-through, I noted that I had everything. A part of me knew I was putting off saying goodbye one last time.

Through a watery smile, I waved at the room of people watching me go and prayed I could hold it together.

Immediately out the door, the wind whistled down the street, hitting me firmly in the face so my lungs burned, my eyes watered, and I cursed my short hair for not keeping me warm. I pulled my coat tighter and looked back at the bakery, not knowing when I'd see it again.

Another stray tear fell. *Damn it.*

"So, have you seen your brother?" I asked Thomas, voice tight. I didn't meet his gaze as I pretended it didn't matter. That I hoped to see Michael before we left because the bastard was growing on me.

It was damn annoying.

We had already said goodbye to his family the day before, but Michael didn't show. Then we stopped by to see Hiram and Evaline, not wanting to upset the child on the day of our departure. Seeing how she clung to Thomas' neck made my throat constrict with emotion. The way he interacted with her and took her well-being into account, I knew he'd be a great father one day. His eyes said it all when they lit up whenever he spotted the girl. I smiled sadly, wishing I could see him with his children someday, knowing that wasn't possible.

Not when I'd be gone.

"Nay, haven't seen him in days." Disappointment overwhelmed me. Thomas bent closer to study my face. "Why?"

"No reason. Let's go."

"Without sayin' goodbye?" a familiar voice asked from around the corner of the bakery. I spun on my heels, beaming at the man who spent hours training me every morning.

"You showed up." I couldn't stop my grin from spreading. "I thought maybe you didn't want to see me leave."

Michael scrunched up his face. "Don't go thinkin' this means more than it is." He pointed at me menacingly.

"You do have a heart," I cooed, ignoring his scowl. He secretly adored me. I knew it. "Were you waiting to say bye to me?"

Michael rolled his eyes to the sky and sighed, and I knew I was right. "Don't forget where ye are at all times." He looked at me pointedly. "I don't want those arseholes pickin' on me wee novice."

My grin faded but didn't disappear as he reminded me of what I had to do.

I surprised both of us when I threw my arms around him in a rare embrace. "Thank you. For everything," I whispered. Then, stunning me, his arms began to lift, coming uncomfortably around me. I laughed as he patted my shoulder.

"Just stick 'em with the pointy end, and ye should do fine."

"You can't just admit you'll miss me, can you?"

"Never." His smile was wicked, and I had to laugh.

This was the moment I had been waiting for. "I guess I should give this back to you," I said, reluctantly pulling the knife out that Michael let me borrow.

He held up his hands, taking a step back. "Keep it."

"Really?"

"Think of it as an early Christmas gift."

"I didn't get you anything, though." He shrugged, and I swallowed around a lump forming in my throat. Michael had shown up for me in ways that made me question whether he was all that bad or if it was just a long-winded charade. I kept my assessment to myself, knowing he'd deny it. I fought back a sad smile as I busied myself by putting the dagger away, allowing my eyes to dry. "Thank you."

"If I would have known ye would be so weepy about it, I would have taken the damn thing back," he growled.

I let out a watery chuckle.

Growing serious, I lifted my chin to the closed door of the bakery. "Keep her safe, will you?"

"Emilia—" Thomas warned.

"Aye, ye have me word," Michael cut his brother off, stunning Thomas into silence. I watched as Michael took in Thomas' clenched jaw and the crease between his brows, his brother's demeanor causing him to straighten. "Look, Tommy—"

"Stay out of trouble, will ye?"

"Ye know I can't promise ye that." Michael's lips curved up in a grin that was closer to a sneer than a genuine smile.

Thomas's eyes narrowed. "Just don't die while I'm gone, aye?"

"I suspect I'll be right here when ye get back."

Thomas raised his brow but didn't question him further. Instead, he looked down, suddenly looking uncomfortable. "Listen. Maybe we can—"

"Kill me some rebels, and I might let ye back in me good graces."

Thomas growled, but Mikey was already backing up, smiling his irritating smile.

"Have a good fight, deartháir!" Michael said, before tilting his hat at me. "Cousin. I knew one way or another ye would make it as a part of this family."

My cheeks flamed as he walked off in the direction of the docks.

"Ye we were good for him," Thomas said with a bit of awe. "It's a mystery to me." He shook his head and turned to me, thankfully not mentioning his brother's comment.

"Ye ready?" he asked, voice gruff. My insides melted as his green eyes burned into me. I didn't know what I did to earn it, but I'd do it again to keep him looking at me like that.

I gave him my best grin and adjusted the pack on my shoulders. "Let's go."

CHAPTER TWO

Michael

December 1861

"Hold on tight, doll," Mikey growled before he shoved himself into the whore he had bent over the back of the bed. He'd done little to warm her up and was rewarded with a muffled scream as he pounded into her, the sound making him feral.

Gripping Keena's thin hips, he looked over her head of long dark hair to the other two women on the bed. A curvy ginger knelt behind the petite blonde, her delicate fingers snaking around to grasp Alma's small breasts.

"Do ye like this, daidí?" Nessa asked, addressing Mikey and not the woman she was handling. *Do I like it? Yes, I bloody well like it.* And the bitch knew it too. Mikey's grin twisted cruelly at the mischief—the sheer unruliness—dancing in her green eyes.

"Harder," he growled even as he picked up his pace.

Alma's head fell back onto Nessa's shoulder, her body shuttering as Nessa's hand skimmed down her stomach to the blonde apex of her thighs, making her moan deep and loud right before she pinched her nipple. Gods, they were a sight to behold.

Alma's gasp had Mikey pulling out, giving himself a minute, lest this end too soon.

Each slag looked towards him, waiting for his demands like good lasses.

It had taken some time for them to learn what he liked, how he want-ed it—compliant, docile, sweet little toys he had molded over the last few months. Though Nessa tended to dance along the edge, pushing slightly against his demands. Mikey swore she liked him riding on the edge of anger just as much as he wanted her to submit beneath him.

He walked around the bed until he was in front of Nessa, her fingers still diving in and out of Alma. The girl looked like she was about to come.

"Stop," he ordered.

A wicked grin spread across his lips at the dejection in Alma's blue eyes—her sweet face flushed as she panted. Oh, she was close.

Good. She could wait.

"Take care of Keena, dove," he told Alma. "Don't ye dare touch yeself."

Alma bit her pretty pink lip as she climbed off the bed. "Yes, daidí."

A crooked finger had Nessa crawling over to him.

"On your back," he commanded.

A devilish smile crested her lips as she knelt there and dipped her fingers into her center. Mikey flipped her onto her stomach, hands pinned to the mattress as he leaned most of his weight on her. His lips brushed the back of her ear, and she stiffened beneath him. "Naughty thing. Just for that, ye are going to be punished."

Her only response was a thrust of her hips, her round ass pushing against him. He flipped her over again, her breasts bouncing as she laughed darkly. His lip pulled back as he held in a growl. He hadn't broken her yet.

Soon. Soon, she'd be begging him.

Mikey thrust inside her, watching her full tits bounce up and down as he took her roughly. Each of her legs up around his shoulders as he pushed harder, deeper until he knew she wanted to moan. He could see it in the tension of her body, even as her green eyes lit in defiance.

He gripped Nessa's hands in one of his own and pinned them back to the bed as his other wrapped around her neck, showing her who was in charge. When she began to squirm, fighting him, he thrust harder. Nessa's head bent back, eyes closing as he squeezed her throat. Oh, she enjoyed this, the damn spitfire. Using all of his weight, Mikey kept moving inside Nessa, kept her pinned so she couldn't move an inch. When she was nothing other than a gash to enjoy, he looked at the other two.

Keena's hips were undulating with the pace of Alma's fingers, her tan body flush with the rising orgasm, her dark hair swinging in sync with her small tits. *Feckin' hell*. He shouldn't have quit her so soon.

Mikey quickened his pace as Keena's head fell back, a loud moan breaking from her and wracking her entire body as it twitched with each rolling quake.

"Feckin' *hell*," he growled, tightening his hold on Nessa's throat. "Did ye like that?" he asked her. Grabbing her chin roughly, he made her look at him. "Do ye want to come?"

"No," she gasped, throat still raw from his stronghold.

Mikey sneered. "Good."

He pushed himself back enough for his hand to come between them, his thumb making quick circles over her center. She squirmed away, exciting him more as her body shattered.

Quick, deep breaths gave him a spectacular view of her creamy breasts, her pink nipples begging him to take one into his mouth.

He did that a moment later, letting it go with a pop.

"Asshole," she grumbled as she went lax.

"Cunt." He whispered into her ear, "Your punishment for warming up."

Mikey pulled out of Nessa, ignoring her sneer—oh, she definitely enjoyed defying him—and motioned for Alma to come to him as he lay on the other side of the bed.

"Hop on, wee dove."

Alma—the youngest and smallest of the three, still unmarked by the hardships of their world, her pale skin flawless except for the rising red in her cheeks—crawled to him slowly. She was a thin thing, hips slightly flared, breasts too small to hold but peaked enough to bounce above him. She straddled his hips and waited, biting her lip at his size.

"It'll fit this time, dove," Mikey encouraged. "Take your time."

Hands behind his head, he watched Alma rise on her knees, her small hand guiding him to her entrance. This was her reward for not coming yet, for being a good lass.

He didn't let himself think of how her family sold her to Nora's establishment, how this sweet girl, just past marrying age, would be used so that her family could eat. How they could sleep at night was beyond him, and he ignored the desire to hunt them down.

No. Mikey shut out those thoughts. Told himself he'd treat her right. As long as it meant he'd be inside her soon. He paid good money to be her first all those months ago and planned to teach her everything he knew before another man touched her. He just needed her body to take him. All of him.

Alma froze, body rigid with pain.

"Help her," he demanded. The thought of Alma enduring any more pain, especially after being thrown to the wolves, by her own feckin' family, no less, made Mikey's stomach turn. He wouldn't exacerbate an already shitty situation. At the very least, he could spare the lass a fate at the hands of a cruel man. A courtesy no one had extended to him after immigrating all those years ago...

Nessa was behind her promptly, hand warming the girl up as Keena began to kiss Alma—hard and savagely. It was a distraction, he knew, to get the lass's body to relax, but he also wondered, not for the first time, if Keena had feelings for Alma. He often caught the two making quick glances at one another.

Mikey's hand roamed over Keena's round ass, distracted by her body. He let out a hiss as Nessa began to push Alma further onto his dick. He froze at how tight she was but didn't move. This was for her. He wanted her to take what she wanted so he could finally be seated so far in her that he'd see stars.

"C'mon, dove. Show me what ye got."

A nervous glance towards Keena. "I don't know—"

Keena's eyes were worried as she looked at Mikey, and he knew what she was about to say.

"I want both of ye to warm her up." His eyes then pierced Alma's. "I'm going to take care of ye, dove. Ye just sit still."

She nodded, her blond hair spilling across her forehead.

"Good, girl."

He grabbed her hips and slowly began to push his way up as he watched the women work Alma. The little devil watched them use her body, her chest heaving with the increasing pressure. Mikey ground his teeth, his muscles taught with restraint from wanting to shove himself inside her in one quick, shattering thrust. He may be a monster, but he couldn't break *this* girl. That was a line he wouldn't cross.

"C'mon," he growled, rotating his hips for a better angle. She gasped as he sunk in another inch. "Feckin' *hell*!" She felt good. "That's right."

The women's hands moved faster, building Alma towards an orgasm, making him slide in farther. "Good girl," he bit out, feeling her body spasm around him. Nessa's hand flew, causing Alma to moan so loudly that he shoved so deep inside her that he choked back a growl.

Her body rocked backward as her orgasm burst through her, and Mikey began to piston in and out of her so quickly that he had to sit up and hold her tiny body to him as he took her like an animal.

Her tiny tits bounced in front of his face. His reward for being so patient. He looked at Keena, his grin nothing but wicked as he watched worry flash in her dark eyes. Oh, there was no doubt about it now. The lass loved Alma.

"Do ye like me inside ye, dove?" he asked Alma loud enough for them to hear while his hand skimmed down her spine, causing her to shiver.

"Oh, yes, daidí." Alma's blue eyes flared with lust as Mikey was finally inside her after taking it so slow.

"Show me."

Mikey lay back down as nervousness overcame her. Keena and Nessa began to guide her when he snapped. "Just her."

Slowly, oh so feckin' slow, she began to roll her hips. Mikey watched, a wicked grin on his face as Keena had to watch the entire thing.

"How often did ye think of feckin' me?"

"I wanted this for so long," she whimpered, hips moving faster as she lost herself in him. Mikey enjoyed watching her blue eyes as they moved from his large arms restrained behind his head, down to the ink on his chest, and then over the muscles rippling through his center, finally coming to rest at the point where their bodies joined. Where the wet sounds of her desire coated him. "Oh, god, it feels so good."

"That's right, dove. Take what ye really want."

Keena's eyes flared.

"Do ye want me to take ye?" he asked Alma.

"Please, daidí." Her small hands gripped his shoulders as her body rolled against him, demanding more. Wanting harder. "Feck me like ye feck Keena."

That had him pausing, his gaze connecting with Keena's.

"That I can do, lass."

He guided her to stand up and bent her over the back of the bed. She was so short he had to hold her hips up as he bent over her for a better position. And without further warning, as his searing blue eyes met Keena's, he shoved in full force.

Alma's cry nearly broke his eardrums, but he could no longer hold back. He was lost in the sensation of her tight, little body, of the rising red in Keena's cheeks—either from anger or lust, he didn't know or care. Feck. He pushed harder.

"Oh, yes!" Alma's screams of pain turned towards ecstasy. "Yes, daidí! Harder!"

Keena's eyes widened as she watched Alma and how she loved him inside her.

Feck the bed. Mikey picked her up and pounded inside her, the sound of their wet bodies smacking throughout the room. All the while, he kept eye contact with Keena. A quick jerk of his chin told Nessa to care for the lovesick woman.

She lay on the bed and sat Keena on her face, devouring her until Keena rode her tongue with soft moans.

He pressed his mouth to Alma's ear. "Ye see the way she looks at ye?" Alma looked at Keena as she bit back a moan. "She wants to be the one inside ye."

The wee dove's body constricted around him at the mention of it. *Interesting*.

"Why, ye filthy creature. Don't tell me ye want her as well?"

Alma's head fell back onto his shoulder as he held her up, still drilled inside her with such force that he was surprised she wasn't breaking apart.

"Watch her as she comes for ye," he said it loud enough for the room to hear.

Nessa added her fingers. *Not a stupid slag, after all*. Keena rode Nessa's tongue hard as she watched Alma. When the blood began to rise in her face, when her pace quickened, Mikey dropped his hand to Alma's center and rubbed. Gods, he was so hard it was painful.

The two women's eyes connected, and they shattered in unison, the view so beautiful that Mikey roared his release right after he pulled out of Alma and spilled all over her back.

He smeared it over her ass, marking Alma's first fully penetrated feck.

He'd found release but thought there would be something more to it. A sense of satisfaction, blissful achievement, or some shite like that.

Mikey scratched his rough stubble, mulling it over, and began to dress. Not sparing the women another glance as they recouped on the bed, Mikey was out the door without another word, ignoring the emptiness that seemed to gnaw at the edges of his soul.

"So?" a familiar voice asked after he thundered down the stairs and entered the saloon.

Mikey paused—reordering his posture, his face—before turning towards his men. He gave Georgie a serpentine smile that had the ginger roaring, pounding his twin's shoulder as he held out a hand.

"I told ye he would break her tonight."

Hughie slammed a wad of money into his brother's hand, scowling as he shifted the brunette on his lap. "Was it worth it?"

"What do ye think?" He sneered.

Mikey went to the counter, ignoring how his gut twisted as the men hollered obscenities behind him. Pushing away the weight settling over his shoulders, he ordered a round for his men. Maybe if he was wasted enough, he wouldn't have to think about the darkness slowly eating at him. Maybe he would believe the lie he told himself that he did her a favor by taking it slow, knowing another man would have ripped her in two without a second thought.

He gloried in the burn of the shot as it warmed the pit of self-loathing in his stomach and turned back to his men with a smile.

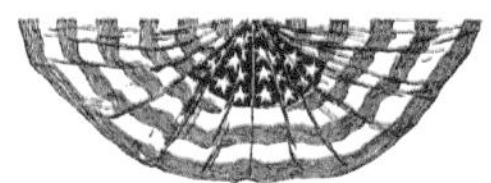

A few hours and a handful of tankards later, Mikey leaned back in his chair, an arm carelessly snaked around Nessa's waist as she sat on his lap. Nessa and

Keena came down shortly after, but Alma was to stay in for the night. He paid enough for her to remain solely his for some time.

Keena and Nessa, on the other hand...

"So..." Hughie leaned in, mischief dancing in his blue eyes. Mikey's body went taught, waiting. "Which of the brothers do ye like to bed more, ye she-devil?" Hughie knew that Nessa was Thomas's usual slag before the gypsy entered town. Asking her this was just to get her hackles to rise. Mikey relaxed. He didn't give two fecks what Nessa preferred.

Nessa studied her nails before slowly raising her gaze over Hughie's body. The twins were nothing special to look at, but with the work Mikey put them through and the fierce competition between the gangs, they had to hone their bodies to survive. They weren't as large as Mikey and Thomas; many weren't, but they had enough muscle to intrigue a woman.

She leaned forward and ran her hands up Hughie's legs. "I'm wondering whether ye and your dearthàir can handle me?"

Georgie raised a red brow. "Ye are something to look at, lass, but I don't think ye are as good—"

"Together," she interrupted.

Georgie choked on his drink as Nessa gave him a lazy smile and flicked a suggestive glance toward Hughie, whose tongue was down the same slag's throat that had been on his lap earlier. "But lose the other bitch," she hissed. "What do ye say?"

Georgie adjusted his pants and took Nessa in—the swell of her breasts and how her corset cinched her slender waist. Clearing his throat, Georgie stood and bent to speak into Hughie's ear.

Mikey watched the brothers, amused, as he drew small circles over Nessa's bare thigh.

"Make sure they're still able to walk when ye're done, lass," he told her. "It's not good for business if they ain't fit for a fight."

Nessa's gaze caught on an older man at the following table with two rough looking arseholes, faces hard as they drank, before her eyes quickly slid away. Mikey wouldn't have thought anything of it if it wasn't for how her body stiffened.

"Who's that?" he asked, tilting his chin to the older man. He looked familiar, but Mikey couldn't quite place where he had seen him. There was nothing remarkable to identify him, besides his grey beard and stark white hair under his hat.

"I'm not certain," she said, turning into Mikey's chest, trailing her lips distractedly up his neck.

Movement caught Mikey's attention, and he found the Callahan twins heading in his direction. He raised his brows, a genuine smile forming on his lips.

"Tell us, lass," Hughie growled. "Can ye take two men at once?"

"Only if ye promise not to hold back," Nessa purred as she rose like a cat eyeing a mouse.

Mikey laughed deeply as he slapped her ass and sent them on their way. "Go easy on them!" he called and laughed again at the grin she returned that would have made most men's knees quake.

Oh, those gobshites were in for a ride, though Mikey didn't envy them. He had his fill, and they could have his scraps. Nay, his craving was to share women, not another man crossing swords. That gombeen would certainly risk losing a limb for trespassing on Mikey's territory.

Mikey's smile faded as he sat back, taking in the room while he took a long pull of his drink. Again, his eyes found the man staring at him. So, it wasn't Nessa he was fixated on. *Interesting.* Mikey raised his tankard and the man returned the gesture.

A moment later, the barmaid set a bottle of whiskey before him.

"I didn't order that, doll," he murmured.

Her brown eyes found the man. "Incentive for a word with ye."

Mikey's brows rose with the glass of the best whiskey that could be purchased at Nora's. He held it up for the man to see, quickly scenting it for foul play before tasting it.

It went down smoothly.

Mikey spread his arms along the backs of the chairs as he watched the barmaid lean in and whisper his message into the man's ear. His gaze met Mikey's, acknowledging the request with a tilt of his hat. Rising steadily, Mikey noticed the older man's still muscular body and tan, indicating years of outdoor work, and wondered what his profession might be.

His two male companions remained at the table, both in their prime and looking as though they could hold their own in a fight, and watched as their mate came to join him.

Mikey threw them a wink before extending a hand for the man to sit. "What can I do for ye?"

Large hands rested on the table as the man sat.

"I should come to you for the type of... business I desire." The deep, strange accent was unexpected. He sounded southern, and probably a rebel at that. Mikey heard many on the docks but hadn't heard anything like this one before.

Mikey leaned back and took in the room, seemingly uninterested. "And what business is that?"

"Weapons."

"And what makes ye think I can attain anything of number? I'm unsure if ye're aware, but a war demands that particular shipment."

The man took a generous sip of his drink before gently placing it back on the table. "Word is, you are just the man to make it happen."

So, the rebel had been prowling. Mikey stiffened. His men hadn't informed him of a new man in the North End, let alone that he was asking around about *weapons*. "Let's say I could. Ye know, hypothetically." Mikey scratched the stubble along his jaw. "What would I get in return? Your money is useless up here—"

"Sugar." The rebel leaned back in his chair, looking like a man used to getting what he wanted. The arrogance practically seeped through his damn skin. Mikey raised his brows. *So that's what he deals in.* "I hear you Northerners have a shortage," he continued. "I'm sure it'd bring a pretty coin for anyone who can scavenge some. And I heard you are just the man I need." He spread his hands out. "Discreetly, of course."

Mikey's eyes flashed as he took the man in and leaned his arms slowly onto the table. "Then ye came to the right place."

He'd send his boys sniffing around later. Mikey wanted to know just who he was dealing with and how the bloody hell he had infiltrated his city without his knowledge. The fact that the man knew how to get by without setting an alarm concerned Mikey. Especially with eyes and ears lurking in all of the shadows. Did he stay on the outskirts? And, if he had the means, why would he come to Nora's and not one of the better establishments?

Regardless—Mikey relaxed and took another deep pull of the whiskey—no matter the man's secrecy, this transaction was too good to pass up, and Mikey would have him in his pocket soon enough.

CHAPTER THREE

Emilia & Thomas

"Over here," the guide for our group yelled.

Someone shoved into me, and I tripped. Before hitting the ground, a large hand tugged my arm, jerking me upright. Thomas stared straight ahead, probably not wanting to draw more attention to us. He had fallen quiet as more men surrounded us, withdrawing so far into himself that he barely looked at me. I busied myself with memorizing the lay of the land, ignoring the sting of his absence.

The 28th Regiment didn't take the ship to Long Island in Boston's Harbor like the previous regiments. Instead, we went farther inland to North Cambridge. The road we walked led from Cambridge Road and cut through the large farm used as our training camp. The road continued, crossing over a brook and a field farther on where we would do our drills.

Wooden buildings surrounded us, teeming with men going in and out of them like bees in a hive. We were headed to the barracks, where we would sleep until we completed our training.

I would have sighed at the relief from the cold when we entered the door at the end of the building, except there were so many of us in the long, narrow barrack that it was almost suffocating. Bunk beds lined both walls as we walked the aisle between them. Men shoved their packs onto the beds, claiming it before someone else.

I went to put mine above Thomas' when a man shoved me out of the way, throwing his stuff on the bed I chose.

My eyes widened at the older man—closer to forty rather than our twenty years. A mustache covered most of his face, his cheeks ruddy from too many days in the cold and sunken from lack of food. Though he was wiry and not much taller than I, I suspected he was stronger than he looked.

"Excuse me," I said roughly, my accent unfortunately cracking.

"Feck off," he snapped.

I began to back away, but he turned to me quickly, causing me to stumble backward in surprise. The man's body caved in, pulled back roughly by his coat. Swiftly righting himself, his fist flew at Thomas' face, which Thomas dodged easily while swinging his own into the man's gut. The guy wheezed, doubling over.

A crowd was gathering around, excited voices calling out to see what the fuss was about.

"Hey, is that Tommy?" a man asked.

Thomas looked over, clearly surprised that someone recognized him. "Sullivan?"

The distraction was long enough for the man who stole my bunk to punch Thomas' jaw.

Thomas grabbed the man, ready to tear into him, when I noticed the men farther away suddenly falling quiet, another man parting them like the Red Sea. *He must be someone important.* I snapped at Thomas, telling him as much.

He was closer now, so I shoved Thomas, making him momentarily lose balance, so he fell back into the bunk.

"What are ye—" Thomas started to ask before the man was barking out orders.

"What is going on here?"

"Who's asking?" a man somewhere in the crowd shouted.

"Captain," he yelled so the whole barracks could hear. "John Brennan. Now, is there a problem here?" His eyes darted between Thomas, now standing at attention, and the other man beside him. The two were the only ones disheveled. "I will not have fighting in my Company. If I find you disobey these orders, you will be punished swiftly. Is that clear?"

Everyone went quiet, standing at attention as he looked from Thomas to the man. No one answered him.

"A day of splitting logs for the two of you." He straightened and turned around to get a good look at everyone else. The group seemed to shrink back, not wanting to face his wrath.

Well, shit.

"It was my fault, sir. Captain. Sir." I stuttered the last out, unsure how to address him. We just arrived and were already in trouble. How much harder could life get?

I really didn't want to know the answer to that.

I felt Thomas's glare—clearly wanting me to shut up—but I didn't dare look at him, let alone snarl like I wanted.

Captain Brennan's eyes bore into me until I had to resist the urge to run. "You?" he asked incredulously.

"I take sole responsibility."

His eyebrows seemed to meet his hairline. "You shall carry out the same form of punishment, then."

"But—" I began.

"Are you questioning me, private?"

"No, sir."

"State your names."

Thomas answered before the captain looked pointedly at me, waiting.

"Eamonn O'Connor, sir."

"O'Connor? Are you in any relation to Private O'Connor here?"

"He's my cousin, sir."

Captain Brennan looked from Thomas to me, noting our height differences and contrast in complexions. His jaw clenched, though he didn't question it, and turned to the man who started the fight.

"Henry Barton, sir," my bully responded, face pinched with disdain as he stared at the wall ahead.

With a mild exasperation, our captain left us with an order to chop logs after our drills the next day, a chore apparently no man wanted to volunteer for. The man whose fault this was shoved past in search of a different bunk as he let out a stream of curses.

"Thomas—" I began.

"Not now," he grumbled, sitting on his bunk with his head in his hands.

"I'm sorry," I mumbled, grabbing my things.

God, am I cursed or something? Not even five minutes in the barracks, and I had Thomas chopping wood as punishment. I needed to do this on my own. Not only to prove it to myself but if I was to mess up or get caught, I wouldn't bring him down with me.

"Where ye going?"

"I wanted to do this," I whispered while the pain in my chest grew. "It is not your job to protect me. I think we should keep our distance."

"Tommy," Sullivan, the man who recognized Thomas earlier, popped up by my side. "Ye didn't tell me ye had a cousin. Where's Mikey?"

"Distant," Thomas said, standing up to shake Sullivan's hand. He looked a little older than Thomas, fresh lines creasing his eyes from days squinting in the sun, but it worked for him. His rugged appearance was softened by his wild blonde hair and blue eyes that twinkled with laughter as Thomas introduced us. They had worked on the docks together until Sullivan found work elsewhere. "And ye know Mikey." Thomas shrugged.

Sullivan shook his head, smirking knowingly. "Not his thing."

"Aye." Thomas smiled.

"Nice to meet ye," I said, pushing past to find another bunk.

Thomas grabbed my arm, but I pulled free, avoiding Sullivan's inquiring gaze.

"I'll see ye later," I said. "It's better if I find me own way and ye yours."

His fingers loosened reluctantly, and he let me go to find a bunk several rows down. A man was lying on the lower one, his arm draped over his face. I stared at him for a minute, wondering how he was sleeping through all of the commotion around him and if I should warn him that I would head on up.

"Are ye going to stand there all day?" he asked tiredly. So caught up in my indecision, I jumped and stuttered out a response.

He rolled over and faced the wall, muttering under his breath.

"Don't mind him," a man said behind me, smiling kindly over a journal he scribbled in. "Names George." He put out a hand covered in lead, his fingers long and surprisingly soft. "George Hall. Ye from Boston or—"

"Aye," I said, glancing at his journal curiously, and told him my name.

His head bobbed. "Ye must just have reached the age limit." He chuckled good-naturedly. "Ye look like a wee bairn."

I pretended to be busy putting my belongings on my bunk so he couldn't see my cheeks flush.

"I didn't mean to offend ye…" Hall said, moving to the edge of his bed as he scrubbed a hand through his short brown hair. "I just have an eye for—"

"Ye just called him a bairn," the man on the lower bunk said very close to my stomach. I stepped away quickly. "No man wants to be called that joining up in a war."

"Ach, I suppose you're right." Hall's eyes crinkled in regret.

"It's fine." I pitied the charming man and gave him a strained smile. "I get it all the time."

The man on the lower bunk unfurled himself, placing his head in his hands and smelling faintly of alcohol. I suspected he was nursing a wicked hangover. "Besides," he said, his brown eyes dancing when he looked at us. "O'Connor here just got in a brawl and was called out by the captain on the first day. That's gotta say something about his character, hm?"

My cheeks flared for the second time in a short span, but I was saved by a man who shoved into my shoulder. I used it as a sign to start climbing up the bunk. "It was just a misunderstanding."

"Misunderstanding or no," my bunkmate said, "the captain will have an eye on ye now. I don't envy ye." He laughed.

My face drained of all color as I plopped down on my flat mattress. How could I have messed this up so much already? And now Thomas was targeted as well. I fell back on the bed, feeling defeated.

"I'm John McNamee, in case ye were wonderin'." His brown eyes popped up beside my face, and I pulled back in surprise. "Most people call me Mick, though."

I quickly glanced at Hall, smiling in his notebook, before looking back at Mick. "I appreciate it, Mick."

He squinted at me. "I've been where ye are. Ye can't let them get to ye, or it'll be twice as hard getting back up."

"I doubt it," I muttered, imagining how he would react if he knew I was a woman. "But ye got a point."

He shrugged, unfazed. "Anyhow, I suppose ye won't be popular for a while. Ye might need a few men on your side." He held his hand out to me. I took it, grateful and a little confused by his comradeship. I tried to figure out their reasoning for helping me even as I noticed Mick's hands were remarkably rougher than Hall's.

Hall nodded. "Ye are going to need it."

"Thanks."

They fell silent as I stared at the ceiling, wondering what I had gotten myself into.

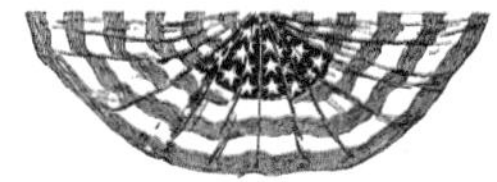

My head shot up, heart racing as a loud noise blasted through the barracks. If it weren't for the adrenaline coursing through me, the abruptness with which I woke would have turned my stomach. Mick swore about the bugle call somewhere beneath me.

I grabbed my hat, shoved it onto my head, and scrambled down the bunk, avoiding the grumbling men surrounding me. A quick glance down the aisle had me freezing in place, arrested by a familiar set of green eyes. I reluctantly tore my gaze from Thomas and faced Hall's back, guilt gnawing at my stomach. The last time I talked to him was before the fight the previous day.

We left the cold barracks in a steady line to the frigid air. The snow fell in soft flurries, lighting the still-dark morning as our boots sloshed through the mud. The cold bit through my coat, but I didn't dare pull it tighter, not wanting to draw any more attention, let alone the lashing I would surely get for falling out of line.

The mess hall blocked the wind, making the chill bearable as we waited to grab the same salted pork and potatoes we had eaten the night before. I reached one of the long tables, sitting next to Hall and Mick. It seemed they had let me into their little group since many others seemed to know each other.

"It's nice to know we get a variety," Mick deadpanned. Hall smiled into his food, not one to complain, and started to shovel. There was little time before we were to begin our drills.

I just lifted a piece of pork to my mouth when my plate was snatched.

"Hey—"

Men started to shove in around us, separating me from Mick. Hall's smile fell as a tall man sat next to him, cracking knuckles that dwarfed Hall's slender hands. I tried to grab my plate, but the man to my right held on. I raised my eyes, ready to snap at the man, and stopped.

Fuckin' *Barton*.

"Kind of ye to give up your portion." He sneered, shoving a significant bite into his mouth. The two other men grabbed the rest of my food and ate it.

"What in the bleedin' hell?" Mick sat forward, ready for a fight. He was the only one out of the three of us big enough to stand a chance.

"Oi, settle down, lad," Barton said. "Just sharing a wee bit with a friend."

"It's fine." I glared, pleading with Mick to stand down.

"Ye can't—"

"I said, 'It's fine.'"

"See." Barton laughed, putting his arm around my shoulders and shaking me roughly. "O'Connor and I have an understanding. Come on, lads."

They stood up, laughing with each other, and sat farther down the table.

"Ye can't let them push ye around like that," Mick scolded.

"I can't draw any more attention to myself." I scanned the area, noticing more than a few men looking at us. Luckily, it didn't go beyond our table.

"And what do ye expect to do without food?" Mick asked. I stared at the table, stung by the harshness in his voice.

"I'll figure it out." *If I survive that long*, I thought bitterly.

Pork landed on my plate. I looked up in time to see Hall giving me some potatoes, too. I muttered my thanks, embarrassed by what had happened.

Hall nodded, but I knew I must do something about Barton.

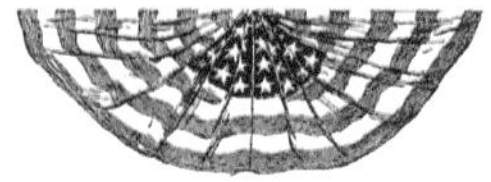

"Heels on the same line, private!" our instructor barked at a man a few rows down.

I kept my head forward, at attention. Our first drilling practice was in the School of the Soldier—learning how to position ourselves while in formation with the others. Shoulders squared, arms hanging with our elbows close to our body, palms slightly forward so that our pinky was close to the seam of our pants, and many other minuscule rules drilled into our heads until they became second nature. Walk forward with your right leg first. March. "No, private! Your feet are too far apart." Halt!

We were to breathe through our noses while we ran to go a greater distance. Not too far into our run, my lungs burned, my legs screamed in protest, and I cursed myself for thinking I could do this. Nearing the end, I doubled over, gasping, burning breaths into my lungs, taking comfort in not being the only one. I kept my eyes straight ahead, though I wanted to check how Thomas was faring. I suspected he was doing just fine, being built for this sort of life.

The rest of the day went much of the same. We had lunch, which Barton and his lackeys picked over, and we drilled in the school of the Company—practicing where we would stand and our placements as a whole. We ended our day with a skirmish drill and a short dress parade that lasted about two to three minutes.

When dinner rolled around, I should have sat down in relief. However, Barton had stolen more of my food, bringing his men around to intimidate us—a power play that he wouldn't have tried if Thomas had been around. Knowing he was not one to mess with, many others avoided Barton and turned a blind eye when he tormented me. It infuriated me to think that he bullied me because he saw me as the weakest link. Mick and Hall encouraged me to stand up to him, but I refused to draw more attention to myself and tolerated his bullshit.

I hid my bitterness that I might need Thomas after all. *No*, I seethed. *I will not bring him into this. Not again.* I was a big girl who could handle it herself.

Right.

I left dinner hungry, irritable, and completely exhausted. On top of it all, we were to report to our additional duties while everyone else finished up their day.

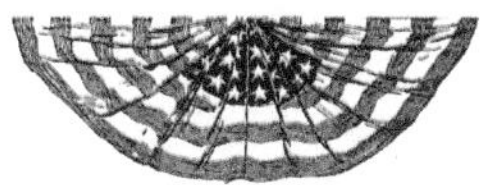

The ax came up in a wide arch and sunk into the wood. And stuck.

Thomas winced as Emilia tried to pull it out, but it was wedged so far into the wood that it just squelched through the mud.

"Place your foot on it and wobble it out."

She didn't look up but nodded, face set in determination. The whole day was spent in drills, pushing them to their breaking points. Though they had their three meals, Emilia visibly shook and tottered to the side.

Thomas caught her, but she pushed him away.

"I got it."

"Too much for ye, *Eamonn*?" Barton sneered.

Emilia didn't comment.

"What do ye think will be for breakfast tomorrow?" Barton leaned back, rubbing his stomach. Thomas narrowed his eyes between the two. "They sure do feed us well here, don't they—Tommy, is it?"

Thomas wasn't sure why rage shot through his veins, but he learned to trust his intuition long ago. "Look here, ye feckin'—"

The lieutenant watching them told them to shut their gab from where he stood. "Finish up so we get out of this bleedin' weather."

The temperature had dropped since the sun went down. Thomas hadn't noticed much, warm from the exertion and now burning with fury. He began to split the logs quicker, picturing Barton's head instead of the wood. Not long after, he tripled their count, and the lieutenant dismissed Thomas and Emilia, asking Barton to follow him.

The look on Barton's face told Thomas that he wasn't through with them. Thomas spat. He was well acquainted with men like him and quickly learned not to underestimate their vindictiveness.

Thomas still seethed inside, but instead of smashing Barton's face in, he held back, trying to be a better man for the woman by his side, even if she still hadn't spoken to him except for her quiet responses while chopping the logs.

Nay, I will not, and he didn't. Instead, he silently strolled through the buildings with Emilia as the snow gently fell around them. It gave the camp an odd beauty, blanketing the ravaged earth that succumbed to the driving force of the army. That and the tantalizing way it danced across the gypsy's cheeks made him wish it was his fingertips.

"Are ye going to tell me what that was about?" Thomas finally asked.

"No."

He sighed, lifting his face to the flurries that stuck to his lashes.

"I don't want you to fight my battles, Thomas," Emilia said softly, dropping her accent as they were alone. Most everyone else found their way out of the cold.

"What—"

"This is something I have to do alone. Do I want you by my side?" She looked up at him, brown eyes so filled with pain that his chest tightened. "Yes. But you can't be. Not now. I have to get through this training alone, not to prove it to you, but to myself, for my Mammina. I'm fighting for her, and if you are constantly saving me…" she let the rest drift off as she shook her head, at war with whatever was happening in her head. "Then I won't ever know if I could've done it alone. I would never forgive myself for being the reason you are punished for my mistakes again. I can't have you get hurt because of me." Her words thickened with emotion.

Though he couldn't see her face, he knew she was close to tears.

"Have ye forgotten why I'm fighting? Is it not the same thing? Though ye think me whole world revolves around ye, have ye forgotten I've got me own people I'm fighting for? That I'm giving my life over to a country I believe in?" He said it harsher than he intended, but she needed to hear it.

She stopped abruptly, nearly making him collide with her. "Of course, I know what you're fighting for." Her demeanor hardened as she turned towards him. "And I never assumed your *world* revolved around me. I'm not that stupid."

"I didn't mean it like that," he growled.

"I know what you meant, Thomas. I'm not trying to push you away; I'm just trying to prove to myself that I can do it on my own."

Thomas gave an angry laugh. She was doing precisely what he'd done to her all those months that he pushed her away. The only difference now was that he knew they couldn't stay away from each other. That they were better together. It was time she figured that out for herself, but he sure as hell wouldn't make it easy for her. Thomas bent so close to her face that she took a step back. "Ye do whatever ye have to do on your own, but don't expect me to come running when ye can't pull yourself out of the mess ye got yourself in."

"That's not fair." Angry tears lined her lids.

Pride swelled momentarily in his chest as she held them back with a strength she'd need in this war, but it quickly dissipated when he uttered his following words. "Life's not fair, gypsy." Thomas said the word without the usual love behind, somehow tainted it to his own ears. He never used it as such and instantly regretted it. She was not to be defined by the prejudices against her people. In fact, he loved her culture as much as the woman before him.

"Well, thanks for the life lesson, *Thomas*," she spat before he could fix his blunder. "How would I ever have found that out on my own?"

Thomas squeezed his fists tightly to keep himself from grabbing this infuriating woman and crushing his lips to hers. To show her that everything else meant nothing when they were together. Either that or to stop himself from punching the building next to him to stop this pointless arguing.

Instead, Irish curses were on his lips as he left her in the snow.

CHAPTER FOUR

Shaylah & Michael

January 1862

Sweat poured down Shay's neck as another contraction wracked her body. She groaned deeply, fists clenching the sheets. The midwife counted how long this one lasted.

Shay withstood the pain, knowing she was in the best of hands. Judy was a fit, sinewy woman, albeit a bit brutish, who did her job exceptionally well. If there was a pregnant woman, they made sure to have Judy with them during delivery. A few months back, Rose called on her old friend and ensured she would be there for this.

"They're getting close, child," Judy said when Shay went slack. "We need to turn that baby."

"Are you sure it hasn't flipped yet?" Rose rubbed her hands together in worry. That act alone sent a shiver of fear down Shay's spine. Rose didn't worry. So, the fact that she stood there with her brows knit together, trepidation turning her lips into a frown, made Shay realize this labor would be long, hard, and dangerous. Would she even make it out alive?

"I've seen worse," Judy admitted, which was believable considering she had been delivering babies since watching her mama from a very young age. She must have seen every horror during childbirth.

A fact that didn't relieve Shay in the least.

"From what I can gather, it's a partial breech," she continued. "But being so far along and in labor, no less, there isn't much room for that baby to move. C'mon." She began to help Shay sit up. "Let's get you in a different position. Maybe a little coaxing will help."

Just then, Mira walked in with a cloth and a pitcher of water, having been keeping Evaline occupied in the bakery below. The poor child had been distraught since the first sign of labor, and Mira had taken it upon herself to distract her.

"I thought you might need this," Mira said mildly, her slim frame approaching Shay's shoulder. Dipping the cloth into the water, Mira wiped Shay's face.

"We could use your help," Judy said, motioning for Mira to grab Shay's other arm.

"I can get it," Shay grumbled, pushing them way. Shay knew her own strength, and she wasn't going to let these women treat her like a damn fragile doll.

Just then, another contraction struck, and Shay's head fell back in a loud cry. Waiting—*God, they were strong now*—for it to be over. Her body slowly softened, and she could sit straight again.

"Good," Judy said, placing a few rags on the floor near the fireplace. "Come kneel over here."

The midwife had Shay on her hands and knees, rocking back and forth and bending her head to the floor, anything to try and get that baby to move; all the while, the uncomfortable push of Judy's hand made Shay grimace as the woman kneaded her stomach.

"I'm sorry, hun," Judy exclaimed. "The baby is breached still."

A loud bang reverberated from the bakery's kitchen, causing Shay to flinch, followed by voices rising from below.

Rose swung towards the door, her hand on her chest. "What in God's name?" She shared a look with her daughter.

Shay wondered again where Mira's small frame had come from. An odd fact to think about, considering the circumstances. And yet...there was little resemblance between the two other than the dark shade of their skin. And that wasn't saying much, considering her own was as rich as theirs. That, and

Rose could scare the living daylights out of anyone who crossed her path. Mira was a little wisp—fragile and meek. Shay almost snarled at the scared expression on the girl's face. She was only a few years younger than Shay's twenty-two years, but she seemed so naïve. Delicate. Useless.

Shay put her head back down, ashamed of where her thoughts had gone. Instead, she concentrated on Judy's hand pushing and prodding her stomach.

She didn't truly hate Mira. Even if the girl had it out for her since she moved into the tiny apartment above her parent's bakery. All of their children moved out except Mira and little Evaline, whom they had taken in as their own. Having some room, Rose and George kindly took her in after some persuasion from Thomas. But Mira turned nasty ever since Shay caught Hiram's eye.

Shay almost rolled her eyes. The man didn't want anything to do with her. They were good friends, and that was that. Even if he had acted like an ass when he found she was pregnant all those months ago. When the thought of those Irishmen using her body had him averting his gaze. Shay knew his stomach turned at the mere thought of one of those white men's babies inside of her. It swayed his attraction, but she found herself surprisingly comfortable in their friendship. Shay didn't want more from Hiram.

She placed her hand on her stomach, feeling sick. Not at her child, but at the pity she saw in some of their faces. She didn't want their pity. Not when those men were rotting in the ground now. Taken care of by Michael and his gang. If it wasn't for Emilia talking to Thomas and threatening to kill the men herself, Thomas may never have convinced Michael to help him. And Shay might still have been looking over her shoulder. Or worse. She could be dead.

More shouting ripped her from her thoughts just as another contraction about ripped her body in half. It was the strongest one yet and pulled a deep scream from her throat as she pushed her ass further into the air, her head pressed to the ground as she tried to ride it out.

Shay gritted her teeth, barely holding it together when the door slammed into the wall, causing her head to whip up and glare at the intruder.

Familiar blue eyes—sharp as ice—met hers.

"What in the bloody hell is going on?" His deep Irish lilt rolled over Shay as he took her in. From her position on the floor to her thin nightgown, soaked with sweat and surely translucent now. But she didn't care what she looked like. What he saw. Not when another contraction was already starting.

Fingers digging into the rag, Shay groaned, holding back the scream that she wanted to let out. But she refused to show any pain in front of Michael. Michael, who had found her at her lowest. Bloody, bruised, but not broken beneath those men in that room. He had seen her when she was quiet. After she had already broken her nails off in the flesh of the previous men. After she already bit, scratched, kicked, and cursed them all. Michael had found her when she lay there, quiet and submissive. A fraction of the woman she was.

She would not let him see that again.

Judy's hands finally paused as she raised to her knees. "You can't be here."

"Get the hell out," Shay growled, jaw still clenched in pain.

Thundering steps came up the stairs, carrying Hiram into the doorframe, blood dripping out of his nose.

Jesus Christ, these men. Shay was going to kill them.

"What happened?" Rose snapped, turning her glare onto the two men.

Before Hiram could respond, Michael started rolling up his shirt sleeves. "What are ye doin' for the pain?" he asked.

"Excuse me?" Judy snapped. "This is not a place for men."

The contraction had eased, allowing Shay to breathe easier and for her anger to grow. "What do you want?" she snapped at Michael.

"I heard yelling."

"That's because I'm in fucking *labor*!"

Michael only grinned, unperturbed by her venom.

Mira snuck out with a whisper of having to find Evaline.

"Honestly," Judy cut in, "you two need to get out. Now."

"I'm not goin' anywhere," Michael said, kneeling by Shay.

"The hell you're not." Hiram still stood in the doorframe, unable to look at her out of respect or disgust; she didn't know. Instead, Hiram directed all of his hostility towards Michael.

Shay sat on her knees and looked Michael in the face.

"Don't make me ask again, a rúnsearc." Something in Michael's eyes, the set of his jaw, told Shay he wouldn't back down. He didn't spare Hiram another glance.

"My lower back," Shay said, watching him take her in unashamedly and, to her surprise, with assessing consideration. Nothing like what she expected from him without her clothes on. Of course, her stomach was as big as a watermelon. That could have turned any man from desire. She didn't want to think about the other reason he might not find her attractive.

God, why was she even thinking about this?

"And what are ye doin'?" he asked Judy accusingly.

She looked about ready to throttle him but reined in her anger. "The baby is turned slightly. We need to—"

"Keep doin' your job. I'll manage the pain."

"Excuse me?" Judy asked as heat rose in Shay's cheeks.

Shay looked towards Hiram, who was about to rip Michael out of the room. "It's okay. Let him stay."

The brutality of his shock would have startled her if it weren't for Michael by her side. Shay knew it wasn't directed at her, but at the whole situation. Hiram had a long history with Michael, and their hate ran deep.

And, for some reason, she felt safer with the brooding Irishman.

"Are you sure?" Hiram asked.

"Get out," Michael snapped, earning him a glare to the back of the head.

"Do you know what you're doing, boy?" Rose asked, staring down at the three of them on the floor.

Shay flinched when Hiram slammed the door behind him but still looked steadily at Michael, curious.

"Me ma had a hard time when Maggie was born. I helped her through it while me pa was passed out on the cot."

"Where was the midwife?" Shay asked, just as she was hit with another wave of pain.

Michael bent her forward, positioning himself in a somewhat scandalous position behind her that had Rose choking on a gasp. His fingers began to dig into her lower back, and to her surprise, the pain eased somewhat.

"How dare you—" Rose exclaimed but was cut off by an appreciative groan from Shay.

"He stays," Shay said through clenched teeth, eyes closed as his hands moved over her.

"We had no one back then," he answered quietly. "No midwife."

"Well," Judy exclaimed, apparently approving of his work. "You do that, I'll work on the baby once this one passes."

"Aye, ma'am."

They kept at it, Michael easing the pain and Judy working on the position of the baby. Shay grew weaker, exhausted by the increasingly frequent and intensifying contractions. When her body felt like it was about to break, when she started swearing that she was going to start pushing, whether Judy liked it or not, the midwife moved her back to the bed.

Judy and Rose helped situate Shay into a good position.

"I'm going to need you to leave," Judy told Michael, who promptly refused. With a sigh of a thousand winds, the woman put her hands on her hips. "I need to check her. It's not at all appropriate—"

"I'm not goin' anywhere."

Sweat coating her body, body limp from the moment of reprieve, Shay looked at him. At his clenched fists. Trailed the muscles and tendons that strained up his forearms. And found his jaw equally tense. She knew if she asked him to leave, he would. What she didn't understand was why he was there in the first place. Why did he care?

Blue eyes met her brown ones, and she froze, seemingly suspended in space, time slowing, and she knew then. She didn't want Michael to go. She didn't care *why* he stayed, only that he *did*.

"He can stay," she said, eyes still on him, though she felt the disapproval of both women.

Judy muttered to herself as she lifted the nightgown. Shay clenched her own jaw, staring at the ceiling as the woman's hand checked the dilation. Her pulse quickened, wondering if she should have sent him away, when a cold rag wiped her brow, swept down her face, and cooled her chest in quick, thorough strokes. Shay looked at him, startled and thankful, but his face was smooth of any emotion. Closed off as he continued his ministrations.

She was about to thank him when her body tensed, and a scream escaped her instead. The rag disappeared as she clenched the sheets, her feet digging into the thin mattress.

Judy crawled onto the bed and positioned herself between Shay's legs. "If you're going to leave, do it now, sir. Push."

Shay started pushing, groaning loudly.

"I found her when it was done," Michael said steadily. "I'll be there when she finishes it."

Judy and Rose exchanged a long look. Shay's hands clutched the bedding, having nothing—no one—else to hold on to.

"Again," Judy instructed.

Shay groaned, digging in with her heels as she pushed again, but little progress was made before the contraction lightened.

She choked back a cry, refusing to let all her anger and pain out. Instead, Shay ground her teeth, dug deep inside, and pushed with all she had. She refused to let the words out. She wished Millie was there, helping her through this milestone like all the others. There wasn't a time her friend hadn't been there for her. Even so, she knew and wanted Millie to do what she had to. She was on her own journey, and Shay could do this alone. If not to prove it to herself, but so her friend could soar.

Shay tried her best not to dwell on thoughts of the unknown father. Not when she lost count of how many men had used her body that night. Their faces blurred until they became one. She refused to let them ruin this for her. To take any more from her. She wouldn't let them win. But having someone by her side while she went through it would've helped. Even if it wasn't her best friend.

Something rough and solid brushed lightly against the back of her hand, so briefly that she thought she had imagined it.

Shay held back a sob and grabbed his hand with a strength she didn't know she had until the slackness of his had her doubting. Panicking. But before she could withdraw, his grip tightened, unrelenting.

In that brief, confusing moment, she had a sense of not truly being alone and had the strength to push.

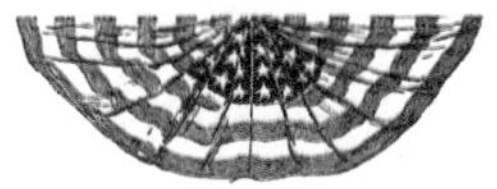

A loud squeal tore through the room, followed by the soft, cooing murmurs from the women.

"A healthy baby girl," Judy said with the affection of a woman who loved her work.

Mikey let out a breath he didn't know he had been holding. There had been some time that Shay had struggled. When the baby wasn't entirely in position, Shay had screamed so loud that he thought there was no way she could do this. Survive it. There was no wonder why men usually stayed out of these rooms. To watch what their woman had to go through, knowing she might not live to see the birth of her child. That the babe had a low chance of survival.

Mikey thanked the stars, spirit, whatever the feck was out there, that he had never experienced this since childhood when he didn't fully understand the consequences with his mother. It was bad enough watching this woman do it. He couldn't imagine experiencing it again. And, thank fuck, he would never have to.

He watched as the midwife placed the baby in Shay's open arms, a rare smile lighting up her entire heart-shaped face until goddamn dimples popped out of her cheeks. He stood back, momentarily perplexed by the sudden tension in his chest. He rubbed it roughly, trying to dispel the foreign sensation, and began to unroll his sleeves. Nodding, he backed up, doing what he'd set out to do. He could finally rid himself of this woman and whatever propelled him to care for her over these months. Well, he could from a distance. He'd keep his word to the gypsy and make sure no harm came to her friend.

A melodic voice had him stopping mid-turn. "Do you want to meet her?"

Mikey paused, wondering if running out the door would be rude. Not wanting to look like a bloody coward, he edged toward the bed and looked down at the slimy, wailing creature in her arms.

"She's white," he said without thinking, his whole face scrunching in confusion as he scratched the dark scruff along his jaw.

Shay gave him a withering stare. "She might take after her father..." The words were like a cold bucket over his head, and an unexpected, burning fury flared deep inside him. "But she'll probably darken the older she gets."

Mikey only nodded, keeping his gaze trained on the babe instead of Shay's long, toned legs still on display. Catching her eye, his breath stopped in his chest at the brightness shining in their dark depths, most assuredly from the little bundle currently in her arms. He'd never seen them sparkle before, and a part of him knew he was seeing a glimpse of the woman she was before he found her.

Mikey swallowed past the tightness in his throat. "Ye got a name?"

Smiling with the brightness of the stars, Shay stroked the babe's cheek. "Liberty."

CHAPTER FIVE

Thomas

JANUARY 1862

"Oi," Sullivan grunted from across the table. They were eating breakfast before beginning their drills for the day. "Did ye see Barton with Eamonn over there? What do ye think that's about?"

Thomas' head snapped up just in time to see Barton and his men stand. Emilia was sitting there, head bent, as the two men she befriended glared at their plates. Thomas placed both hands on the table, ready to stand, but forced himself to remain in place. "Don't know," he said, looking down at his food.

"Think we should do something about it? I mean, your cousin is a wee bit of a runt. Don't tell him I said that, though."

Thomas couldn't believe people actually believed their outrageous lie. He didn't think it'd bother him, but Sullivan was a good man. He didn't like lying to someone he could trust. Thomas might not have considered himself a good man, but he tried to uphold his honor whenever possible.

"Me cousin wants to make his own way," Thomas answered. "Let him."

Sullivan leaned back, taking in the change in Thomas. "Something happen between ye? I thought that was your boyo."

"He made it clear he doesn't want help."

Sullivan let it go, though Thomas could feel his frequent stare as he finished his food.

In the back of his mind, Thomas knew Emilia was right. She needed to find her own way. But did it have to be in a war? These men were going to eat her alive, and they weren't even in the thick of battle yet. How selfish was she to put those close to her in danger, risking their necks to keep her alive?

Thomas stood, noticing Emilia's plate was empty. Good. Even angry at her, Thomas considered her well-being, and she needed it with all the work she'd been doing. But what in the bloody hell was Barton doing over there? "I'll keep an eye on him," he said to Sullivan, who agreed and volunteered to do the same.

It looked like men naturally wanted to protect Emilia, even when they thought she was a man. Even when she didn't want it.

Wanted or not, gypsy, ye are stuck with me.

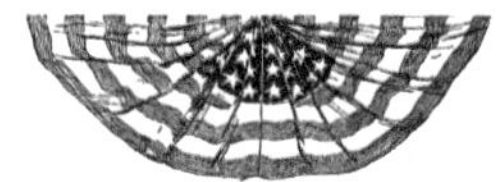

Rain pelted them in freezing sheets until they were thoroughly miserable. They had been at it all day and were nearly finished drilling.

"Get up, Private!" their sergeant yelled at a man a few rows up. "Is it too much for you? Shall we send you back home to your mama?"

"No, Sergeant!"

Thomas could feel the blood drain from his face when he heard Emilia's peculiar accent. What had happened to gain the sergeant's attention?

"Then get yourself out of the mud and get yourself cleaned up."

"But—"

"I want you out of here! I expect you to be at your best tomorrow."

Thomas' hands shook with fury as Emilia broke rank and began her way to the barracks, face and clothes covered in mud. It took everything in him to not break rank, slam his fist in the sergeant's face, and race after Emilia.

"Now, march!" the sergeant yelled. "Unless you all want to pansy out like O'Connor? Should we just retreat now and let the damn rebs win this war?"

"No, Sergeant!" they all yelled and began marching, practicing their formations.

"What's with your cousin?" Byrnes asked after they had finished for the day. Patrick Byrnes was a small man in his mid-thirties with the mindset of a bull. He was a Teamster, often in control of six horses while they pulled his large wagon of supplies. If one saw him on the streets, they would quickly learn that he used up all his patience on his horses. It was best to stay out of his way when regarding people.

Thomas liked him.

"How should I know?" Thomas snapped, more worried about Emilia than annoyed by Byrnes. "I'm here with ye, now. Ain't I?"

"No need to get your knickers in a twist." Byrnes exchanged a look with Sullivan. "All I meant was if ye thought something was wrong with him? It's not every day ye see a man collapse for no reason."

Thomas stopped abruptly, causing Sullivan to ram into him. Thomas mumbled an apology before grabbing Byrne's arm. "Are ye saying ye saw what happened?"

Byrnes didn't see anything funny happen, only that Eamonn's steps faltered and collapsed into the mud. "It was quick." He shrugged. "I didn't see anyone do anything to him, though."

Thomas let go of his arm, and they made their way to the mess hall. If no one touched her, then she was either injured or she passed out. But why?

The mess hall was already half full as they entered, but Thomas immediately found the back of Emilia's head. He grabbed some food and found a place close enough to see Emilia while being far enough away not to draw attention. The others followed him, talking with each other as they let him be.

Emilia's uniform still had large portions of dried mud, though her face and hands were wiped clean. She shoveled food in her mouth like she hadn't eaten in days. Now that Thomas was thinking about it, she did look thinner, which was strange. She shouldn't have been losing weight yet, not when they had steady meals.

A cold draft of wind blew across the room, bringing in a group of men with it, but Thomas wasn't paying attention. It wasn't until Sullivan elbowed him, pointing to Barton and two of his men, that Thomas noticed where they were headed. Barton took his place next to Emilia, who seemed to wilt in his presence, hunching over her plate like a wild animal guarding its prey against other predators as his lackeys sat at the following table. At that moment, Thomas was hit with the sudden realization of what Barton had been up to, and a slow fury began to burn through his veins.

"Feckin' gobshite!" Sullivan realized the same thing. "What do ye want to do, Tommy?"

"Ye gonna let him treat your boyo like that?" Byrnes asked when they filled him in.

"C'mon." Sullivan began to stand, but Thomas put his hand on his arm.

"Sit." Thomas recognized the look on Emilia's face, brown eyes focused on her food as a line of concentration creased between her brows. He hadn't seen it in a while but had many times when she was ready to tear into him. Her mind was set, and Barton was at the receiving end. Thomas' jaw clenched so tight that pain shot through his teeth, yet he held still, fully prepared to jump in if needed or give Emilia his food at the very least. "Let's see what happens."

"Are ye sure?"

Thomas forgot what he was about to say when Barton went to grab her plate. Quick as a snake, her hand shot out, somehow pinning Barton's arm to the table with a loud thud into the wood. His men stiffened, leaning forward as if waiting on Barton's order.

"What the *fuck*?" Barton said loud enough that those around them went quiet.

Thomas leaned forward for a better look and spotted the fork she had used to pin his sleeve to the table. When Barton tried to tug his arm free, Emilia's other hand slammed down, causing the whole table to fall silent and stare. Barton's face paled as he took in the dagger between his fingers.

"Ye feck with me food again, and I will cut your bloody finger off next time." Emilia's voice was low, but the table was so quiet they could hear the vehemence behind her words. "Do ye hear me?"

"Ye dare threaten me?"

"Aye. Ye know who me family is? Do ye know the O'Connors?"

"Common name for a common—"

Emilia hummed, nodding her head as if she was prepared for this. "What of Michael O'Connor? Since ye seemed daft when ye met me cousin Tommy over there." She tilted her head towards Thomas. He sat straighter, impressed that she knew he was there. He hadn't seen her look up from her food since he entered. Emilia watched Barton as the blood drained from his face.

"I've heard of a Mikey O'Connor?" he growled. "But I haven't heard of a cousin."

"That's not what matters." She began to twist the knife, so the blade came closer to slicing his fingers. "What matters is what Mikey would think about ye tormenting his family? And not to mention ye insulting me blood over there." She raised her eyebrows, and Barton looked at Thomas. Everyone turned as well.

Thomas clenched his fists with the attention on him but kept his hardened gaze on Barton.

"Do ye know what Mikey would do to ye?" A man said down the table.

"Feck Mikey," someone else chimed in. "What is Tommy going to do?"

Emilia pulled the fork and knife out simultaneously, causing Barton to flinch. He cursed, holding his hand. It appeared that Emilia angled the blade so that it sliced between his fingers. Barton stood, blood dripping from his closed fist, avoiding Thomas' glare as he left the hall without another word.

Emilia grabbed Barton's plate and started eating off it, noticeably avoiding eye contact with Barton's two glaring men. They turned to one another, probably whispering some half-assed plan that would only piss Thomas off further.

Chatter broke throughout the room.

"I take it back," Byrnes said. "I'm impressed."

Sullivan nodded, shoving more food into his mouth. "Looks like it runs in your family."

"I'm nothing like Mikey."

Sullivan shrugged. "Maybe so. But they think so, and in times like this, ye could use that to your advantage."

Thomas sat back and sighed, knowing what he had to do. Every time he tried to be a decent man, something set him back to his base nature. Made him into the man he had fought so hard not to be. In truth, it was easier for him to be like Mikey because it ran in their blood. An instinctual biological tendency to do whatever it took to survive—whether it was harmful to others or not. What made him unlike his brother was his desire to live a more honorable path. To fight for what he so desperately believed in the right way. But when pushed, it was like flipping a switch. Very little could stop him when Thomas let his instinctual proclivities take control.

He was a force to be reckoned with.

That's why Thomas denied it daily—deep down, he knew he was capable of far more destruction than his brother could inflict, and it scared the hell out of him. But Thomas was willing to destroy himself if it meant protecting his family.

Thomas stood. "I suppose ye are right."

"Where ye going?" Byrnes asked suspiciously.

"Not to worry." Thomas focused on Barton's men. He was heading out of the hall.

Sullivan raised his brows. "Ye need help?"

"I'm just going to have a wee chat." Thomas kept his eye on his targets, wanting to maintain sight of them. "Do either of ye know your letters?"

"Aye," Sullivan said around the food in his mouth. "What is it ye need?"

"If I procure the materials, do ye mind writing a letter?"

Sullivan shrugged and agreed.

Thomas slapped a hand onto Sullivan's back, leaving them to look quizzically after him as he went outside, looking in each direction for the man until he saw a flash of fabric disappear around one of the buildings. He hadn't made it ten paces when a voice behind him called his name.

"Wait!"

Thomas let his head fall back, knowing he wouldn't be able to catch up to him. It'd have to wait until later.

"Where are ye going?" Emilia asked, keeping up her accent in case anyone overheard them.

"Ye're talking to me now?"

"I just wanted to make sure ye wouldn't do anything stupid."

Thomas glared at her, and she actually smiled. God, help him; she was getting used to his moods. And now that he saw her this close, he could see just how much weight she'd lost.

"What are you doing?" she stuttered when he stopped abruptly, grabbing her chin. He turned her face back and forth, inspecting her sharp cheekbones. Emilia's face had always been angled but in a soft, delicate way. Now, harsh lines defined her face, hardening it in ways that tugged at his chest. She was no longer the gentlewoman who walked into his life many months ago.

"When's the last time ye ate?"

"I just did…"

"Before that," he growled and let go of her face when she winced. "Sorry, lass."

Emilia looked away. "I didn't want to bother you."

"Ye can always—"

"I told you I wanted to do this on my own."

"This again—"

"Yes, again!" She stabbed her finger into his chest, face reddening. "You can't save me all the time. I need to solve my own problems!"

"And look where it got ye!" he yelled. "Have ye taken a look at yourself?"

Emilia pulled back, hurt crossing her face. She touched her cheek, running her fingers over her face as if the thought had never occurred to her. "Is it really that bad?"

"Yes!" he shouted and winced when she recoiled at the cruelty of his words. "I mean, no. What I meant was that you need to take care of yourself. How can I expect ye to care for yourself out there, in the thick of it, when ye can't even do it here?"

"I did take care of it!" she yelled.

Thomas looked around, worried someone had heard her normal voice, and began to tug her toward the barracks. She pulled her arm free but kept walking next to him.

"I only meant that I'm worried for ye," he said, knowing he let his emotions get the better of him. If it wasn't for Barton, Emilia would be doing remarkably well; he knew it, but he couldn't admit it to her. Because if he told her the truth, what he really thought, it would crush her. Deep down, Thomas wished she stayed home where it'd be safer. It scared the hell out of him every time she was put in danger. "That's all."

"I think he'll leave me alone now. I won't let him take my food anymore if that's what you're worried about."

Thomas smiled reluctantly, remembering the look on Barton's face. "How did ye get such good aim?"

Emilia smiled up at him. "Mikey was a stickler for precision."

Thomas gave a thoughtful nod. "Good to know he listened to at least one thing I taught him."

She looked at him quizzically.

"Who do ye think trained him?"

"He—" She stopped talking, visibly reviewing everything she'd been taught. "Who trained you then?"

"I worked for a butcher for some time. He showed me a few moves when he saw I was roughed up a wee bit one day. The rest I learned on the street." He shrugged, turning his face to the sky, heavy with dark clouds.

"I guess I have you to think for that, then."

"No, that was all Mikey. He did what I could not, and I'm glad for it." He could feel her eyes on him, but he watched for people instead, not wanting anyone to overhear them. They stopped in front of the barracks. "Ye scared the shite out of him, ye know that? A hair over, ye would have cut his finger nearly off."

Emilia smiled, as if remembering how it played out. "About that." She paused, looking up at him meekly. "I missed."

"Missed?"

"I aimed correctly with the fork, but I really wanted to take off his finger. I've been so hungry and mad that I—" Emilia ran her hands over her face in exasperation. "I know it was wrong, but I just snapped."

Thomas shrugged. "I think ye should have taken the damn thing off, but if I'm speaking truthfully—I don't think ye missed."

Her eyes flicked between his before staring into the distance. She seemed to subconsciously pull her coat tighter against the chill while her mind was elsewhere. "I suppose you're right."

Thomas barked out a laugh, startling Emilia.

"What?" she asked, staring at him like he'd lost his mind.

"I think that's the first time ye agreed with me."

A group of men came out of the barracks, speaking loudly and laughing so that Emilia and Thomas had to step aside lest they be trampled.

"Try to stay out of trouble, aye?"

Emilia side-eyed the men walking by but pulled her shoulders back instead of shrinking under their presence. She was really coming into her persona. "Where ye going?" she asked him when he turned away.

"I've got some bones to cross."

CHAPTER SIX

Michael & Shaylah

Mikey opened the letter and wondered for the umpteenth time what the feck had happened. They were clearly his brother's words written by someone else. Asking *him* for help? Again?

A familiar knot tied his stomach. Mikey had gone to school when they docked in America. Thomas—Thomas, being the elder, went straight to work. He never learned how to read well or write. Mikey might not be a poet, but he sure as fuck knew more than Thomas.

Swallowing past the age-old guilt, he focused on the letter's contents. It seemed the gypsy had gotten herself into trouble again. When he had read how she nearly cut the man's finger off, a loud laugh burst out of him, startling the barkeep and himself, if he was to be honest. The woman had more balls on her than most men. He wouldn't tell her that, though.

Alma giggled loudly, drawing Mikey's attention from the letter to the two women on the bed. Keena whispered into Alma's ear, her dark hair draping the young woman's face as their naked bodies melded with one another. Mikey folded up the letter and put it back in his shirt pocket.

Alma turned her blue eyes to him, smiling. "Are you going to join us, daidí?"

"It looks like ye two are handling it." He raised a brow, and she blushed deeply. He motioned for them to continue.

"But—" Alma looked between Mikey and Keena.

Keena moved toward Alma and gently turned her face toward hers. Slowly, Keena lowered her tanned body over Alma's, and they kissed. Mikey almost felt as if he was an intruder, watching two lovers in a private moment, no matter that he had paid them.

Shaking his head at these intrusive thoughts, he leaned back and watched.

Lost in the moment, his eyes closed, bringing the sudden, vivid image of much darker, toned legs wrapped around him.

Bloody hell. *No.*

Mikey's eyes sprung open. He forced himself to watch the two women before him, afraid of what fantasy his mind might conjure.

Mikey flipped up his collar, trying to stave off the bitter cold as he stared at the tiny house before him. If it could even be called a house. The thing was feckin' tiny. And with all the goddamn barren trees around them and the town a half mile out, it was like a ghastly rural wasteland. He was already itching to get back to his city.

Mikey sent the twins toward the back of the house, blocking the exits. He wanted to oversee this job, not trusting the boys to overreact.

Making it up the walkway, Mikey's giant fist pounded the door, setting off a wailing from within. *Christ.*

The door cracked, revealing a brown eye. "May I help you?" a woman's unsure and undoubtedly southern voice asked. The door remained cracked. Smart lass. Though it wouldn't keep him out.

"I have matters to speak with ye."

"Matters of what kind?"

"Your husband."

The door opened farther, revealing a plain face lined with worry. "Is he well? They haven't left—"

"May I enter, ma'am?"

"How do you know Henry?"

Mikey smiled, a sight that had her paling as he pushed his way in, causing her to stumble back. He surveyed the small room, picking up and setting down random items and skimming through the papers on the small desk in the corner.

"Excuse me!" she sputtered. "You really—"

"Your husband needs to know his place, ma'am."

Mikey looked at the small sitting area, not much room for more than a few people. A kitchen led through the back. He straightened his jacket and sat, trying to ignore the babe screaming in the bassinet in the corner.

"I'm sorry?"

"Has he had any problems with his colleagues at the factory?"

Mrs. Barton looked startled. "I believe there is a misunderstanding," she stuttered, eyes darting towards her screaming babe. "Henry has enlisted. He no longer works—"

Michael shifted, pulling a long dagger from his jacket to lay it across his legs. He smiled with no small amount of satisfaction as the woman's face paled. "I asked ye a question, ma'am. I will not react kindly the next time it is ignored."

She shook her head, tripping over her skirts, making her rear end land hard on the arm of a small sofa. Her hand shot to her breast, and Mikey's gaze caught on the modest ring on her finger. "I—I don't believe so. Of course, there were some fights that men tend to get in, but Henry—"

Michael nodded and started cleaning his nails with the dagger. He didn't have to look up to find her watching his every move. "Does Henry tend to lose his temper, Mrs. Barton?"

Lips pressed tightly together, face strained, she shook her head. *Lie.*

Mikey raised his brow. "Has he ever laid his hands on ye?"

"How dare—"

The back door slammed open, causing Mrs. Barton to scream and the babe's wailing to turn into angry guttural cries that almost had Mikey going to the child to see if it was getting in any bloody air.

Mikey snarled at the brothers. "I told ye to wait outside."

Georgie leaned against the doorframe, folding his arms cockily as his brother pushed his way into the room.

"Got tired of waitin'." Hugh sneered at Mikey before he continued circling the bassinet. "Loud little bugger, isn't it?" He lifted part of the blanket before letting it fall back down.

Mrs. Barton looked like she wanted to go to her child, but her eyes darted between the three men. "What is it you want?" she asked, voice wavering.

"Your husband has gotten himself into a bit of trouble," Mikey answered, tired of this shite and the godforsaken noise. "Now, I'm not in the business of repeating myself, but I will give ye this one. Has your husband ever beat ye?"

Her eyes grew wary, but Mikey didn't miss the way she had grabbed her wrist. A defensive position, usually at the cost of an old injury.

"I don't see how this is any of your business," she snapped.

Mikey's patience was about to snap when movement by the bassinet drew his attention.

"Shall we make it our business?" Hugh asked, cradling her screaming child.

The woman paled when she saw the knife precariously close to the babe's face. She started forward, but Georgie came up behind her and grabbed her, causing her to shriek and recoil.

"Shall we take ye in the back?" Georgie asked. "I bet I can get a few answers out of ye when I have ye under me."

"Enough!" Mikey barked, and Georgie's hands paused their pursuit across Mrs. Barton's body. This was why he wanted them outside. "Put the feckin' wean down," he told Hugh.

It looked like Georgie wished to protest, but he listened with a snarl. The babe continued to wail as Hugh put it down and backed away.

Mikey let out a slow breath. "And take your bloody hands off of Mrs. Barton, or I will have ye flayed."

Georgie let go, and the woman stumbled, catching herself on the sofa before running to her child.

"Outside," Mikey growled, and his men let themselves out of the back.

"I'll tell you whatever it is you want to know," Mrs. Barton said, bouncing her babe.

Mikey eyed the thing. "Is he hungry?"

"What?" Her eyes crinkled in confusion.

"Feed your feckin' child, and we'll talk."

When understanding dawned on her features, she looked at the door.

"Don't be plannin' anything, Mrs. Barton," Mikey drawled, making himself comfortable in the chair he occupied previously. "Me men are outside. I will let them in again if ye plan to leave."

Her complexion greyed. "Of course," she said and turned, intending to go to another room.

"Ye can feed your child in here."

"But—" Something in his expression made her redirect to the sofa.

Her face reddened with each unbuttoning of her white shirt. Mikey watched as her thin neck was uncovered, and with the swipe of her hand, her shirt opened, exposing her small breast. He sat there in morbid fascination as the child latched on, and the room fell blissfully silent. Only when he wondered if Shay was doing that very act did he ashamedly look at his hands tightly balled into fists in his lap.

With a quick clear of his throat, he stated, "Your husband is not a good man. Am I correct?" He ignored the churning in his gut at the hypocrisy of his statement. At the task, he had planned out coming here.

Mrs. Barton wouldn't look at him but nodded her agreement.

"And can ye tell me why a southern man would fight for the Union? A lovely southern woman like yourself surely has ties down there."

Mrs. Barton looked as if she was going to vomit. "We moved here several months ago. Henry had promising business—"

"Business?"

"He—he just said there was business." She shrugged. "I assumed it was the factory. It hadn't been easy..."

That had Mikey sitting straighter. Something was odd about the whole situation. Why would a southern couple move North? Unless they believed in the Union? Whatever the reason, it was evident Mrs. Barton wasn't privy to it. Instead, he asked. "He placed his hands on ye?"

"Henry has a temper," she said slowly, stroking her babe's face as she thought. "He often gets in fights at work."

"And at home?"

"I try not to displease him."

"Would ye say he is a bully?"

"Yes."

Mikey nodded, adjusting himself in the chair, his knife in his lap. "Does he pick his victims at random?"

"Has Henry done something?"

"It has been made clear to me that your husband needs to learn there are consequences to his actions. He has targeted someone very close to me."

Her throat bobbed again. "I truly am sorry for whatever—"

"That is not enough." The sharpness of his words made her still.

She quickly shifted the babe to the other breast before she pleaded. "Please. You can do whatever you want to me, but I beg you not to harm my child."

Mikey watched the back of the babe's head, the way the mother's hand cradled it as if already shielding it from him. At the ring on her finger. He quirked a brow, an idea forming.

When the babe finished, Mrs. Barton put the sleeping child in the bassinet and walked over to him, shirt still open.

"Stop," he demanded.

With shaking hands, she started to pull back her shirt. Mikey rose and grabbed her shaking hands. His eyes never left hers as he buttoned her shirt, the rough fabric the only barrier between his fingers and her chest.

"I do not want ye," he said, noticing the flinch as if he slapped her. "Not that ye aren't—" He shook his head. He needn't explain to her.

She stopped him only to press his hands over her breasts. "I can—"

"No," he snapped, pulling away as he tried to dispel the shock of her brashness. Had she been put in a similar situation before? "Put your hand on the table, ma'am."

"My hand..." Her words trailed off when she spotted the dagger. "Please."

Mikey ignored the fear in her voice. The way his stomach knotted simultaneously with the shot of adrenaline through his body.

"Your hand," he growled. "This will only hurt as much as ye fight me. I suggest you answer my next questions very carefully." Mrs. Barton slowly moved toward him. The leather creaked as his grip tightened on the dagger, and the babe's wails pierced the night moments later.

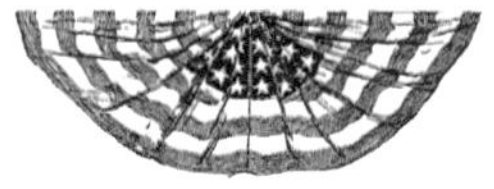

"You can't be here," Shay heard Rose exclaiming loudly downstairs.

A familiar brogue rumbled up. "Rose, darlin'. Ye missed me."

Shay gasped, looking at the mess of discarded baby stuff and then down at herself. Yes, that was definitely a food stain from earlier and some spit-up on her shoulder that she hadn't gotten around to cleaning up.

Shit, shit, shit.

She ran around the room, throwing dirty towels into the corner, and as she grabbed a clean one, dipping it in the pitcher of water to scrub at her dress. There wasn't time for it to dry, but at least—

Footsteps on the stairs had her tossing the rag before steadying herself. Her body still hadn't completely healed, and sudden movements were a strain. With a deep breath, she went over to Libby, who began to fuss on the bed and carried her over to the rocker just in time to find Michael still flirting with Rose.

Shay had to hide her smile when she saw the venom in Rose's glare.

"I'm sorry, child," Rose said to Shay, her face softening. "Are you up for company?"

Michael leaned against the wall, smiling lazily. "Are ye up for me, lass?"

Shay puckered her lips, giving him a withering stare before telling Rose he could stay. Michael's smile turned smug, and Rose made her thoughts loudly known as she descended the stairs.

Shay narrowed her eyes at the package Mikey put in his jacket pocket.

"What are you doing here?" Shay adjusted Libby in her arms.

"I was just walking through and thought ye—"

She gave him a look but stopped when her eyes caught on the bulge again. "What is in your pocket?"

"Oh, just—" He stopped—Was he nervous? It couldn't be. Whatever it was disappeared and was replaced with a crooked grin. "Never ye mind."

He sat down at the small table in the center of the room. This close, Shay noticed the strain in his features.

"Did something happen?" she asked hesitantly.

Michael sighed, resting his arms on his knees and rubbing his face. "It seems our gypsy had gotten into a wee bit of trouble."

"What?" Shay snapped so loud that Liberty flailed her little arms, her lips wobbling before Shay could hush her. "It's okay." She rocked. "It's okay." After a soft hiccup that didn't threaten a deafening wail, Shay turned back toward Michael. "What happened?"

Michael stared at her and the baby with an odd expression. "Nothin' ye have to concern yourself with. Just some trouble in the barracks."

"And she told you?" she asked incredulously.

"Jealous?" A sly smile grew, transforming his whole countenance.

Shay's breath snagged as she was caught in the intensity of his blue eyes. She looked down at the baby, not wanting him to notice how he'd started to affect her. She could kick herself for the stupidity of it. Even if it was a miracle that she'd want another man again after what her assaulters had done to her. She couldn't remember when the desire returned or if it had increased since Michael had stayed for Libby's birth. She'd blame it on not being with a man in over a year. Well, not one that gave her any satisfaction.

Damn, when was the last time she'd been decently touched by a man? Her cheeks heated. Apparently, a long damn time if *Michael* affected her like this.

Shay ignored the swirling thoughts and admitted, "I haven't heard from her."

The chair creaked as he leaned back, tone suddenly serious. "Tommy told me. The matter seems to be settled. Don't trouble yourself, lass."

Shay nodded, ignoring the tightness in her chest—the worry for her friend—and raised a brow. "Is that all?"

"Do ye want it to be?"

"Do you ever just get to the point? Or do you always have to dance around it?"

"What would be the fun in that?"

Libby's face scrunched up, her little mouth rooting for her mother. Shay's face heated again, and thanked the stars that her complexion most likely hid it from him. They had about five seconds before Libby would explode.

"She's hungry," Shay said just before Libby pierced the room with a shriek.

Michael nodded and stood. "Well, I'll leave ye to it then." He paused as if hesitating for a minute. Shay held her breath and tried to ignore the twinge of disappointment. *What the hell is wrong with me?* "Do ye need anything before I leave?"

Shay rocked Libby, trying to get the babe quiet so she could pull her thoughts together and get a bearing on her fluctuating emotions. Did she want to throttle him? Kick him out? Or climb him like a glorious, overbearing, very muscular tree? She tried not to snort at that thought, even as desirous heat flared over her body.

Instead, she reluctantly chose indifference. "You don't have to keep checking on me," she informed Michael, voice flat to hide the truth. He couldn't figure out how much his visits thrilled her. Made her feel *alive*. A nearly impossible feat since... Shay paused, shaking the memory out of her head before continuing, a strained tightness in her tone that hadn't been there earlier. "I can handle it myself. You probably have a million other things you would rather be doing."

Michael hesitated, already at the door. Something flickered in his expression before he sneered, and Shay's stomach bottomed out. "Don't flatter yourself, dimples."

The new nickname sent butterflies fluttering in the chasm of her belly before his following words torched them to embers.

"I have a woman—or several—warming the bed as we speak. Ye were just on the way."

He gave a sultry wink and was gone, leaving Shay cursing him and his *women*, unable to stop the onslaught of images that *that* scenario entailed.

She shifted in her seat, hating how much that turned her on, even as jealousy brewed deep. Yes, she hated that even more than the relief she desperately needed. Besides, she didn't even know if she *could* find relief. She'd been too afraid to try since the birth.

It wasn't until after she fed Libby and set her down to nap that she found the package in the chair—a tiny ragdoll inside. Shay's head whipped towards the door as if Michael would be there. As if it could make any damn sense of the infuriating Irishman.

CHAPTER SEVEN

Emilia & Shaylah

January 1862

Excitement rippled through the ranks, practically humming with each word carried across the lawn. We worked hard for this and were so close to completing our training. I stood tall as the wind cut through my coat, too enthralled by Governor Andrew and other speakers presenting our flags.

Christmas had come and gone, and with it, the New Year. The men had celebrated with some drinks, food, and letters from home, but nothing like with our families. I sent a letter to Shay but had no idea if she received it in time and received nothing in return. Thomas had found a rope that he knotted into a design to fit around my wrist. Obviously, he thought it wasn't enough, but I loved it and wore it ever since. I tried to give him my rosary, as my promise that I wasn't going anywhere, but he refused, claiming that our first Christmas together was enough. I couldn't disagree.

We stood in front of the State House, nearly in the same spot I was in all those months ago, when a burst of patriotism burned through me. I presently felt a slow-burn satisfaction for standing among the men. I hadn't known that was what I desired, but standing there, my heart knew this was where I belonged. I had broken insecurities and barriers that I didn't even know existed, and I emerged stronger because of them. I was beginning to feel at peace about who I was as a person, rather than just going through the steps of everyday life.

I looked over to find Thomas already staring at me. Our eyes locked, everything else fading away as I fell into his emerald depths. The sadness I wasn't prepared to see stopped my breath, and I felt myself deflate. He wasn't looking at me with the pride I mistakenly searched for, but as if he was missing the woman I was before. I turned away, feeling the sting of tears threatening to break free.

The back of Thomas' hand brushed against mine for a split second, so subtle that I almost mistook it as a hair or a kiss of the wind. The slight touch sent shockwaves up my arm, and my throat tightened. It was enough. It had to be. He may disagree with me, but he still supported my choices. With that, I finally let out the breath I was holding.

The men around me were becoming restless, ready to finish our training and get out in the thick of it. The flags flew high, the gold stars standing out on the deep blue of the national flag, making them look dirty compared to the white snow blanketing everything around us. The state flag billowed in the wind, the state's seal and red regimental ribbon in the center barely visible from where we stood.

"...To you and all your soldiers," the governor continued speaking to Colonel Monteith. "From all the inhabitants of this land today begins an indebtedness which it will take long to discharge, and by future generations will you be remembered. Inspired, sir, by the purposes of patriotism, you, as adopted citizens, will know no other allegiance than that due to the United States of America, now the mother of us all."

This was why most of the men enlisted. Fighting for the Union was like giving a big middle finger to their oppressor. What better way to liberate Ireland than to fight for the Republic that England so dearly despised. If the Union won, Ireland would win in the hearts of the men around me. They practically hummed with anticipation.

I smiled, squaring away the knowledge only Shay and I knew.

Governor Andrew finished the speech, and we cheered, the hum of battle already hot in our veins. Once dismissed, we began to walk away, falling into formation as we had been drilled to do for so many weeks.

Though I kept my head straight, I could see citizens standing at a distance, trying to get the best view of the ceremony without interrupting. An older man stood off to the side, under one of the large trees, as he stared in our direction. My brows scrunched at how sharp his three-piece suit was, a tall top hat adorning his gray hair. He looked like he was born into money, starkly contrasting the men I'd been around lately. However, something about him was familiar from how he held his shoulders back as if he was used to demanding attention. Or was it the hard set of his face? A prickling sensation of unease overcame me, and I was thankful he was far enough away that I didn't have to engage.

A fight had broken out on the other side of the street, drawing the attention of most of the men without breaking rank.

"What is it?" I mumbled to Thomas, though I was looking the other way. The shouting became louder, and I tried to see around the man in front of me.

"Looks like a fight," he said blandly.

I shot him a look. "Obviously."

I could've sworn his lips twitched, threatening a smile.

We came around a bend, and I could glimpse a group of men pulling apart the two who seemed to be grappling with one another, taking punches awkwardly wherever they could.

"Could ye see what started it?" I asked.

Thomas collided into me, causing me to curse and nearly fly to the side. If it wasn't for him catching me, I would have fallen on my ass.

I looked up at him, disgruntled and a little irritated.

"Do they have to have a reason?" he said as if nothing had happened. He only straightened his jacket and smoothed his hand over the front. "I wouldn't give it much thought."

"Did ye trip?" I hissed, looking around to see if anyone noticed.

"Aye. Sorry."

I turned back to the commotion, but the men were already walking in separate directions. Apparently, it was only a minor scuffle. And then, one of them pulled his hat off, revealing bright red hair, and I gasped, noticing his long, thin features. "Is that Hugh?" I asked Thomas, squinting to see better. "Or Georgie?"

Thomas shrugged, though his face was notably erased of any emotion. "They aren't the only lads with red hair, aye?"

I gave him another look. He was acting fucking weird. The last few minutes were too, but I didn't question it further. "It just looked like one of them," I mumbled.

We crossed the street, and I felt my heart accelerate. It had begun to snow, large flurries falling over the bare tree. We turned the corner, walking in front of it, and I dared to look around Thomas for the nicely dressed man I had seen there earlier. I let out my breath when I saw he was no longer there.

"Did ye see a man there earlier?" I whispered, not wanting to draw anyone else's attention.

"Who?" Thomas' brows drew down.

"There was a man by the tree."

Thomas kept his head straight, trying not to make any movements that would draw attention to us. "Nay. Someone we know?"

"I don't know," I said, my stomach tightening as an unexplainable jolt of fear and déjà vu overcame me. I shook my head. "No one, I guess."

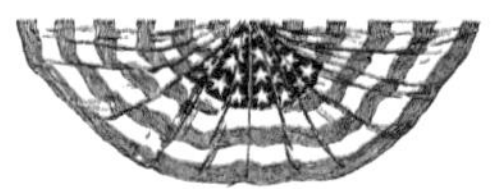

The smoke billowed high in the air, the sharp clang of the train's whistle ringing across the crowd. Shay held Libby tighter, swaddled against the cold, and buried deep within her coat as she descended the stairs.

Hiram parted the people around them, and Michael trailed close behind.

She couldn't miss this. She had to see Millie before she left on the train to New York. The previous day, she had missed the speech and presentation of the flags at the State House. She'd been furious with Michael for keeping her from it, and only found out from Hiram after it had finished. And for the life of her, she couldn't figure out why Michael didn't tell her.

A familiar set of shoulders towered over the crowd, revealing a dark head of hair and pale skin. A look to the side showed the shorter form that Shay knew, like the back of her hand.

"Over there." She pointed until Hiram found them as well. "Wait!" Shay yelled over the crowd. "Wait!"

Emilia had stopped with one foot up on the step of the train as if she heard her friend over the crowd, hanging onto the handle in her ridiculous oversized uniform. Her face turned, and Shay nearly collapsed with relief even as her stomach pinched with worry. She'd never seen Millie so thin.

"Eamonn! Thomas!" Shay screamed again.

"I think they heard ye, lass," the familiar brogue rumbled into her back; he was so close.

She shot Michael a glare even as her body betrayed her, igniting at his proximity.

People grumbled at her and Hiram until they saw Michael following behind, and then they seemed to part like they had leprosy. Shay shook her head, still angry with him even though his reputation made navigating it easier. She ignored the stupid flutter in her chest and what that might mean.

"Remind me again why you're here?" Hiram snapped at Michael.

They were close enough now that Shay could no longer see Millie above the crowd.

"Can I not visit me, dear brother?"

Hiram muttered something Shay would rather ignore and thanked the stars that Michael didn't hear. She could not deal with the fighting between them right now.

Finally, the crowd parted and—

"What are ye doing here?" Millie's fake brogue floated over to them, and Shay had to suppress an odd mixture of a laugh and sob. Millie took a step down and rushed toward them, Thomas following.

"She wouldn't shut her gob until we agreed to come," Michael said as the two women hugged. Shay couldn't even be angry with him anymore. She was too happy that her friend was in her arms—arm. She pulled back and looked down.

"You could've stayed behind," Hiram grumbled, accepting Thomas' hand with a quick embrace.

"And trust the lass with ye?"

"Oh my God!" Millie hissed, pulling back the coat a bit. "Oh my God!" She looked up into Shay's face, eyes wet with tears. "She is so beautiful." Millie ran her fingers over Libby's sleeping face. "You're a momma." She smiled.

"I am." Shay's throat felt thick, tears springing to her eyes. "A girl."

"What is her name? Michael hadn't told us." Millie threw a glare at Michael and punched him in the arm.

"Ye look like shite, gypsy."

Millie's face paled as she looked at Thomas. "Training was hard."

Michael nodded, but the raise of his brow said he didn't believe her.

Shay looked between them. "Did something happen?"

Millie shook her head but wouldn't meet her eye. "Nothing I can't handle."

Shay stepped forward, but a slight pressure on her lower back made her look up. Michael shook his head and leaned around her, listening to something Thomas said in his ear.

"I didn't know we were coming today, deartháir," Michael said, running his hand agitatedly through his dark hair. "It sure as hell would've been a whole lot easier."

Shay eyed the two men suspiciously but turned toward Millie instead. "Liberty. Her name," she clarified, looking down at the bundle, and smiled. "I like to call her Libby."

Millie glided a finger over Libby's face and smiled sadly. "I'm sorry I wasn't there."

Shay's throat constricted, and she had to swallow before speaking. "It's okay, Mill. I know you would have been if you didn't have something important to do." Her eyes flicked to Michael while she whispered, "Michael was there."

"What?"

Shay grabbed Millie's arm and turned her when Michael noticed them staring.

"He showed up and just stayed," she clarified.

"Do you have any idea why?"

Shay shook her head.

Millie widened her eyes dramatically. "Did he see her like...come out?"

Shay cringed, and heat rose in her cheeks as she looked at the man in question. "He saw everything."

Millie reared back. "Why?" she dragged the word out again. "Have you guys..."

"When would we have done that?" Shay said a little hysterically. "When I was nine months pregnant and ready to pop, or after and still bleeding everywhere?" Millie cringed. "Because I'm still sore. It was awful!"

"I'm sorry." Millie frowned, clearly learning more about childbirth than she was prepared for. "It's just you two seem so—"

"He's not interested. What man would be after what happened?" Shay's stomach twisted in embarrassment at what Michael saw that night and how it affected his view of her. How disgusted he must be. Besides, it wasn't like he showed any interest in her like *that,* anyway. He felt a sense of obligation, and that was it. Shay worried her lip. Was this some sort of savior complex? Because if it was, she needed to get over it really quick. Michael had plenty of women. He didn't need another one with misbegotten stars in her eyes.

Millie's gaze filled with a sadness Shay didn't want to acknowledge.

"Any man would be lucky to be with you," Millie said. "And if they think anything other than that, then they aren't a man worthy enough to be by your side."

Shay felt Millie trying to catch her gaze, but Shay wouldn't look up from her baby.

"I didn't mean to—"

"It's fine." Shay sighed, finally meeting Millie's eyes. "It's probably just the hormones." She gave a half-hearted smile.

"We can't stay long," Hiram announced just before the train whistled its last call.

Shay glanced at Michael and was startled to find him staring at her, face stony and almost...*angry,* mixed with something else she couldn't discern. She averted her gaze and hugged Millie instead.

"You stay safe," she said.

"Of course." Millie's voice was heavy, full of the trickling sadness that Shay felt. "Remember to go if you need to," she whispered into Shay's ear. "Don't be afraid to leave. Leave the vials with someone, and I will find them when I return. Do what you need to do." Millie backed away quickly, aware of the stares they drew around them.

"Not without you." She rocked Libby, a defiant stance that her friend was all too familiar with. A posture that could start wars.

Millie's smile trembled when she mouthed. "I love you."

"You too, Millie Billie."

Shay watched as Millie turned quickly to Thomas, who was looking oddly at his brother. "Are ye ready?" Millie asked him.

Shay's heart squeezed at the love written all over the man's face as he stared at Millie, and, not for the first time, she had the deep, sinking inclination that her friend might never leave this time.

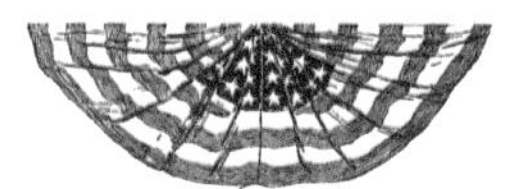

We said goodbye to our friends for the second time in just over a month. This time was different, though.

Then, I realized just how much I had committed to this time.

I wasn't looking at a few months, but possibly years, before I could return to Massachusetts, let alone go back to the future. I thought I knew what I signed up for, but looking at Shay, I started having doubts.

With one last glance at my best friend, I knew she'd be okay. Especially with the two men towering behind her, keeping everyone else at bay like an impenetrable wall. I smiled and stepped back on the train's step, finding a seat next to Mick, who spoke animatedly with another soldier across the aisle.

I pushed towards the window, careful not to hit him in the face with my pack, belatedly wondering why Thomas and Michael had been acting so suspiciously.

It took me a minute to find Shay outside, but I finally spotted her and tried to wave. She was laughing at something Michael said, and my heart squeezed at how he looked down at her and the sweet little babe in her arms.

I sat down heavily, amazed at how much those two had grown. *When did that happen?* Clearly, both felt something for one another and were fools to think otherwise. I knew Shay enough to ascertain where her feelings lay, but Michael? If he hadn't yet, it would only be a matter of time before he realized it, too. I smiled, thinking of all the ways my friend would torment him.

I only wished I could be there to see it.

The train started with a loud whistle, moving past a sea of faces. As they sped by, I waved at my friends. A tall top hat suddenly caught my eye behind them—the only thing seen over the families crowding around to wave to their men. I stood up, trying to see his face, my heart pounding.

I told myself that it was a popular hat. That it couldn't possibly be the same man. And after a while, I started to believe it. It would only be weeks until it had escaped my mind entirely.

Maybe if I had listened to my intuition, I'd have saved us from the pain. Perhaps the subsequent events in our life would have turned out differently.

Maybe, just maybe, he would have survived.

CHAPTER EIGHT

Emilia

FEBRUARY 1862

"**A** what?" Hall asked, probably thinking he heard Mick wrong.

"A goddamn finger! In his bloody bunk."

We were on Governors Island, having left the train to ride the ferry over to the fort the previous day, now heading across the yard to the southeastern portion of the island to be drilled. Word around camp was that Barton had woken up to a severed finger lying next to his head.

My stomach turned as a feeling of uneasiness washed over me.

"Why do ye think?" I asked, keeping my eyes on the horizon.

"A warning, I'd guess," Hall answered seriously.

Mick gave an enthusiastic nod. "That's not all." Anyone would have found that disturbing, but what adorned the finger had Barton nearly in hysterics. Luckily for him, most everyone left before he started tearing the place apart and blaming everyone who came close to him. "The word is that it's his wife's ring."

A wave of nausea washed over me, and I turned quickly, puking up my breakfast.

"Aye!" Mick drug the word out, laughing. "O'Connor 'ere hasn't got the stomach for this. I thought this was a common occurrence in your family."

"He just got off the boat, gobshite," Hall said, side-eyeing Mick. "They all don't need to be misogynistic. No offense," he added quickly to me.

"None taken," I answered, but my head was already elsewhere as they bickered back and forth.

Had Thomas done this? Suddenly, so many blurry instances I had looked over became vividly clear. Michael's remark regarding my appearance. Thomas had been oddly quiet about the matter since the incident in the mess hall. I thought he finally accepted my independence, realizing I could handle it myself. But now I was thinking maybe he backed off because he had already set a plan into motion.

The sudden realization had my stomach turning again. Did he not think I could handle it myself? And would he really hurt an innocent woman to protect me? How he found the time to do it was beyond me.

My thoughts ran wild, and I knew I had to speak with him. Bile rose in my throat at the possibility.

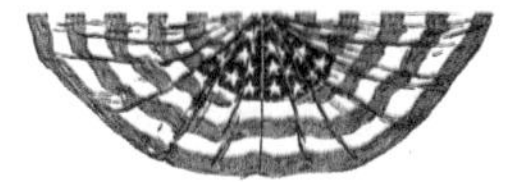

The wind off the water pierced my coat like a million sharp knives until I shook in my boots. I pretended it didn't affect me like the other men. Or maybe we were all just pretending.

We fell into line, drilling endlessly until we could do it in our sleep. Once our instructor was satisfied with our positions, we moved on to our rifles now that we all had our weapons. They quickly taught us how to use them since we were already expected to know the basics of shooting. My heart sank, realizing I may be farther behind than anyone else.

"Right hand, Private!"

I squeezed the rifle tighter, my hands shaking with nerves and the cold. "But I'm left-handed, Sergeant."

"And what does that have to do with what I told you? Should we throw the whole lineup off because of you? Would you want one of your men to perish because you couldn't follow a simple order?"

I felt Mick stiffen to my left. We were in line with two other men. All of them had automatically used their right hands. My face heated under the scrutiny.

"No, Sergeant." I switched hands, the rifle feeling unnatural this way.

"Your arm is too low!"

I raised it more.

"Right shoulder higher! Goddamn it, soldier. It's as if you never shot a day in your life."

I kept still, perfecting my aim. No way in hell I would tell him I was a rooky.

"What is your name?"

"Eamonn O'Connor, Sergeant!"

"O'Connor, aye?" He eyed me up and down, but I kept my sight straight ahead. "Any relation to Thomas O'Connor?"

My heart sped up, not sure how much to reveal to him. "Junior or Senior?"

"The answer would be the same. No?"

"Aye, Sergeant. He's me uncle."

He stared at me for so long that I wanted to fidget out of nervousness. "I haven't heard of a nephew."

"Distant relation, Sergeant. Me ma was of Italian stock. I didn't make the journey over from Ireland until recently."

"I have to say, I can't place your accent. What part of Ireland did you say?"

"Lansdowne, Sergeant."

He stared at me as I shook, until finally moving on to his next victim. I lowered my weapon in relief, my arms nearly giving out from holding it up so long. I made a mental note to work my arms and back to build strength. We had been running, but it was evident that I had to develop my upper body strength to keep up with the men. Hell, I'd need to do it just to get through the days of carrying all of my supplies.

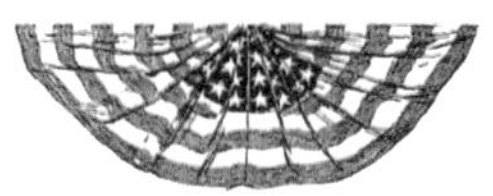

"How'd ye get away with it until now?" Mick asked later that night. We sat around one of the many fires the men had made in the clearing.

"With what?" I asked, my body stilling as my heart nearly burst out of my chest. Did he find out I was a woman? Was I not careful enough?

Mick looked pointedly at my hand. "They didn't beat it out of ye when ye were a lad?"

I stared at him, my pulse still galloping as I thought of what to say. I'd spent all day kicking myself for forgetting the superstitions and restrictions of this time. I should have anticipated using my left hand would cause some controversy. Ridiculous as it was…

"Runs in me family. Me ma took pity on me." I shrugged like that was enough information.

Movement caught my eye. I stood quickly, following Thomas without another word. They all watched me leave, probably wondering about my abrupt departure, but their conversation started back up as I was still in earshot.

Thomas was heading to one of the other fires. I saw Sullivan and a few of the other men he usually hung out with. I hadn't realized how much we separated ourselves from one another since joining the army. I was the one to blame, really. I wanted to make a name for myself and do it on my own terms without relying on anyone else. What I hadn't expected, though I should have known, was that Thomas would be looking over me, whether I wanted it or not. He always had.

"Tommy!" I called, not liking the way it sounded on my lips.

He stopped and waited for me to catch up but didn't turn to look at me.

"I need to speak with ye."

He tilted his head for us to walk off. The frozen air suddenly felt heavy. He knew what I wanted to speak with him about.

We walked a few paces, heading away from the groups of men as I attempt-ed to gather my thoughts. I peeked up at him. A frown creased his brows, his jaw tense as he watched our boots crunch through the snow. Clearly, something was bothering him. I prayed it wasn't what I suspected.

"Did ye do it?" I asked.

"Do what?" His frown deepened.

"Ye really are going to pretend like ye don't know?" I hissed it, stepping closer to him.

He looked at me from the corner of his eye before turning his face to the clear sky. All the stars were out tonight as the moon shone silver over the sharp plains of his face. For a second, I was jealous of its caress, wanting nothing more than to run my fingers through his dark whiskers. "Can't ye just leave it be?" he asked.

"No. Did ye?" The words stuck in my throat. I leaned in, whispering the next part. "Who did it? Who cut off her finger?"

"Mikey." His eyes darted to me and away just as quickly. "But it's not what ye think."

"How can it not be?" I yelled a little too loudly, gaining some attention from men close by.

"It's not her finger," he growled.

I took a step back, my heart nearly stopping as the meaning of his words sunk in. We stopped in the middle of a clearing, practically spitting fire from our eyes.

"Then whose is it?" I asked incredulously. "Do ye just go cutting off people's fingers? They said it had her ring."

Thomas swore at me in Irish, but I could see his resolve crumbling.

"If ye must know," he said, grabbing my arm to drag me farther away from the other men. "It's from a corpse. Mikey scared her into giving us the ring and put it on the finger. When Georgie and Hugh—"

"So, it was them!" I said, putting it together. They were the men who were fighting the day we received our flags.

"Mikey snuck me the finger when everyone was looking at them."

"A diversion."

"Aye."

Relief washed over me. Thomas hadn't ordered for another woman to be hurt. In reality, they had just taken a ring, and now Barton had it again. No harm other than frightening him. The man needed to be taken down a notch, and a healthy dose of fear might have been good for him. But—my brows scrunched. "Why didn't he give it to you at the train station? Why go through all of the trouble at the State House?"

Thomas's laugh was harsh as he ran his fingers through his hair. "That's what I said. The damn gobshite didn't know he'd be there. Apparently, Ms. Banks didn't take too kindly to him keeping her from the State House.

Hadn't even planned to tell the lass about it. She'd heard from Hiram. When Hiram agreed to take her to the train station, Mikey wouldn't let her go without him. Whether from guilt or his dark soul actually being worried for her…" He shrugged.

I started walking again, trying to make sense of the warring emotions within myself. I was happy that Shay put Michael in his place, even with how he and Thomas had helped me. But there was also an anger brewing within me, directed at the man by my side.

"You lied to me," I whispered. "When I asked you about Hugh, you made it seem like I was crazy. You kept me in the dark about all of it." My accent faded the more pain I had felt.

Thomas shoulders drooped. "I thought it best ye didn't know."

"You didn't trust I could do it on my own?"

"No," he snapped, then the tension in his face softened. "I mean yes, but I wanted to make sure. Men like Barton need to be put in their place."

I nodded. We were behind one of the buildings, the soft lap of waves in the distance and faint laughing from the men in the camp the only noise surrounding us. We were alone.

"Thomas, I'm sorry." I held my hand up when it looked like he was about to stop me. "I'm sorry I keep pushing you away. I just want to do this so badly. But the truth is…" I swallowed a lump forming in my throat. I was so *tired* of pushing everyone away. "I need you. I don't want to do it alone anymore. I don't want to waste another minute."

I watched his chest expand, his breath coming faster the more I talked.

His hand glided over my cheek, and I rested on it. With my sigh, I let go of all the tension and responsibility I had put on myself, and when I breathed in, I accepted that sometimes it was okay to take help from others.

I closed my eyes, cherishing the warmth radiating from his hand and pooling straight into my belly.

"I'll always need ye, gypsy."

That had me looking up, searching his face and finding nothing but genuineness. "No more secrets?"

Thomas closed his eyes briefly. When he opened them, the heat swirling inside seared me. My breath caught. "No more secrets," he breathed. I should never have kept it from you."

I turned my face into his palm and pressed my lips against it. He inhaled sharply, causing me to smile. Suddenly feeling brave, I grazed my teeth up his hand, wanting to sink them into his flesh until he pulled me into him. He did just that, slamming my back into the building, and pulling my head back by my hat.

"I miss that hair of yours," he growled into my neck, running his lips up it until I shivered. "The things I would do to ye."

"My hair is what's stopping you now?" My voice shook, making me flush in embarrassment.

He pulled back, eyes searching mine. "Ye know what's stopping me. It's not safe—"

"What if I don't want you to stop?" I asked softly. "What if I want you right now?"

My words had the opposite effect on him, and he pulled back. "I don't want to compromise ye." He looked towards the camp even as his hands gripped me tighter.

"No one is here to stop us." Doing this with him didn't mean I was any less capable of handling myself and my problems. This was about him and me, feeling and sharing a moment as if it was just us. Like we were back in Boston, and the war wasn't exploding around us.

Frankly, if he didn't touch me, I might combust.

Something predatory entered his gaze as he stepped in, flushing my body with his. Thomas's lips firmly captured mine, unrelenting until I opened for him. Snow fell on us as I ran my hands through his hair and over his strong jaw, savoring each touch like it was the last. I wasn't sure when I would be able to hold him again. I just knew I wasn't going to waste my chance.

"We should stop," he said, his lips still pressed against mine even as his hand slid into my shirt, gripping my breast. A moan rumbled through me. He looked down, watching his fingers as he said, "Someone might see."

Well, *someone* was definitely watching.

I grabbed his hand and squeezed harder, wanting the ache. "We have a little time."

My nose brushed his, tilting his head up so I could nip his lip, making him growl as I moved my hand around his neck and deepened the kiss.

His hand left my breast and deft fingers began to unbutton my pants before sliding in. The gasp that escaped me was heady, needy, *desperate*. I didn't care and widened my stance.

"Is this what ye wanted, Emilia?" My name on his lips sent a shiver through me.

"Yes," I said breathily, my hips bucking. "God, yes. I want you so bad, Thomas." His large fingers slid over my entrance, spreading the wetness over my center and making me moan so loud that he had to deepen our kiss to muffle me.

"Any louder, lass," Thomas' warm breath danced against my lips, "and they'll hear ye."

My body thrummed with desire even as a spike of fear shot through my veins. "I'll be quiet," I promised.

Thomas made a guttural noise in the back of his throat, expressing his disbelief.

I ignored him and did quick work of his pants. I wrapped my cold fingers around him, making Thomas hiss in both shock and desire. His tongue swirled over mine, devouring my mouth as our hands moved quickly, knowing this had to be quick lest we be caught.

"Feck, Emilia. What ye do to me..." His body curved over mine, pulling me closer, shielding me, demolishing me. He pushed his fingers into me, and I gasped, the intrusion brutal and exhilarating as Thomas covered my mouth with his hand. I stared into his green eyes as he quickly, roughly pumped into me, entirely at his mercy. My hand jerked, unsteady, as I tried to keep up with his ruthless pace. Unable to look away from the all-consuming desire darkening his eyes.

The way that we watched each other work ourselves into a frenzy, the snow falling around us, men's voices in the distance, our pace quickening. Hell, it was so hot that my body began to spasm.

"Thomas," I moaned into his hand, though the word came out as a guttural, incoherent growl.

Thomas's hips thrust into my hand, fucking it as my body tightened, lava concentrating to my center, and—and detonating. Bursting into a million brilliant stars.

My legs gave out. Thomas held me up, thrusting into my hand as I curled into him and fell apart. His mouth replaced his hand covering mine, inhaling the deep moan rumbling out of me. Thomas' strong hand now held my face still as he used my body.

I dropped to my knees, causing him to lose his grip. His curse was cut off as I pulled him out of his pants.

"Emilia—"

I didn't wait for him to deny me. I shoved him into my mouth so quickly that he jerked down my throat. I gagged, unprepared for the size of him. Pulling back, I looked up to watch his tight features as I ran my tongue up his shaft.

"*Hell*, woman."

My tongue swirled around his tip, making he groan. I pulled back and looked up at him through my lashes.

"Use me, Thomas." My voice was unrecognizable—confident, husky, pleading.

His green eyes were consumed by black. It only took one indecisive second before he grabbed the back of my head and shoved in—quickly, viciously. Tears sprang to my eyes as he pushed deeper. I focused on hollowing my mouth, holding onto his hips, encouraging him faster.

"That pretty wee mouth is mine, ye understand? None of these men—Christ." He groaned, closing his eyes as his head pressed against the building. "I'll kill any man who comes near ye. Your body is mine. *Ye're* mine, goddamn it."

The pure, feral possessiveness of his words set my body on fire. I groaned, the vibration of it making him curse louder. I drew back and he pulled out of my mouth with a pop.

I looked up at him, eyes big and innocent, and I felt an unusual moment of courage that befell a woman when she knew she had a man at her mercy. "Am I doing it right?" I gripped him as I ran my tongue slowly up his shaft. "Because I've never done this before." My words were sweet even as I swirled my tongue around his head, watching his face tighten and his eyes nearly glow with need as a low growl vibrated through his chest.

"Aye—" His words were choked off as I sucked him in deeply. "Ye're mouth..."

I pulled back, smiling up at him before I teased him into my mouth again, cutting off his words momentarily. One taunting suck, then I gave him permission that would be our undoing.

"Fuck my mouth, Thomas."

He grabbed my head and shoved in, slamming down my throat and making me gag again. I gripped his hips, encouraging him to keep moving. Faster. Harder.

"God damn it, woman." His thrusts became uneven as he started to lose himself. "That pretty mouth of yours will get ye in trouble."

Tears fell down my face as his long length pushed down my throat, cutting off my air even as I held him tighter, wanting him to use my mouth as much as he enjoyed it.

"Fuck!" he growled, trying to be quiet even as he spasmed down my throat, holding my head to him as I swallowed every last salty drop.

Thomas fell to his knees, eyes narrowing on my mouth as I licked my lips. "Christ, lass." I never heard his voice so gruff. It sent chills all over my body. He brushed my tears away and rested his forehead on mine.

I chuckled, holding onto his arms to keep myself upright. Pulling back, he scanned my face before returning to my mouth, slowly brushing his thumb over my lips as if in reverence. I opened them to say something, but his mouth was on mine, his tongue pressing in deep and rough, swirling around, and I knew he could taste himself. I moaned, pressing my breasts to his chest.

Several minutes passed until we were dangerously close to doing it again when Thomas pulled back, forehead on mine.

"Where did that come from?" he asked.

"I missed you..."

"I missed ye too, lass, but that was—" He shook his head, seemingly at a loss for words. His head slowly rocked back and forth against mine. "I didn't hurt ye, did I?"

"No." I ran my hands up his chest. "I like it when you use my body."

He pulled away to look at me. A deep crease deepening between his brows. "Ye are so much more to me than that. Ye know that, right?" I tried to pull away, but his strong arms locked around me. Thomas turned my face to him, so I had to look him in the eye. "Emilia?"

"Yes. I just—" I tried to think of the proper words to convey my feelings. There were so many emotions swirling through me that I didn't want Thomas to misinterpret. "I never did any of that with someone before. And you are the first person I *wanted* to do that with. I just—this is new to me. Wanting this. And knowing I want to with you, actually doing it with you is a way I can show you how much you mean to me."

His quiet scrutiny lasted long enough to make me squirm. When I began to pull away, his hands encompassed my face, and his warm lips gently pressed between my eyes. "I love ye, too, gypsy. Ye're it for me. Deep down, I knew that when ye walked into my life, there would be no one else for me. There never has been. I was just too damn stubborn to realize it. I've been with many women—" When I gave him a look he placed a finger over my lips, smiling abashedly. "But I never made love to one. What me and ye do..." He shook his head, face lit with the same emotion swelling inside my chest. "I never experienced anything like it."

I pressed my lips softly to his. A kiss that was warm and unhurried, conveying what I felt and everything I hadn't said. The previous ones satisfied our bodies, our temporary desires. This one warmed me straight to my soul.

We couldn't stop our smiles as Thomas helped me stand and we straightened our clothes.

He bent down for another long, slow kiss, taking his time. Savoring each moment we had together because we didn't know when would get another. He held me when we finally pulled back.

"There's one more thing ye should know," he said, face suddenly serious. My pulse skipped a beat. "It might not be anything, but something Mikey said had me thinking..." He straightened but kept his arms around me. "When he went to see Barton's lass, he did a sort of interrogation. No harm." Thomas smiled when he saw my reaction. "Mikey said the lass wasn't sure why Barton volunteered. Word is they're from the South and he was a known secessionist."

I stepped back to see him better, grabbing his arms to steady myself. "Why are they in the North, then?"

Thomas shook his head. "She said they up and left their home a few months back. Barton told her he had a job lined up. It could be the factory job he'd been working for, but Mikey couldn't get a straight answer about why he's a turncoat."

I thought about it a moment. How he didn't get along with anyone other than his two cronies. But that didn't necessarily mean he was a turncoat. But if what Mikey said was true...

"Do you think he is a spy?" Maybe that was why he had it out for me. If he suspected I wasn't who I said I was... I shook my head. "We need to figure out if he has any ulterior motives."

"That's what I'm planning to figure out."

I put some distance between us, straightening my uniform unnecessarily while I thought. "Don't get into trouble," I said. "Maybe you should leave it alone. It could have nothing to do with us."

"Trouble? Me?" His words were teasing, but his eyes gleamed with a barely controlled violence. "Why would ye think that?"

I worried my lip, knowing that I couldn't stop him.

"What's troublin' ye, gypsy? Ye don't think I can handle him?"

"Oh, I know you can," I said, fisting his coat. "That's what I'm worried about."

His brows scrunched, making me want to punch and kiss him simultaneously. "Ye're worried because I can handle him?"

"No, I'm worried that you will do something reckless."

"I spent most of my life reckless, lass. It's time I had a little fun again."

I stared at him. Thought of the way he said it as if he missed running the streets with his brother. As long as I knew Thomas, he fought to be a better man. Controlled the monster sleeping deep inside of him. I knew he struggled to keep it contained but I never once thought he might *enjoy* letting it out. I always thought he despised what he had done to survive, but now I thought he might despise how much he relished it. How easy it was to let the monster out to play.

I looked at Thomas as if it was the first time, and I wasn't sure if my heart pounded from fear or desire. Or a mixture of both. And I was slightly concerned about what that meant about me.

"What is the worst thing you've ever done?" I was unsure what prompted me to ask that question, but I had to know.

Thomas froze, his face hardening and green eyes blazing through mine. One step toward me had me bumping into the building at my back. Caging me between his arms, he bent so that his face was even with mine.

"What exactly do ye want to know, Emilia? And why do ye suddenly have the nerve to ask?" I looked away, but his strong hand gripped my chin and forced me to look at him. "I told ye I was no good for ye. Are ye suddenly realizing it?"

I watched his lips form each word, the way his jaw clenched, the dark stubble over it, and how his eyes boar into me, waiting for my response.

"You are good for me." Deep down I knew it was true. "It's just—"

"What, gypsy? It's just what?"

I glared at him. He was trying to intimidate me. It would have worked when I first met him, but I had enough monster in me now to not shrink back. Not anymore.

"Do what you got to do," I said, watching the anger slowly melt away. "I trust you. I'm not going anywhere, Thomas. I'll love you even if you have to let the monster out."

He pushed me away, and I flinched, not out of fear, but the intense emotions emanating from him felt tangible. "Ye don't know what ye are saying."

"Please," I snapped sarcastically, realizing I wasn't even a bit afraid of him anymore. "You're the one who admitted to wanting to be reckless, and now that I say go on ahead, you want to argue with me?"

Running his hands through his hair he looked up at the sky. "It's an argument I have with meself daily. Ye don't know how hard it is to control that part of myself. How many times a day I almost snap." He moved so fast that I didn't even flinch as he gripped my face again, his mouth nearly on mine. "How many times I wanted to take ye? Feck the others. I want ye, and that is the worst thing I ever done. Ye are too good for this world. This kind of life. I should never have let ye be a part of this."

"You don't get to decide that." I grabbed Thomas' face and looked him dead in the eye as we glared at each other. He didn't get to say that, believe it. And I knew there were far worse acts that he committed. "If you have to be a monster, then I am one too. Because, like it or not, this life is mine now, and I am not backing out, O'Connor."

I'd said the last name hundreds of times most of my life, but for some reason, in that moment, it sent tingles down my spine. Maybe it was because I recently reclaimed my Moretti name. It could have been a case of nostalgia. I didn't think much about it. I just knew, either way, I had a burning desire to be an O'Connor again.

I kissed him hard and pulled away, backing towards the camp. "Deal with it."

He prowled toward me, but I pointed to the camp in a silent order. Thomas growled, looking like he wanted to devour me.

"I like that name on your lips," he said as he drifted past, sending tingles up my spine. "I like that they all think it's yours." My stomach lurched, getting the uncanny sensation of him reading my thoughts. "And I love that ye used it while looking at me photograph in your time." He stopped, his gaze laying heavily on me as I stood frozen. "So, in a way, ye were always mine. Isn't that right, gypsy?"

I swallowed past the tightness in my throat. My entire being believing every goddamn word he said.

A slow, wicked grin spread across his face as he watched how he was affecting me. "Aye. I think ye rather enjoy that as well. Don't ye, Emilia?"

With a wink Thomas rounded the corner first while I tried to get my breathing under control. I barely moved when I heard a sharp crack somewhere behind me, causing me to jump and my heart to gallop with the speed of a thousand horses. Scanning the dark landscape, it was hard to tell anything among the shadows of the building. And yet—a flicker of something by the other building. All the little hairs stood up on my body as I looked closer. Was it there earlier? I wracked my brain, but I'd been too distracted by Thomas to pay particular attention to the landscape.

I looked up at the bright moon and how it distorted everything. It had to be a trick of the light. A quick scan revealed only vacant buildings and large shadows from a few crates and barrels. No sound. No movement.

Laughter rang out in the distance again and snapped me out of my growing unease. Knowing it was almost time for lights out, I shook off my paranoia and quickly rounded the building to join the guys.

CHAPTER NINE

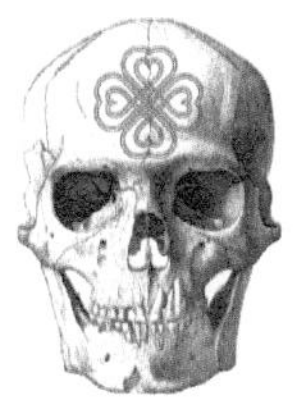

Michael

19 FEBRUARY 1862

Mikey straightened his blue jacket, pulling at the uncomfortable fabric out of pure repulsion. He cursed himself for sending Henry to procure the disguise for this particular mission. Once they had what they needed, he'd feckin' burn them.

"Not like that." Hugh spat, drawing Mikey's attention back to the task at hand. "Goddamn it!"

The tree groaned and swayed high above them but had not yet fallen across the train tracks they had targeted. They were in the middle of godforsaken Massachusetts, with only trees and a large group of his own stinkin' men. Even the wildlife was sparse. Good thing, too. Distractions could be fatal.

Georgie deepened the angle of the cut. "Think that'll do?"

"How the feck am I supposed to know?" Hugh snapped. "Like I go around cuttin' down feckin' trees for the fun of it."

"Well, ye're the one talkin' out of your arse like ye bloody know what to do. If ye know so much, why don't ye cut the damn thing down?"

Hugh cursed, and they began sawing the tree's other side.

"How much ye want to bet it lands on one of them?" Henry asked Mikey as they stared down the tracks.

The sky was overcast, and the air bit sharply through his clothes, but there was no sign of snow. *Thank the gods*. The carriages wouldn't make it if there was any build-up. The mud was bad enough, and it had taken him several days just to find the appropriate route to not get the damn things stuck.

"Is it done?" Mikey asked, ignoring Henry's bet.

"Aye, it's ready."

Mikey nodded, and the seriousness of what they were about to do weighed heavy on him. The telegraph wires were cut, and the train would be barreling down these tracks within the hour.

A loud crack and groan had the men scurrying away before a loud thud rocked the earth. Mikey's eyes widened, and a big grin spread across his face this time. He slapped a big hand onto Georgie's shoulder, the man smirked as they stared at the large tree lying across the railway tracks.

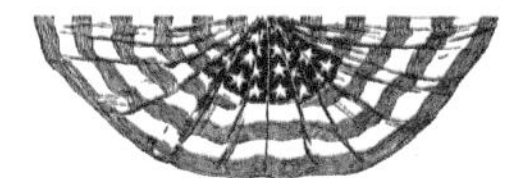

The snow had just begun to fall lightly as a rumble came from the distance. Crouched behind a tree, Mikey caught glimpses of the men he had placed strategically to accomplish their mission.

They didn't have to wait long. The sound of a loud horn down the tracks, followed by the shriek of breaks jolted through Mikey's body like an electrical current. The conductor must have noticed the fallen tree across the tracks. The train slowed, squealing as it struggled to stop before it hit the tree with a roar, sending bark and branches into the air as the train nearly derailed before coming to a stop, the tree wedged tightly under the pilot.

With a quick wave of his arm, Mikey and select men took off through the trees, heading farther back to the flatcars containing weapons and ammunition. They had only moments before the men would try to disembark and, with it, a blood bath if they didn't move fast enough.

The adrenaline coursing through Mikey had his feet flying over the ground, hurtling toward the train and onto the rail, thanking the gods he was blessed with his height.

Georgie appeared to his right, and Mikey hoisted him up as another man pulled him onto the flatcar. Removing the crowbar from the bag slung over his shoulder, Mikey pried open one of the crates just as someone started working on another. They started loading the bags with rifles and passing them to men, who took them to waiting wagons. Once loaded, they were to go immediately, leaving Mikey with his designated wagon. He wouldn't take any chances of getting caught.

A yell had Mikey's head snapping to the front of the train, and a gunshot rang out. Swearing under his breath, he started packing the rifles faster and lowered another bag to a young man.

"Go."

The boy took off into the trees as Hughie emerged from the front of the train, out of breath and a manic look in his eyes.

"One of the cars wasn't secured."

"What the feck ye mean it wasn't secured?" Mikey let out a string of curses that could make a grown man weep. More shots rang out as the soldiers from the cars began to move through his men.

"They didn't get the chain on before the feckers—"

Mikey closed his eyes, trying to keep his rage down when another loud shout had them springing back open.

Georgie lowered a bag as Mikey ordered another man to take his place.

"Keep filling them," he told Georgie before swinging over the side and jumping down.

The snow fell in earnest now, significantly reducing the visibility and hopefully working in his favor.

As he made his way to the front, men hollered from inside the cars, banging against it as they tried to escape. It was only a matter of time before they were out as well.

A soldier was up ahead, pinning one of Mikey's younger boys to a car, screaming for answers. Without hesitation, Mikey lifted his pistol and shot him through the head. He fell with a thump, the spray of the wound coating the fresh snow.

"Are ye all right?" he asked the boy when he neared. The kid was visibly shaking. Why the feck did he bring someone so young? Was he fourteen, at the least? The job was supposed to be simple. The boys he brought were only supposed to take the filled bags and get to the wagons. There was no need for them to be involved in anything else.

Apparently, that plan went to shite.

The boy nodded, head jolting up and down awkwardly as he struggled to get ahold of himself. Mikey pushed him toward the back, where he could grab a bag and get the hell out of there. A shout had Mikey lifting his pistol again, only to find Hughie already running a wicked blade across the man's neck. A movement to his right had him point it at another, only to find a young soldier, not much older than the boy he'd just saved, with his hands up in the air.

"Please, sir." His voice cracked. "Don't shoot."

Mikey's finger tightened on the trigger, gritting his teeth as he stared the boy down. Looking into his eyes, he could only see the same green as his brothers. It wasn't supposed to go down like this. No one was supposed to—

A gun exploded, and the boy went down, his brains splattered across the snow as his lifeless eyes still watched Mikey.

"C'mon," Hughie snapped, his pistol still smoking from the shot.

Mikey had a hard time pulling himself away from the scene. From the eyes that reminded him of the man who was a soldier himself, not too far from here. It could have been Tommy. It might—

Hughie swore, colliding with another soldier before slitting his throat. The distraction propelled Mikey through the men, the chaos, and the blinding storm. Bodies, soldiers, and his men alike fell across the ground. This was a feckin' disaster.

"Who forgot this car?" Mikey screamed at Hughie, trying to be heard over all the noise.

Hughie shook his head. "They were already comin' out when we got there. Someone hit Jack over the head, feckin' bastard." Hughie spit. "The feckers came pouring out after that."

Mikey cursed, looking at the scene around him. The snow still fell, obscuring most of it as the dark bodies continued to fight. They were close enough now to see that it was too late. All the soldiers were already out and would be working on getting the others out next.

"Pull the men back," Mikey growled. No one was supposed to die. He wouldn't have his own men's blood on his hands; some of them could barely find two hairs on their cheeks. Mikey ground his teeth, assessing the carnage.

"Ye can't be—"

"Tell them to grab as much as possible and get the feck out."

"No! We need to blow the damn thing."

Mikey fisted Hughie's coat, his face contorted in rage as he glowered at the smaller man. Fear flashed in his eyes so quickly that Mikey almost missed it. Hughie was a sick fecker, but he knew not to cross Mikey. It looked like the man hadn't killed off his remaining common sense after all. "If we blow it up, what do ye think will happen with all the damn ammunition? Ye damn fool."

"Then—"

"Ye contradict me again, and I'll make sure ye're just another damn body out here."

A quick shove had Hughie stumbling backward before straightening his coat as he glared at Mikey. Mikey squared himself, ready for the fight, but his friend thought twice and nodded curtly.

Mikey watched him go, wondering if he should be worried. Hughie always rode too close to the edge and flirted with insanity more than some. He was sadistic, unrelenting, his best torturer, and unhinged in the best of ways. Mikey could always trust Hughie to listen. Since they were kids, the Callahan twins followed him around, terrorizing the city while following his every command. But it seemed that Hughie might be questioning Mikey's choices, and he couldn't stand by that. He needed to put Hughie in line before he did something stupid.

A bullet tinged the train next to him, and Mikey ducked. Lifting his pistol, he shot the soldier in his next breath. Without another glance, Mikey made his way through the men. *We need to get the hell out of here.*

A sharp whistle had his men falling back with the rest of the bags.

"Get the hell down from there," Mikey yelled up to Georgie, who still passed bags down to men.

"We're almost—"

Mikey swore at him in Irish so profusely that Georgie tipped his hat and threw the last bag down to him. Catching it with a grunt, he slung it over a shoulder, scanning the area around him while he waited for Georgie to descend.

The storm hadn't let up. Several inches had fallen already, and if they waited any longer, they'd have a shite of a time getting the wagons out of here. Mikey cursed. Nothing could go as planned, could it? Not only did some dumb shite completely feck up the chaining of one of the cars, but even mother nature was giving him the finger. The number of men with bags was the only reassurance.

It would have to do.

They made it to the trees, his other men already retreating into the woods as they left the soldiers behind them. Mikey cursed them, cursed his men, cursed the whole damn world. At least the cover of the trees slowed down the blizzard.

They crashed through the underbrush and jumped over logs. His legs strained, but he didn't dare stop. Mikey wouldn't have wanted to, even if he could. The burn and adrenaline pumping through his veins were as intoxicating as any drug.

He looked over to Georgie and saw the same exhilaration he imagined was on his own face.

This. This is what they lived for. They weren't killin' themselves by working on the docks or some godforsaken job run by men that would give them a paltry wage if they hadn't turned them away first. Mikey may not follow the law, but he lived by his own rules, and he wasn't going to let some assholes tell him where, when, or how he could live.

Feck that. Feck *them*. Those pretentious, arrogant pricks could shove their systems up their arses. Mikey would take what he wanted and burn the rest down while doing it.

He smiled wickedly, sprinting up a short hill that led to their wagon. Grabbing some roots, Mikey pulled himself up, his feet slipping in the mud, before handing the bag to Georgie.

"Good work—"

Georgie slung the bag over his shoulder, his grin suddenly falling. Everything happened in slow motion: The widening of Georgie's eyes, how he stared at something behind Mikey while yelling at him to get down.

As Mikey ducked, a shot echoed through the woods, and Georgie lurched to the side. A deep breath escaped Mikey until he saw deep red blossoming over Georgie's chest.

No.

"No!" Mikey growled, rolling across the wet ground as another shot sprayed dirt around him.

Crawling on his hands and knees, he made it to the top as more shots went off, and he winced as one grazed his calf.

"Come out here, you damn coward!"

Mikey lifted his head just enough to see the man waiting at the bottom of the hill, pistol drawn and trained on him. The soldier couldn't have been much older than him. Mikey ducked down just before another shot went off. The horses stomped, pulling on the ropes that tied them to the tree. If they weren't secured, the damn things would have taken off by now.

"What makes you think you can take our supply and run off? Where were you going to go? It takes a certain kind of bastard to steal from men fighting for *you*."

Mikey scoffed, and his stomach tightened, a fire burning intensely within his soul. No, it wasn't guilt that churned like the man intended.

Loathing. Pure, unbridled hatred toward the man.

The Union soldiers weren't fighting for *him* or his people. Not one of them gave a helping hand or a bit of food when they landed in America. His mother and father had to beg for a tenement with over a dozen others living inside. Huddled there like rats in a sewer, starving and smelling just as bad.

Where were these men when he was a boy, and his stomach growled, and he had to pick discarded, half-rotten food out of the trash just to survive? They were the ones who beat him for it. They didn't need to give them handouts, but they sure as hell didn't need to turn the Irishmen away at every job. The cooks and bakers didn't need to post signs saying the Irish weren't welcome. They never had a chance, and this man represented everything Mikey loathed.

Pushing himself further over the hill, his leg throbbing with each step, Mikey descended along the side until he could get a clear view of the soldier. The man still had the pistol drawn, aiming for where Mikey used to be. Backing further into the trees, he kept his eyes on the man circling behind him.

No longer did Mikey regret how the job went down—the men that he killed. Consumed by a blinding rage, that would be the end of this privileged, senseless, Union-loving, discriminating asshole.

He killed Georgie, for gods' sake. His closest friend, Georgie, still held a shred of humanity left that Mikey had been lacking, and Hughie lost altogether. He was the only one of the three that made sure they didn't take their jobs too far. *What are we going to do without him?*

One thing was clear to Mikey. The bloody bastard killed the wrong man, and he would pay for it.

The hard pull of the trigger sent a thrill through Mikey, and the soldier lurched forward as the bullet went through his shoulder.

Mikey bounded over the remaining distance and grabbed the soldier's jacket, flipping him over, wanting the feel of his fist colliding with his face rather than the distance of the gun. The first blow broke the man's nose, the second smashed it, but as he raised his fist for the third, a burning sensation flared across his chest.

The soldier had sliced through Mikey's uniform, the blood already darkening his clothes. Catching the man's hand, they wrestled for the knife, Mikey using his weight to outmaneuver the injured bastard. Slamming the soldier's fist repeatedly into a rock, the knife finally clattered to the ground as he let out a stream of curses.

A brutal hit to Mikey's side had his breath going out in a whoosh.

Feckin' hell.

The man's fist collided with Mikey's jaw, sending him backward.

"Ye are going to pay for what ye've done," Mikey growled, wiping the blood from his split lip.

The man sneered, revealing his crooked front tooth. There was no light in his brown eyes—just reciprocated hatred. "Scum like you ruin this country. Miserable pricks, cloggin' up our streets, wantin' our jobs, our housin', breedin' with our women. You all should have died on the boats. Fuckin' parasites are what you are. Your friend?" His grimy smile widened. "He got what he had comin'."

Mikey's vision went red, blinded with rage, body thrumming with the power he'd been holding back. He landed on the soldier, grabbing him by the jacket and lifting him just enough to give him a bloody smile before slamming his forehead into his. He grabbed the man's neck, squeezing as hard as he could, enjoying how red his face was turning, how red he imagined his own was from the force of it. The way the large vein in the man's forehead bulged as he fought for his life. The soldier's hand fumbled with Mikey's face, trying to push him away. Mikey pulled back, trying to protect his eyes, when a sharp, blinding pain shot through his side, and he fell back.

The knife stuck between his ribs. "Shit," he growled and pulled it out. Blood gushed out of the wound, coating more of his coat. Soon there would be barely any blue left of the damned thing.

He didn't know how many times his fist collided with the soldier's face, if the blood on his knuckles was the man's or his own. Only that the soldier was barely conscious when a strong arm came up around Mikey and pulled him back. Mikey slammed his elbow into the assailant's side until he heard the familiar cursing.

"Leave him to me," Hughie gasped, holding a hand to his injured ribs.

Mikey's eyes quickly flicked from Hughie to Georgie's limp body—whose shock of red hair was stark against the snow. Anger and guilt rippled in his chest as he settled his hateful gaze on the soldier who murdered him. The man tried to get up but kept slipping in the snow and mud.

Mikey gave a curt nod. "I'll wait for ye."

Hughie shook his head. "Me wagon is up a ways. Ye should go. Get the rest of the men out. I want to take me time."

Mikey eyed him, considering whether or not this was a shit plan. "If they come for ye, we won't be able to get ye out."

Hughie nodded. "If I'm not out in time, then I'll fall where I'm meant to." He'd die as his brother did, is what he meant. Mikey knew it. He also knew there was no convincing him to leave the soldier.

Mikey laid a hand on Hughie's shoulder. "I'll take Georgie, if ye just help me with the body."

Hughie nodded, face strained, as Mikey gasped in pain up the hill, holding his side to staunch the bleeding. At this point, there was so much of it that he didn't quite know where to compress it. Mikey threw the bag into the wagon before helping Hughie pick up his brother. Grinding his teeth, they heaved Georgie's limp body into the back, covering him with the tarp meant to cover the guns.

"Don't take too long," Mikey suggested, but Hughie was already ambling toward the soldier, his blade out, flipping it between his hands. He knew Hughie was already going through a dozen ways to torture the man for murdering his kin.

Mikey turned from the scene and untied the horses from the tree before hoisting himself into the wagon. His side pulled and he had to bite back a loud groan escaping his bared teeth. Taking shallow breaths, he flicked the reins and started down the path that led to the meeting point.

It had to be miles before the man's screams no longer trailed behind him.

CHAPTER TEN

Emilia

Liquid sloshed up my front as we exited the water, getting ready to lay the planks so we could haul the large artillery from the flatboat.

"Feck! Watch where ye are fucking putting that!" Mick whispered vehemently when another man smashed his hand between one of the timbers.

I grumbled for him to be quiet, reminding him of our orders to make as little noise as possible. Still, I turned to him, worrying that more harm was done, but seeing his hand in the dark was nearly impossible.

We had spent a month training on Governors Island before making our way to Hilton Head, South Carolina, much to our regiment's disappointment. We thought we were to make the Fourth Regiment of Meagher's infamous Irish Brigade. Even with little time in this century, I had heard enough talk and news about Meagher. He was a sort of a celebrity among his Irish people—being an Irish revolutionary leader in Ireland and then America. It would have been a great honor to serve under him, and we felt slighted. Thomas told me that there was even talk of Meagher's troops going on to fight for Ireland's independence after the Civil War. I just shrugged when he asked me if I knew anything about that. I didn't, and my time travel was still a sore spot between us. I could tell he was beginning to believe me, but his mind kept fighting against it.

When we neared Hilton Head, I couldn't reconcile the difference between the wild-looking island before us and the vacation destination I was so used to it being. I should have been used to it, having spent almost a year in nineteenth century, but now that I had left Boston, the open world left me speechless. It was a world of in-betweens, not precisely as wild as when it was untouched by settlers, and not quite as tamed as the future. It was a mixture of the Natives' land and those who were tearing it down for a slow progression of industrialization. My heart squeezed at the beauty as my body shuttered with the knowledge that danger lurked behind every shadow.

We arrived in South Carolina a little over a week after Governors Island, where we were to serve under Major General Benjamin Butler. I was in Company C with Thomas and the men we had become close with and left with four companies for Tybee Island, Georgia. It was our job to set up the artillery in the middle of the night so as not to draw the attention of enemy fire. Hence, the orders are to do it quietly lest we be shot.

Mick was swearing under his breath but continued laying the platforms so we could move the artillery across them. It was hard enough to push the heavy equipment, let alone through water that came up to our waists. My arms screamed in pain. Though I'd been working on building my strength, I didn't have time to see much improvement, and each task made it glaringly apparent that my body wasn't built like the men's. Fortunately, some of the other men struggled as well. Each day I could keep under the radar was a blessing.

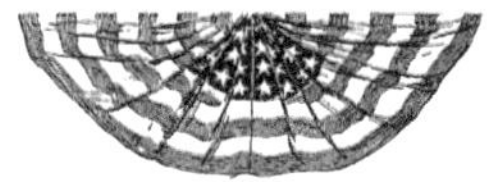

"How's that healing?" I asked Mick, nodding to his bandaged hand as he lifted the pot of pork and potatoes off the fire. We had been on the island for two weeks since his injury. The hand may have been broken, but he was lucky enough to be able to use it while bandaged. He refused to see a doctor, often hiding his grunts and grimaces with each jolt of his fingers.

"Still works," he grumbled.

Hall shook his head, thinking Mick should have had it looked at. Hall was still scribbling in the book he always carried around. I watched his long fingers, and admonished myself when I found myself relieved that it wasn't Hall's hand that was injured. I had suspicions that Hall was some sort of an artist but hadn't the nerve to ask him yet.

"Gimme that." Brophy, a soldier in his mid-thirties, took the dinner pot away from Mick, swearing under his breath. "I'm not eating that shite ye boiled up yesterday." The other men laughed as Mick's face reddened in anger.

The companies had broken up into groups to our allotted campfires. Sullivan and Thomas found their way to ours, along with a few other men. It was shocking how little these men knew their way around their food.

I went to cut my portion and found the pork still pink inside.

"What are ye doing?" Brophy snapped, eyes lasered in on me when I went to place it back in the pot.

"It's not cooked thoroughly."

"Not cooked thoroughly? Ye sound like a goddamn woman. Shall I call ye lassie?"

All the blood rushed out of my head and I wondered if I was white as a sheet. Thomas didn't look up from his plate, sitting rigid but leaving me to defend myself.

"Nah." I shrugged, trying to show Brophy he wasn't affecting me. "Just don't want to shit me drawers all night, is all."

The group laughed again as each man dumped their food back in.

"O'Connor's got himself a job then," Brophy snapped, sitting down to eat.

I stirred the salty contents, wishing for a cheeseburger or an extra cheesy pizza slice while stealing glances at Brophy. He ate the meat, though it clearly wasn't done. The man was going to be shitting himself the next day.

We ate our small rations, joking and reminiscing. Many of the men left family behind. But it didn't take long for the conversation to shift toward more... lustful thoughts. Talk quickly turned towards prostitutes who tended to follow the army. My stomach turned as I eyed Thomas, wondering if he wanted that. It was stupid, I knew how he felt about me, but he had needs like the others. Didn't he?

I concentrated on my food, making myself eat it. I couldn't take the chance on missing a meal. Feeling eyes on me, I glanced up and found Thomas studying me, his eyes slowly taking in all my features. A jolt shot to my core, equal parts nervousness and exhilaration. He shouldn't be looking at me. Not here.

Still, the heat in his gaze had my stomach flipping. I desperately wanted to be alone with him.

"What about ye, O'Connor?" Bryant asked loudly. Thomas and I looked at him, our tether breaking with a sharp, almost painful, snap. Neither one of us knew who he was talking to, until I noticed everyone looking at me. Mick's arm wrapped around my shoulders, jostling me so much that I almost dropped my plate.

"Goin' to get ye a lass?" Bryant was older than most of us, in his forties, and liked to pick on the young ones good-naturedly. "Ye look like ye haven't had much of them."

My face flamed as all the men laughed.

"Don't pick on me good friend." Mick smiled at me. I ducked from under his arm and took a few steps back. "He's a wee bit shy." His eyes lit up mischievously. "Maybe we should give him a few pointers, aye?"

A few men dove right in, and I cringed at their expletives. Thomas forced a smile when Sullivan nudged him, laughing and participating in their fun, but he mainly avoided looking at me. They began to pick on one of the other men, and I found it was the perfect time to sneak away.

I backed up slowly, ensuring everyone was preoccupied as I blended into the shadows. I had hoped to get a few minutes to go to the bathroom for a while. Finding privacy wasn't easy, and I often had to hold it until they were distracted so I could sneak behind a bush.

Pushing through the foliage, I slapped a mosquito, praying to God that it didn't carry malaria. Men had been dropping of sicknesses since we landed on the mosquito-infested islands. I pulled down my trousers and squatted. Mid-pee, a branch snapped close by. I had my pants up swiftly, feeling someone behind me as my fingers fumbled with the buckle.

I turned, seeing a figure in the trees. I cursed silently as Mick stood frozen, looking at me as if I just murdered a baby.

"What the feck?" I cursed, trying to distract him. "Can't a man piss in peace?”

"Why were ye squatting?" Mick's face contorted, and my stomach bottomed out.

I hadn't seen him this prickly since I first met him, so my worst fear was probably happening. "I just told ye—"

"Ye told me ye had to piss."

My blood ran cold despite the humidity. "I… thought I had to shit, but can't do it with ye damn well here, can I?"

"Who are ye? A spy?"

"What? No!" I hissed, going closer to him, hoping to persuade him to be quiet.

"Then ye better tell me why ye have an ass like a babe?"

"Is everything all right?" Thomas asked, making me jump. Where the hell did he come from?

"Fine," I snapped, throwing each of them a glare. "Just heading back."

"That's right, your cousin." Mick laughed without humor. "Are ye a spy as well?"

"Ye get that from me having a smooth ass?" I growled.

In one swift movement, a blade was in Thomas' hand as he positioned himself between Mick and the camp.

"Don't." I held a hand out to Thomas and turned towards Mick. "I'm not a spy. Neither is he."

"Then please explain why a woman is in the Union army?"

My heartbeat frantically, threatening to break through my sternum. *Oh, God. No one can know. He can't tell anyone. They'll lock me up, throw me into an asylum. What will I do?*

Thomas let out what sounded like a remarkable string of curses in Irish, cutting off my panicked thoughts. Suddenly, he was on Mick, his knife pressed against his throat.

"Stop! Yes, I can explain." I shoved between the two men, holding my shaking hands out while avoiding accidentally piercing myself with Thomas' knife. "You're right, but it's not what you think."

Mick blanched at my lack of an accent as Thomas cursed from behind me.

"I will explain everything if you promise to keep quiet."

"Emilia..." Thomas warned.

Mick's eyes widened as he looked at my face in a new light. I knew he had suspicions, but this was far beyond what he expected. "Are ye two even cousins?" He looked between us, noting our contrasting skin tones and lack of familial resemblance.

"No," I said at the same time Thomas said. "Aye."

I glared at Thomas. "I have to be completely honest with him if he's going to believe me."

"It's dangerous."

"It's our only option."

We stared at each other, our battle of wills playing out in front of Mick, who was beginning to get restless.

"Give me one reason I shouldn't report ye," he threatened.

"My mom was a slave." The words came out unbidden, but it was hard to make them stop now that they flowed. He looked at me incredulously. "A gypsy slave. They're not as common, but enslaved nonetheless." I went closer to him, ignoring Thomas' attempt to stop me. "They killed her." Tears clogged my throat, leaving me momentarily speechless. "Please," I said, grabbing his arm. "You have to believe me. I have to fight for my people, too."

He pulled out of my grasp, a deep line between his eyebrows as he focused on where I touched him. His brown eyes slowly found mine again. "I won't tell anyone." My sigh of relief was cut off swiftly. "But me and ye, we're done." He thrust his face in front of mine. I took a startled step back, hurt by his admission. "There's no place for women here, and I don't trust ye. Let me guess, ye two are a pair?" His face scrunched up in disgust when we didn't answer him. The loss of his friendship was like a knife in my gut, twisting my stomach painfully.

Mick took a step to leave only to have Thomas cut him off. He searched Mick's face until he found whatever he was looking for, then, moved to the side with a nod. Mick crashed through the trees and passed the fire, heading to his tent without another word.

I stood there long after he disappeared.

"What are ye thinking?" Thomas asked after a long silence.

"It doesn't matter."

"Ye have to be more careful."

"You don't think I've been careful?" I rounded on him, fuming. "I nearly piss my pants every day, waiting for a time to go when no one will see me. I have been careful!"

I watched as shock swiftly replaced anger on his face. "Ye knew what ye were getting yourself into. Maybe ye should go—"

I growled in frustration. "Don't you dare tell me to go back to Boston. I will not desert the cause. I never complained. I will not have you tell me what I should and shouldn't do, when you don't even know what I must do to survive this."

He watched the camp over my shoulder, his nostrils flaring as he struggled to control his anger. "Fine."

"Fine?"

"Do what ye must. If I see ye go off, I'll keep a better eye on the other men so that it won't happen again."

"You don't have to do that," I said, softening under the kindness. I rubbed my eyes, already tired. "I can be more careful." It was my choice to come here. My mistake. I didn't need to take it out on Thomas.

I looked up at the sun that was just falling behind the trees. We still had a whole night of work to do.

Thomas shrugged. "It's a small task."

I frowned.

"Ye are upset about your...friend." He said the last word like a question.

I reluctantly smiled at his grimace. "Yes, friend. I don't have many of those here."

Thomas nodded, face somber. "Aye, me either. He'll come around."

I watched Hall continue to draw in his book as the other men laughed about some joke.

"I hope so."

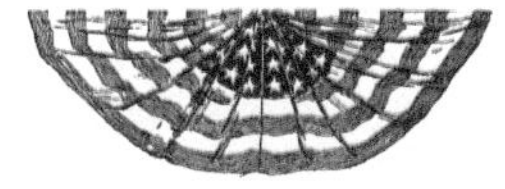

"Can't wait to be rid of these godforsaken islands."

"Ye are about to leave one for another. It might be a while."

Grumbles sounded all around me as we marched through the marshy land, our boots squelching in and out of the mud. I swiped sweat off my forehead, cursing as the southern humidity covered us like an unwanted blanket. Thankfully the trees provided some shade from the relentless sun.

A deep cough made me turn to the side, studying the man several yards to my left. I noted the sickly yellow of his complexion as he gave out another rattle of coughs and cringed. He was staggering, struggling with the mud and whatever parasite had infected him. I suspected malaria like the others.

We kept walking, knowing that the boats were waiting by the shore. I watched my feet sink in and pull out, my boots nearly slipping off before breaking free. I was counting the seconds, wishing we were almost there, when yelling had my head snapping up.

A crowd circled around an area, standing back, but focused on something in the middle. I pushed a man to the side so I could see. Men shoved their hands into the puddle, searching for something as bubbles broke the water's surface. Thomas' arm disappeared up to his shoulder in the deceptively deep puddle.

"What happened?" I asked anyone who'd listen.

"A man fell in," said a young man with patches of red whiskers struggling to come in.

I stared at him in horror, looking back to the puddle. "Do ye know who?"

"Shite!" Mick cursed, crouching on all fours, trying to get as close as he could without falling in.

The boy shrugged. "Some guy named Hall, I think."

Hall.

"What? No! No, no, no." I was nearly hysterical, looking around for anything that could help as my heart threatened to crack my ribs. I turned to one of the men, seeing that he had a long rope tied to his pack. "Give me that," I demanded, ignoring his puzzled expression. I was already taking off my pack and boots.

"What?" He scowled, the deep lines in his face nearly cracking under the scrutiny.

"The rope. Tie it around me waist."

"Feck that. Get your own damn rope."

I unsheathed my knife and had it to his throat before I was even conscious of what I was doing. "Give me the damn rope. Do ye want a man's death on your hands?"

He snarled at me but started fumbling with the rope, unwinding it as I grabbed one end, securing it around me. I ripped the rest out of his hands and returned to the scene.

"Tom! Catch!" I yelled, throwing him the end of the rope. He caught it out of reflex.

Confusion quickly changed to anger. "No."

"What?" Mick snapped, looking between us.

"I'll give it a tug when I have a grip on him."

"No." Thomas' voice was strained with barely contained fury.

The bubbles slowed and I knew it wouldn't be long before Hall drowned. We didn't have time to debate this, and I wouldn't give him the chance to volunteer. He'd be too heavy to pull back up. Thomas' green eyes widen in horror as I stepped in, but I trusted that he would hold on to the rope.

Murky water bubbled around me, the first feeling of coolness since coming to this blasted island, while the mud gave me the worst case of claustrophobia I'd ever had. I could barely see through the dirty water, as I flailed my arms around me in search of Hall. My fingers grazed something flat and loose, like a jacket over an abdomen. I grabbed it, pulling myself closer as I felt higher, finding shoulders and a face.

Hall. He was no longer moving, which sent adrenaline through me, so that my fingers deftly untied the rope from around my waist. Now that I found him, I wasn't sure I could pull him out. But I could hold on to him. The rope came undone as my lungs screamed for air, bubbles coming out of my nose like a volcano ready to break the surface.

I reached around his waist, thankful he was thin and tied the rope. I tugged the knot to ensure it was secure and wrapped my arms around his neck and under one of his arms. Pulling the rope from above, I wrapped it around my wrist for good measure.

A hard jerk had me nearly screaming as a sharp pain shot through my wrist. I kept my hands clutched together, knowing if they couldn't get him out,

I would surely drown. My lungs burned, and a stabbing sensation ripped through my chest. There were more pulls as my vision started to go black, stars dancing around the inside of my eyes. The only thing keeping me conscious was my desperation to live.

It felt like hours, but I knew it had to be no more than a minute when we broke the surface. The sun pierced my eyes through the mud and water, causing me to blink rapidly while the dark colors of my surroundings spun like a kaleidoscope. My hands broke free of Hall when someone grabbed under my arms, pulling us apart as I fell back with my rescuer, hitting solid ground. I turned over and spewed water out of my lungs.

"Are ye bloody mad?" Thomas yelled, slamming his hand on my back repeatedly.

"Stop," I rasped, pushing his hand away when I no longer felt like vomiting water.

"It was bad enough ye jumped in, then ye take off the damned rope? What is wrong with ye? Ye could have drowned!"

I ignored the anger working its way up his neck and under his beard in a red flame. My hands sunk into green-covered mush as I tried to push myself up enough to see Hall. Mick alternated between pounding on Hall's chest and breathing into his mouth. Men were still gathering around, a whispered hush spreading through the marshland as we waited.

My breath rasped in and out, still not convinced I wasn't drowning. Hall convulsed, and Mick flung him to the side as he heaved up lung full after lung full of water.

Finally, a full, relieved breath entered my lungs, and I fell back, letting the warm sun cake the mud on me. A bird flew overhead, and I began to smile.

He was alive.

Quiet cheers rang out as soldiers clapped each other on their backs even while knowing we could come under enemy fire any minute. Faces appeared in the blue sky, smiling and telling me a job well done. I swatted them away so that I could stand.

"All right, back it up, boys." The voice had me standing at attention.

"Sergeant Coffey," I said, a little breathless and sick, already preparing myself for his reprimand. "I know I didn't wait for your orders, Sergeant. I was afraid there wasn't enough time."

"You'd be right in your assumptions, Private."

I held my head high, taking in his stern face and unyielding posture as I waited for my punishment.

"If not for him—" Thomas' defense was cut off by Coffey's raised hand.

"What ye did was brave, O'Connor. Any more time down there and he'd be dead. Well done."

I let out the breath I'd been holding, my shoulders relaxing. "Thank ye, Serg."

"We need men like ye. I won't forget this."

Men began to pat my shoulders, nearly sending me tumbling back into the hole. I made my way to Hall as the men began to depart. We didn't have much time to make it to the boats, even when one of our own almost died. The man who had let me borrow his rope grabbed it and left, grumbling about it being wet.

I knelt by Hall who had been propped up against a tree. Mick fumbled through Hall's pack, trying to salvage anything that wasn't water-damaged.

"I'm fine." Hall's words came out raspy, his throat strained from the water. "Mick said ye saved me." He gave me a smile; his teeth gleamed white under all the mud on his face.

Mick avoided my gaze and kept scowling at the pack.

A tall, wisp of a man crouched by us, and I recognized him as one of the surgeons. I sighed in relief.

"I'm fine, O'Connell," Hall mumbled.

"Ye just spent several minutes underwater. I'll let ye know when ye are fine." O'Connell pushed his wiry brown hair back with sweat, making his unruly hair stick out farther.

"How are ye, O'Connor?" he asked me without turning away from Hall. "Any problems?"

"I'm fine."

Hall watched me as the surgeon peppered him with questions, and I became uneasy. I didn't want any unnecessary medical attention.

"Are ye hurt?" Hall asked when O'Connell finally declared him well enough to go on.

My arm throbbed in answer, and I looked down at the wrist I'd been cradling. With all the commotion, I forgot that I'd hurt it. I shrugged. "Probably just a sprain."

"Let him see it." Thomas towered behind me, throwing me into his large shadow.

"It's fine." I glared, standing up quickly. I explained about the rope as I retrieved my boots and pack. Most the men had already set off again.

Mick stood. "We should go."

"I should have a salve in me pack," O'Connell said, rummaging through it. "Here. Just rub it on. Ye shouldn't need much, it not being that bad." After wiping the wound, he wrapped it and told me to avoid using it when possible for the next week.

The doctor left as Mick and Thomas helped Hall up.

We hobbled the rest of the way to the boats. Men already scurried over ours like bees in a hive, preparing it to set sail for James Island. It didn't take long before we found Sullivan and Byrnes.

"What happened to ye?" Byrnes asked from his seat on the ground, eyeing the mud falling off my uniform as I shrugged out of my pack.

"O'Connor was trying to be a hero," Mick snapped before disappearing into the crowd.

"What's up his ass?" Sullivan turned back to us and grimaced. "Ye two smell like shite."

Hall ignored him, sitting down heavily, and I followed suit. I was exhausted and had no patience for explanation. I sat with my feet outstretched, not caring about being a nuisance to the men having to walk around me.

Sitting silently, I listened to Thomas explain what happened as Hall rummaged through his pack. He pulled out his book and growled at the graphite.

"Is it ruined?" I asked, catching a glimpse of soldiers sitting around a fire, heads bent over their food. I caught a glimpse of a cabin drawn with so much detail it could have been a photograph, confirming my suspicions about his art.

"I might be able to salvage them."

"That's quite good. Why didn't ye tell me ye could draw?"

"I was a painter back home. I just don't talk about it much." He shrugged.

"Didn't think anyone would be interested."

My brows rose with disbelief. Many of these men would probably pay for a sketch of a loved one, and I told him as much. "Ye should really think about it," I continued, though he looked skeptical. "Might earn some extra cash in the meantime. Would ye mind showing me one of your favorites?"

He nodded, and I allowed him his privacy by watching the choppy water as he flipped through the pages.

A wet page molded over my hands, and I pried my head from the wall instead of letting sleep overcome me.

It was of a group of children, arms outstretched and feet bare as they reached for the loaf the baker was handing them. The desperation on their faces was so prominent that my throat constricted with emotion.

"Didn't ye get enough of that without sketching it down?" Sullivan asked.

"I like to remember where I come from," Hall said, taking the page from me and putting it back in his leather book until he had somewhere to dry it later. "He gave the children a loaf of bread every morning. Sometimes it was the only food they would get the entire day. But this man gave it to them at his own expense, even as he struggled to keep his business afloat. To him those children were more important. I couldn't let that be forgotten."

"I can understand that." Thomas sat on the other side of Hall.

"I rather just leave all that shite behind and be done with it," Byrnes grumbled.

"Aye." Sullivan nodded, staring at the island receding into the distance. "Don't think I'll be forgetting that much."

"Now, if ye draw me a woman..." Byrnes laughed, breaking the tension, and Hall soon had a few men asking for commissions. I smiled weakly, glad he was getting the attention he deserved. I just hoped I didn't start something he didn't want...

Sometime later, the constant rumble of the ship vibrated beneath us, and we fell silent, waiting for it to take us to our next destination. As my eyes closed, the drawing of the little hungry faces burned into my mind and continued to haunt me in my restless dreams.

CHAPTER ELEVEN

Shaylah & Michael

FEBRUARY 1862

S hay kneaded the dough the way Rose had taught her, rolling and balling it before putting it aside to rise. Libby napped by the fire, and Shay glanced at her daughter again, worried about the heat or a wayward ember that could catch the whole bassinet on fire. And, for the umpteenth time, she thought about how dangerous this time was. How this entire century was fucking terrifying.

Oh, the woes of not having modern heat.

Shay sighed and leaned against the counter, enjoying the silence of the bakery and the soft crackle of the life-threatening fire.

They were alone this morning, a rarity in the usual bustle of the business. The bakery was closed, and Shay felt confident enough to pick up the baking that must be prepped for the next day. Rose had left her shortly before, and George had already left for his second job. She didn't even have to watch over little Evaline; the school day was not over for a few more hours.

Shay let her head fall back, her eyes closed, and her body relaxed. She knew the moment was fleeting and that the world would storm through that door shortly and, with it, its problems. But these moments were so rare—when she could just be herself without the expectations of the times—she had to soak it in and let it be. If she didn't, she would have lost her mind ages ago.

"Do ye always take naps in the middle of the day?" *His* voice was rough and loud in the little area.

Holding in a scream, Shay grabbed her chest as she took in Michael's knowing smirk.

"What the hell are you doing here?" she snapped, more from the fright than his presence. How did he get in without her hearing?

"Ye really should lock the door when no one is with ye." The seriousness of which he said it kept her from snapping at him like she wanted. That, and he stood oddly, stiffly, as if it hurt.

"What's wrong with you?" Shay started to go to him before coming to her senses. Would he even want her to help him? She balled her hands into fists, angry for wanting to help. Maybe they should just keep their distance...

He trailed each movement with calculating certainty, putting her on edge. Loosening her fists when he didn't answer, she sighed. "I've got work to do."

Shay began rolling more dough, ignoring the scrape of a stool on the floor. From the corner of her eye, she noted how gingerly Mikey sat—as if he was afraid of moving too quickly—and the slight grimace he tried to keep off his face.

"What if I was a murderer?" he asked, and she raised her brow. He squinted, a glint in his eye. "I meant after ye. We both know what I am. I was practically on ye before ye noticed."

He glanced down at her neck before scanning the rest of the room. What was that about?

For some reason, she didn't feel any fear and had to keep herself from rolling her eyes. "You were twenty feet away." She paused, really looking at him. He looked so tired—dark circles offsetting his blue eyes, his skin pale and taut. "Are you sick?"

"Nay." Even as he said it, he frowned.

"Cut the bullshit," she snapped. Michael's brows rose as she skirted around the counter, watching every movement until she was right before him. God, he was intimidating, even as he sat, looking up at her with those damned eyes so blue they could be ice. She placed her hands on her hips. "What did you do?"

He smiled, an honest-to-God, genuine smile that stole her breath away.

Michael never smiled. "Got in a wee tiff." She waited for him to explain. "Fine, if ye must know, the wrong end of a dagger may have grazed me."

"What?" She all but yelled, before wincing as she glanced toward Libby, waiting for her to wail. When her babe didn't wake, she turned back to Michael. His grin was even bigger, the bastard. "Let me see." She grabbed his shirt before she came to her senses, pulling her hands back as if burned. "I'm sorry." It came out hoarse, and she stumbled back.

The guarded look on his face almost had her running from the room. "It's nothin'."

She nodded, looking around at the floury counter, shelves, baked goods. Anywhere that wasn't him. She hated her reaction. What they'd turned her into. Before those men—she ground her teeth. Back in her time, Shay would never have balked before touching a man. She would have flirted and tested, touched and teased. The woman she was now wasn't even a flicker of who she'd been. And it killed her inside that this man, this indestructible, brutal, tempting man, only saw her weaker side. From the first goddamn moment he met her.

She tried to blink back the angry tears.

"Look at me."

When she didn't, a deep guttural noise had her gaze snapping back.

He watched her stare as his deft fingers unbuttoned his cotton shirt, and all her troubled thoughts disappeared. He did it slowly as if not wanting to startle her. With each button, Shay began to see the dark artistry expanding on his broad chest. Something tightened in her stomach, and she stepped forward, wanting a better view of the tattoo. She didn't even know tattoos were done in this time. A dumb thought, she knew, but one that she never even considered.

It was a large skull with a Celtic symbol of intricate lines woven into it, shaped almost like a four-leaf clover, carved into its forehead. The eye sockets were black and penetrating and seemed to be focused solely on her.

Shay shivered. It took her a minute to realize she wasn't breathing, just staring at it as her mind raced. What was the reason behind this tattoo? Did it represent his journey to America? Somehow, she knew it wasn't just the design that intrigued him. A dark, prickling sensation ran across her skin, and she shivered.

It was then that she focused on the large bandage wrapped around the side of his pectoral and across his upper abdomen. Her mouth fell open. "Grazed you? You were fucking butchered!" She didn't have to remove the bandage to know it was terrible.

"I love the mouth ye have."

That was enough to tear her startled expression from the wound to his sparkling eyes. How was he joking right now?

"What happened?" she snapped, wringing her hands to prevent herself from lifting the wrap enough to see the wound. Except that smug look on his face set something dangerous burning within her. An old spark that caught, one she didn't quite want to extinguish.

Fuck it. She went to Michael and lightly pulled it back. He winced. "Sorry. How bad does it hurt?" The muscles twitched beneath her touch. God, it was awful. The long slash was more profound than she imagined and so *long*. Why didn't he have it stitched?

Her hand slid along the wrap, noting how her dark fingers contrasted with his light skin. They grazed Michael's abdomen, and she watched in fascination as the stiff muscles rippled beneath her touch. They stopped on another wrap that covered his lower abdomen. The man didn't have an ounce of fat on him.

"And this?" she whispered, hoping he didn't hear the quiver in her voice.

"The pointy end stuck in a wee bit more," was his only explanation. Shay's fingers trailed across his uninjured skin as her throat closed, keeping her from responding. When her hand fell, he said, "Just a job. Nothin' to worry over."

"Some job. How did it not hit anything? How are you even alive?"

"Aye, made out pretty well, if I say so." Apparently, he was going to completely dismiss her questions and worry. Typical, stubborn man. "Lost Georgie, though."

Shay looked up, startled, and her breath froze at their nearness. She contemplated whether he intended to confide in her. Michael rarely opened up about his emotions. Georgie was close to him, and one of the men who'd saved her, but if she was being honest, she didn't like the man. Nor his brother. They had a mean streak and clearly hated her people.

Still, it was hard losing someone close to you.

"I'm sorry," she said, so quietly she wasn't sure if he heard.

The fire crackled while they stared at each other, unmoving and so close that Shay could count the few freckles on Michael's face, the whiskers a day away from turning into a beard, the long lashes framing darkening eyes that made her stomach flip.

She swallowed and licked her lips nervously. Her body thrummed when his gaze fell to her mouth, sending a thrill straight to her core, twisting and heating in a delicious way that she hadn't felt since coming here.

A calloused thumb brushed her bottom lip, and her breath caught as his large, warm hand delicately cradled her cheek. Shay was frozen, partly because she didn't want to break the moment, but also because she believed she was hallucinating the whole thing, not believing he was capable of such a sweet gesture. His eyes glazed in a way that she'd never seen before. Well, not directed toward *her*.

It was thrilling, even terrifying. Suddenly, Shay's advice to Emilia came to mind, and she knew.

No.

She stepped back, a tearing sensation ripping through her as his hand fell away, her heart screaming at her to stop even as her body refused and took another step backward. This may have been the man who saved her, but he also didn't hide the hatred that dwelled in his heart.

Something flashed in Michael's eyes before she could decipher it, and his expression shuttered, endlessly hiding whatever was behind his hard exterior.

"I should get going," he said, buttoning his shirt as he stood.

She nodded, at a loss for words, unable to look at him again in fear that he might read the emotions on her face.

A tense moment hung between them, a silence filling the room and making them acknowledge whatever it was between them. Because there was something between them. If Shay could just put her damn finger on it.

Michael turned to leave.

"Why did you come?" she asked, the words coming out in a rush as her heart threatened to beat out of her chest. What was with these overbearing, domineering, nineteenth-century men? Why did he care? It wasn't as if he owed her something. And she sure as hell didn't need Michael's help. He didn't even do anything when he was here, either. Other than confusing the hell out of her.

Michael's jaw tensed, his nostrils flaring. Shay waited tensely, wondering why the question would garner such a reaction.

"I don't know."

If it weren't for the confused look on his face, she would have demanded a better response. *Well, figure it out.* She wanted to snap, even as a knowing, prickling sensation told her he spoke the truth. He didn't know. And yet, he kept showing up.

An inkling niggled at her that maybe Michael kept coming around for the same reason she reacted so strongly to his presence. Ever since he'd found her, saved her, they were connected. Forged in a way that neither could understand or refuse. It kept pulling them together like a tether, and she had no idea what would happen if they no longer fought against it.

With a final, painful grimace, he left without another word.

As the door swung shut behind him, Shay yelled, "Get that stitched up!"

Libby's startled cry pierced the quiet room. Except now, it no longer felt peaceful.

It just felt lonely.

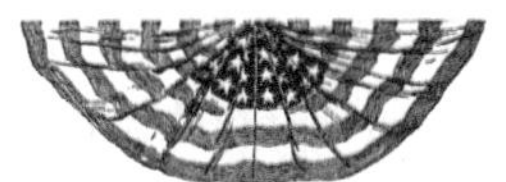

The tension in his chest hadn't eased since he left Shaylah—gods, even her name was beautiful. His throat burned as he thought it. When had he started being such a soft gobshite?

That wasn't even the worst part. After Mikey left the bakery, he followed Shay's bloody advice and got some damned stitches.

That was a day ago, and he still recalled the softness of her skin. The fullness of her lip beneath his thumb. How he wondered what she tasted like. He'd almost done it, nearly kissed that mouth...if she hadn't backed away, shuttered herself from him.

That had stung.

Didn't he bloody well prove himself yet? That he would never hurt her. And why the feck did he care?

Mikey's stomach rolled even as his heart soared. He didn't think about lasses other than for feckin', and he sure as hell didn't fancy them.

He scoffed at his train of thoughts, grateful that the sentiment was adequate while on the filthy street he occupied. He spit to the side, knowing the thick tobacco of the chew would disgust the gentleman next to him. He had to suppress a smug grin at the slight shift in the older man, probably in preservation of his expensive suit.

"Your man is late." Pierre's thick accent rumbled as he straightened his cuffs as his men shifted, getting anxious in the cold, probably unused to the northern winter.

Mikey remained motionless, glaring down the alley with his back against the massive warehouse, and adamantly refused to retrieve his watch or look at Henry for any reassurance. Where the bloody hell were they? They were merely a few miles from Springfield and should have arrived there a quarter of an hour ago. Mikey would have overseen the matter himself, except the whole damn city was teeming with people in preparation for this bloody war. Besides, Henry's cousin lived here, and it would draw less attention if they handled it. And yet, there was still a significant chance of running into trouble, and without him there, the whole deal could be fecked.

It had taken a day's ride to travel across the state, leaving them tired, irritable, and forced to spend the night in this feckin' city, making Mikey itch. Too many things could go wrong back in Boston while he was gone, and if he wasn't there to fix the situation, who knew what the gobshites would feck up while he, Hughie, and Henry were gone. That, and... He shook his head. *Feck that.* Mikey refused to think about her. Instead, he should have left Hughie back home to handle things. He could scare any man into submission.

"You'll get your supply," Mikey responded simply.

Pierre had already taken him to his storehouse, where he revealed four carriages filled with sacks of sugar. This commodity would surely fetch a pretty penny when inflation on the southern-grown crop went through the roof. It may take some time, but the guarantee was inevitable, and Mikey was a patient man. As for the warehouse, Mikey didn't have a bloody clue when the rebel acquired it during his brief time in the North.

Mikey spat again and straightened when a low rumble of wheels across the dirt road carried over to them.

About damn time.

The three men flanking Pierre straightened as well, adjusting their coats to cover the pistols that were surely hidden beneath as Pierre stood patiently. Or not, considering the annoyed expression on his grizzled face. Mikey refrained from rolling his eyes as he and Hughie waited. A sharp pain speared his gut, and he refused to look at the empty spot Georgie should have been standing in.

The carriage stopped, and Henry jumped down, bowing deeply and sweeping his hat with a flourish.

Mikey rolled his eyes.

"Fellas." Henry chirped. "May I introduce ye to me cousin, Jimmy."

The young boy looked like he was two seconds away from shitting his pants. What had Henry been thinking? Mikey pulled Henry to the side while Pierre and his men followed Jimmy around the back.

"Ye didn't tell me he was a feckin' babe," Mikey grumbled.

"That's why he'll pull it off." Henry smiled cockily, making Mikey want to punch him in his bloody face. "No one will suspect him."

Mikey fisted the front of Henry's jacket, pulling the man to him as he growled in his face. "If this plan goes to shite, it is your head. Do ye hear me?"

"Is this all of it?" Pierre's voice rumbled to them.

Mikey let go of Henry, shoving him back and went around the carriage in time to hear young Jimmy. "Just a glimpse, sir."

There were stacks of rifles, barrels of pistols, and enough ammunition to take down an entire city. Mikey nodded in approval.

"The rest will be at the station," Mikey said, drawing Pierre's attention. "I'll have a few of me men overseeing its transportation."

"As will my men." He extended a large hand toward the cargo. "Upon arrival in Virginia, they will meet yours and take charge of the transport from there."

Mikey nodded. The sooner it was out of his hands, the better.

"However," Pierre drawled. "I would like to see the rest. I'm sure you understand…"

Mikey held in a curse and shoved his hands into his pockets against the cold. "The station is overrun with military personnel. I highly recommend ye leave it to me men who know how to play the game."

The older man stiffened, and the creases between his brows deepened. "You expect me to just believe you? After I went out of my way, presenting all my supply." Pierre extended to his full height, an imposing figure if Mikey didn't already have a few inches on him. "Why should I trust you?"

"Oh, I can assure you, sir." Jimmy insisted. "My brothers and I secured them last night."

"Your other cousins, I assume." Pierre leveled a disbelieving gaze toward Henry.

"Aye." Henry smiled, leaning his slim frame against the side of the carriage. "Ye have me word."

Mikey fought to keep his face free of emotion as annoyance surged. "It's too dangerous to take ye where they are holding it," he explained. "Ye are more than welcome to check what we have here, but I am unwilling to feck up this deal because ye want to be reckless." Mikey leaned in, incapable of controlling his unstable temper. "Your men take inventory when it's in their own hands in Virginia. I'll even leave your end of the deal open until ye hear of it. A guarantee on both of our parts. Now, does that suit ye, or are we done here?"

Mikey waited while Pierre visibly reined in his anger. Judging by the flare in his eyes and the clench of his jaw, no one dared to speak to him in such a way, let alone a younger man. No. Pierre was used to people falling to their knees in acquiescence, bowing to his will or suffering the whip. But he was also the type of man born into that position. Taught it as a small child and took up the vile throne with the little effort it took to pass one crown to another.

Aye, Mikey knew men like Pierre. Even understood them. Some would even go as far as throwing Mikey into that category of reprehensible men. The difference was Mikey wasn't given shite. He stole, beat, and slaughtered to get where he was. He built his throne from the feckin' ground up until he rose above the masses. Until all feared him, not for a position someone else had given him, but for every goddamn day he'd dug himself out of the cesspit that so many of his people succumbed to. He knew what it was like to be the lowest dregs of society. Mikey didn't bow then, and he sure as hell wouldn't bow now.

The two men stared at each other, neither breaking as the others waited for them to make a decision.

Mikey had to hide his smirk when Pierre held out his hand.

CHAPTER TWELVE

Emilia & Thomas

MAY 1862

We arrived on James Island, the beach packed with soldiers and equipment. A hot air balloon flew high in the distance, scouting the island. Men shoved around, each with a specific job to do. After setting camp, immediately searched for a piece of the river far enough away that no one would spot me.

Taking a deep breath, I sank into the cold water, relishing my first bath since joining the army. I didn't get away from the men often, and they didn't think of hygiene much.

The mud was my breaking point.

Sweet, glorious water. Thank you. I'm never going to let myself get this dirty again.

I scrubbed at my muddy clothes still on my body with the only bar of soap I owned. Made with the dreaded lye. Though I hated the stuff and missed my vanilla body wash terribly, I couldn't help but relish being clean. I took the clothes off, hung them on a few warm rocks to dry, and deposited the soap. Not wanting this blissfully quiet moment to end, I went back in, floating as I stared up at the blue sky, the sun warm on my face.

The soft gurgle of water over my ears lulled me into a meditative state, all the troubles and hurts floating out of my head and emptying until I could enjoy the moment. Something that didn't happen in the middle of a war with men constantly surrounding you. I refused to deny myself this.

The trees swayed in the light breeze, their branches throwing shadows and light across the peaceful land, and I let myself be.

Minutes passed, and my muscles finally relaxed until a voice broke through the silence, and I sat up in alarm. Heart beating out of my chest, I scanned the trees, lowering myself further under the water. Glancing at my clothes, I knew I couldn't make it to them without showing whoever it was my figure.

"Ye should have told me." The familiar grumble had me sinking in relief.

"I didn't want anyone to notice we were both gone." My gaze flipped between the trees, trying to find him.

"It won't be long before more have the same idea."

Quickly, and then there—a dark form loomed, partially hidden behind a large tree several yards into the woods.

"Then we should be fast," I said, allowing myself to fully float on my back before I lost my nerve. I was thin now but still had some curves that were on full display. I drifted there for a minute, my heart thundering in my chest. When Thomas' silence became too much, I sat up and scrubbed my short hair nervously.

"Don't hide on me account. I was enjoying the show."

My cheeks flared, and I sank until the water was up to my mouth. "I thought you might join me."

His dark form hesitated, not sure whether to come or stay put. "I should keep watch."

"Of me or possible gawkers?" I stood up, letting the water fall down my body.

My boldness had snapped whatever indecision he was struggling with, and he came to me, hands already working the buttons on his shirt. He pulled it off, and my eyes traveled his chest, roaming the plains of muscle down his stomach before moving back up to the firm set of his jaw. I admired how the sun tanned his skin, making his light freckles more prominent. His eyes were bright with mischief.

My head dipped low, and I was suddenly insecure with my body and short hair. Would he like the changes war had done to me? The loss of some of my curves?

Thomas' calloused hand grazed my cheek, and I leaned into it, closing my eyes.

"Ye're beautiful, gypsy."

"I thought you might miss the way I used to look."

His hands cupped my face as his thumbs tilted my chin up to meet his mouth. The brush of his lips sent a fresh wave of warmth through me.

"I don't think there's any way I wouldn't want ye."

His lips molded over mine, teasing them open so that I had to grab his forearms to steady myself as he deepened the kiss. We went further into the water, our lips never breaking as I wrapped myself around him. Our slick forms driving me mad as they touched bare for the first time in months. I began to fumble with his pants, trying to unbutton them until he stopped me. I lowered my legs and stepped back, gazing into the captivating green depths of his eyes. The gold flecks practically vanished, and dark heat overtook them. He wanted me. So why stop?

"I'm ready." The want in my voice made me blush.

"I can see that." He grinned, eyes roaming over my naked body. "But it's not time yet."

My head fell back as I let out a growl of frustration and pushed him away, rewarding me with a rare full belly laugh. "Really, Thomas. What do I have to do for you to want me?"

His hands wrapped around my waist, pulling his body flush with mine. My hand played with the hair on his chest as his hands moved higher, his thumb brushing my nipple. I gasped, looking up at him, but he was distracted by my body's response to his touch.

"I've always wanted ye. Ye just deserve more."

"We already had this discussion." The irritation in my response came out strangled by the desire flaring inside me.

Thomas kissed across the hollow of my shoulder and neck, making his way up until reaching my ear. "Just because I want to wait until I marry ye..." That confession sent a shiver up my spine, and I pushed aside the thought that I couldn't stay. Not when I still planned to go back with Shay. "Doesn't mean we can't do other things." His fingers skimmed my side and finally reached between my legs as his breath tickled my ear. "I can't stop thinking about what we did in that room."

My knees about gave out as his fingers began their ministrations. I gasped, and he took it as a sign to capture my mouth, his tongue sweeping in to devour me as his fingers plunged into my center.

I moaned shamelessly. "Thomas."

His lips trailed my chin, my neck, and he shifted, bending me back and sucking my nipple into his mouth. My gasp came out ragged and desperate, the pressure building inside of me. *Stop.* He had to stop or—I tried to push him away.

"Thomas, wait." I shoved him, but his arms were like a vice around me, his muscles strained and controlling as he made my body light up in a myriad of nerve-endings. "Wait." I gasped as another finger entered my body, pulling me tighter than I had ever been.

I let out a cry when he shoved deeper, deliciously painful as I held on, unable to do anything other than succumb to him. He was in control, and all I could do was take it. I tried to make him stop, to return the favor, but he kept working me until my head fell back, and I moaned, my body spasming with desire as his lips skimmed up my neck, stopping at my ear.

My whole body stiffened, rippling with waves of pure ecstasy. "Thomas!" I screamed, unable to stop saying his damned name.

"Ye know better than to try to stop me," he whispered, his mouth brushing the edge of my ear, sending another set of shock waves through me. "Not when I know your body better than anyone else. Isn't that right, Emilia?"

I whimpered, nodding jerkily as his short beard abraded my cheek.

"Say it," he demanded.

I squeezed him tighter to me, my breasts flush with his chest as I held on, wishing we could stay like that forever. "My body is yours," I promised. My hands ran up his solid arms and corded neck and buried themselves into his dark, thick hair, pulling until he looked me in the eye. "Everything about me is yours, Thomas. You stole my heart when I first saw your picture." My lips gently pressed to his. "You captured my soul when you did everything you could to save Shay and help me." I swept my tongue into his mouth in a gentle caress. "And I gave you my body all those months ago. Do with it as you will."

Thomas's hands moved up to my face, holding it like it was the most precious thing he ever cradled. His eyes flared, something akin to desire and an emotion that made my heart swell in my chest to near bursting.

"I love ye, gypsy."

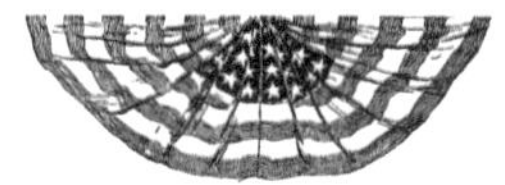

Thomas held Emilia tighter, careful not to hurt her, as her hand finished him. With a shuttering exhale, his embrace softened, and she stilled. Whatever chance he had of making out of this intact was obliterated long ago. There was no going back.

If only he could keep her in his arms, where he knew she'd be safe. His hand brushed down her back, unmistakably feeling the muscle and strength that wasn't there when he'd first met her. A part of him mourned the woman untouched by the world, soft by the ease she lived, and naïve with the cruelty of mankind. And yet, it was nothing compared to how much pride she inspired in him at how far she came. She was no longer just a woman. She was a warrior. And Emilia was perfectly capable of holding her own.

"Was that okay?" she asked softly into his neck, too shy to look him in the eyes again. He loved that she could still be this way around him. One minute, she would threaten his life; the next, she was meek as a kitten.

"Aye," he said, biting her shoulder lightly so she'd squeal. "Ye were perfect." After a minute, her body tensed. "What are ye thinking?"

She lay her head on his shoulder. "When we return to the mainland, will you see the girls with the other guys?"

He struggled to keep his face straight as a smile threatened to slip. "Girls?"

"You know, the 'girls.' Prostitutes," she spat when it was clear he had no intention of letting on.

"Oh, those 'girls.'" He shrugged. "Now that ye bring it up, I was thinking I haven't had some fun—" She shoved his chest, growling, her face scrunched up and so feral that he couldn't stop the laughter bubbling out of him.

"Asshole," she muttered, going lax as she realized he was teasing.

Pressure built in his chest with so much love for this woman. He held her tighter when she began to squirm out of his arms. "Gypsy, if I remember correctly, ye spent plenty of time with those women." When she glared at him, he gave her a half-smile that would make most women swoon. "There's no one for me but ye."

"But you've seen them since you met me?" She did everything to avoid his gaze.

Grabbing her chin gently, he guided her face toward his and gazed into the most entrancing mahogany eyes he'd ever seen. "Only one, and I regretted it immediately."

The hurt that flashed across her features made his stomach fold in on itself. He was such a feckin' gobshite. He only slept with Nessa to get Emilia out of his damned head.

"You didn't have to," she said quietly. "Regret it, I mean."

Thomas shrugged. "Wasn't really me choice. Just didn't feel right to do that with her anymore."

Emilia ran her hand over her short hair. Avoiding his gaze again. "Who was it?"

"Does it matter?" He sighed, knowing the trouble this was going to cause. "What good is knowing going to do?"

Her brown eyes crinkled sadly. With the sun on her skin, her freckles were more prominent, bringing the color out in her cheeks, and he wondered yet again how the men didn't see her for what she was. "It matters to me."

Thomas held onto her as he backed out of the water to the bank, lying her down on the small rocks as the water glided over their legs. He restrained Emilia's hands over her head and used his body to pin hers. "If ye must know..." He paused, watching the sun turn her eyes to amber as he weighed the outcome of telling her. *I'm going to regret this...* With a heavy sigh, he admitted, "It was Nessa."

Emilia turned her face away.

"Don't do that," he said. "Look at me." She turned back to him. "Ye wanted to know, and I won't lie to ye, gypsy."

"Is that what you want?" She looked down at her body. "I don't exactly have milky white skin and bright red hair. I'm boring."

Thomas couldn't help but laugh, finding the thought so ridiculous that he laughed even harder, his sides aching. He had to use all his body weight to keep her from squirming away, pressing his face between her neck and shoulder. "Boring? Dia cabhrú liom. Tá tú ar buile, a bhean." He put both of her wrists in one of his hands so he could use the other one to skim down her side, smiling when she shivered while he took extra care of her breast. "Ye are far from boring, gypsy. Ye are the most exotic thing I've ever had the pleasure of putting me hands on. And if it is up to me, ye will be the last woman I ever touch again."

She squinted at him. "That's a lie."

He nipped her lip. "No, it's not. Ye're mine, and I never plan to let ye go."

"Never?"

Thomas stared at her and wondered if she was the reward for all the sacrifices he made for his family. Or would she only be taken away? A punishment for all the crimes he committed. For all the harm he'd done.

His features must have contorted because Emilia's face softened, and she pressed her beautiful lips to his.

"What does that mean?" he asked after she whispered something in Italian against his mouth.

"I'm yours."

Thomas's chest nearly shattered, having never felt so much love for someone before. It was terrifying.

"Well, isn't this fookin' touchin'," a male voice rumbled from behind the large rocks.

Thomas shot up, pushing Emilia behind him to keep her out of sight. *What in the bloody hell?* Thomas cursed himself for not hearing his pursuit. For being distracted and unaware of his surroundings. It was bloody ignorant when so much was at stake for Emilia.

The man was Barton's smaller lackey, Jeremiah Driscoll. With a face as flat as a bulldog and skin as cracked as leather, he squatted near Emilia's clothes and played with something in his hand.

"A little late for modesty, aye?" He raised a dark brow. "Already saw all her nice bits. Shame to cover them up in lads' clothing. Can't blame ye for wanting to keep the lass all to yourself, though." He straightened, letting

Emilia's rosary dangle from his fingers. Emilia gasped softly behind Thomas. "When he gave us this job, I thought, 'Nah, no way this wee shite is a lass. Jesus, Mary, and Joseph, was I wrong." Driscoll's sneer held every sick thought going through his head. Thomas's stomach turned as fury flamed inside him.

"What job?" Thomas asked.

Was this fecker working for Barton, or were they both hired by someone else?

"Now, I can't believe me luck," he continued as if not hearing Thomas. "Not only will I collect this—" Driscoll put the rosary in his pocket "—but I might get a piece of the lass, too."

"How will your employer feel about that, aye?" Thomas's brow rose, hiding his wrath under indifference.

Driscoll shrugged. "What he doesn't know won't hurt him." He turned his seedy eyes to Emilia. "Ye won't tell. Will ye, lass?"

"Fuck you," she snapped, spitting at him.

Thomas eyed the man, trying to locate the weapons on his person. There was a small revolver on his hip and probably several knives that he couldn't see. Thomas eyed the pistol and knife he'd left by his boots when he joined Emilia in the water. If only he had a distraction, he might be able to get to them before Driscoll took a shot.

Thomas' stomach turned when he realized what he needed to do. "Do ye trust me?" he asked quietly enough for only Emilia to hear.

"Yes," she said without hesitation.

Thomas grabbed Emilia from behind him and pushed her forward. She immediately tried to cover herself and tried to struggled in his grasp. Thomas held her in front of him.

"I was done with her anyway," Thomas said, feeling sick to his core as his instincts screamed to cover her.

Driscoll's sneer turned to confusion as his dark eyes scanned her body. Thomas would have dived for his weapons then, but he didn't want to risk endangering Emilia. Driscoll had to be completely distracted.

"Ye play me for a fool?" Driscoll asked.

"Nay." Thomas sighed, acting bored. "The lass was a nice plaything for a while. But I like mine willing, and this one doesn't put out." Thomas took a step closer to the shore, grimacing at Emilia. She stared at the water, refusing to look at either of them.

Driscoll laughed. "Aye, I'd seen that. I don't have a problem with a little force. Need to put your women in their place, ye know?"

Thomas chuckled darkly, wanting to ring the man's neck. He took another step to the side that went unnoticed. The look in Driscoll's eyes was dark and hungry with desire. Thomas' lip peeled back when Driscoll returned his gaze to Emilia and the thought of all the potential things Driscoll planned to do to Emilia.

Only a few more steps stood between Thomas and his gun. "And, with all honesty…" Thomas drew Driscoll's attention back to him, "I prefer mine milky white with hair like fire. Ye know what I mean? A little feisty. But this one…" Thomas jutted his thumb at Emilia, trying to ignore how her own words cut her when on his lips. "I think ye will like her nice. I hear she has a little gypsy in her. Why don't ye give him a show, peach?"

Thomas sneered at Emilia but swallowed hard at the look of betrayal on her face and how she shook.

"No," she spat, backing away from Driscoll. He wasn't more than ten feet from her.

"Barton said ye two were a piece." Driscoll's brows bent in suspicion. "I could've sworn—"

Thomas shrugged. "It was fun for a while. I don't like to keep one for long."

Driscoll smiled darkly, the curve of his lips grimy as he nodded and turned back to Emilia. "I did hear about your reputation with women."

"Oh, aye? Then see this as my gift to ye in exchange for no trouble on me part." Thomas winked and turned to Emilia. "C'mon, siúcra. Do a little spin for us." Thomas' Irish accent deepened the farther he went into his act, and Emilia noticed, looking at him the same way she did in the alley the first time they met. She was terrified. And she should be. He told her he wasn't any good, and she'd be better off far away from him. Maybe this *was* the real him, and everything else was just an act.

He spun his finger around. "Why don't ye lift your arms up, to?"

Emilia glared at him, arms outstretched as she slowly turned. It was remarkable how tan her face and hands were compared to the skin usually hidden under her clothes. Driscoll whistled as he slid down from the large rocks, so enraptured by her, he didn't seem to notice that he had splashed into a foot of water.

Thomas was already in motion through it all. He dove for the pistol and, not bothering to get up, took a shot at Driscoll. *Feckin' hell*, he swore when the shot missed. Emilia ducked down, running to shore as Driscoll let out a string of curses, disappearing around the large rocks.

Thomas grabbed his knife as Driscoll slipped and recovered before hurrying his way into the trees. Thomas broke into a run, cursing the stones and sticks, stabbing his feet.

Would pants be too much to ask for? Runnin' bare arse through the feckin' trees...

Driscoll had a head start, but Thomas had a more considerable stride. He quickly caught up to him and tackled him to the ground.

Driscoll raised the gun, but Thomas was quicker, grabbing the man's arm and pounding it to the forest floor before he could get off a shot. In the chaos, the gun went off into a tree. *Damn ye!* Thomas slammed Driscoll's hand on a rock hard enough to break a bone. *What ye well deserve.* Driscoll yelled, fingers going loose long enough for Thomas to grab the gun and throw it to the side. Thomas wished every misery upon him. *Ye will* burn *for threatenin' me woman...*

Without realizing what he was doing, Thomas had his knife pressed to the man's neck. "Tá tú ag dul a aiféala an lá a rinne Dia tú."

"Ye'll regret *this*," Driscoll threatened.

Thomas felt like he smiled, but Driscoll's eyes widened in fear. This was Thomas buried far deep beneath the surface, emerging like a monster that came out to play.

"Tell me..." Thomas went on as if he hadn't heard him, his blood thrumming with the need to see the life fade from his eyes. "Do ye want your fate in me hands or those of your employer?"

Driscoll spat in his face, earning him a backhand and a bloody lip.

"Tell me who hired ye."

"Feck ye."

Thomas punched him several times, dazing him. "Is Barton in charge?"

When Driscoll didn't respond, Thomas cut his shirt open, struggling against Driscoll's grip when he realized Thomas's intent. Both hands on the handle, pushing down against Driscoll's hands, the blade cut into his chest as Thomas's knees pinned the slighter man to the ground.

Driscoll screamed.

Thomas faintly heard Emilia calling his name somewhere behind him, but it was as if his head was underwater. He stopped after a few more bloody gouges.

"Who is in charge?" Thomas growled.

Driscoll spit in his face, and Thomas started the following letter, slowly and deeply, while the man bucked ineffectively, no match for the hulking man on top of him.

"Is Barton the man calling the shots?"

Driscoll panted, beads of sweat breaking out over his brow, but didn't answer. Thomas pushed against the knife again. He might not know how to spell a whole lot of words, but he knew this one.

"No, wait." Driscoll sputtered, eyes wild. "A man hired him. I never met the bastard. It was Barton who recruited us."

Emilia said something from behind him, but he ignored her, finally getting some answers.

"For what?" He pushed the knife down again, though he didn't have to cut.

"The girl. We were to follow the girl."

"Why?"

"That's all I'm saying, ye goddamn bastard. Ye can rot—"

Thomas's fist fell like a hammer, and blood spurted from Driscoll's nose, cutting off what he was about to say.

"What do ye want with her?" Thomas shouted in his face. He would tear him apart for targeting Emilia. He began to carve again, Driscoll yelling when a hand grabbed Thomas's arm.

"What?" Thomas asked, his eyes still on Driscoll. He fought Emilia's attempts to pull him away.

"We have to go," she said.

"I'm about—"

Thomas heard the voices then. He turned back to Driscoll. "Tell me why, and I'll let ye live."

Driscoll smiled, blood seeping out his nose and in between his teeth. "Go feck yourself."

Thomas placed the knife at Driscoll's eye, ready to cut it out to speed up the process.

"No, we have to go." Emilia became more frantic the closer the voices were.

Driscoll stayed still, afraid to move. "Okay, okay. There are possessions on her that he wants. The rosary. I—I don't know. Barton said the gypsy bitch was his. I figured the rosary might be worth something if he's going through all this damned trouble for it." Did they not know about the vials? *Interesting…*

"Barton claims the gypsy?" Thomas asked, unclear.

"No… feck. Can ye remove the damn blade? The man who hired Barton. Said she was his property or some shite."

Thomas stood quickly, knowing he shouldn't let him live.

"Don't," Emilia said, reading his mind. "He already has that on his chest." She pointed to the word Traitor slashed across it. Her face paled. "Leave him here for the others."

Thomas knelt by Driscoll again. "Ye no longer work for Barton, do ye hear me? If I so much as hear a whisper of ye, I will gut ye and let ye bleed out slowly."

"Aye," Driscoll said, either unable or too tired to move.

Thomas kicked his face, instantly knocking him out.

"Jesus Christ!" Emilia sputtered but was already bending down to grab his things. She must have retrieved them when she heard the men. She was fully dressed and ready to go.

Thomas dug into Driscoll's pocket and pulled out Emilia's rosary. He handed it to her and quickly put his pants and boots on. Without another word, they took off through the trees while he shrugged into his shirt.

They took a long way back to go around the camp in a different direction without much notice.

"Lass." Thomas grabbed her arm. She'd been quiet since they left Driscoll, and with what she witnessed, he wouldn't blame her for being frightened. It'd be a miracle if she ever wanted to be around him again. "Are—"

Emilia's fist slammed into his shoulder with surprising force.

"Feck, woman!" he grunted, holding his arm.

"Don't ever do that to me again!" she growled. "Do you know how humiliating that was?"

Thomas stood there, dumbfounded and more than a little impressed. "Ye aren't scared of me?"

"Scared of you?" She nearly screamed it a second time before he cut her off.

"Christ, be quiet!"

Emilia shoved him. "I was naked, Thomas!"

"Believe me, I was well aware."

She growled and shoved him again, hitting his chest with her fists with only a fraction of the force of the first. He caught her wrists, holding her to him as she struggled to break free of his grip.

"I'm sorry, gypsy."

She still shoved, but he could feel her half-hearted, angry charade fade into quiet tears. These weren't the actions of an enraged woman but of one who felt used and embarrassed. His gut twisted in guilt. Maybe he should have thought of another distraction.

"Emilia, stop. I am sorry. Truly. I didn't want to have to do that to ye. I probably should have thought of a different way."

"You think?" Her voice broke, and she went weak in his arms as he wrapped them around her. She was shaking, for Christ's sake. God, what had he done? He was so overcome with fear for her that he did the only thing he knew to do to get to the weapons, damned the consequences.

"I'm sorry," she whispered. Thomas froze, thinking he had heard her wrong, and was about to say as much when— "I know you needed a distraction. I just—" She rolled her forehead against his chest in dismay. "I should never have hit you. It just was humiliating, and I was just so scared."

"I would never hurt ye."

"I already told you I wasn't scared of *you*, dumbass." Her candor almost had him choking on a laugh. If only the situation wasn't so serious. "Someone is looking for me."

"I know, lass. But who?"

"Someone besides my family had to find out about the rosary and vials. It has to be. Maybe someone overheard us? Or found out from my family?"

"Ye think they would betray ye?"

"No. That would put them in danger as much as me. That type of knowledge would be devastating. Do you think they're okay?"

Thomas squeezed her tighter, running his hand reassuringly over her back, though he had a sinking sensation that this was only the beginning. "I'm not sure, lass. I hope so." And he meant it. She'd only just found her father. "One thing I do know," he continued. "They won't stop until they get what they want."

Despite the heat, she shivered in his arms. "I am really sorry for punching you," she mumbled, dark eyes looking up at him.

Thomas smiled. "It was a good swing."

As he bent down to kiss the top of her head, Thomas looked around the empty woods, hearing nothing but crickets and frogs and the faint sound of hundreds of men camped in the distance. He knew then that they had more than a war to fear.

This threat was aiming straight at his heart.

CHAPTER THIRTEEN

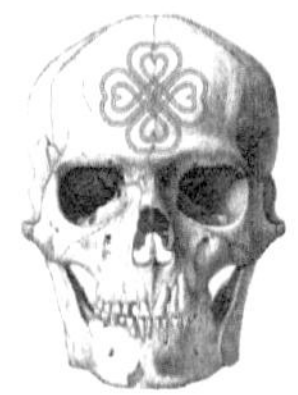

Michael

MAY 1862

Mikey took another swig of the liquor, smiling behind the glass as he won another hand.

The other men protested and threw their cards down, cursing him and the game.

"Ye're bloody cheatin'," Henry grumbled. "There's no way ye are winnin' so damn much, honestly."

Mikey scooped his winnings toward him, doing little to hide the cocky grin from the men around the table. Pierre clapped slowly, and the grin fell as everyone's attention turned their way.

"Congratulations," Pierre rumbled, his deep accent penetrating through the noise in the brothel. "I dare say I haven't met a card player as renowned as you."

Mikey nearly snorted. What bullshite was he spouting now?

Pierre leaned over and offered Mikey a cigar. Mikey nodded, accepting it as Pierre leaned back in his chair. "Sucre," the man called, snapping his fingers at Nessa, who was at another table in another man's lap.

She looked over, clearly irritated, until she saw who was calling. Mikey had to refrain from rolling his eyes as he practically saw dollar signs light up in her eyes. "Yes, sir?" she said, uncoiling from the man slowly, knowing full well that whatever attention she didn't have, she now attracted by her practiced movements.

"I want to buy a night for my man here," he said, gesturing to Mikey, who scratched his beard with a thumb, his cigar between his other fingers.

Mikey raised a brow, ignoring the jolt of aversion that went through him. What the feck was that about anyway? Nessa had been one of his girls for some time now...

Nessa smirked and made her way over to Mikey, draping herself over him. He had to do everything in his power not to dump her right on the floor.

"Hey!" the man who she'd been with yelled over. "That's me girl."

The table turned to him, abruptly cutting him off. He muttered something incoherently and turned back to his drink.

Mikey lifted an arm to accommodate her and puffed the cigar. "I believe it is I who should be buying ye a night," he said, watching amusement play on the old man's face. Nessa stiffened and turned her attention to him, bending so her cleavage was in his face.

"Where have ye been?" she whispered into his ear, gliding her hand over his broad shoulders. A distraction, he knew. Nessa wanted Pierre's money, but it'd be Mikey if it was a choice of who would enter her bed. He wondered how the hell he was going to get out of this.

But why?

"A wee bit of business," he admitted, absentmindedly rubbing a palm up her thigh.

It had been over two months since they completed the trade with Pierre. Mikey had been avoiding Nora's and dealing more with some of his other investments. It wasn't that he had been avoiding the women in the brothel. He was a busy man, he told himself, and he refused to think more about that matter. But it wasn't until earlier this day that they received news from the south, in a coded letter from one of Pierre's men, that the shipment made it to its destination without a hitch, and the sugar began to sell. Naturally, Pierre wanted to rejoice. Mikey just couldn't figure out why the whole thing left him unsatisfied. The money was definitely cause for celebration, as he could finally purchase his planned long-term investment. He leaned into Nessa instead and whispered, "Nothin' to worry your pretty peaches over."

She scoffed, but recovered quickly, plastering a smile on her face.

"He's being humble," Pierre drawled, lifting his glass to his mouth.

Mikey raised a brow. Humble would be the last word used to describe Mikey.

"We made quite the transaction. One that I believe will be financially beneficial and a promise of future business together."

"Oh?" Nessa cooed and leaned closer to Mikey, already sinking her claws at the mention of money.

What was he playing at? Mikey had other plans, and none of them concerned Pierre. But he didn't need to know that.

Mikey gave a strained smile and raised his glass. The whole brothel cheered as if they would be a part of the damned deal.

"Come," Nessa said, grabbing his hand and dragging him out of his seat. She pulled him all the way up the stairs and to the room. However, to his surprise, the usual rouse of excitement faltered, replacing it with a deep emptiness in his gut.

The door closed with a soft click as she leaned against it. A mischievous look lit up her eyes. "It's rare when we get the room to ourselves," she purred.

"That's because I prefer three," Mikey drawled. His pulse spiked when she tried and failed to cover up the flinch. Good. He liked it when she was angry. "What, minx? Don't like to share?"

She prowled toward him, unlacing her corset slowly. So, it was going to be that type of night. It was rare when he saw her completely bare. His eyes roamed down her creamy skin—

"Tommy always took me alone," she admitted, mouth quirking up.

His gaze snapped back to her face, causing Nessa to pause at the scowl. "Don't speak of me brother when I am in a room with ye."

"What?" She was outright sneering now. "I thought ye liked to share?"

His blood boiled, and he was on her in an instant. Flipping her onto her back and pinning her before she could finish the scream that she let out. His hand took up her whole face as he crushed it between his fingers. "Still pining over that fool, are ye?" A part of Mikey wondered at what fueled his anger. He never cared that Thomas had slept with Nessa. Never really thought about it other than taking what his brother desired. That gave him a particular satisfaction. Only now, a creeping sensation crawled up his chest. Not concerning his brother, but—

Nessa's knees raised, and Mikey's troubled thoughts eddied out of his head as she trapped his hips between her thighs. "Why would I when I have my pick of men to adorn me bed every night?"

Mikey scoffed, watching her bloodred mouth as she said each word. "Those men pay ye to open your pretty legs, minx. Do not fool yourself."

A flush of anger spread across her chest, and his pulse betrayed him, rioting in his chest. By the smile on her face, she could feel how much it excited him. He started to tug the corset off, wanting to see the rest of her.

"Tell me, how did the gypsy take it?" she asked.

His hands stilled, and he pulled back, genuinely confused. "Take what?"

"Tommy leaving. I'm sure she must have been crushed."

Uneasiness overcame him. What did she know? If Nessa found out...

"The gypsy left awhile back," he lied. There was no way she could know the truth. Emilia went into hiding weeks before enlisting. The story was that she was uprooted and gone like the usual wanderings of her people. So, what was Nessa getting at? "Jealousy doesn't become ye."

"Nay, not jealousy. Just wonderin' where the wee bitch went, is all. Can ye blame a lass?"

Mikey's stomach tightened, still running his hands over her, but his head was remarkably not focused on the woman beneath him.

"Gone," he growled. "Ye don't have to worry about her anymore."

Her gaze collided with his, something flaring in the green depths. *But what?*

Mikey wound her hair in his fist and yanked hard, bringing her head back sharply and exposing her neck. Running his teeth up the creamy skin, he ripped the rest of her corset off.

Nessa practically mewed when he roughly grabbed her breast. They were a fecked up pair, that was the truth. Nessa enjoyed the pain as much as he liked to inflict it.

"Good," was all Nessa said before leaning up and running her mouth up his throat as she began to move underneath him. Her hands slid across his chest, and he held back a wince. Mikey had been good at hiding the pain, but her hands paused along the bandages, and her green eyes widened. "What befell ye?"

Mikey stood, buttoning his shirt back up. "Nothin' to concern ye."

She lifted onto her elbows, giving him quite the view of her tits, but instead of pouncing on her, a strange sense of—of what? *Guilt?* Nay, that couldn't be right. What would he feel guilty—

A pair of dark eyes flashed in his mind as she held up the babe to her breast. And his pulse quickened for an entirely different reason, a flood of warmth flooding his veins.

What. The. Feck.

Would he never be able to look at another pair of breasts again? The thought staggered him back a step, and the warmth quickly evaporated, fury consuming him. What the hell sort of predicament was this? He wasn't attracted to the damned suckling babe, that's for damn sure. But he was getting the feckin' warm and fuzzies.

Mikey scoffed, spinning away from Nessa. He *did not* feel the warm and fuzzies. That was something the damned gypsy would describe. Not him. He wasn't even sure he was capable of it.

"What happened?" she asked again as he headed for the door. "Is that what is troublin' ye?"

"I need to go," he said, raking his hands through his dark hair and pushing it out of his face. "Ye can keep his money. Take the night off."

With that, he was out the door and down the stairs in seconds. A few more, and he told Hughie and Henry that he was heading out.

He needed to walk the cold streets to get his damned head on straight. There was too much at stake, and he wouldn't sacrifice everything he worked for by letting something as small as feelings get in the way.

CHAPTER FOURTEEN

Shaylah

May 1862

Shay placed Libby in the bassinet and adjusted her dress, covering herself before turning toward Rose. "Are you sure you'll be okay?" Shay asked. "What if she's hungry—"

Rose cut her off with a stern look, rolling a rag between her hands. "I've had four children of my own, child. She just ate. She'll be just fine until you get back."

Shay looked toward the door leading down to the bakery, where Hiram was waiting. He promised to take her out now that the weather was warming up.

Between the snowstorms, waiting for them to clear the streets, and for the low temperatures, she began to pace restlessly, countlessly asking Rose if she needed any help until the woman took pity on her and offered to babysit. Hiram happened to stop by and offered to take her anywhere she wanted to go.

Having saved up some money, Shay wanted to buy a few things for Libby. She had been fortunate enough to borrow Evaline's old baby things, but Shay wanted to buy something just for her child from her mother.

"Thank you." Shay smiled but couldn't ignore the concern softening the woman's eyes.

She straightened her dress and took the steps two at a time, catching Hiram's eye. He paused, running his hat through his hands—a nervous tic she had learned to recognize over the months. Instantly, she went on alert. Although they may have had a budding attraction initially, they had settled comfortably into friendship after learning about Libby. At least, she thought they had. So, Hiram had no reason to be nervous around her. Unless something happened...

"Did they send news?" Shay asked when she approached him near the door.

Hiram shook his head, his half-smile contrasting his sad, caramel eyes. "None since the last letter. I think they are well. As can be expected."

She let out a gust of air, the relief flooding her system instantaneously. "Good."

Unable to afford a carriage, they set a brisk pace down the street toward the city's center. The cool spring air caressed her skin, a promise that the long winter was nearing its end. It felt so damned good to get out of the bakery.

"Do you mind if we make a couple of stops on the way?" he asked.

"Of course not."

They made their way through the city. Stopping by different stores, checking on the families who had worked with Hiram in the past, and exchanging information on war efforts and what they could expect to come out of them. Shay often stood silent, wringing her hands to keep herself from spewing out what she knew.

She couldn't help them. Maybe make a few suggestions and drop a little history that wouldn't be suspicious. But beyond that—

"Did you hear?" the older woman asked in a quaint little toy shop Shay had been wanting to visit for weeks.

Shay paused, holding a miniature wooden horse as she turned toward Hiram and the woman. The woman grasped his arm, either out of earnestness or to steady herself, her dark tones contrasting with Hiram's golden ones. Shay looked back down at the horse and put it down. Instead, she picked up a small doll, its face porcelain and...creepy. She immediately put it back on the shelf.

"Hear what, Louisa?" Hiram asked patiently.

Shay kept her ears trained on the conversation as she kept looking. What did she expect to find anyway? She just wanted one damned thing to be from her.

"That Mary, the First Lady, I mean. Well, talk around town is that she's been holding seances in that big ol' house of theirs. People say she's trying to talk to Willi."

It had been a couple of months since the boy passed in February, but Shay's heart still dropped into her stomach, her eyes closing. Lincoln wasn't loved by many of her people. He wasn't fighting for their freedom or their rights. But he *would be* the man to emancipate them. Soon. If the talk around town was correct, he already started the gradual process. But the death of a child? No parent should have to endure that. Since she had Libby, she empathized for the man and his crazy wife.

Shay felt Hiram's gaze rather than saw it, choosing to stare at the figurines instead. They fell into a comfortable discussion that she tried to ignore.

It didn't last long, her ears perking up when the word abolitionism fell.

"...but with Davis as their President," Hiram continued. "If they are cut off, what will happen to all those in the south—"

The bell over the door dinged, and a large man, face as dark as his hair was white, walked in. His round face broke into a wide grin when spotting the two. "There you are, Louisa."

Shay's heart warmed at the love between Louisa and her husband. She had met them a few times at events Hiram brought her to, and they always brightened when their spouse walked into a room, as if the world dulled when they weren't together. Shay wanted that kind of love so very much.

She placed her hand on her now flat stomach, willing herself not to fall into those familiar thoughts. She had Libby, and that's all she needed. Walking farther down the aisle, she spotted a shelf of toy soldiers. One had a rifle up to his shoulder and dark hair remarkably like Thomas's. Another kneeled on the ground, its rifle held up, and she smiled. They could be a teeny Thomas and Emilia.

"Those just came in," the store owner said, startling Shay. Baptiste Lacoste had a deep Creole accent that could bring down cities. Having been introduced already, she discovered he had moved to Boston after leaving New

Orleans in his twenties. He built the store from the ground up, being one of the few black owners in this area at the time.

"Do you know what they're made of?" she asked, praying it wasn't lead.

"Tin, I believe, ma'am."

She gave him a genuine smile and grabbed a few that reminded her of those she knew. "Do you have any with darker skin?"

His warm eyes softened, but he shook his head. "I'm afraid not, ma'am."

"That's okay. I'll take these."

She went to purchase them at the counter. The bell above the door rang again, announcing the departure of the others.

Hiram made his way to the counter, picking up one of the soldiers. "It looks like him," he said with a sad smile.

Shay grinned back. It really must if they both came to that conclusion.

"These are very popular with the children," Baptiste rumbled.

"I just want to make sure she knows who's fighting the good fight," Shay admitted. "For her. For us." The stricken look Hiram gave her had her backtracking quickly. "That's why I wanted a darker one too. To represent this one." She jutted her thumb at Hiram. "I know he'll leave us as soon as they say he can."

Hiram's face darkened, a storm brewing within him. "They'll never let us fight."

"I think this war is going to get very bloody." Her voice came out softer and sadder than she expected. "I think they'll soon find out they need any hands they can get."

"I believe the missus is right," Baptiste agreed, startling them both into looking at him. "I've lived in the South. I'd be surprised if they aren't using our boys down there by now. It's only a matter of time before Lincoln sees the benefits."

Shay nodded and grabbed the paper bundle of toy soldiers Baptiste had wrapped for her. Paying him and giving her thanks, she turned to leave but paused, swinging back to him. "May I ask you something?"

He bowed his head, his dark eyes seeming to know more about her than she knew herself. It was unsettling, really. Shay was accustomed to hiding her thoughts and emotions behind the wall she'd built since—she swallowed, the awful night flashing through her mind unbidden—but it seemed the wall was beginning to crumble. Whether it was from Emilia enlisting, the godforsaken hormones burning through her body, or the stupid brute of an Irishman constantly confusing her—she didn't know.

"Was it worth it? Escaping the South?" She continued in a rush. "What I mean is, are you treated vastly differently in the North than the South?"

Baptiste set down a few things he'd been organizing, his face growing solemn.

"I'm sorry," Shay started, feeling like she overstepped.

"No, child. It is all right." He sighed and looked off into the distance as if he could see something buried deep in his memories. "I was a free man in Orleans. I even had me a woman." He gave her a smile that made her heart clench. Baptiste didn't have a woman that she knew of. "And she was the most magnificent, kind-hearted, strongest spirit I'd ever encountered. She was a force to be reckoned with, that one." Tears pricked Shay's eyes as she watched Baptiste reminisce. "We were happy. Free," he clarified, dark eyes landing on Shay. She squeezed the package, knowing this story wasn't a happy one. "For a time, in that part of the country, I felt free. As if I could do anything a white man could. See, I was born free, but Célestine was not. She'd been freed when she was no older than ten. We were not married three months when a runaway came across our doorstep. Célestine couldn't turn the poor girl away. We kept her hidden in the cellar a few days, planned to get her out when the authorities showed up." He looked down at the desk, the heartrending emotions bowing his shoulders, visibly tearing the man apart. Baptiste shook his head. "I was at the shop when they came. They took them both. Returned the child and sold Célestine at the next auction. I tried to buy—God..." His deep voice broke. "I tried to buy my own woman, but another, richer man had outbid me. All the money to my name could not save her from him."

Shay reached across the desk, gripping his strong hand in her own. "You did all that you could."

"Did I?" Anger flared in his gaze. "It could have been any number of other owners that wouldn't have touched her, but this one was notorious for buying the pretty ones. Everyone knew most of the children on that plantation were his, and he still sold and used them as he saw fit. Six months later, his babe was growing in my Célestine."

The doorbell rang as Hiram exited. Being a child of a slave owner, she expected this was too much for him. She tried to apologize to Baptiste, but he shook his head, giving her a sad, understanding smile.

"I know of Hiram's own sad tale. Do not worry." He patted his other hand on top of hers. "I tried to break her out. I had it all in place, but we had to wait for the child to be born. Except when she'd gone into delivery..." He trailed off, and Shay knew. Remembered her own complicated birth in this time.

"I am sorry I asked you about this," she said, tears falling down her face.

"You asked me if it was worth it." His eyes hardened to a quiet resolve from years of going over the same thing. Knowing what could have been. "I left when I had nothing left. Started over in a new town, where no one knew me or what had happened. But if I'd have come sooner, if we moved, I may still have my Célestine. I believe if we made it out, she would never have been sold back into slavery. We could have had our own family—" The word stuck in his throat as he broke down.

Shay skirted around the desk, wrapping the man in her arms, and comforted him in the way only a woman could comfort a man who'd lost the love of his life.

"I'd always been a free man," he said, patting her shoulder before backing away. "But the fear of losing my loved ones has never lessened. The threat lurks over us, whether in the North or the South. There is no escaping what they could do."

Shay nodded, already knowing the answer. She just—she just what? Wished someone could give her any sort of hope? A miniscule chance to do what she'd been considering for weeks now.

She had her hand on the doorknob when she thought to ask, "What happened to him? The man who'd bought your Célestine."

"Heard he was shot in a hunting accident years back," Baptiste grumbled, returning to his cleaning. An uneasiness settled into Shay, one that she couldn't quite place. "It wasn't until years later, when I was too old and tired to return, that I heard he lived. The damned bastard. Of course, he still plagued this earth." Baptiste's dark eyes collided with her own, and a surge of fear went through her. "Never trust a Boudreaux, child."

The world seemed to fall from beneath her feet, sweeping her into danger-ous waters. Waters that might drown her and everyone she cared about if he found out Emilia was back. Or that Shay had what he wanted.

There was only one person Shay trusted with this information. With her life. And he'd been avoiding her for weeks.

CHAPTER FIFTEEN

Shaylah

June 1862

Shay clutched the letter in her fingers, feeling sick to her stomach.

They know, Shay. Emilia's words were like an arrow to her chest. *Who could have hired them?*

Shay had already sent a letter to Emilia, warning her that Boudreaux was alive, but Emilia's letter, telling the scary tale of what happened, had already arrived. The two letters must have crossed each other on the journey to get to one another.

Please, Emilia pleaded.

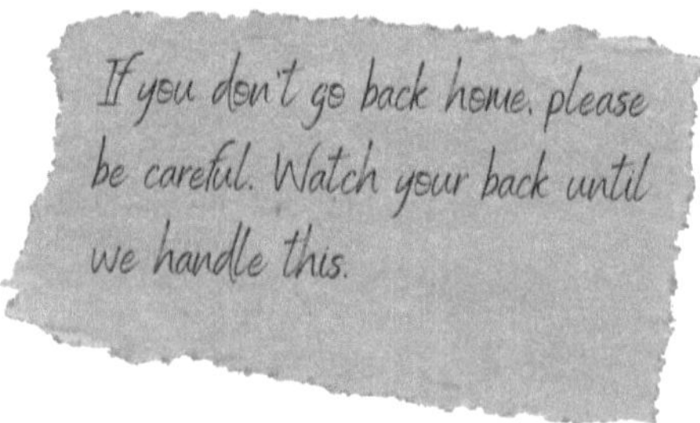

Shay stood abruptly, startling George and Rose who sat at the table with her.

"What is it?" Rose asked, looking toward the letter. "Is all well?"

"I have to go out," Shay said, folding the letter and grabbing her things.

"It is after dark..." Rose protested.

Shay halted, looking toward the staircase, almost forgetting that she had a child upstairs, fast asleep with Evaline and Mira. "Can you watch Libby?"

"A lady—"

"It's important," Shay interrupted, clutching the letter to her chest. "They are okay, but if I don't get to someone..." She shook her head, not sure how to explain. "People can get hurt, and I don't have time for these *stupid* rules."

George placed a hand on his wife's arm, momentarily stalling the wrath that was indeed to come. "Let her go, Rosie."

She swatted his hand away, but kept her icy stare on Shay. "Of course, we'll watch over Libby. What concerns me is a lady walking the streets after dark."

"I'll be careful," she promised. "I wouldn't if it couldn't wait." Not one more minute could be spared. She cursed the slow mail and lack of technology. A simple phone call could save them so much trouble.

"And where will you be going? Do I even want to know what type of questionable establishment will let you in at this hour?"

Shay stared rather sheepishly. "Probably not."

Rose scoffed but threw her hand up. "Go. But I don't want to hear any complaints when the town talks about your reputation."

Shay's spine stiffened, blood boiling. The town already *did* talk about her reputation. As a single mother, word spread fast. And if they knew she didn't even know who the father was—shame heated her cheeks.

"Go, child," George's voice was gentle, as if he could read her thoughts. With how he looked at her, she wouldn't be surprised everything was written on her face.

Embarrassed, she looked at the floor and nodded. "Thank you."

She was out the door and down the street in moments, tying a small hat on her head more out of a sense of concealment than necessity. She shook her head, knowing that the damned thing didn't conceal shit.

A brisk clip through the streets had her at Nora's faster than expected. Her breath came out in sharp gasps—and she cursed herself, mentally taking note to get back in shape—while trying to come up with the right thing to say to

Michael.

A flutter broke out in her stomach. She hadn't seen Michael since he'd stopped in the bakery a few weeks ago. He'd been good about visiting until he just...stopped. It left her confused and a little hurt. And, in all honesty, pissed. He'd been the one adamant about checking in on her and to just stop, cold turkey?

What the hell.

Shay forced the door open more aggressively than she intended, causing those sitting close to the door to turn and stare. They fell silent, staring now because of the color of her skin.

Shay straightened and walked in, refraining from giving them the middle finger like she so desperately wanted. A quick glance around revealed no Michael, causing her heart to gallop out of her chest. Was he upstairs? She scanned the crowd and found no fiery redhead. She knew that much, at least. Her throat constricted, and her heart fell into her stomach. What would she do if he was bent over the woman? Just the thought had her wanting to stomp her way upstairs and rip the slut off him by the hair.

Instead, she headed over to the small woman in the back, schmoozing the men around her as they all laughed and eyed the scantily clad women around them. She was almost there when a small girl, blonde curls bobbing, stopped her.

"Ye Emilia's friend, aren't ye?"

Shay paused, looking across the bar at who she knew was the madam, but if she could avoid the woman altogether...

"Yes," she said, letting the girl guide her away.

"What are ye doing here? Have ye heard from her?"

Shay shook her head, noting the worry softening the girl's blue eyes. How old was she?

"I'm sorry," Shay began, hesitant to tell the girl anything. "Who are you?"

"Oh! Pardon me," she said, smiling at an old, balding man as he brushed past her. Shay held back her look of revulsion. She couldn't comprehend how these women did particular acts with some of these men. They must put on quite a performance behind closed doors.

"I'm Biddy. Emilia stayed in me room when she first came to town."

"Nice to meet you, Biddy," Shay said, meaning it as she recalled Millie mentioning the woman. "Emilia is out of town. I'm actually looking for Michael. It's really important." Shay's eyes betrayed her and flicked towards the stairs again.

"Oh, he hasn't been in weeks."

Shay's head snapped back so fast that she nearly hurt her neck. "Weeks?" she asked. She hadn't seen him in weeks either. "But you know he's okay, right? Nothing happened?"

Biddy grabbed Shay's arms, probably seeing the panic rising her, and started rubbing them reassuringly. "I haven't heard anything. Here," she said, guiding Shay over to a table. "Let me ask one of the boys."

Biddy ran a hand over a middle-aged gentleman and smiled sweetly, plopping down in his lap. She whispered into his ear and giggled as his hand roamed high up her thigh. Biddy was innocent, girlish, and had a sense of youth that would attract certain men. The thought alarmed Shay, but she knew the woman wasn't as innocent and young as one may think.

Shay stood to the side, trying not to draw attention to herself, even as men side-eyed her and whispered. A prickly sense of unease ran down her spine, and she held back a snarl at the nearest man.

A few minutes and Biddy bounded back, a smile on her face. Was this girl always happy?

"Word is he is in ol' Duffy's establishment," she whispered, leaning in. "They fight down in the lower level."

"Fight?"

Biddy nodded. "It's real rough to watch," she admitted. "Blood spraying everywhere with the way they pummel each other like the brutes they are. Mikey goes there to take bets some days. Some days, he fights, but it has been an age."

"He what?" Shay asked a little too loudly, causing all those near them to turn toward her again.

Biddy gave her a sad grin that one might give a young child. "I'm sure he's doing just fine."

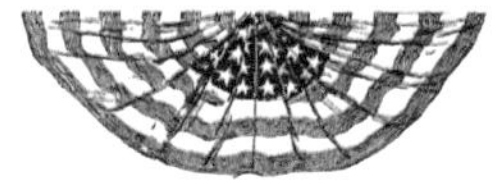

Fifteen minutes later, Shay found herself looking up at a two-story build-ing, technically a pub, illegally running an underground fighting ring. A thrum electrified her as she prepared herself to enter. A part of her was nervous—only God knew why; the man was infuriating—the other sent a thrill through her that she didn't dare acknowledge.

Shay took a deep breath and pushed in, jostling between the rowdy and drunk, straight to the back where the stairs led down, per Biddy's directions.

Dodging a man, she turned to descend when a large arm shot across her front. Shay pulled back. *What the hell?*

"What business do ye have here?" the thick Irish accent rumbled down to her.

Slowly, her eyes lifted from the massive meaty fist, following along the curve of his arm that was as thick as a thigh, before finally resting on the barrel of a chest so large, she nearly turned right back around. The man's grizzled face scowled down at her; even his horseshoe mustache seemed to frown its disgust as he waited for a response.

"I have to see someone," she admitted, looking around him toward the yelling that erupted down the stairs.

"And what makes ye think someone like ye would be welcome?"

"Fuck off," she snapped, all the tension and anger from this shithole of a century bursting out of her. She bent down quickly, spinning around him and descending a few stairs before his hand wrapped around her dress, yanking her backward.

"Get off me!" She tried to break out of his bruising grip. The next moment, his snarling face was in hers, and she reared back in repulsion.

"Let go," she growled, wrenching her arm to no avail as he began to yank her through the pub, skewing her hat and causing her to stumble through the crowd. She wouldn't—couldn't—turn back now. Not when she so des-perately needed to talk to Michael. There was no other option. No fleeing this brute of a man. "He's going to be pissed when he finds out what you did to me."

The man snorted, still dragging her. "And who's that? No man here wants ye. They'll be thanking me when I rid the place of ye."

"Michael!" she thundered, knowing he couldn't hear her, but everyone around her sure as hell could. "I'm here to see Michael."

The man stopped, beady dark eyes squinting down at her as she pulled away from him, finally stumbling out of his grasp in his distraction. "What are ye playin' at?"

"Michael O'Connor!" She pointed a finger into his chest. "You know him?" Shay turned, meeting each eye that would find hers. Men and women stopped talking, looking at the scene over their drinks. "Any of you know him? Because I need to talk to him, and this guy—" She jutted her thumb to the bouncer "—won't let me."

"Ye know Mikey?" a young man asked, looking skeptical. "What would he want with ye?"

"Why don't you ask him and find out?"

Everyone looked toward the hulk of a man behind her, and she had to bite back a grin. Let the man burn.

"She's lyin'." He sounded remarkably unsure.

"Want to test that theory? Or is that too complicated for your silly, little brain to understand?"

His face reddened like a tomato, and Shay worried she may have overstepped, even as she straightened her shoulders, preparing for a fight.

"Come," he rumbled and grabbed her roughly, pulling her back to the stairs. She smiled and nodded at those blatantly staring at the scene, glad they couldn't notice her shaking.

They descended the stairs briskly, entering a large room. A crowd stood and cheered toward a roped-off open floor. A man threw a punch, sending sweat and blood into the air as the other man's face twisted to the side.

Shay cringed even as excitement thrummed through her. She craned her neck to see more, but Hulk pulled her to the far left, obscuring her vision.

"Stay put," he said, giving her a death glare before turning to—

Shay paused, finding a tall man with dark hair swept back out of his face. He was watching the fight as if studying the customs of an undiscovered culture, learning and plotting all the ways to pillage, decimate, and conquer.

He fights. Biddy's voice came back to her. Only now did she fully understand what it entailed. Shay's head whipped to the bare-knuckled boxers again, trying to see them through the crowd.

Hulk spoke into Michael's ear, pointing in Shay's direction. Her heart shot into her throat when piercing blue eyes found hers. Time slowed and muted the cheers around them until there was nothing but him and her and their shallow breaths between them. Almost as if someone else was controlling Shay's actions, she felt her hand rise, giving an awkward little wave.

His eyes narrowed to slits as he nodded to Hulk and stalked over to her. She resisted a retreat homeward and settled for watching Michael saunter over. Her heart raced as he stopped before her, his hands in his pockets, studying her face.

"Word is ye've been asking about me?"

"He wouldn't let me down." She glared at Hulk. "It's the only way I could get to you."

Michael's expression darkened, promising an unfortunate fate for Hulk. It lasted only a moment before something shifted, propelling him to guide her to the fight, his warm hand pressed lightly to her lower back. Heat pressed against Shay as Michael drew closer, his breath whispering over her ear, sending a shiver down her spine. "You shouldn't be here," he said, his voice tense.

"Why? So, you could avoid me some more?"

His hand gripped her upper arm, stopping her so quickly that she swung to face him, their chests touching. Shay knew she should step back, but her body froze, prickling at the contact.

"What makes ye think I've been avoidin' ye?"

"Oh, I don't know. I haven't seen you in weeks and..." Shay trailed off when his eyes sparked.

"Miss me, dimples?"

"No," she scoffed. "You've been plaguing the bakery for months. I thought maybe—"

"Ye were worried about me?" Michael's cocky grin made Shay want to pinch him until he winced, but she settled for swatting his chest. The defined hardness of it was a fact she refused to acknowledge.

"I need to talk to you," she said instead, trying not to get distracted.

He stared as if trying to figure out what was happening in her mind. His smile dropped, and he nodded. "After the fight."

"But—"

"After."

His sharp tone sent a tantalizing jolt straight through her.

What's wrong with me? She should *not* like how he bossed her around, leaving no room for argument. She was a strong, independent woman, damn it. No dominant men had a place in her life. They were *not* attractive.

Michael guided Shay to the fight, ignoring the whispers and stares thrown their way. Screw them.

Lifting her chin, she stood beside Michael and watched the fighters take punches that made her wince. They were crazy for not using gloves. The number of concussions and internal wounds had to be exponential, and she wondered what a fighter's longevity of life had to be.

Michael leaned in to tell Hughie something while Shay tried not to make eye contact with the other gang members. They still made her feel uncomfortable, knowing they didn't like her even if they had orders to do no harm. They weren't the only ones staring, though. Her spine stiffened at all the attention, and she moved closer to Michael, needing to feel the security of his presence, a truth that pissed her off. She'd never needed a man before she entered this century, and here she was, leaning into one so the rise of panic didn't overwhelm her system.

"Ye get used to it." The proximity of his voice startled her, and she stared up at him, his face breathtakingly close to hers.

"Excuse me?"

"The stares," he explained. "Ye get used to them. Don't let the feckers get to ye. They have nothin' better to do than put others down to make their miserable lives feel like somethin' special. There are people in this world who make a life out of shitting on the rest of us. And then there are those who don't give a feck and throw them the middle finger. They don't know what they have comin' for them."

"What about the ones who genuinely care about everyone?" she asked, raising a brow.

The fact that Michael felt partly what she experienced surprised her. She never considered how much immigrants were affected by forced assimilation and the prejudices against different cultures. Of course, there were the indigenous peoples and those trying to get across the border in the twenty-first century, but in Boston, she had never been fully immersed in it. And here she was, still in Boston, witnessing firsthand the terrible ways people could treat others. Why couldn't people accept those who were different from them? Why did they always have to find faults instead of learning and authentically enjoying diverse cultures and rich heritages? The world would be entirely dull if they were all the same.

"Aye," Michael grunted, rolling his eyes. He grabbed a drink out of Hughie's hand and took a swig. She held back a smile as Hughie glared at Michael and left to get another. "Thee holier than thou shites who do nothing wrong and sing their hymns, praying to a god that doesn't hear their pleas."

She glared at him. "Just because you care for everyone doesn't make you religious. It just makes you a good person."

Michael snorted. "Aye, sure, lass." Clearly, he was unable to separate good people from religion. The thought almost made her give a bitter laugh. How many times had the church oppressed and abused those who didn't follow their faith? Many good people were not religious, just as many "religious" people did unspeakably cruel acts under their so-called "faith."

The ludicrousness of this man was infuriating, and there was no changing his nineteenth-century outlook in the middle of a fighting ring. She tore her eyes away from him and changed the subject. "Why have you been avoiding me?"

She felt rather than saw him stiffen beside her, lifting the drink back to his lips as he watched the fight before them. One of the men swayed, his face swollen and unrecognizable. He wouldn't be on his feet much longer.

The smell of sweat and body odor overwhelmed the area, but a pleasant spice wafted over to her, and she had to keep herself from leaning over and smelling Michael. She sucked on her lips, thinking of all the smelly people around her instead. That doused the flame of desire threatening to engulf her.

Shay almost thought Michael wouldn't respond, pretending to study the men fighting rather than talk to her until: "I've been busy."

She rolled her eyes. "Okay."

The taller man in the ring swung a solid punch at the swaying man, knocking him out cold. Michael hollered something in Irish, causing Shay to jump. She stared up at him like she'd never seen him before. He gestured to the fighters, yelling at another man who must have been a referee. She looked between the two, not understanding a damn word.

The crowd started to disperse, those clearly pissed about the loss as others smiled smugly, counting their winnings. Michael heatedly spoke with the man who argued with him.

Hughie came up to her, sipping his drink. "Ye don't belong here."

Shay glared, lip curling upward. "That line is getting old."

"Nay," he scoffed, gulping down the liquor impressively. "I don't know what it is about ye, why he feckin' gives' ye the bloody light of day, but ye are goin' to get the man killed. If not by your stupidity, then by his."

"Fuck you." Even as she said it, her stomach sank. "I didn't do shit."

Hughie's face was in hers, causing her to stumble back, even though he was several inches shorter. The man scared the shit out of her. "Ye're a damned distraction. Ever since ye came around, his head has been up his arse."

Shay looked to Michael, watching him gesture wildly with the man still. Was she a distraction? She hadn't gone out of the way to see him. If anything, he always came to her.

"Leave him alone," he continued. "If ye bloody well know what's good for ye."

She stared into his eyes, hatred burning through them. There was nothing good in Hughie's soul, and being next to him made her want to flee. "Is that a threat?" she said with more force than she felt.

"Oh." His laugh made her stomach turn. "It most definitely is a threat, lass. If ye don't back off, what those boyos did to ye will be feckin' child's play." He leaned in, whispering into her ear, making her whole body tremble. "Good men died because of ye."

"Good men?" She scoffed. Good men didn't tie up a woman and take turns using her. "I'm glad they're dead."

His lip peeled back, revealing a chipped tooth. "Learn your place," he growled, sending a chill through her. "I would love to get ye under my knife, ye bloody slag. Ye deserved what ye got. Women like ye have never been his type. He likes 'em creamy and willin'. If ye get me meanin'." His gaze shifted to Michael, his eyebrows rising as he took in the redhead who had suddenly appeared and placed her hand on his chest, smiling as he conversed with someone else.

Nessa.

"Looks like he can't keep away from 'em even with ye here." Hughie's grin made her want to slam her fist into it. She balled her hands to keep from doing just that. "Shame." He tsked. "And ye came all this way…" Jealousy Shay never knew flared so bright she saw red. "Why even try? No one wants a—"

"Listen up," she hissed. "I've had enough of your shit. I didn't come here to listen to your insults or your half-assed threats. If you don't like me, fine. I don't give two shits what you like. But if you think you can stand here and berate me, you have another thing coming for you."

Hughie laughed loudly as he scratched his beard, the scraggly mess several shades darker than the red mop on his head. "Ye have no idea who ye're talkin' to…"

"Oh, I know exactly who I'm talking to. An insecure little man who takes orders from the big man over there." She tilted her head toward Michael. "But you want more. Don't you, Hughie? Tell me, how does it feel taking the orders when you so desperately want to be *him*?"

"Ye little slut—"

"Aww." She smiled, even as her heart nearly imploded. "That's cute. Do you talk to all the women like that?"

Poking the sadistic murderer, Shay? Real smart.

"Ye don't know what ye're feckin' talking about." His face twisted in anger; his knuckles white from gripping his mug so tightly. Lifting her chin, Shay stood her ground, not giving him the satisfaction of seeing her fear. "Go back to whatever hole ye climbed out of. It's pathetic, the way ye come around." He grinned, looking back at Nessa. "Me man will be with his three slags by the end of the night, and ye will be alone and—"

Shay leaned forward, smiling wickedly, knowing she must seem a little unhinged, but she had no more fucks to give. "That's because he never had a woman like me. He wouldn't even remember one of those whore's names after I'm through with him. Not when I'm riding—"

Someone cleared their throat loudly. Shay's head whipped around, finding Michael, blue eyes burning through her. Her spine straightened and she swallowed thickly, unsure how much he'd heard.

"Let me introduce ye to Mr. Pierre," Michael said, jaw stiff with—what? She held back a wince, unsure if she wanted to find out. He scratched his beard with one hand, trying to hide his emotions and failing.

Shit. Shit, shit, shit.

She hadn't meant for him to hear. She didn't mean it, really. Hughie just made her so angry, and she *used* to have men stumbling over her. Now, though—her throat constricted. How could she ever be the same after what had happened?

But if what Hughie said was true...maybe they would never have worked. She couldn't imagine submitting to a man, not when she so quite liked to take control. To make them beg. And if what she heard was accurate, Michael was the same way. They were incompatible. Hell, maybe she would never be ready to be with a man again, anyway.

Shay looked at Nessa, finding the woman's green eyes on her and looking none too pleased to see her either. Good. The hussy could eat dirt for all she cared. And yet...Shay cocked her head, considering. Nessa didn't look like a woman who would willingly submit either. Perhaps...

Ugh. Why was she even thinking this?

Finding Michael's gaze, one brow high, Shay suddenly realized she had been lost in her thoughts, and they were waiting for a response. She tore her eyes away from him, face burning, as she focused on the middle-aged man Michael gestured to. Deep wrinkles cut his weathered face, but they in no way detracted from his impressive build, his body still straight and strong from years out in the sun. Still blushing, Shay held out a hand to him. "Nice to meet you," she said.

Pierre swept her fingers up in a gentle embrace, surprising her by kissing them lightly instead of the handshake she expected. She held back her grimace and smiled sweetly instead.

"The pleasure is mine," Pierre rumbled, the accent stiffening her back. It sounded awfully like— "I was talking with Mr. O'Connor here, and I could not keep my eyes away from a woman of such beauty."

Shay's eyes flicked to Michael's, noting how his jaw ticked. She pulled her hand away, unsure if he was angry with her or Pierre's affections.

"Thank you," she said, returning her gaze back to Pierre. The nicety was like an ice pick to the eye.

"Are you a free woman?" Pierre asked.

Shay drew back, eyebrows slamming down in a glare that made him chuckle deeply. The bastard.

"I am only asking if you have a man." He spread his hands out, looking around the room.

"I don't see—" she started, but Michael turned into her, placing his large hand on her lower back, the heat reassuring.

Nessa scowled at them, shimmying up next to Pierre instead, hand trailing up his white sleeve.

"She is spoken for," Michael's voice boomed as his fingers splayed on Shay's dress. Did he realize what he was doing?

"Of course, of course," Pierre said, still chuckling even as his blue eyes focused on the hand on her back. "I understand." He winked at Shay. "If you'll excuse me..."

Michael watched the older man until he walked from the room, something calculating in his gaze.

Shay's heart beat rapidly. *What just happened? And why is he acting like this? It's almost...territorial.* The though had her biting her lip, unsure what to do with that assumption.

"Are you okay?" she asked, confused.

Her voice seemed to bring Michael back into the moment, but the hardness around his eyes didn't soften. "Hughie," he said, voice rougher than she ever heard as his gaze seared into her soul. "Get the feck out of here."

"Mikey—"

"I'll deal with ye later," he growled, propelling Shay forward.

She looked back to find Hughie scowling. "He's going to be pissed," she told Michael.

Michael pinned her with a stare that had her steps faltering.

"I don't give a feck," he snapped, gaze scorching over her body in a way that stripped her bare. All the air seemed to suck out of the room, immobilizing her at his following words.

CHAPTER SIXTEEN

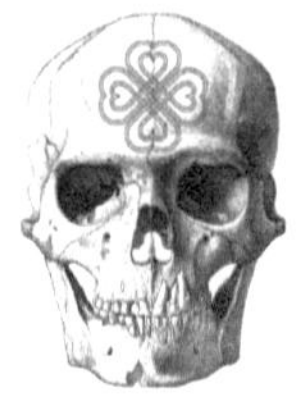

Michael

"**N**ow, tell me, grá. What were ye two talking about?"

"What?" Shay's cheeks darkened and her steps faltered. Mikey grabbed her elbow to keep her from shying away.

"Don't play dumb with me, dimples," Mikey teased, liking how her body reacted to him, even as a jealousy he'd never known consumed him.

They veered around people, making their way to the rear of the room where a small hallway led to a few doors. He pushed one open, shoving her in.

"Hey!" she started.

"What man are ye takin' to your bed?"

"What?" she asked, looking around at the pantry, the jars covering the shelves, and the large barrels of spirits. A small window just above the street outside let in some light, but not much. Mikey fiddled with the lantern hanging inside the door, and light bloomed around them.

Before she could say anything, Mikey's hands wrapped around her waist, slamming her chest into his. She gasped, his hand wrapping around the long braid she had been wearing lately. He pulled it, making her look up at him, loose curls falling into her eyes.

"Don't make me repeat meself," he growled, concentrating on her lips.

"I..." Her words trailed off, probably trying to find a way out of this. He'd be damned before she left this room without giving him answers. "He was saying things—"

"Hughie?" His gaze flew up to her big, brown eyes. Gods, she was beautiful.

She nodded. "I was just..." She winced, and Mikey's chest tightened, wanting to erase whatever discomfort she felt. "I was just irritated."

A deep line formed between his brows, his jealousy quickly shifting to fury. He would kill the man she wanted so badly. "I swear to the gods," he growled. "If ye don't—"

"You!" she yelled, slamming her hands against his chest. "I was talking about you, damn it! God, you're insufferable!"

He stood there, momentarily stunned, as he tried to piece together what she said. He didn't dare hope. Not when he didn't understand why he cared in the first place. Still, he needed more clarification. "Ye were talking about me?"

She swallowed and nodded.

"About riding me..." His one brow rose, a rising excitement thrumming through him, resurrecting his usual confidence.

"Yes," she growled, brows scrunching adorably. "Riding *you*."

Mikey's gaze dropped to her full lips, wanting to know what it felt like to suck one into his mouth. He smirked when she inhaled sharply.

"Wait," she said, an unexpected smile forming. "Were you *jealous*?"

Mikey's neck heated, shocking him. Was he jealous? Feckin', gods. That's the unbearable feeling that overtook him whenever she spoke to Hiram? Shown a man any attention? For Christ's feckin' sake.

"Are you blushing?" She giggled, the sound surprising them both. He would have killed to hear that sound again.

Oh, she was in for it.

His stance shifted from stiff to predatory, causing her to retreat from his arms so quickly that he didn't stop her. He prowled after this infuriating woman until her back hit the door, jostling the lantern and sending light bouncing around the room, striking up every crevice and curve of her tantalizing body.

Mikey put a hand on each side of her head, barely bending to see into her eyes. She was the tallest woman he'd ever met, but if he remembered correctly, the gypsy said women tended to be larger in their century. Even Emilia was bigger than average. However, where the gypsy had temptingly lush curves, Shay's body was thin, her lithe muscles promising a subtle strength that made his pulse rise in a way that no one ever tempted him. He thought of her long, bare legs he wasn't supposed to see all those months ago and the thousands of ways he imagined them wrapped around him.

Ignoring *that* memory, he snapped, "I don't get *jealous*."

"Are you sure about that?" Her flirtatious words contradicted the way her body stiffened.

His eyes narrowed. "What was that?" he asked, guiding Shay's chin up gently to look at him.

"Nothing."

"Ye flinched."

"It was nothing," she snapped, ducking down and maneuvering away from him impressively.

"Ye were fine," he started, looking between her and the door, realization dawning.

He was so feckin' glad he killed those feckers. Just by the few things she said, he knew she was a wraith of the girl she'd been before those assholes got a hold of her.

"I *am* fine," Shay said, turning the jars around randomly.

Mikey held his hands up, stepping closer as if she was a deer ready to flee. Shay rolled her eyes, making him feel a wee bit foolish.

"Don't," she said in warning.

He had no intention of stopping. What he had in mind was to erase every gods-damned memory of them, replacing their cruelty with his own torture until Shay screamed with pleasure. "I'm not going to do anythin' ye don't want," Mikey said, slowly closing the distance.

She scoffed, crossing her arms over her chest and glaring.

"Ye forget, lass," he said, stopping before her. "I was the one who found ye."

She snarled so fiercely Mikey had to restrain himself from taking her right then. Gods, she was savage, and he loved every bit of it.

"I didn't forget shit." The gravel in her voice had the opposite effect on his body than she undoubtedly intended.

He reached behind her, wanting to see how her wild curls framed her face, and pulled the ribbon tying her long braid. He ignored the way Shay's body jolted, the fear that was a constant wall between them. A wall he planned to feckin' demolish until the only thing between them was their own feral appetites.

"What—" she started, his hands removing her hat and moving into her long curls, taking it out of the braid. "You're going to mess it up!" She swatted at his hands as he bit back a smile. "You don't know—"

He pulled it over her shoulders, gently laying it across her breasts. He forgot to breathe as he stared at the goddess before him. The way her breasts heaved, remarkably larger now than when he'd first found her. He knew it was from nursing the babe, but he couldn't seem to give a damn. He'd thank the wailin' brat later.

"I just wanted to see it." The roughness of his voice had to betray his thoughts.

"See what?"

"How ye look undone." Mikey's eyes roamed over her curls—unruly and magnificent—down her throat to where dark, smooth skin met her creamy dress. He bit his lip to keep himself from tasting her. He looked up. "I've been with a lot of women..." His mouth hooked upward when she glared. Lifting a hand, he slid his thumb over her lip momentarily before weaving it in her hair, pulling her head back as his other slid around her waist. Shay's little gasp electrified Mikey's every nerve. "I know why your body reacts the way it does," he admitted, wishing it was her desire for him rather than terror of what they'd done. She swallowed, eyes filling with tears that tore through him. "I saw what they did to ye. And I killed every gods-damn one of them for it." His grip tightened when Shay stumbled back, grabbing the counter behind her as if trying to create some distance between them.

He'd have none of that. His hand gripped the skirt of her dress, pulling her closer.

"You didn't like me then," she stated weakly.

"Aye," he agreed, knowing it'd hurt her. But he'd be damned if he lied to her now. "I've had some time to gather me thoughts."

Shay quirked a brow. "And?"

"Gods strike me, I can't keep away. Every time I feckin' try, I just end up right back here."

"In a pantry?" she asked, eyes lit with amusement.

"No, ye devil." Mikey leaned in, face close to hers as his rough hands slid gently up her sides, trailing her shoulders to skim over the sensitive skin of her clavicle. She shivered, and he smirked.

Gods, curse him now. How was he ever going to recover from this?

He took his time, not knowing when he'd get another chance, and admitted what he'd been denying for weeks. "Near ye."

A heavy silence weighed on them as what he admitted sunk in.

"Why?" she whispered. "What is so special about me?"

He fixated on his hands, cupping her face, how his pale skin contrasted with her darker pigment, looking out of place while feeling—like what? Like the shores of Ireland when he was a boy? The way he laughed with his siblings in the fields before the famine? Not quite, but close. His heart beat faster as his mind raced. More like the way life was before everything went to shite.

Like going home after a long journey.

Gods. It'd been years since he felt at home, wandering these streets, taking what he wanted to make it feel a wee bit like his. Even though it never gods-damned did.

His heart swelled, his body taking on an ethereal sensation as he cradled the most precious thing he'd ever encountered in the most unexpected person.

Feck. He cradled home.

Mikey felt Shay lean farther into the counter, watching him as he struggled to comprehend what he felt. How could he ever be good enough for this woman? When he'd done everything to push her away. When he fecked up so many times, insulted her and her people. How could he ever expect her to want a no-good gangster like him? He didn't deserve her, and sure as hell couldn't put her through all the shite that was sure to come with a relationship like theirs. Hell, she probably only tolerated him as it was. Realizing that everything he strived for didn't reside in a land but in a living being brought every fear to the surface.

He couldn't do that to her.

Mikey started to pull back, ready to apologize, when something in Shay's expression shifted, stealing his breath. Her strong hands gripped his shirt right before her body slammed into his. He barely had time to register the contact before she surged onto her toes.

And kissed him.

The world stilled. Mikey's body went rigid as Shay pressed her soft lips to his. Grabbing his face, she deepened the kiss, opening for him. But his mind struggled to understand, struggled to move, as a woman surprised him for the first time in his life.

She gasped and pulled back, embarrassment and shock written all over her. "I'm sorry."

The little restraint Mikey had snapped. He wove his arms around Shay's body as he captured her mouth with his. Mikey shook, holding himself back so as not to startle her. She opened her mouth, swiping her tongue over the seam of his lips, asking for the entrance they so desperately wanted. *Craved.*

Mikey gave her just that, his tongue sweeping in to devour her. The she-devil moaned deeply, shattering the rest of his restraint. Mikey gripped Shay's thighs, lifting her onto the counter and making jars clatter. Shay gasped, landing back on her hands. He smirked, watching how he affected her before his gaze dropped to her breasts.

Taking advantage of his momentary distraction, Shay yanked Mikey closer between her spread legs. He held back a growl as her thighs tightly squeezed around his waist.

Her breath tickled his ear, sending shockwaves of pleasure through him, when she whispered, "I know for a fact you never had a girl like me."

The growl he'd been holding back erupted through him. She had no idea how damned right she was, and he wanted to make her pay for it all in the best ways.

A fire lit in her eyes, daring him to do just that. "If you have the audacity to look, you better take good care of them."

Mikey's jaw tensed, his hands gripping the fabric of her dress instead of where he wanted them. If she'd been any other woman, he'd already have her bent over the counter, moaning for him. He swallowed, arms shaking as he admitted, "I'm tryin' to do it differently with ye. Ye're makin' it damn hard."

She smiled, shifting closer. "Not the only thing that's hard."

Mikey closed his eyes, feeling her run her hands up his arms, a special kind of torture as he tried to be the man she deserved. Gods, he wasn't, but he'd try for her.

Only for her.

Shay ran a finger up his chest, and Mikey swore, eyes springing open as he bent her backward and was rewarded with a little gasp. His lips skimmed up her soft chest before hitting that sweet spot between shoulder and neck, practically making her mewl in pleasure. *Feck.* The way she clung to him made him want to…

Feck it.

Mikey's tongue ran up Shay's neck, tasting of sin and everything denied of him. His hands gripped her tighter, pulling their bodies flush with each other. She wrapped her legs around him, and he grazed her jaw with his teeth to keep himself from sinking them into the tender flesh of her breasts heaving beneath him. The temptation was only denied by the way she bent into him, reclaiming his mouth.

They both moaned simultaneously, lost within each other. He skimmed his hand up her leg, pulling the fabric up so he could grip her thigh, almost bruising in his want. Her body stiffened beneath him, her mouth still pressed against his, but her tongue withdrew as they both breathed each other in.

What had he done? He clearly crossed a line she wasn't ready to cross. Gods, he wanted to take it slow with her. What had he been thinking? He knew he should have waited, shouldn't have even *tried*.

Mikey pulled back, putting distance between them even as he took in the delectable sight of her spread for him. Mikey spun on his heel, running a hand through his dark hair as his stomach turned. She didn't want this, and he looked at her like a feckin' treat. Now, he looked at anything but her.

How he would leave this room without tasting her again was beyond him.

At the end of the day, he didn't deserve her. And she didn't deserve a man like him to take any more from her. What they needed was a distraction. He spun back to her, remembering she'd come to him with information. He'd been so blinded by jealousy that he'd forgotten.

"What did ye have to tell me?" he asked suddenly.

Her face contorted in confusion, eyes boring into him as she clung to the counter. "What?"

"If we keep this up, I'll take ye here right now. Ye're not ready for that." He gave her a pointed look. "So, what did ye have to tell me?"

"Who are you to tell me what I'm not ready for?" she snapped and started straightening her dress.

He stared at her, mind completely blank, not knowing how to react to this sudden change. Shay widened her eyes, waiting.

"I just thought—" he started, but she scoffed, hopping down.

"Right, you thought. That tends to get you in trouble, doesn't it?"

Confusion and need swiftly turned to annoyance. "What the feck is that supposed to mean?"

"Never mind." She shook her head, running her hands down her cream dress as if she could smooth the wrinkles out. Sighing, Shay finally turned to him. "Millie thinks people are after the vials and rosaries. She sent a letter warning us."

She explained the altercation that led to the letter and the reason for sending her own letter when she froze, face paling several shades as she stared at him, looking as if she'd seen a ghost.

"What is it?" He went to her, hands gripping her shoulders as she shook her head. Whatever spooked her scared the shite out of him. Though he'd never admit it.

"It can't be."

"What?" he growled, frustration eating at him. "What is it?"

She shook her head again, loose curls flowing around her face. "There is a man, a shop owner from Louisiana," she explained—rather slowly, in Mikey's opinion—but he waited silently, rubbing his hands up and down her arms. "He mentioned Boudreaux. Michael..."

His name on her lips sent a thrill through him at how she looked at him. As if he could solve all her problems. Right before everything went still at her following words.

"Boudreaux is alive."

"Alive?"

Shay nodded. He didn't know her face could pale any more than it already had, but it sure as hell did as she explained to him the shop owner's unbelievable tale. Shay went to Mikey, grabbing his shirt in desperation. "Pierre," she said, searching his eyes like she was waiting for him to realize something. "I knew when I heard his accent something was off. I heard it before. It is the same accent as the guy in the shop. Who is he?" Her voice rose with each word. "Is that his full name?"

He opened his mouth, shaking his head, holding her hands in his. Gods, what had he done? "Mr. Pierre from Louisiana," he admitted, feeling sick. "Marcel—"

"Pierre Boudreaux," she finished.

The room seemed to fall out from beneath them, sweeping them up in a storm of shite that went farther than either of them could have imagined.

Emilia's master was alive. In town. Wanting her and the keys to time. Going as far as hiring men in her regiment. How he'd done it, found her, was beyond Mikey. Why hadn't he taken her when she was in town? Had her disguise hidden her that well?

Feckin' gods above, how had he not realized this?

Mikey should've known. Should've known he'd been working with the enemy for months. The damned bastard had been planning this, shuffling them like pawns in a game, until he took what he wanted and left everything to shite. But how far would he go?

Mikey straightened, pulling Shay to him as he pressed a gentle kiss to the top of her head, mentally preparing himself for what must be done.

Pierre. *Feckin' hell.*

CHAPTER SEVENTEEN

Emilia

16 JUNE 1862 ~ BATTLE OF SECESSIONVILLE

It was dark as we made our way across a cotton field so overgrown with weeds that we had to break our lines and proceed at a much slower pace. We set out hours before the first light, something I would have struggled with a year ago that I was surprisingly growing accustomed to. Our regiment joined with the 8th Michigan, 7th Connecticut, and 79th New York Highlanders.

As we neared, our left flank proceeded into the marsh, bogged down and clogged to the point that the narrowing field made the travel dreadfully slow for the rest of us.

Two hundred yards from the fort, Colonel Lamar of the damn Confederates ordered a collection of sharp materials to be shot out of the cannon and straight into our center. Men called out as broken glass, grapeshot, nails, and other atrocities tore through their bodies, even as we kept pushing forward. Panic filled my veins as I heard the screams, and I had to control my breathing in order to keep a level head. Luckily, the 28th was farther back, and I knew my men weren't hit, though that time would come all too quickly.

The closer we got, the fear turned into the exhilaration of battle, and I wondered if the men around me felt called to push harder, faster, as I did. It wasn't our first time under enemy fire. That had come a few weeks ago under a series of skirmishes. Then, I was frightened beyond rationality, worried that those who were close to me would be injured. I almost laughed at my naivety then, knowing what I experienced could only be described as a practice run. Indeed, we'd lose more than five of our men in the impending battle.

I couldn't see it in the dark but would soon discover that the 8th Michigan made it to the parapet, shooting into the Confederates. It wasn't long before hellfire shot into us. I ducked down while still trying to keep in position, praying I wouldn't get hit. My entire body surged with adrenaline, heart racing and limbs tingling as I tightened my grip on the rifle, scanning for any sign of the enemy.

Those of the Connecticut were told to charge, but they quickly lost their path and stuck into the pluff mud, marsh overcoming them as our regiment slammed into their backs. My feet sunk into the brown gunk of despair, making it nearly impossible to keep my balance. A man fell, and his rifle fired into the group. Whether or not he shot one of us went unknown, we were still being hit by the Confederates.

The men around me were packed shoulder to shoulder, front to back, unable to move. We were at a stand-still, our ranks disorganized as our Colonel spit out profanities. He was doing his best to get us back in line, but each second that passed was another taken from the aid of the 8th Michigan.

The Highlanders, a beautiful, fearsome sight to behold, came to our aid, splitting our regiment with a thunderous roar that echoed through the battlefield, not even the mud could bog them down. Their prowess and relentless determination carried them to our struggling Connecticut regiment and surpassed them as well. The site left me breathless with the determination and strength that enabled them to conquer the seemingly impossible. I should have felt disheartened that they achieved what we could not, but it only bolstered my faith in the North.

With them, we can do this, I chanted internally. *With them, they will lead us through the charge.*

The Highlanders didn't falter as the cannon shot down their middle. My stomach surged into my chest as they seemed to defy all odds, breaking through barriers like gods coming down from the heavens.

"Jesus Christ," I muttered. "It's like a whole goddamn regiment of Jaime

Frasers."

No one heard my outburst.

My eyes searched through the lightening dawn and landed on Thomas, who was dragging a man out of the mud. My heart swelled at the sight of him. The soldier must have been shot, and Thomas was trying to get him out of the line of fire. Rifle at the ready, I went to cover them, searching through the swarm of men for any rebels.

Soon, the order came for us to fall back, and the man Thomas helped staggered away, swept up in the group of men moving to the hedgerows. Pops continued to blast throughout the field as our group retreated. I was just behind them when I heard another pop and grunt of a man in pain.

Turning around, I found three Confederates on horseback who had ventured farther away from the fort. They were headed straight for a man trying to stand on an injured leg, made worse by the mud. My breathing hitched as I found my regiment already yards away.

There was no time to get help.

The closest rider lifted a pistol, aiming for the injured man. He hadn't seen me yet. I let out the breath I'd been holding, lifted my rifle, and fired.

I didn't have time to dwell on the sick feeling in my stomach, I was already tearing the next cartridge with my teeth before dumping it down the barrel.

"O'Connor!"

I ducked just as Mick raised his rifle and shot the second rider. I stumbled forward in my desperation to get to him. *My God, it's Mick.* I thought he was a random soldier. My desperation to get him to safety intensified.

Mick was loading his rifle when he was shot again. He reeled back, the bullet going through his shoulder. *Shit. Oh, shit.*

I lifted my rifle again and fired but missed, the last rider veering off. *Damn it!* I cursed myself for missing, my stomach plummeting with our predicament. *Cowards!* I seethed. *I hope you* rot.

Turning to Mick, I pulled his arm around my shoulders. "C'mon," I said. "Ye need to get out of here."

"I'm not leaving without you." My voice broke on the last word. *What do I do?*

I searched the area around us for any sign of help but found none. Our best bet was to make it to solid ground to move easier. A tree stood in the distance, lit by the sun like a golden beacon of salvation. I turned Mick in that direction, hoping we could use it as cover.

"Leave me," he grunted. Blood oozed out of his shoulder and covered his pants.

"We're almost there." *Please, God. Get us there.* This was too much. An absolute nightmare. But if he was in it, then I was in it too.

Another shot had birds scattering out of the tree.

Almost there, come on!

Hooves pounded behind us. My chest heaved in and out as I tried to catch my breath, my legs screaming as I pushed them to their limit. Finally, we reached the tree, falling to the ground and rolling into its embrace. I lifted up just enough to see around the trunk even as black spots danced around my vision.

"Do ye see him?" Mick gasped, his hand staunching the flow of blood seeping from his shoulder.

I shook my head. "Maybe he turned back."

I helped Mick sit against the tree and began to undo my belt.

"What are ye doing?"

"We have to stop the bleeding."

I wrapped the belt around his leg and pulled tight, ignoring the hiss that escaped his lips.

"Why'd ye do it?" he asked, his face contorted in pain as the sun lit up his skin, almost radiating out of him like a golden angel.

"Do what?"

"Enlist. Why are ye here?"

I thought about it momentarily, ordering my thoughts into something that would make sense.

"I realized I never fought for anything my entire life. I was comfortable singing in my family's pub. I was fine not knowing my birth parents. Until life shoved it into my face and opened my eyes."

I secured the belt and looked for the lone rider, grabbing my rifle just in case. "When I found out what happened to my mammina—when I remembered—I knew I couldn't be comfortable anymore. Not when my friend was targeted just because of her race. I'm sick of it. I'm sick of my loved ones getting hurt because of other people's hatred. I knew I wasn't going to be comfortable ever again. Not knowing what I know now. What I *see* now."

He quietly watched me, a solemn expression softening his pained features.

"I have to fight because if I don't, I'm just another part of the problem. I know when I'm comfortable again, I'm not doing enough."

Mick's face contorted as he tried to straighten himself. "Some say that is the goal." A brief pause. "Ye aren't what ye seem."

I shrugged. "Why'd you enlist?"

"I guess I wanted to show them we could do better." He heaved a sigh. "That maybe if we helped them win their war and preserve the Union, they might look at me for what I am rather than what they think of me. That the Irish deserve more than leftovers. That we deserve equality as any other man in this country."

"And woman."

Mick smiled. "Aye, and woman."

Tears sprang to my eyes, and I looked everywhere but at Mick, not wanting him to see how much that meant to me.

"You know by your answer," I said, trying to divert the topic a bit, "we have to free the slaves." His expression showed I hadn't hidden anything from him, and I smiled weakly back. "We have to give them just as much a chance to make it in this world as everyone else."

He let his head fall back, and I worried he lost too much blood. "Stop talking sense, woman. I can't handle any more of it."

My smile bloomed, taking part in a win. "Thank you."

His head rolled to face me. "For?"

"Not telling anyone about me."

"Guess I couldn't bring meself to turn in someone who keeps saving our arses."

I laughed even as doubt flooded me. Instead, I focused on scanning the field around us. We were alone, our regiment past the hedgerows and the fort far enough away that stragglers weren't passing us.

"And that man of yours, I figured he'd hang me by me bowels, that one. Scares the living shite out of me."

I blushed. "He wouldn't—"

Mick stopped me with a look, and we both laughed, knowing Thomas would.

"I guess you're right," I agreed. That man would do anything for those he loved, and after seeing what he did to Driscoll, I would never doubt how far he'd go again.

"Aye, I know it."

We sat silently for a few moments, just taking in the morning and not the battle happening elsewhere. I shifted on my knees, knowing our time was running out.

"Ye need to go," Mick said, his thoughts coinciding with mine.

"Not without you."

"They will be on us soon enough. Ye are still intact. Ye can't let them take ye prisoner."

I swallowed. I didn't want to leave Mick behind, but he couldn't put weight on his leg, and I couldn't carry him as quickly as we needed to move. I could get someone to help me bring him to safety if I ran.

I looked in the direction that our regiment went. Thomas would be searching for me soon—if he wasn't already—and I couldn't risk him being hurt or captured.

"I'll bring someone back," I promised.

Mick nodded and pulled out his pistol, lying it on his lap as he struggled to position himself to see around the tree. "Go."

"Mick," I started but hesitated, unsure how to express my feelings.

"God damn it, lass. Ye never turned your back on your men, and ye aren't now. It's time for me to have yours. Go!" He growled the last bit.

I grabbed my rifle and ran faster than I'd ever run. Arms pumping, bag bouncing off my back as the mud from my boots flew off in chunks, my breath coming in and out in sharp puffs.

Pop.

A tight burning shot through my arm, and I held back a scream.

Another *pop* and the field was silent. I turned, raising the rifle the best I could with an injured arm. A horse ran in the direction of the fort, riderless. Mick must have shot the man who hit me.

I caught Mick's gaze across the distance and gave him my nod of thanks. He saluted me in the old-fashioned way, palm out.

I made it over the hedgerow and didn't stop until I heard the faint sound of soldiers. In the distance, the heavy smell of smoke and wood burned on the air.

I didn't take the time to figure that out.

Finally, I made it to a few men and tried to explain the situation, but they wouldn't return. It'd be against orders.

I pushed through a growing crowd, searching their faces for one familiar.

"Please, help me," I practically begged.

Each man denied me.

"Where have ye been?" someone grumbled, but I was too frantic to comprehend the words.

A hand grabbed my arm, and I yelped.

"What happened?" Thomas demanded, looking pointedly at my arm. Shocked by the ferocity on his face, I glanced down, almost forgetting I'd been shot in my desperation, and explained to him about Mick.

Thomas scanned the group around us, each man slowly walking their retreat, and nodded. I sighed in relief, knowing I could count on him.

"We need to wrap it."

"There's no time. C'mon." I tugged on his shirt until he relented, knowing time was of the essence.

We made it to the clearing and hid behind some hedgerows. I muttered a curse upon seeing a scattering of Confederates.

"What are they doing?" I asked.

His green eyes scorched the field, estimating the distance while calculating our chances of making it to the tree unnoticed. "Gathering the prisoners."

My stomach dropped, and I felt slightly queasy from being awake so early, getting shot, and the trauma of the day. I grabbed his arm for support.

"Let's go," I said, already taking a step.

"Wait." Thomas grabbed my waist and pulled me down. "Look."

He pointed to a few Confederates surrounding the tree, pulling Mick up. I went to stand, lifting my rifle, when Mick shook his head, staring right at us. Thomas pulled me farther into the long grass, pointing at more soldiers swarming the field for prisoners.

"It's too late." Thomas's voice was full of regret, but I didn't care. His reluctance pissed me off all the more.

"We have to do something," I hissed.

"They outnumber us six to one, gypsy. If we go out there, we won't make it back."

I didn't make it a step when my legs were pulled out from under me. I crashed to the ground, struggling against Thomas's grip.

"We have to try," I snapped, trying to kick him away.

Landing a solid blow against his shoulder, he grunted and lost his hold. I made it a few feet, crawling army style, when he grabbed my ankle, yanking me back before crawling on top of me.

"I'm not letting ye get yourself taken."

I bucked unsuccessfully, his weight crushing me as I grabbed the long grass to pull myself forward. Thomas flipped me over, face to face, as his strong hands pinned my arms.

"What do they think they'll do to ye when they find out you're not their ordinary soldier?" he asked. "He's gone, gypsy. He wouldn't want ye to risk yourself—"

I headbutted Thomas, faintly aware of his grunt of pain as I kneed him in the groin and shoved him off me. I didn't make it a few feet when Thomas landed on my back, knocking the wind out of me with his hand around my mouth.

"I'm sorry, lass. I cannot let ye do this."

Thomas dragged me behind the hedgerow, kicking and flailing against him as my tears landed on his hand, coating each of us with my grief. He didn't stop, though, his grip remaining strong until we were far enough away.

We were in the middle of a cotton field when he finally let me go.

"How could you?" I spun towards him and shoved him backward. "He's my friend! We can't leave him behind."

"He knew we couldn't make it to him!" Thomas yelled. "I know ye saw it. He knew it. I knew it. Now ye need to accept it. This is war, gypsy. We're not all going to make it out. But I will be damned before I let ye throw yourself away."

"That wasn't your call! I could have made it."

"Ye couldn't!" His words stung like a slap, and I flinched, recoiling from him.

"You don't know that. At least I know I would have gone down trying."

Thomas shoved his hat off his head and grabbed his hair so hard I thought he would rip the dark strands out of his scalp. "Ye can't save everyone. It's the first thing about battle ye need to grasp. Ye can try, but ye can't always save everyone."

I shook my head, not wanting to listen to him anymore, and started walking away.

"Where ye going?"

I grabbed my arm, trying to put pressure on the wound.

"Gypsy," he called, but I didn't stop. "Emilia!"

"I failed him." *I promised him. It was too late. I was too late.*

He grabbed the back of my shirt and spun me around, holding me by the shoulders, careful to not hurt my wound.

"Ye didn't," he said, his face so close to mine that I couldn't ignore the worry written all over it. "And ye might not like it, but I know I did what was needed to protect ye. Because when I have to choose between them and ye, it will always be ye. No matter what. I will die before I let anyone hurt ye. And it's about time ye wrap your head around that."

My face was damp with tears as my heart broke. God, I promised Mick that I would bring someone back. I was so sure I could save him. Take him back to camp, and instead, he'd be stuck in some horrible POW camp, starved and beaten. Worse?

"I failed him," I gasped again, doubling over. Thomas caught me, holding me upright as I sobbed, the tears gushing from my eyes as my body shook with anguish.

Please, I begged Heaven above. *Please save him. I am so sorry.*

"Thomas…" I clutched his arms, seeking something to anchor me as my breaths came in gasping sobs. Thomas held my head to his chest, but it didn't ease the guilt clawing its way through my ribcage. "I promised I would bring someone to help. I promised him."

"Ye did, gypsy. Ye did."

My body folded in on itself, trying to protect my mind from the pain that wracked it. When I collapsed, Thomas swung me into his arms and sat, cradling me in his lap.

"Ye can blame me," he whispered, his cheek pressed to the top of my head as he rocked me. "I failed Mick."

I shook my head, not wanting Thomas's false reassurances. We both knew it was *I* who failed Mick. I couldn't blame the man who continually showed up for me. Who came to save my friend and chose me every time.

But I also knew that it wasn't safe for us to stay there. We were in the middle of a war, and I was here, sobbing, unable to get past my own guilt.

My fault. I hiccupped through tears. *It's my fault.*

I tried to pull myself together, focusing on Thomas's hand rubbing circles into my back, the strength in his arms, and his deep breaths to steady my uneven breathing. Closing my eyes, I listened to the firm beat of his heart, slowing my own until, eventually, my sobs subsided. Without my grief overwhelming my senses, I cracked my eyes open, taking notice of the cicadas and crickets around us, the sun higher in the bright blue sky, and gave one last shuddering breath.

"Maybe I'm not cut out for this." I kept my head down, not wanting to see the truth in his reaction. I tried to wipe the tears and snot away, disgusted with myself. "All the other men are probably at camp while I whine like a baby. I'm so sorry I brought you into this."

"I can guarantee others are suffering losses as well, lass."

"It just hurts so much." More tears fell. "What are they going to do to him?"

His strong arms squeezed me tighter, protecting me against the world but unable to block out the horrors that would befall Mick.

"All ye can do is hope for the best," he admitted.

Thomas moved me off his lap and removed his bag, digging inside it to pull out a torn cloth he had saved for times like this. He tied it around my arm while I stared at the large weeds overtaking the field, strangling the life out of anything good that once grew there.

"Tell me something," I said, watching how his rough hands gently took care of me.

"What?" Crouched before me, he leaned back on one of his heels, scrutinizing my face as if trying to read my thoughts. Maybe he could.

"If it was me injured, would you have gone out there? Would you have tried to save me?"

"Aye," he said without hesitation, his face like stone and green eyes blazing. "I'd travel through hell to get to ye."

I nodded, his answer reaffirming what I already knew. I just wasn't sure if it made me feel better or worse, knowing we'd risk it all for each other over everyone else.

CHAPTER EIGHTEEN

Michael & Shaylah

July 1862

Mikey saw the opening and slammed his fist in his opponent's ribs, jabbing his left hand into Carter's nose. Blood spurted, and he pulled back before Mikey could get another punch. They circled each other, throwing jabs, trying to find a weak spot. Carter punched and Mikey dodged, swaying to land another blow to Carter's kidney. The man grunted, earning hollers of sympathy from the crowd.

A flash of dark red caught Mikey's eye, distracting him for a split second, but that's all it took. Carter's fist slammed into Mikey's face, sending him backward a step, his face throbbing as he straightened. A growl tore through his throat. He shook his head, trying to clear it of the pain and the sight of Shaylah Banks descending the stairs.

How the feck did she know he was fighting this night? They've seen each other the past few weeks, discussing what should be done with Boudreaux and whether or not Mikey should eliminate him or wait for the gypsy's response. As it was, the man was far more protected than what Mikey felt comfortable with. He already had the coppers in his pockets, who knew if he had the voice of the politicians.

Mikey didn't need that amount of shite on his shoulders. It was a feckin' suicide mission. A blight on this city. Mikey cursed the moment they found out that Boudreaux was the one terrorizing them. He would've gladly worked for the devil if Boudreaux didn't damn well threaten Tommy or the insufferable women Mikey couldn't seem to part from.

They had enough to discuss without revealing the fight he'd been training for.

Another fist landed straight into Mikey's gut, causing him to grunt as the muscles in his abdomen tightened, the only barrier keeping him from barreling over. He wiped the sweat from his brow, vaguely aware of the flash of a red skirt by the side of the ring.

Gods damn it, the woman would be the death of him.

"Is that all ye feckin' got?" Mikey growled, grinning savagely as he stared into Carter's swollen blue eyes and blonde hair plastered to his skin. Blood seeped from the bastard's brow, and still flowed out of his nose and down his pale chest.

"Never learned how to shut yer gab, did ye?" Carter sneered.

Mikey used the distraction to throw a couple punches, causing Carter to raise his fists to protect his face, exposing his ribs. Mikey didn't hesitate, pummeling Carter's abdomen in quick succession until he stumbled back. The crowd roared, with some cheering and others screaming obscenities in both Irish and English, depending on who they bet on.

Carter swayed on his feet, his hands dropping low in his exhaustion. The opening Mikey needed.

Putting all his power in one solid punch, Mikey's fist snapped across Carter's eye, sending him spiraling downward, knocked out cold.

The room erupted in screams, cheering as Mikey held his fists into the air, turning around so they could see the smirk on his face. Carter had been one of the best fighters, taking down good men for weeks.

Until Mikey.

"Ye crazy bastard," a familiar brogue rumbled, a hand slapping on Mikey's shoulder.

Mikey smiled, turning toward Henry, blinking the stinging sweat from his swollen eyes. He could barely see as it was. "How'd we do?" Mikey asked, allowing Henry to pull him to the edge of the ring.

"Quite fine," Henry chuckled. They had worked the crowd, betting on

Michael while convincing others to bet on the wrong man, earning their money.

"And the other investment?" Mikey asked, taking a towel to wipe the sweat and blood from his face. They started selling the sugar at a low rate, making sure to knock all competition on their arses. With the amount they had, they could slowly increase the price and still make a good buck as the product demand increased.

"We're in business." Henry grinned, and Mikey smiled back.

Soon, he'd have enough to purchase what he'd been planning for quite some time.

"Business with who?" An enchanting and all too maddening voice skimmed over Mikey's skin, sending a thrill through him, much to his dismay.

"Nothin' a lady needs to worry herself over," Mikey said, turning on his heel to face her.

Shay snarled, even as her eyes roamed down his body. He froze, aware of how the new, puckered scars looked across his chest and abdomen. "I'm no lady," she said, licking her lips as she continued to peruse his bare skin without any inhibitions.

Michael couldn't hold back his smile. "See something ye like, dimples?"

"Mikey—" Henry started, but Mikey smacked the soiled towel to Henry's chest and nodded him away. "But—"

"Later," Mikey growled, steering Shay in a different direction.

She looked behind them, brows drawn. "What was that about? Are you hiding something from me?"

He leaned in, sweeping a stray curl behind her ear. "I simply can't talk business when ye are lookin' at me like that."

"Don't flatter yourself." She scoffed, crossing her hands over her chest as he retrieved his shirt from a chair and shrugged it on.

He smirked as her eyes dropped back down to his chest. "Aye, if ye are going to look, ye better make it feel good," he said, repeating what she told him that day in the pantry. He was rewarded with a deep blush to match her red dress.

"Why are you fighting?" she asked instead, brown eyes flaring as they met his. "You haven't taken enough of a beating?"

He raised a brow, rolling up his sleeves before he pulled the suspenders over his shoulders. "Did ye not see me win?"

"Oh, I saw you get a fist to the face. You look awful." The words would have stung if she hadn't bitten her lip.

"Ye sure about that?" Mikey's smile widened. "How did ye even know about the fight?" he asked when Shay rolled her eyes staring at the other's coming and going.

"I asked Hiram when the next big fight was," she admitted.

Jealousy shot through Mikey, rearing its ugly head. He clenched his fists to keep from responding.

"Mikey," Hughie interrupted, handing him his pistol and blades.

Mikey grabbed them without taking his eyes off Shay.

"What were ye doin' with him?" he asked her more sharply than he intended.

Her eyes found his, causing him to pause as a wicked grin spread across her face. "Jealous?" she asked.

Mikey's eyes flicked to Hughie, hoping he didn't hear their exchange before he realized his mistake. Shay's grin fell.

"I shouldn't have come..." She turned quickly, moving through the crowd while he fumbled with his weapons, trying to follow her.

"Wait!"

"I don't know why I even came," he managed to hear her say over the noise.

"Wait," he growled, grabbing her arm and spinning her to him. "Just bloody wait a minute."

"I thought..." She shook her head.

"Thought what?"

"That maybe things changed since..." She swallowed, the hollow of her throat bobbing.

His gut twisted in shame. He fecked everything up like usual.

"I'm stupid," she said, the sadness in her voice pummeling him worse than the fight. "I knew that you couldn't..." She made a disgusted noise in her throat. "I don't know why I would even think that we—" Shay's gaze pierced through him.

"We?" he asked, closing the distance between them. Suddenly, he didn't feckin' care about anyone else in the room. Shay's breathing increased, betraying the emotions swirling inside of her. Could he hope? "What—"

"I need to go." Shay spun away, dodging a group quickly as she ignored their complaints.

"Feckin' hell," he growled, turning to find Henry standing a way off, a look of disapproval on his weasel-like face. "Collect," was Mikey's only demand as he took off after the infuriating woman.

Mikey cursed those stopping and congratulating him on winning the fight, some slapping him on the back even as he propelled himself away. Mikey pushed himself up the stairs, grimacing as his ribs protested with the extra exertion. He passed the new bouncer. The last one had taken ill a few weeks back, losing his job in the process.

Mikey rubbed his knuckles, the new swelling reminding him how it felt to break the arsehole who dared to treat her that way.

A flash of red up ahead had Mikey pushing people out of his way. He cursed when ale sloshed over his arm. "Bloody, watch it!"

"Ye were the one crashin' into us, ye bastard!"

A blonde woman cut in front of Mikey, smiling sweetly. A blind man couldn't ignore her blue dress cut daringly low on her tiny chest. "Mikey, dear," she purred. "I haven't seen you in an age."

"Cora." Mikey sighed, looking over her head, finding Shay's eyes across the room before she slammed the door behind her.

Gods damn it.

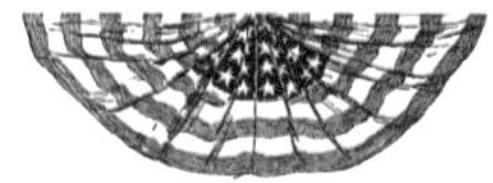

Idiot, Shay seethed, storming down the street, not caring if she looked like a lunatic. *Let them judge. I don't give a fuck.*

The pubs were still filled enough that she could hear the ruckus of laughter from one of them. She scowled, any form of happiness making her want to punch someone in the face. Particularly a tall, blue-eyed fiend.

Shay growled under her breath, wishing she could wrap her hands around his thick, muscular throat. How could she have thought he changed? That he no longer cared what other people thought? Of course, it could have been all his visits, the way he checked on her and Libby. Michael's eyes sliced into Shay's as if he could see straight into her soul as she did his. It was all in her imagination, an unsettling, profoundly delusional infatuation gone wrong.

Or his scared ass could only act that way in the secret confines of the bakery, where no one could see them bat their lashes at one another.

Asshole.

Shay grumbled again, getting a strange look from a man passing by. It wasn't until she turned the corner, entering a darker street, that she considered her safety. Her pace slowed as she took in the silence, her soft footsteps the only sound in the immediate area, the loud laughter now nothing but a murmur in the distance.

A clang rang out behind her, and she spun, finding nothing but a dark street, one lone streetlamp reflecting off a puddle in the cobblestones.

"Just a rat," she muttered, turning around to collide with a large body.

A scream erupted from her as she punched instinctively, hearing a muttered curse as she grabbed the dagger she'd hidden in her dress.

"Touch me, and I'll fucking gut you," she growled, raising the knife only to halt mid-stride. "Jesus Christ!" she yelled, turning the knife so she could shove Michael without stabbing him. "You scared the shit out of me!"

He held up his hands in a placating gesture that made her want to stab him all over again. "I told ye to feckin' wait," he said, backing away from her as if he knew her intent to do him bodily harm.

"So, you sneak up on me in a dark street? Why didn't you say something?"

"I only just got to ye, lass. Calm down."

"Calm down?" she screamed, her heart and body in fight or flight mode.

She knew she was experiencing PTSD and that she didn't want to have this reaction. And yet, she couldn't control it. Couldn't slow the sharp gasps that tore through her throat and the way her limbs shook.

"Look at me." He said it with such authority that she instantly obeyed, calming in the presence of the man who'd saved her. "We are here." He spread his hands out, reminding her of the street around them. "No one else. It's just me and ye, dimples. Ye have nothin' to fear."

Shay's breathing slowed as she lowered the dagger, staring into Michael's cerulean eyes. He dropped his hands, his body relaxed as he kept muttering reassuringly, slowly pulling her back to reality without coming to her. Somehow, knowing if a man touched her, she'd flee.

"You really do look bad," she admitted, wincing at his bruised and swollen face. It'd look like hell tomorrow.

"I thought the women loved a fightin' man?" he smirked, the expression crinkling his swollen eyes to slits.

Shay shook her head, hiding the dagger back in her dress. "Not with a face as pretty as yours."

His brows rose at that, his hands sliding into his pockets in a way that could only be described as smug. Shay rolled her eyes, realizing too late that she puffed up his ego.

"Go on," he purred, falling in step with her as she continued her path down the street. "Tell me how much ye like to look at me."

"You first," she said without thinking, falling back into her old rhythm. God, she missed flirting.

To her surprise, he didn't respond immediately, and heat flared across her skin in embarrassment. She saw him from out of her periphery, shocked to find a solemn, contemplative expression in dire contrast to their playful banter. Was she completely misreading Michael? God, she hated making these mistakes with him. Of even worrying about it. She was about to say as such when he spoke first. "Why did ye come to the fight today?"

That's what he was thinking about? Not the daring red dress she chose with him in mind, knowing how good she looked, the way it made her skin practically glow. Of course, he wasn't thinking about that because he was embarrassed to be around her.

I am so stupid.

Shay kicked a small stone down the street, listening to it tumble as she thought of what she wanted to reveal. Hell, why was this so much harder than flirting? Why couldn't he treat her like the other girls so she didn't have to admit what she wasn't ready to reveal yet?

"Why did I go to the fight?" Shay repeated, stalling. She wouldn't tell him because she found his technique, form, and powerful build downright attractive. Hell no. His ego was already inflated to almost popping as it was. Nor would she admit that she worried he might get hurt. She'd never hear the end of that one. But the other reason, the only one that she could use as a valid excuse for going, wasn't about him at all.

"I think we should ensure that Pierre is one hundred percent Boudreaux," she admitted. They came to the conclusion, all signs pointing to him. Evidently, it was the same man who plagued them, but she had to be certain. She couldn't, in good conscience, blame or plot against a potentially innocent man.

"It's him, lass." Michael sighed, shoulders stiff. "But we can guarantee it if it would please ye."

"It would."

"That's why ye came to the fight?" His look was dumbfounded, even when swollen. The man needed some ice. "Why didn't ye just tell me the next time I saw ye?"

"I didn't know when that'd be."

"What's the real reason then, hm?" He put out an arm, making her stop and look at him. "Ye know well and sure that could've waited." His head tilted in thought. "And information is hard to come by when ye are beatin' someone's face in. Did ye plan to come in the ring with me?"

Shay's chest tightened, knowing the one thing she didn't dare admit to herself. The one thing that propelled her out of that bakery and into the night. She couldn't lay alone in bed, listening to the snores of the others, the soft hiccups of Libby. Not when her mind had been racing, her body burning for some sort of affection, or hell, just for someone to touch her. To acknowledge that she was more than just a mother. More than a victim who shied away from any man who came near her now.

She was not that woman, damn it. She was strong and independent. She didn't care what other people thought. Nothing got in her way, and she loved exploring her sexuality.

Or at least, she did.

Shay sighed, looking around the street, hearing someone yell something in one of the tenements above them, and shuffled on her feet. Michael waited patiently, studying her face more than she wanted.

"I need..." she paused, throat closing, and shook her head.

"Ye need what, dimples?"

Shay threw her head back. "I need a man to touch me." The words came out in a rush, her mortification at the admission making her want to shrivel up and just die there on the dirty street.

The silence grew. Shay refused to look at anything but the dark sky. The tension rose within her, tightening her skin and coiling deep in her core, building until it exploded out of her in another horrible admission.

"I can't take it anymore. I wasn't sure if I could want it again, not after—" she choked on the words but continued past the lump in her throat "—But I need it. I want it, Michael. I haven't been touched in so long. Not in any way that matters." She looked at him then, tears falling down her cheeks. "But who is going to want someone like me? Do you think any man who finds out what they did to me would want to touch me? Or that I don't even know who my child's father is? They'd take one look at me and cringe in repulsion." She gestured to her body, not even trying to decipher the anger written on his face. What did *he* have to be angry about? "But I'm not broken." Her voice cracked. "And I *need* it, Michael."

She grabbed his shirt, needing something to hold her upright as her silent tears turned into frantic, anxiety-ridden breaths. Slowly, as if approaching a frightened animal, Michael lifted his hands and stroked her hair. Soothe her with his swollen hands. Comforting her with his bruised body. Grief swelled in his eyes, shattering her heart in two.

How could she ask this of him? The man found two others using her body in unspeakable ways as other men watched, already having their turn. Why was she seeking comfort in the man who had seen her at the absolute lowest point of her life? There could be no way he felt anything other than repulsion at the sight of her.

Shay's head fell to Michael's chest with a thump, defeated. "I need to feel wanted," she whispered, more to herself than him.

He cupped her cheeks so gently that a new wave of tears cascaded down. He guided her head upward, his large hands encompassing her whole face, protecting and guiding until she saw only Michael and his own battered body.

"Ye are wanted." He kept Shay from shaking her head, blue gaze drilling into hers with such an intense resolve that heat flooded her limbs, deceitful hope warming her. Michael didn't look away as his following words began to fill the cracks within her soul. "I never wanted anythin' more in me life."

With a tenderness that she didn't know he was capable of, Michael brought his lips to hers. Shay let him take control, guide their movements, and wrap his arms around her as she clung to him. In all honesty, Shay needed it. She needed a man to take care of her when the others hadn't. For a man to remind her that she could be wanted, if not cherished.

Their lips parted simultaneously, and their tongues swept in, exploring each other slowly, methodically, so unlike the feral way they had in the pantry. No, this kiss could be felt to her core, spreading out through her whole body. Michael pulled her tighter, the embrace comforting and protective. Shay's hands moved up his chest, feeling how his muscles rippled beneath her fingers, reacting in a way that ignited a deep need within her. She didn't just need to feel wanted; she needed it to be with *him*. Shay knew that she wouldn't feel safe with another man. That thought alone almost had her giggling nervously if Michael hadn't started roaming his hands down her back.

"Are ye sure?" he asked, hand going dangerously low.

"Yes," she breathed, the word barely out before he cupped her behind, pulling her flush with him. His other hand skimmed to her breast so softly that she shivered. Shay felt as if she was floating, his caresses tickling and heating her in a way she never experienced before. She knew Michael wasn't like this, that he had particular preferences, but how he cared for her...

She had no words for what he was making her feel.

"Is this all right?" he asked, his large hand cupping her whole breast, fingers skimming her bare flesh just above her dress. She nodded, his breath increasing as his fingers drew soft circles over her skin.

Michael's hands roamed her, possessed her in a quiet exploration. Fulfilling her needs without making it crude or entirely lustful. Showing her that a man could treat her body for what it was and not a plaything.

Shay looked up, brows scrunching, when Michael pulled away. She didn't have time to question him when he turned her, pulling her back into him, her ass fitting exactly where it needed to be against his hardness. She gasped, looking over her shoulder in question.

"This is about ye tonight, dimples." He smiled, bending to place a kiss on her neck.

The street was empty, but he pulled them into the closest ally, still holding her to him as his other hand began to pull up her dress.

"What are you doing?" Her words came out breathy as her hand stopped his pursuit.

"Do ye trust me?"

She nodded and let go.

His hand found its way into her dress and to her center with apt precision. She gasped, letting the back of her head fall to his chest. She held his arm as he began to rub her, feeling her wet and ready for him.

"Are ye still tender?" he asked, making her laugh.

"It's been almost six months," she said. "I hope not."

"Are ye tellin' me ye tested this out?" His tone had a teasing lilt to it, but she still froze.

"No," Shay admitted. "I—" She shook her head. "I couldn't. My mind just kept—"

Michael's free hand glided up her throat, pulling her face to him for a deep kiss, one that made a woman forget their own name, let alone what they were about to say. His other hand picked up the pace, working her up into such a state that her hips began to move of their own accord, begging for release.

"Michael," she gasped, squeezing her nails into his arm, her other holding his hand still gripping her jaw.

His hand slid lower, dipping gently to her center so swiftly that she gave out a little moan. "That's right," he said, breaking off on the last word and betraying how much he was affected by this. "Let me take care of ye."

"What about you?" she managed to get out, body writhing against his hand.

"I have all I need."

Shay's legs gave out as Michael continued to work her, and he had to hold her up as she began to spasm around his finger. She moaned, low and long, their movements unhurried and tentative, building a tightening so deep within her that she knew she couldn't hold off much longer.

Michael slipped another finger inside her, stretching her in a way that made her eyes roll back in her head as his palm picked up the pace, moving in quick circles until she was on the verge of begging.

He must have sensed it, felt her body tightening, beginning to spasm, because he slid a hand into the top of her dress, squeezing her breast tightly as he plunged his fingers deep inside her.

Shay shattered, body spasming around him as she called out, her scream echoing down the alley as she became dead weight at the mercy of this infuriating, glorious man. She let out another half-scream, one that made Michael groan, his cock thrusting against her, his pants and her long dress the only things stopping him from what he so desperately wanted.

She lifted her arms, reaching behind her to encircle them around his neck, the position pressing her chest outward, allowing him more access to her body. Michael's hand grabbed both breasts, squeezing them gently until she mewled in pleasure. A few more pumps and her body went lax, contented for the first time in half a year.

Michael's lips roamed over her neck, her shoulder, across her cheek as he murmured sweet reassurances to her. "Ye did so good," he muttered, his hand now rubbing her hip, down her thigh, and back up. "Ye are so beautiful."

Shay's body gave one final shudder, and her hands fell, going limp as she leaned against him. "Thank you," she whispered, unable to turn around and look at him.

"Ye have nothin' to thank me for."

"What about you, though?"

"What about me, lass?"

"You know what I mean." She turned in his arms, staring up at him. He didn't look like a man unsatisfied. In all honesty… She quirked her head. Had he…?

"I will be fine," he said.

"Going to see one of your dolls?" She grimaced.

"Jealous?" He smiled infuriatingly.

Shay looked away, hating the doubt eating at her, knowing his preferences. "Have you seen Nessa lately?"

"Nay, dimples. That particular slag has been gone for some weeks now. Or so the boys tell me. I hadn't been to Nora's more than necessary."

"What?" She looked up at him. "Where'd she go?"

Michael shrugged. "Found work elsewhere, I suppose. None of them came outright and asked Nora. Could ye blame them?"

Shay shook her head, wondering where the witch could have gone. Actually, she suddenly didn't care. One less woman she had to worry about. But the other two...

"And what about the other girls?" she asked. "Going to visit them now?"

Michael tried not to smile. "I really do like ye when ye are jealous."

She scowled. "Well, whatever this is, we aren't a thing. You have free reign, so I wouldn't be surprised."

That had a line forming between Michael's brows, his grin dropping so fast she almost backed away. "Is that what ye plan with another man?" he asked. "Now that ye got what ye needed."

"No," she snapped, slapping his chest. Even with their bickering, they still clung to each other, knowing these moments were short and might not get another chance. "But you didn't get what you needed. And you have your girls—"

"I haven't been with a woman in months," he growled, squeezing her tighter.

The confession stole every thought out of her head. Even her breath paused in her chest as her body thrummed with excitement. "Months?"

"Aye, ye siren. Looks like ye ensnared me, so I can't have me fun."

"Then go have your fun!"

"I don't want it if it's not with ye," he growled so loudly she flinched.

Shay ran her hands up his chest, reveling in the thickness of it, at the rough line of his recent injuries, and marveled at the tattoo she couldn't see but thought of nonetheless. "Okay," she said, finally believing him.

"Okay?"

"I hear you," she said, suddenly feeling playful. "You only want me when the other two girls are present."

"Och." He groaned, turning his face to the starless sky. "How many times—"

"I'm curious," she cut him off. "Would you be with me while you watched them, or would you want to watch me with them?"

His head snapped to hers, eyes wide and darkening. She bit back her grin, liking how he reacted to her teasing. "Be careful..." he warned.

"Or what? You'll take one of them in front of me?"

He twirled her so fast she squealed, her back hitting the wall as he caged her in. "Is that what ye want, dimples? Will it help ye if there were other women present?"

Shay's heart accelerated; her chest tightened with need as her joke became more tangible. "Maybe," she admitted, knowing it might calm her. But then jealousy reared its ugly head again as she thought of him with another woman. Of him watching them, comparing her body to theirs.

He must have seen her inner turmoil because his stance softened, his thumb brushing her cheek. "I don't want anyone but ye. If ye wanted it—needed it," he corrected. "I would take ye there. Have ye try it. But if it was me choice, I'd be the only damned person worshippin' your body. I'm a greedy bastard, lass. I never could share somethin' I wanted to keep." His eyes widened, and his face paled as he realized how much he revealed.

"And you want to keep me?" she whispered.

His hand returned to the wall next to her head, his fists tightening with some emotion. She almost didn't hear him and had to strain to understand his next words. "A twisted fecked up fate, mine is. Life presentin' me with the one thing I can't have."

"But you can," she said, eyes flicking between his sad blue ones.

"I pride meself on takin' what I want." He laughed darkly, running his teeth over his bottom lip as if he hadn't heard her. "Maybe that's it. A curse for all the shite I'd done. I never wanted to keep me a woman, and life just threw me the finger, knowin' ye were the one thing I couldn't take."

"So, take me!" she said louder than she meant, shocking them both. "Take me. What's stopping you?"

Michael threw his hands out to the world, turning around to show her that there wasn't one damn thing working for them.

"I can't!" he screamed back, his voice cracking with emotion. His hands fell down with a slap. "I can't take ye, and it's damn near killin' me! Why do ye think I stayed away? That I avoided ye. Aye." He sneered, seeing the truth in her face. "I knew I couldn't keep ye even if I tried. Not when they will do everythin' they can to stop it. I won't…" He shook his head in defiance, a bull being told he could no longer charge. "I won't let them hurt ye. Ye been through enough. Ye shouldn't have to endure one moment of what this would be."

Shay's shoulders slumped in defeat. "So, this could—whatever this is—could never work. You're sure?"

What had she been thinking anyway? She didn't plan to stay in the 19th century forever. Why start something that would end? Still… "You make everything else work. Am I not enough to try?"

"Don't," he snarled, pointing his finger at her. His imposing figure took on a rage that should make her quake, but she only straightened. Ready for his wrath.

She smiled widely, pushing him to fight. Showing him that she wouldn't back down.

Straightening her dress, she fluffed it in a show of indifference. "I'm worth fighting for, Michael." She loved his name on her lips. "You never played by the rules. Why start now?"

The way he flinched, how his whole body recoiled, sent a shot of pain through her. "Ye can't ask that of me. Ye can't expect me to risk your safety. What type of man would that make me?"

"Mine."

Silence fell as the world narrowed to the tether connecting them. Goosebumps covered her body. She hadn't meant to say it, yet somewhere deep in her soul, she knew its truth. Every time their eyes met when one entered a room, the way they found each other through a crowd. It wasn't natural, nor was it something everyone experienced. Only those who had felt it, lived it, with another being would understand. And she finally found it.

She'd be damned if she let it go now.

"Yours." The word caressed her, smoothing over her skin and subduing her qualms as he stalked toward her. "And how do ye plan to keep it that way?" he wondered.

"We'll figure it out."

Michael shook his head, his countenance solemn and defeated as he pulled her toward him. "I finally did it," he said.

Shay drew her brows down in confusion. "Did what?"

"Found a woman crazier than me."

She hit Michael's chest but laughed, her head falling back, her long hair flowing over his arm wrapped around her back.

Michael picked up one of her stray curls and twirled it on a finger. "I love your hair like this."

Shay smiled. She had taken to wearing it naturally, painstakingly caring for the curls so they flowed down her back. When she first entered the 19th century, she'd worn braids. After that, she didn't care enough to take care of it, allowing the other women to put it up in the style of the time. It felt good to have a piece of herself back to normal, even if people tended to look at her longer for standing out.

"Thank you," she said, meaning it. Shay knew she didn't need his approval, but it pleased her nonetheless. "I like it too."

Michael smiled in a rare, quiet moment where they only existed. Even if it was in a dirty alley that smelled particularly bad. Even with the world against them.

"Why me?" he asked, still twirling her curl.

Her mouth opened and closed, unsure how to answer the heaviness of that question. "What do you mean?" she finally asked.

"Why did ye trust me with this? Ye know I'm not the best..." His finger stilled as he fought whatever intrusive thoughts bombarded his head. "I'm not the best of men. I'm sure ye could have found someone more...suitable." He grimaced, and she chuckled.

"I have no idea," she admitted, still laughing at his scowl.

When he looked away, the tension in his face made Shay's stomach turn over uneasily. She swallowed, squeezing his shirt in an attempt for him to look at her. She pulled on it, but he refused.

"That's not true." She corrected. "I guess I feel safe with you. And..." she trailed off, unexpected tears flooding her eyes. "And I can't see myself doing what we did with anyone else. I don't *want* to do it with anyone else."

"Ye have to know this won't work." The anguish in his voice was like a bullet to her heart. "That they don't accept people like ye bein' with people like me."

Shay brought her hands up, tugging his damaged face, pleading for him to look at her. She watched her dark fingers smooth over his swollen cheekbone, his light skin already turning black and blue, as an intense wave of hatred for this time overcame her. She hated that someone else with no say in their relationship could drastically change their life course.

"You know," she said, fingers still smoothing over his rough beard as if she could magically heal his wounds. "You and I could be together in my time."

That caught Michael's attention, his blue eyes flaring. "Truly?"

She nodded. "Could even get married if they wanted to."

"Ye're bloody lyin'," he scoffed, his head falling back against the building behind him.

"Nope." She let the word pop on the last syllable. "A lot changes in the next century and a half." *It's not always easy, though,* she thought bitterly, unable to disregard the racism that still existed in the country. "What I don't understand is how you went from hating me to this." She pulled on his shirt to emphasize her point.

Michael sighed, shoulders sagging as his hand fell away from her hair, circling her waist in an embrace. "Ye were the first person to make me realize that I was using every bad experience in me life as an excuse to say feck it. I hated your people because I saw them as more trouble we had to face, keeping us from jobs and from putting food on our tables. But for the first time in me life, I had something in front of me that showed me the other side of the coin. That ye were a victim in this whole feckin'—" Michael waved his hand around in the air "—world. I *needed* to help ye. Then every time I saw ye, ye kept pushin' me. Kept treatin' me with the respect I wish I always showed ye. Ye fought for me, dimples." He grinned sadly, but it didn't reach his eyes. Michael brushed away a few tears from her cheeks. "It was feckin' annoying." Shay gave a watery chuckle that earned her a full grin. "But ye kept at it when ye should have given up on me. I know I didn't make it easy on ye."

"Does this mean I'm your girl now?" she asked, only half kidding. The other half of her couldn't bear the thought of leaving this question unanswered.

He chuffed, shaking his head in what she saw as wonder. "Aye, dimples. Ye're me girl, as ye say. Am I your man?"

"Oh, you're mine."

They grinned, relishing in the broken barrier between them.

Michael walked her home, refusing to let go of her hand the whole way.

And Shay sent up a silent prayer, begging God to let her keep him.

She refused to acknowledge the silence.

CHAPTER NINETEEN

Thomas & Emilia

AUGUST 1862

Thomas took another swig of whiskey, relishing how it went down as he sat apart from the group.

They were just out of Centreville, having taken the waterways back to Virginia. Now a part of the 9th Corps, they traveled around northern Virginia, joining Pope's army at the Rappahannock River and marching to Centreville, where they stayed to help with an artillery battery.

"O'Connor!" Sullivan hollered.

Thomas feigned ignorance. Emilia wasn't around to answer the call. She'd been staying in her tent, mourning and blaming herself for the past month. They received word that John McNamee—Mick—had died a month after his capture from his injuries. He never made it out of the Confederate prison camp.

"Tom." Sullivan wrapped his arm around Thomas' shoulders and shook him. He wreaked of alcohol. The men were getting unruly, often getting into the drink and fighting when they weren't with the camp's slags. "A fiery little redhead has been asking about ye."

Thomas shook him off, thinking he was blowing smoke, and took another pull. "Not interested."

"She's insistent, boyo. Says she knows ye from Boston."

Thomas straightened, studying Sullivan, who had turned to laugh at something one of the other men said. Though he knew many redheads, he saw only one frequently in that profession. But what would she be doing here?

Thomas looked toward Emilia's tent, knowing she wouldn't like it. But he had no interest in Nessa anymore, nor any other woman. Besides, what would the odds be that it was truly her? He told himself he'd get some answers and, if by some hellish fate, it was true, he'd tell Nessa not to call on him anymore.

He walked with Sullivan through groups of men and camp followers until the tents began to thin out. A short distance away, loud laughter drew his attention to a group of tents on the edge of the camp. Though he never visited this part—never straying too far from his gypsy—he knew they were almost there, even before seeing a flash of bare flesh and hearing a woman giggle.

Sullivan laughed, pulling Thomas towards the group of slags flirting with the men. Some disappeared into empty tents, while others lingered at night, draping themselves over their more than willing victims.

"Ye have been strung so tight, I thought this lass could loosen ye up," Sullivan said. Thomas bristled. He couldn't tell his friend that his tension wasn't from sexual frustration but more from the inability to console Emilia. "When's the last time ye've been with a woman? That's not the O'Connor I used to know."

"I'm not the same man anymore." He said it loud enough for Sullivan to hear, but the man was either too intoxicated or distracted by the scantily clad women around them to respond.

"I coulda swore she was over here." Sullivan spun around in search of her location. He caught a glimpse of a tall brunette and slapped Thomas's back. "I'll bring her back to ye when I find her." Sullivan wrapped his arm around the brunette before Thomas could respond.

Sighing, Thomas searched for Nessa, knowing Sullivan would be preoccupied for some time. The fire flickered, and he caught a glimpse of red, a set of pretty curls cascading over a man's face as she straddled his lap. He was heading for her when a small, dark-haired woman exited a tent just in front of him, still in the process of covering her breasts. Thomas looked away, trying to ignore that they were still visible under the thin fabric.

A slow smile spread on her angular face as her eyes roamed over his body. Thomas was well aware of a woman's attraction toward him, and she obviously had no problem drawing his attention to her body. Her eyes sparked with desire when she noticed him studying her, causing Thomas's pulse to quicken with familiarity. They were as dark as Emilia's, and she had close to the same complexion. If he was to guess, she had a small amount of Indian blood in her. He took a step back, needing distance.

"Somethin' tells me ya know how to handle a lady," she said in a surprisingly southern accent. She took a step into him, gliding down her hand down to his belt, and pouted when he grabbed her wrist. "My name is Edith." Her eyes flashed as she tried not to smile. She seemed to like the chase, a game he'd like to play, but not with this woman.

"I'm flattered, lass. But me bed is warmed elsewhere." He gave a half-smile, momentarily catching her off guard. Her cheeks pinkened, and she wet her lips. Thomas watched her tongue make its slow pursuit, and his grip tightened. "Those days are behind me, I'm afraid."

She laughed, throwing her head back in a move that drew a man's eye to her slender neck and exposed chest. "I can't tell ya how many times I've heard that." She leaned in as if telling a secret. "I won't tell if you don't. She'll never know."

Thomas whispered into her ear, "Believe me, she's not the type of woman ye want to mess with."

"Back off, Edith," a familiar voice warned. "This one's mine."

Nessa sauntered from the shadows and into the firelight, red hair aflame in a mass of brilliant curls piled on top of her head, her green dress significantly more expensive than the ones she wore back home. He studied the rich fabric, wondering how she found enough means to buy one. He knew his mistake when he caught her smile, the one she would give whenever she caught him looking her over. It always led to the removal of their garments.

Thomas let out a breath of surprise when Edith stepped in front of him, arms crossed over her chest in defiance. "I saw him first." Apparently, this girl didn't know Nessa's reputation, or she just didn't care. "This one seems to have a woman. I'm going to change that."

Nessa raised one of her brows as she studied Thomas. "Does he now? It couldn't be that gypsy slut, could it?"

Thomas's face hardened, and Nessa had enough sense to look momentarily worried before covering it up with a sneer.

"Will ye excuse us?" he said to Edith. "I have matters to discuss with Nessa here."

"Who's the gypsy?"

Thomas glared at the woman starting to get on his nerves. When he didn't answer, she rolled her eyes and left them with a few choice words.

"What are ye doing here, Nessa?"

She certainly didn't look like she had been sleeping with the men. She was significantly more dressed than the others, though the neckline cut daringly low, and the dress looked as if it had been ironed. He sensed a new air of authority that rivaled Madame Nora's.

She smiled. "Let's talk somewhere more private."

Nessa led him to an empty tent. He scanned the area around them before following her in. No one was paying any attention.

"Why did ye leave Nora's?" he asked, eyeing the unrumpled blanket on the ground. She sat on the only stool, positioning her skirts so he could see her slender legs.

Nessa pulled out two tin cups. "First, we drink. Will ye hand me that?" She pointed to the decanter of whiskey hidden behind a small trunk. Odd, it wasn't placed by the cups.

Retrieving the alcohol, Thomas looked at her meager belongings as she poured the drinks.

"The war suits ye," Nessa purred. Thomas found her holding out one of the cups to him. "The beard is a nice touch."

Thomas scratched his jaw, surprised at how long it had grown. He hadn't taken the time to shave in a few months, and he never would have let his hair grow to his ears. He shrugged. "What's with the dress?"

"Do ye like it?" She ran her hands over it almost self-consciously. "It's taken some getting used to, but I wouldn't mind having a few more." Nessa always dreamed of making it out of the Irish slums. Maybe she was finally going to see that happen.

"It's nice." And he meant it, just not how she hoped. "Tell me. Why have ye been asking for me?" He downed the drink, trying to calm the irrational, growing anxiety inside him. He wanted to be done with this.

Nessa watched him swallow the drink with a strange fascination, smirking as he put the cup down.

"Why don't ye take a seat?" She patted the blanket.

Thomas's head swam. He must have drunk more than he realized and agreed to sit for a minute. He bent and suddenly was lying face down, struggling to roll over onto his back.

"What did ye do to me?" He didn't recognize his own voice.

Nessa's face appeared before him as a smooth finger glided slowly down his cheek and into his beard. "He paid me nicely to keep ye out of her bed."

She began to unbutton his shirt. Thomas attempted to push her away, but she effortlessly swatted his hand aside, his limbs feeling as heavy as lead. Thomas was helpless when he felt the tug of his belt, and she stood, tugging his pants down. Nessa huffed, pushing her hair back as she began to sweat in the hot summer heat.

"When he found out the dirty little gypsy had never been touched," Nessa continued, "He wanted to make sure no man would. She is his property, after all. Except, the wee wretch disappeared before he could take her. It wasn't until he spotted ye two leavin' that horrible wee bakery ye always went to, ye all resplendent in your uniform, that he knew the game. The wretch was goin' with ye." Nessa pouted. "And Mikey seeing you off, no less. I'd been havin' fun with that one." Her pout turned up slightly, and Thomas's stomach rolled as he thought of her with his brother. *Poor bastard.*

"Anyway," she carried on as she finished undressing him. His gut began to knot at what she had planned. "Pierre went on and hired some men to protect his property, he did. If only he could have nabbed her and saved us all the trouble." She shrugged. "I think I like havin' a wee bit of fun here anyway." Nessa gave him a sly grin, lifting her skirts to straddle him. "He paid me a fair amount to keep ye occupied."

Thomas strained to keep his eyes open when he felt her weight around his waist. He tried to roll her off, his words slurring as he swore at her.

She pouted. "I told him it wouldn't be a problem, but ye haven't been to see the girls. What's happened to ye, Tommy? Ye aren't the same man I used to know.”

Why does everyone keep feckin' saying that? he wanted to ask, but he no longer could feel his mouth.

Nessa tugged her dress down, exposing herself. There was a hitch in her voice, but she continued on talking. “And then I couldn’t find the whore among the camp followers. Tell me, Tommy.” She bent over him, pressing her bare chest to his. “Where are ye hiding the slut? What keeps ye going back to her? If it’s true and ye don’t occupy her bed, what does that gypsy trash have that I don’t?”

He knew he made a mistake coming here, and a mountain of regret crashed over him as his vision went black.

“Soon, that little tripe will be his, and we can forget all this.” Her finger blazed a path down his chest, and just before he lost consciousness, Nessa whispered in his ear, “Ye’re mine.”

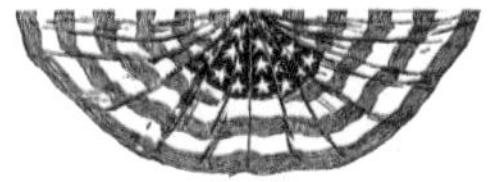

I woke before dawn, a habit I hadn’t broken since training with Michael. A feat not even my parents could have instilled in me. The thought that he’d be pleased to know I kept it up while adding strength training kept me motivated. That and my arms were never as toned as they were now. After completing a few sets of push-ups, I left the tent and headed to the latrines to find a secluded spot before more men woke up, which made it increasingly difficult to find privacy.

On my way back, I paused by Thomas’s tent, debating asking him to train with me. It would be fun to explore the differences between the brothers, especially since Thomas had trained Michael. A thrill shot through me, and I unconvincingly told myself it wasn’t sexy to engage in hand-to-hand combat with my— Could I call Thomas my boyfriend?

I shook the ridiculous thought out of my head and had to remind myself that I hadn’t been talking to him much lately. The loss of Mick was a blow that I hadn’t expected, and I wasn’t quite sure how to deal with such a loss, never having experienced it before. I didn’t blame Thomas and knew it was wrong to let him think that. I just didn't know how to face him without seeing my pain reflected back to me.

Fuck it.

"Hey." I ducked down into the tent and stopped short. His pack and blanket were still rolled up in the corner. I stood there, momentarily confused. Maybe he had woken while I was gone?

There were only a few men by the morning fire, none of them Thomas.

"Have ye seen Tom?" I asked Sullivan, his head in his hands. A lump formed in my throat that I could barely swallow. Sullivan had been drinking more lately. Thomas thought I didn't notice much, but I was well aware of his friend's interests and that Thomas had been doing his best to avoid him lately.

Sullivan looked up, wincing as he looked at me. "Tom? No, I—" He stopped and smiled. "Aye, took him to see a red-headed lass last night. Guess he must have had a better time than me." He shook his head, clearly thinking about his escapade last night.

I saw red.

"Man, ye should have seen the..." He held up his hands, mimicking a pair of melons that must have been attached to the front of the woman. Sullivan sighed and dropped his hands, reminiscing. "Anyway, she was a bit dull, I'm afraid. She..."

I refused to stick around to hear the rest.

"Oi!" Sullivan called. "Don't be too hard on the lad. He needed a good tussle! Maybe ye could use..."

"Oh, no. I prefer ye, gypsy," I mocked under my breath. *And yet you're with another red-headed whore.* I shook my head in disgust. What made me think I had changed him? That he actually loved me? I was just another conquest in his book.

A fool.

I stormed through the camp, finding the group of tents quickly, and even startled a few women by poking my head in. With quick apologies, I stopped short of the larger tent in the middle, feeling unease creep up my spine. I somehow knew, without proof, that I would find Thomas in the tent.

This tent was taller and had a flap for privacy, so I had to pull back the tanned canvas slowly. The rising sun gave off enough light for the world to have a soft grey hue but not enough to see clearly into the dark tent. I went inside and let my eyes adjust, noting the two cups set out and a large trunk to the right. To the back of the tent, there was a dark mass that I would have dismissed for a pile of blankets if it weren't for the milky white skin sticking out of one side.

I bent down to look closer, rubbing my rosary between my fingers. A mass of red curls cascaded over a bare, muscled arm. I sat back on my heels, heart thundering in my chest as I studied Nessa's face, willing myself to look over at the man. Thomas's features were strained, as if he was dreaming about something that upset him. Tears welled up in my eyes, and as I started to back away, I suddenly paused.

Had he been sleeping with her all this time? Harboring feelings for Nessa while proclaiming to love me? I was such an idiot. Yet a part of me felt that this wasn't right. After all that we'd been through, I owed him a chance for an explanation at least. Even if he was buck naked with the woman draped over him.

I sat down and waited, willing my hands to stop shaking.

Fifteen minutes had passed, my pulse slowed, and the shaking subsided when movement under blankets sent my whole body into a panic again.

"I'm not seeing any customers," a sultry voice laced with sleep said.

I continued to pick dirt out of my nails with my large dagger, my face hidden under the brim of my hat. "Then what is that in your bed?"

Nessa stayed quiet as if hearing something beneath my accent. "He's the only one that gets me services."

Something was wrong. Thomas was a light sleeper, often waking at the squeak of a floorboard. Now, he hadn't even stirred by our voices.

"What did ye do to him?" I asked.

"Tired him out, I guess." She stretched back, letting the blanket fall around her lap, revealing her perky breasts and slender waist; it was a body that I couldn't blame Thomas for admiring. For the first time, I wondered just how young Nessa was. She couldn't be more than twenty if that.

Not much younger than me, I thought bitterly.

"Stop the bullshit," I said in my normal voice, shocking her. It was almost fun watching all the emotions flit across her face before it went blank. I took off my hat. "And tell me why the hell Thomas is in your bed."

Nessa flinched as if I had slapped her. "A soldier?" She eyed my uniform, grimacing. "How the hell did ye land that, *gypsy*?" She soured the word that Thomas used so lovingly. "Ye quake at the thought of a man touchin' ye, let alone fightin' one in a feckin' battle."

"What can I say? People change." I shrugged, standing up. "Now answer my question." I twisted the dagger around so she could see it clearly.

She smiled lazily, looking completely sated. "He's in me bed because that's where he belongs. I know how Tommy likes it, and he always crawls back, beggin' me for more. Tell me, does he moan me name when he's in your bed? Because, surely, he can't see any beauty in that."

Embarrassment scorched through me as her gaze descended my body.

She started to arrange her curls, enjoying the attention. "He belongs with his own."

Sweat coated my palms, and I had to tighten my grip on the dagger. "What are you doing here, Nessa? Really?"

She stood up, ignoring the dagger, and came towards me. "He's mine. It's time ye backed off."

"He loves me. You're nothing but a worthless whore, who doesn't know when she is no longer wanted."

I must have imagined the hurt in her eyes before a sharp slap landed across my cheek. My hand flashed out and latched onto her hair. Before I knew what I was doing, chunks of it fell to the ground as my dagger sliced through it again.

"Get off me!" she hissed, grabbing my arms. I kept hacking, feeling completely unhinged.

I was so tired of Nessa meddling in every damn aspect of my life. Tired of her trying to steal the man who was mine. *Mine, damn it.* I had enough of her. Enough of her games.

I'm going to make you as ugly on the outside as you are on the inside, I promised.

A large hand grabbed my fist, yanking it away from Nessa. Thomas pulled me back and pinned my arms down. We stumbled back half a step, Thomas having lost his balance.

"Let me go!" I growled at him, wanting to tear into his flesh as much as hers.

"Not until ye calm down!"

"Calm down?" I snapped. I pushed his arms away, his grip weak. "You're in bed with *her*."

Thomas let out a stream of Irish curses. "I know how it looks, gypsy. Just hear me out. *Quietly*. We can't let anyone find out about ye."

Nessa was grabbing her hair off the ground. "What did ye do? Ye feckin' bitch!" She began to charge before stopping mid-stride, her eyes flicking between us.

I don't know what Nessa saw just then. Thomas had wrapped his arm protectively around my waist as I held up the dagger, ready for her to pounce. Maybe it was how we moved as if in extension of each other, or perhaps it was just how naturally he came to my defense. Whatever she saw made her deflate. It was almost comical, with her hair sticking up in wild curls. It wasn't enough to ignore the fact that both of them were still naked, though.

I pointed the dagger at each of them in turn. "I think it's time for you two to get your pants on." I eyed the sun starting to light up the tent. We would be missed soon. "And explain. Quickly."

Thomas let go of me slowly, probably thinking I would pounce. He picked up his pants and hastily started climbing into them. Nessa put on a long robe that left little to the imagination. I rolled my eyes.

"Gypsy, I swear—"

"He's been coming to me for two months now. I thought ye were out of the picture."

"Ye lying, tramp!" Thomas seethed. She sat on the only stool and gave her best look of innocence. "What did ye slip in me drink last night?" he continued. "The last I remember is drinking it, and then I'm laying naked with ye two going at each other like feral cats!"

We both glared at him. That explained why he was sleeping so soundly.

"Why were you even here?" I asked Thomas.

"Why are ye playing pretend?" Nessa countered.

Thomas quickly explained what Sullivan had told him the night before.

He was suspicious of her presence and thought he could settle the matter.

Apparently not, I thought miserably.

Nessa began to protest, but Thomas admitted he couldn't remember anything after drinking the whiskey. Nessa bit her lip, but I could have sworn she was hiding a grin.

My stomach sank.

"Fucking convenient. Isn't it?" I scoffed, backing up a step and trying to ignore the hurt that flashed across Thomas's face. "Stay away from me."

"Emilia—"

I shook my head, not wanting to hear anymore. I looked into his eyes, knowing I needed the connection to drive my point home. "I don't believe you."

My whole body shuttered when his face hardened, shutting out every emotion. I wasn't sure I was going to survive this.

"Gypsy—"

"Please, don't follow me."

Thomas grabbed my arm, stopping me from leaving. I pulled out of his grip.

"I hate you," I hissed.

My stomach turned when I saw Nessa smile. This is what she wanted.

"I would never betray ye," he growled, his hurt turning to anger. "Ye have to believe me."

I slapped him as hard as I could. "Sono tuo."

Thomas halted, studying me and what I had said. Finally, when I thought I couldn't take it anymore, he growled, "Feck it. Ye were boring me anyway."

His sneer made me want to throw up, and as he took a step backward, my whole body revolted. Nessa's eyes widened when he put his arm around her waist. I wanted to tear her eyes out. To rip her arms from her body and beat her with them.

"I think ye staid your welcome," Nessa said, practically glowing as she snuggled into Thomas.

My eyes stung, and I had to leave before either of them could see me cry. The image of Nessa raising on her toes to kiss Thomas on the lips burned into my memory. My pace quickened as I heard her giggle.

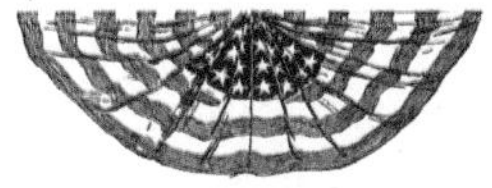

A shadow fell over me, but I kept my eyes on my food. I'd been sitting on one of the logs that circled the fire, trying to forget that Thomas was with Nessa. Sullivan had left, probably to sleep off his hangover. A few other men were playing dice and taking bets.

"Can we talk?"

I sighed and handed Thomas a plate of hardtack and pork. "I made sure to boil out the weevils," I grumbled, aware that I would have gone green at the thought of bugs in my food just a year ago.

"I'm surprised ye didn't leave them for me."

"I thought about it."

We sat silently for a few minutes as Thomas choked down some pork.

"Think she believed it?" I finally asked.

"Aye." Thomas pushed his food around, unable to look at me. "I believed it until the end there."

Sono tuo.

"I told you, 'I'm yours.' And I meant it. Nessa is a conniving—" I shook my head. She wasn't worth it. "Your story makes sense, and I don't trust her. You've proven so many times that I can trust you. I won't throw that away that easily. Not anymore."

"Ye believe me? Just like that?"

A smile tugged on my lips before vanishing just as quickly. "Well, I didn't like seeing you two naked together." My throat constricted, and I had to stop for a minute. "But I waited to hear you out. I'm glad I did. I really didn't like seeing you kiss her either."

I saw him shake his head out of the corner of my eye. "She kissed *me*, gypsy. I didn't want it. I am sorry ye had to see it, though." He paused to make sure the other men weren't listening. They were sitting far enough away and paying us no mind. "Boudreaux hired Nessa as well."

"What?" I straightened. "What makes you think that?"

"She admitted it last night."

"I thought you didn't remember?" I snapped.

"Aye, it took me a bit, but once ye weren't at each other's throats, the memories started returning to me." Thomas leaned forward, his arms on his knees, the plate forgotten in his hands. "She called him Pierre, but it was clear enough. I suspect she thought her wee act would be convincing enough to keep ye away from me." He looked at me from the corner of his eye.

It almost did, I wanted to snap.

"She called ye his property. Admitted he hired Barton and the others to watch over ye."

Thomas studied the scars on his hands while my thoughts went haywire. Why did Boudreaux let me enlist? Was it really too late to capture me? And how would hiring three other men be any easier? I could have died in this war, for God's sake. What was his reasoning?

When Thomas didn't continue, I felt my face drain of color. "Tell me."

Sighing, he set his plate down, turning toward me. "He knows ye are a virgin. He sent Nessa to keep me away from ye. Hell, she probably told him herself. Whatever the case, he found out in Boston and wants ye for his own pleasure."

Tears stung my eyes. "Nessa told you all of this?"

He nodded, a deep line creasing his brow as he studied me intently.

"Why didn't he just take me back to Boston? Why go through all of this trouble?" It didn't make sense to let me go to war.

Thomas shrugged. "I don't know. Me guess is that your family had been protecting ye far greater than they let on. Another assumption would be that your disguise was quite good. He could have hired Barton after he found out ye enlisted."

I let my head fall back and watched the puffy white clouds cross the blue expanse. I suddenly wished planes existed in this time. I'd take Thomas and never look back. Then, a sickening thought came to me.

I whispered Thomas's name as if Boudreaux was there to overhear me. "I left the vials with Shay. If he's looking for them and in town with them…"

Thomas's face hardened. "I'll get word to Mikey. He'll take care of it." He shook his head, sighing. "When Shay sent the letter, I had a hard time believing he was still alive. And now in town? Feck." He cursed profusely in

Irish. "How long had he been in Boston without our knowin'?" Thomas's green eyes found mine, the worry turning my stomach. "He could have had ye. What if..."

"Don't," I said, refusing to go down that train of thought. "He didn't, and that's all that matters. I'm here now. We dealt with his lackeys. We'll handle him." I reached for his hand before catching the slip and let it fall to my lap instead.

"Ye're right. We'll warn them. Mikey can handle it."

I just nodded, unable to voice my concerns. We'd send another letter, but who knew if it would even make it to them before it was too late. Nausea surged to my throat at the thought of Shay in danger. It'd be my damn fault if she got hurt. I should have sent her back to our time, gone with her just to keep her safe. My only hope was for him to believe that I still had the damned things.

"He would have told me if something was amiss. He has eyes, gypsy." When he saw my confusion, he clarified. "Mikey. He and his boys keep watch of the city. He knows to protect Shay even if he doesn't know of Boudreaux yet."

"I hope so." It wouldn't be the first time I'd wished for modern technology. A letter would take far too long to get to them.

While Thomas finished his meal, my mind decided to dwell on every problem I faced. Finally, I couldn't take it anymore and had to ask him: "If you remember..." My voice broke, and I had to look away. "Did you have sex with her?"

"I remember her pushing me onto the ground and pealing back me clothes." He hesitated.

I swallowed past the tightness in my throat and reached out to squeeze his hand before quickly realizing my mistake and withdrawing. Instead, I looked at him and found him watching me with solemn understanding.

I nodded. "You can say it."

Apparently, he remembered Nessa undressing both of them and passed out with her straddling him. My stomach turned at the implications, and angry tears burned behind my eyes.

How dare *she.*

"I'm going to kill her," I growled through clenched teeth. If I didn't want her gone before, I did now. It was one thing to target me, but Thomas? That's where I drew the line.

He blew out a frustrated puff of air, running his hands over his face. "I won't lie to ye, la—" He eyed the men again. "I won't lie to ye. We could have, but I swear I wasn't part of it. And frankly, I don't see Nessa taking it that far. I think she did all of that for show."

"You think she expected me to show up?"

"She sent Sullivan after me. Said she couldn't find ye in the camp followers. Aye, I think she was drawing ye out. To turn ye away from me."

We looked at each other then, realizing we couldn't ignore this. We had to do something about it. Why did Boudreaux want me so badly? It was ridiculous. He could have any woman. Any woman would be easier than going through all this. Then again, no other woman could control time...I cocked my head, wondering. Was it not just the ability to travel through time and the appeal of owning me, but were the two interconnected? Was it in my blood? No. I sighed. Shay traveled back in time, too. It couldn't just be me. I ran my hands over my face. Was his obsession with my mother so great that it passed down to me?

I swallowed, revolted by that thought. I turned to Thomas, needing to get out of my head.

"You should have come to me," I said. "I could've gone with you."

"I didn't expect her to feckin' drug me," he growled, and I grimaced. "I thought she might have some information, then I'd leave. If I'd known, I would never have gone."

"Well, one thing's for certain."

"What's that?"

"You sure know how to bring a girl out of mourning."

He sighed, running a hand through his beard. "What can I say? I have my way with the ladies." When I glared, his lips twitched, not quite grinning, before growing more serious. "Tá grá agam duit."

"Ti voglio bene anch'io."

I just wished we didn't have to fight so hard for our love. Then again, the last year had taught me that the best things in life are worth fighting for.

It was time everyone else understood that.

CHAPTER TWENTY

Thomas & Emilia

SEPTEMBER 1862

That very same day, Thomas and Emilia had sent a letter home warning them of Nessa. It would be in Mikey's and Hiram's best interests to hide the vials and watch for any sign of the man. Thomas insisted that their letter be sent as soon as possible and even gave the mail carrier some extra coin to ensure its expediency.

The end of August came, and the 28th Massachusetts fought at the Second Battle of Bull Run. While their regiment controlled the battery support, they came under heavy fire, driving Thomas nearly mad that he couldn't keep track of all those close to him. Instead, he concentrated on the battle before him, believing they could take care of themselves. By the end of the day, they retreated with 135 casualties. They were not among those, though Thomas had been grazed by a musket ball on his upper arm.

Thrown back into battle on the first day of September, they joined the Cameron Highlanders of the 79th New York. Thomas shook his head as they lined up with them in their indigo jackets and tartan trousers.

"They remind me of Jamie Fraser," Emilia said by his elbow.

Thomas felt an unfamiliar pang of jealousy that he tried to push down. How the woman talked like they weren't about to run into battle completely dumbfounded him. "What are ye talkin' about?" he asked sharply.

A smile played on her lips, damn her. "Just a character from a show—I mean book. He's Scottish."

He raised his brow. "Should I be worried?"

"About a fictional character?" she laughed, but it didn't last. Her face grew somber. "No. He kind of reminds me of you, though."

"I'm Irish," he growled. This conversation made him prickly. "And ye were talking about them." He pointed to the Scottish men lined up in front of them.

"I meant his mannerisms." The smile was returning. "The way he fights for the ones he loves. And when he does something bad for the right reasons." Thomas turned his face to the side, focusing on the bedlam around them and the darkening clouds rather than letting Emilia see how her words affected him. "Someone you can count on." She said it quietly so only he could hear, and so candidly that he shifted on his feet, uncomfortable with her conviction.

They turned towards the fight, hearing the call to charge. Thomas gripped the rifle tighter, preparing himself for what was to come.

Inhale. Exhale.

Hundreds of feet stormed through the cornfield, tripping over the bodies of their fallen soldiers, blood soaking the ground. Over halfway through the field, the rebels began to fire from the cover of the woods, causing them to stagger.

A horse flew by them, and the loud call of General Stevens: "Follow me, Highlanders!" had them cheering. They continued to charge.

Bullets rang out around them, and the heavens roared, opening up until they were drenched to the bone. They shot at the rebels, some hitting their marks, others being shot themselves. Thomas fired as quickly as he could load, unsure if he hit his mark before aiming again. Their boots sunk deeply into the mud, making it harder to avoid being hit. Thomas's hand shot out, grabbing the back of Emilia's uniform as she slipped in the mud. She gave him a nod of thanks and turned back to the rebels.

Thomas lifted his rifle and aimed at a man just beyond the edge of the woods.

Click.

His rifle was soaked, unable to fire. He looked around at the men around him, struggling the same. He'd have to use the bayonet.

Thomas ran into the woods, but sensing Emilia behind him, he stopped. "Ye should stay back." She squinted at him as rain cascaded down her face. "Do what ye can from a distance."

Emilia slung her rifle over her shoulder and pulled out Mikey's old dagger. "If you're going in there, then so am I."

Movement flashed to his right, and Thomas barely ducked in time. He brought up the bayonet to find the man's eyes wide with surprise. With a jerk, Emilia pulled the dagger out, blood spurting out of his neck as he dropped.

"Thank ye."

"Sure," she muttered, even as she stared at the man, looking as if she was going to vomit.

Another man ran at them. Thomas parried with the bayonet as Emilia put her blade up through his jaw, killing him instantly.

Thomas took down three men rapidly as they charged into the woods. Both sides were already in the midst of hand-to-hand combat. The darkness of the woods and the storm made it almost impossible to distinguish one person from another. Thomas and Emilia kept at each other's backs, finding they fought better together, with eyes on each side.

A man came at them from the trees to their right, slicing Thomas across the chest. The flash of a blue jacket had Thomas reeling back. "We're on the same side!"

The man kept thrusting his bayonet at Thomas. Emilia yelled out, causing Thomas to turn towards her before receiving a blow to his head that sent him to his knees.

"Ye don't know when to quit, do ye?" a familiar voice said to his left.

Two men descended on him, struggling to tie a rope around his wrists. Barton had Emilia with her own knife to her throat.

"Change of plans," Barton yelled over a crack of thunder. "Boss is tired of waiting."

He began pulling Emilia through the trees, away from the battle and camp. Thomas struggled to stand, needing to reach her, only to be wrestled by Driscoll and Currivan until one of them slammed the butt of his rifle into the back of Thomas's skull.

"Thomas!" Emilia screamed.

"Shut up," Barton snapped, dragging her away. "I said shut up!" Barton backhanded her, and she stumbled a step before he pushed her forward.

"Ye're going to regret this," Thomas growled.

"What are ye doing?" Currivan muttered when Driscoll hit Thomas again and rolled him over. "Just finish it."

"I have a little business to take care of first."

Thomas managed to open his eyes in time to see Driscoll unsheathe a large knife from his belt. It was difficult for him to lift his head as his skull threatened to split open. His head fell back into a mass of wet leaves as he tried to make sense of the bloody, watery mess on his chest. Had someone stabbed him?

"Ye should have killed me when ye had the chance," Driscoll growled, kneeling down in front of Thomas.

"Aye." Thomas coughed, turning on his side, his body sluggish. "I won't make that mistake again."

Driscoll shoved Thomas onto his back again. Thomas winced as the rope cut into his wrists when he felt something give. He let out a slow breath, keeping his sights on them.

"We need to go," Currivan said impatiently, scanning the chaos through the trees. Driscoll also looked, knowing a man could stumble upon them any minute. Thomas pulled in another deep breath, fortifying himself.

"Not yet," Driscoll growled, revenge distorting his lined face as he pressed the knife to Thomas's throat and watched the blood mix with the rain.

Thomas smirked, a chilling expression born from nightmares and rooted in destruction.

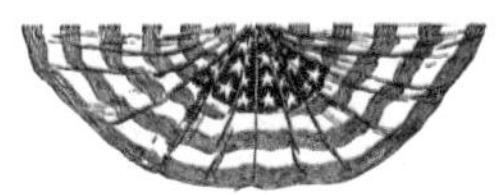

"What are they going to do to him?" I tried to twist from Barton's grasp, but his fingers only dug deeper.

"Kill the fecker. The man's been a bloody thorn in me foot." I flinched under his tightening grip. "If we would have done it from the beginning, I'd be sunk balls deep into me woman right now and not dragging some gypsy whore around this godforsaken shithole."

"I'm surprised you found a woman who would let you touch her."

He shoved me to the ground, flipped me over, and backhanded my face.

"Did I touch a nerve?" I grinned, spitting blood to the side. My time with the O'Connor brothers apparently wore off on me. I never would've talked so boldly before.

Barton grabbed my throat, bruising and cutting off my air supply. I thrashed, trying to loosen his stronghold. "I'm starting to think killing ye would be easier than going through all of this. If it wasn't for the pretty cash he gave me, I'd use ye up and throw ye to the crows. Damn thorn in me side since day one."

He lifted me by the throat and pushed me deeper into the woods, leaving me to cough and sputter. It seemed forever before we came to a clearing and stumbled upon a wagon carefully concealed behind a copse of trees.

Under a tarp in the wagon was a rope that he tied tightly around my wrists before throwing me in and securing the other end of the rope to the rail. I had to inch up, positioning myself against a crate so I wasn't face down on the wet dirty, wagon bed.

Barton pulled himself onto the front seat, and the wagon shot forward with the snap of the reins, nearly making me face plant again.

I scanned the trees, hoping to find Thomas. *He can't be dead. They can't kill him.* I refused to believe those assholes could get the better of him.

The fighting hadn't reached this far yet, and the only thing that stirred was a few birds scattering at the sound of the wagon jumbling over the deep ruts.

"What about the others?" I yelled over the pouring rain. "Shouldn't we wait for them?"

"I'll knock ye over the head if ye don't shut up."

I pulled on the rope until my hands went numb. The knot wouldn't budge. Through the slot of the front bench, I saw my knife sitting in plain sight next to Barton's ass in his haste to flee. I tried to contort my body so that I could reach it. I'd been at it awhile, long enough for my arms to go weak with the struggle, when the wagon stopped abruptly, throwing me back to the ground.

We sat there until the rain started to let up. So long, Barton began to get antsy, fidgeting back and forth on his seat and continuously looking back into the woods.

"He's going to kill you, you know," I said, losing all pretense of my fake accent.

Barton's shoulders stiffened. "Your fella is beginning to rot in one of 'em ditches. The boys will be meetin' here soon."

I laid my head against one of the wooden beams, staring at the dark clouds as I tried not to let his words bother me. Thomas couldn't be dead. I'd feel it. Wouldn't I?

"It's taking an awfully long time," I said. "You sure it's not your boys rotting in the ditch?"

Barton slammed his hands on the bench and turned around so fast I barely had time to pull away before he ripped me from the ground, holding me upright by the front of my jacket.

"Do ye know how to shut your gab?" he growled, spittle landing on my face, making me cringe.

"I've never had the pleasure of anyone saying that to me. You must bring out the chatter in me."

Barton shoved me down, causing my head to slam into the side of the wagon. We sat there some more, the rain dripping down my face, mixing with my silent tears as Barton fidgeted in his seat. I tried to keep still and not agitate the growing bump on my skull.

A rustle in the thicket and the snap of a branch alerted us to a new arrival. I tried to sit up, hope clogging in my throat.

"It's about damn time," Barton began. "I was starting to think he got the better of ye."

The click of a revolver had Barton sitting straight. The man's hat was low, concealing his face, and so much blood covered his chest that I wondered how he still had any in his body. I scanned the trees for anyone else.

"Let her go." The familiar brogue had me jumping up without thinking.

Barton grabbed a fistful of my jacket and threw me to the ground.

"What did ye do to them?" Barton asked.

"Let her go, and I won't give ye a demonstration."

"Over me dead—"

A shot rang out, and something wet splattered my face, causing me to recoil. I touched my cheek and tried to make sense of the sticky red that came away. Blood and a chunk of...what? My stomach heaved when I realized it must have been the inside of Barton's skull. I managed to keep from vomiting as Thomas appeared by the wagon, lifting himself in to crouch before me.

"Are ye all right, gypsy?" he asked, untying my hands.

I think I nodded as he helped me out of the wagon. My feet hit the ground, and I found Barton lying sideways on the seat, a bullet shattering his skull.

"Gypsy?" Thomas asked, arms holding me upright.

"You killed him." I was still in shock, trying to get my bearings.

"The bastard talked too much. Thought I would cut matters short and get ye out of there."

I stared at him, wondering if he was real, and touched the blood on his chest.

"You're hurt."

"It's not all mine." Thomas grabbed my arm and began to pull me back into the woods. "We have to get back before anyone notices where we've been. Let them think the secesh got 'em."

"How did you know where to find me?"

"Pulled it out of Driscoll. Finally, the pain was enough, and he spilled his guts, quite literally, if I must admit." He looked at me from beneath his hat, eyes burning with fury. "Told me where to find ye before that."

I turned and heaved up what little food I had in my stomach. Thomas rubbed my back soothingly as I dry heaved, gagging on nothing but the atrocities that befell us.

When I finally finished, I wiped the back of my hand over my mouth and managed to ask, "What about Currivan?"

Thomas side-eyed me. "He won't be botherin' ye anymore."

CHAPTER TWENTY-ONE

Shaylah & Michael

SEPTEMBER 1862

*A*nswers that *question*, Shay thought, anger boiling up within her.

She folded the letter, hiding it in her dress to burn later. Looked like Nessa joined Boudreaux's team. Shay wasn't surprised. The wench had a vendetta against them since they entered the nineteenth century.

"Good news?"

Shay's hand flew to her chest, twirling toward Mira. "Jesus! Don't do that!" Shay snapped. The girl could sneak through a room like a wraith in the night.

"Sorry." Mira rolled her eyes as she placed some bread on the counter, wrapping it for delivery.

"Well, not great news," Shay admitted. "But they're okay, so that's good."

Mira nodded, her small frame folding in on itself far more than usual. Shay was about to ask if something was wrong when the bell above the door rang. A little girl ran through, giggling and twirling in her usual way. Shay couldn't stop the smile that Evaline always brought her when a considerable form filled the doorway, blocking the sunlight.

Hiram.

"I got a lollipop!" Eva announced, waving a small candy in the air.

"You spoil her," Mira said, giving Hiram a pointed look.

He just shrugged. "Someone has to."

A baby's wail descended from the stairs, and everyone turned their heads toward the noise. *Libby.* Shay sighed, looking at the clock. Only a forty-five-minute nap.

Better than nothing, I guess.

"What are you guys up to?" Shay asked Hiram as she walked around the counter, wondering if he was just dropping off Evaline or here to see her.

"I was hoping to catch Ms. Mira here."

Mira's head whipped up from her work, dark eyes wide as she stared at him. Hiram pulled his hat off his head, running his hands through it.

Oh. *Oh*, Shay thought, eyes darting between the two. She smiled.

"I have to..." She waved her hand at the stairs, her words trailing off as she realized the two weren't paying attention to her. She bounded up the stairs, taking two at a time to get to her baby.

Opening the door, she gasped, finding Libby sitting straight up, her caramel curls sticking in every direction as tears glistened on her face. "You sat up!" Shay squealed, running to her daughter. Libby's hazel eyes squeezed shut in consternation, and she sobbed uncontrollably. Shay laughed, grabbing and swinging her around, the motion stopping her wails out of utter shock.

Libby sat up before, hunched over and with Shay's help, but this was the first time she'd pulled herself up and sat on her own.

"Good job, sweet girl," Shay said, kissing the top of her head as they danced around the room.

The excitement didn't last long. Libby screamed anew, shoving her little hand into the top of Shay's dress and pinched her boob.

"Ow!" Shay yelled, removing Libby's hand. "Fine, I'll feed you, little fiend."

They just sat, Libby nursing happily when Rose walked in, muttering under her breath. "That girl is going to be the death of me."

Evaline swept by her, running to a rocking horse in the corner of the room. "Who? Shay asked.

Rose looked up as if she just noticed her there and sat some laundry on the table. "Mira. Hiram is escorting her through town."

Shay smiled. It was completely innocent, Shay having gone with him plenty of times, but she knew this was different. Mira had a crush on Hiram for years, and it wasn't until recently that Hiram and her parents were aware of Mira's feelings. His request was practically a declaration of his intentions. Hiram was a good enough match, a great one, actually, if it weren't for Rose and George wanting their children to marry above their station. Hiram, being a dockworker, did not fall into those plans. Shay snorted, shaking her head.

This time is wild.

"Hiram is a great man," Shay said, trying to nullify Rose's concerns.

"Yes." Rose sighed. "We know. Mira couldn't have picked a better one. I just worry."

"Struggling with the right man is far better than being miserable and financially stable with the wrong one." Shay raised her hand when Rose opened her mouth to argue. She couldn't help but look at Evaline and what her mother sacrificed to escape her father. And even at Libby, who was the result of a depraved man. She bit her lips, trying to calm her emotions before speaking again. "You think she won't regret it, years down the road, when she's five babies in with a man she despises? That she won't cry herself to sleep wondering what could have been with Hiram?"

Rose's brows furrowed, her fingers playing with the laundry as Shay continued.

"Maybe they will find they don't even like each other. Maybe they won't get married, and you won't have to worry about this. But do you really want to take that choice from her?"

Rose blew air from her nose, and Shay switched Libby to her other breast. She smiled down at her child, the slight green of her eyes sparkling up at her.

"Of course," Rose said, putting the laundry away. "You're right. I shall give them a chance, as you say."

Shay turned her grin to the woman. Maybe someone could find love in this godforsaken place. The thought turned her mind elsewhere, and she had to ask, "Can you watch Libby again tonight? I won't leave until she's asleep."

"Of course," Rose said, waving a hand as she went back down the stairs.

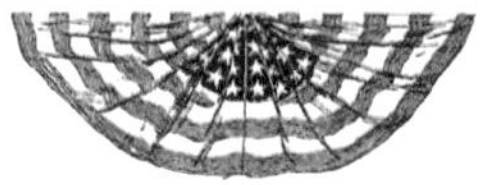

Mikey leaned back in the chair, throwing down more cards as he watched Pierre—No, Boudreaux, he corrected—out of his peripheral. It still chafed that he hadn't figured out the man's identity long before. He'd been so caught up in their deal, too busy making plans, that he hadn't properly looked into his background.

Feckin' hell.

Boudreaux let out a deep, hoarse laugh, sweeping the money from the table. "Looks like I have you beat this time, young man."

Mikey tried to smile, hoping it wasn't complete shite as he adjusted himself in his seat and took another swig of whiskey. He'd need another bottle if he was going to survive the night. *Young man. Who the feck did he think he was?* It was all Mikey could do not to put a bullet through the pompous arse right then and there.

That, and the girls had been circling like a pack of wolves, trying to sit on his lap and making offers he'd have taken just a few months ago. He only came to keep up appearances with his boys, but it was getting more challenging and complicated each day.

Mikey chugged the rest of the drink and held up the glass. "Next rounds on me," he told the table.

There were enough cheers and back clapping that Mikey hadn't seen the door open until a light breeze swept the room. They were busy pouring drinks and taking shots when Mikey's eyes widened, his entire body igniting.

Shay glared at the half-naked girls walking around while she searched the room. Finally, her eyes found his, and the rope that bound them tensed, pulled tight as everything spiraled down to them. She scanned the rest of the table, and her shoulders relaxed in what he guessed was a relief. Did she suspect a woman with him? That thought had him grinning.

Jealous woman.

Gods, that cream dress accentuates every curve and dip in her lithe figure.

Mikey's teeth worried his bottom lip, watching Shay come to him as he imagined the various possible reasons she arrived, most ending with her skin on his.

"Oi!" Hughie yelled, pointing his finger at Shay. "What are ye doin' here?"

Shay's glare could have set the man on fire.

"Ah," Boudreaux purred, leaning into his chair. The hairs rose on Mikey's arm. He'd kill the bastard. "Welcome, lady…"

"Banks," Shay said, face hardening even more. What had possessed her to come here?

"Beg my pardon, Miss Banks," Boudreaux continued. "It is a pleasure to keep your company. Please—" He held a hand out to a seat. "Sit."

Hughie kicked his foot on the remaining chair, making Mikey see red. Before he could kill his friend, Shay skirted around the table and promptly sat on his lap. He raised his brows but settled, amused by her apparent show of possession.

He leaned in, relishing her shiver as he whispered into her ear. "If I knew ye would be this much trouble, I would've pursued ye months ago."

And he meant it, even if his gut twisted in anxiety, knowing his men's eyes were on them. They didn't accept her. He didn't give a shite, honestly, but their loss of respect would mean the death of him, quite literally. Mikey very much wanted to stay alive and for this mad woman to keep safe.

Shay rolled her eyes. "No one ever sat on your lap before? How scandalous." She held up her hands and wiggled her fingers in a way that was so cute he wanted to sink his teeth into her.

He slapped her hip, making her gasp as everyone's eyes turned to them. Mikey scowled.

"So," Shay said to the table as if nothing happened. "Don't let me stop you. Who's winning?"

"Mr. Pierre," Mikey answered, raising his glass to the man.

"I have to admit—" Shay smiled sweetly at Boudreaux "—I've never heard an accent quite like yours. Where are you from?"

Mikey froze, waiting for Boudreaux's response. This was not the way to go about it. Did the lass have a feckin' death wish?

"Louisiana," Boudreaux responded and took a long pull of his drink. "Though it hurts me…" He turned to Mikey, "That Mr. O'Connor hadn't mentioned myself."

"Your business is your own," Mikey said, his smile tight.

Boudreaux nodded. "Respectable in its own right, I suppose."

"What brings you here at a time like this?" Shay asked, and Mikey's arm tightened around her in a warning. "Surely this war is enough for you to want to be with family?"

"I have some business in the North." Boudereaux's eyes sharpened, skimming down her in a way that made Mikey straighten, adjusting her on his lap so he could easily reach the pistol on his waist. Shay wrapped her arm around his shoulders as she flashed him a puzzled look.

"Oh!" Shay said a little too enthusiastically. "A businessman! I do admire a hard worker." Her one finger began to trace circles along Mikey's chest absentmindedly. However, he wondered if it was deliberate when it caught Boudreaux's attention. "What type of business?"

Boudreaux signaled for Keena across the room before answering, "I own a sugar plantation."

"What can I help ye with?" Keena purred, skimming a hand along Boudreaux's shoulder as she played with her long dark hair.

With a jolt, Mikey realized that she had close to the same coloring as Emilia. How had he not noticed Boudreaux's preferences before? It was staring him straight in the face, in the girls he picked. Though he had liked Nessa, which threw him off.

And where is she now, ye bloody fool?

Mikey cursed silently. Boudreaux had been using her for an entirely different reason. Could he be the reason for her disappearance?

Boudreaux pulled Keena onto his lap. "Keep me company, pet."

Keena smiled, but Mikey could see the strain in it. Had he been bothering her much?

"Well, that sounds exhausting," Shay said, ignoring the slag. "Have you many workers?"

Boudreaux's grin made Mikey sick as the man took Shay in, his thoughts written plainly on his face. In the cocky way he held himself, the superior way he talked to her as if she was a child or something he could own. Mikey had to lift his glass to keep Boudreaux from seeing his snarl.

"Glad you asked, my dear." His rumbling voice grated on Mikey. "Something your people should know enough about." He laughed, holding out his glass to her before chugging it. Shay stiffened in Mikey's arms. "A few hundred of my slaves keep the plantation working exceptionally. I only keep the finest of them. I am proud to have the strongest men and finest women. So, when they're not in the field, they keep me occupied in other ways."

The men around the table hooted as Boudreaux sneered, running his meaty hand up Keena's bare leg.

"I do say, you are not my usual type, dear," Boudreaux continued to talk to Shay, "but have you ever thought of being a house servant? I would pay you reasonably."

A loud bang rang out as Mikey's fist hit the table, startling the room into immediate silence. Shay's finger stilled as she rested her palm on his chest. *Relax*, it said.

How she smiled at Boudreaux was beyond Mikey.

"That is a compliment, indeed," Shay responded, with a voice as smooth as honey. Mikey thought his neck would snap by how fast it whipped toward her. Had she lost her feckin' mind? "But if I am not your type, then may I ask who is?"

My gods she was flirting.

"Ah." Boudreaux leaned back, staring at the ceiling in reminiscence. "Bronzed goddesses that my family have kept pure for generations."

Shay's face scrunched in perplexity. "How does one do that?"

Boudreaux laughed. "Of breeding them, of course. Really, do you know nothing of our ways?"

Shay's face darkened in what Mikey knew was a flush. He squeezed her tighter, wishing he could reassure her, but there was no dampening the atrocities men could devise. Instead, he cut in, "I must know. What type of women are these? They sound..." His mask fell into place in what he hoped was carnal interest. "Exotic."

"Oh, a troubled, poverty-ridden sort back in France." He waved it off, answering the question without giving any detail. However, the gobshite gave them all they needed, and Shay began to shake. He needed to get her out of this godforsaken room.

Mikey signaled for Nora, who was across the way. He held back a smile as she came to him, knowing how much she despised being summoned.

"I require a room," he told her.

Nora nodded. "Your usual?"

Feck. Shay stiffened.

"An empty room."

Nora's eyes flicked between him and Shay, and she scowled. "Are ye sure—"

"I'll pay your fee," he growled. "Just give me a damned room."

"There's my boy!" Boudreaux called out, laughing with the other men.

Boy.

Mikey could have punched Hughie's laughing face. Whose damned side was the man on? At least Henry looked a bit apprehensive. "I have a switch if you want to show your pet what a plantation is like. I find it gets the best responses."

Mikey lurched forward but was stopped by Shay's hand circling his neck and her mouth on his ear. "Take me now," she said low enough so no one could hear, no longer shaking. When he pulled back, he only found a quiet resolve in her relaxed features. "I'm ready."

She turned back to Boudreaux and smiled sweetly. This woman was a damned performer if Mikey ever saw one. She worked a crowd better than himself. "We might have to try that," she told Boudreaux. "I always wanted to put this boy in his place."

The room broke out in raucous laughter, causing a deep flush to work up Mikey's neck. *Oh, the lass is goin' to pay for that one.* But Mikey only sat there and let them laugh. He would not try to belittle her or make them think differently than she intended. Shaylah Banks had enough of that from men like him, and he'd be damned if he didn't treat her like a gods-damned queen.

"Aye," he agreed, lifting her with him so they both stood. "I've been a bad lad lately, hadn't I?"

Shay's lip quirked up, her eyes sparkling in a way that made him want to sweep her off her feet and carry her up the stairs. Alas, he refrained and threw money on the table instead, paying for the drinks. He slipped more to Nora before weaving through the tables, his hand protectively on Shay's back. Too many men were eyeing her for his liking.

They had just reached the steps when Boudreaux called behind them. "Let me know how that friend of yours is doing." Mikey's blood froze in his veins, a deep yawning sickness sweeping over him. Boudreaux continued, "Haven't seen her in some time. Emilia, was it?"

Shay halted on the first step, turning so her face was even with Mikey's as his hand tightened around her waist. He gave a brief shake of his head.

"I beg your pardon?" Mikey said with such politeness that it sounded fake to even his own years.

"Your friend," Boudreaux explained, still running a hand over Keena. "She reminded me of someone. Gave a lasting impression, I dare say."

"She's with family." Shay's fake smile faltered.

"Family?" Boudreaux's laugh was bitter, grating on Mikey's nerves. "What does she know of family?"

"Excuse me?" Shay sounded genuinely confused, and rightfully so.

"Oh, nothing," Boudreaux lifted his drink to his mouth. "Just wondered about her family name. Anyone I may know?"

"I doubt it." With that, Shay grabbed Mikey's hand and pulled him up the stairs, receiving hoots and hollers from his men below.

They reached the top of the stairs, and Mikey swung her around, pinning her against the wall. "What the bloody hell was that?" he seethed. "Ye have a feckin' death wish? Why don't ye come right out and ask him everythin' in front of everyone?"

"I got our answers, didn't I?" she growled, getting into his face. Heat surged through him as she pushed back as much as he gave.

"At what cost?" he growled through his teeth. "I cannot—" He ran a hand through his hair, spinning around on his heels before turning back to her. "I will not lose ye. Not to that bastard."

Shay's face softened. "You won't."

"Ye cannot know that. After all that has happened, how can ye run straight into danger?"

"I can't spend my life being afraid of little men!"

"But ye can bloody well die from them!" It came out harsher than he intended. Seeing her flinch was the last thing he wanted, but it would be necessary if it ended up protecting her. Made her think before making impulsive decisions. "I'm sorry," he continued, holding up his hands. "I didn't mean…"

"I know what you meant." Shay stepped away from the wall, her eyes not holding the anger or hurt he'd expected but a grave knowledge that left him momentarily speechless. Her soft hands, softer than any woman he'd known, cupped his face. "You care." She smiled when he frowned. "Have you ever cared about anyone? Or did you just not want them to see how much?"

Mikey's chest tightened, and the secrets he didn't want to be known or acknowledged threatened to crush him. "I care for no one."

"That's a lie." Shay's head tilted as she studied him.

"Ye should go," he said, his eyes shuddering as he looked down the hall. "There's a back door." He grabbed her hand to take her there. "Come, I'll see ye to it."

Shay tugged on his grip, planting her feet so his arm jolted. Mikey looked down, aggravated by her resistance. The sooner she was at the bakery, the safer she'd be. She was a bloody fool for coming here, and he was about to tell her as such when, with a slowness that made his heart thunder, she lifted on her toes and kissed him.

Mikey grabbed the skirt of Shay's dress, holding her to him with a gentleness that he wasn't used to, but came naturally with her, nonetheless. Their tongues danced together, sweeping in, exploring leisurely, memorizing every taste and detail. Something in him swelled, daunting and magnificent, a feeling that tore down every wall and made him want to build new ones. It was his own fear, his own self-loathing, that made him want to shut her out. Shut these unwanted feelings out.

And yet…

Mikey wrapped her in his arms, lifting her off the ground without breaking their kiss, and headed for the room. Fumbling with the handle, he pushed open the door, and they stumbled in.

"We really should talk about what to do with Boudreaux," she said against his mouth.

For feck's sake.

Shay didn't want to go home but wanted to talk about another man when she was in his arms?

He didn't take his mouth from hers as he mumbled, "Don't mention that bastard when me lips are on yours."

Shay kissed him harder, but he felt her smile. "It would be stupid of us to do this when he's downstairs," she continued. "He seemed like he knew. Didn't he?"

Mikey pulled back with a growl, glaring down into her beautiful face, her dark brows drawn down and mouth pouting in worry. Even her damned dimples were out, softening him to her worry. "If ye rather talk about him, then I suggest ye take it out of this room."

"No," she snapped, pushing away from him. "I just thought we should talk about it. But if you're going to be like this..." She backed away, untying the laces on her dress. "Then, I guess it can wait."

Mikey couldn't stop watching her hands at her dark skin contrasted against the light dress. Gods, she was beautiful. If she wanted to distract him, she bloody well was doing it. "We'll discuss it tomorrow," he acquiesced.

She smiled. "Tomorrow."

Mikey pulled his teeth over his bottom lip, needing it on her skin but not wanting to startle her. He wasn't sure what she could take, but he did know his usual style would be unwise. Instead, he lifted his hands and asked, "May I?"

Shay nodded, dropping the laces and letting him slowly lower her dress. He noted how her breathing hitched then sped, her chest heaving as the fabric fell from her shoulders to pool on the floor. He took her in, tracing a finger over the slender curve of her shoulders, over the tops of her breasts, across the slip, until he couldn't take anymore and grabbed the material at her waist and pulled her flush with him.

Her hands were in his hair, pulling him to her mouth without hesitation. They both groaned, opening for one another as she started unbuttoning his shirt, shucking it off and to the floor. They made quick work of his pants, their mouths still devouring one another while they stumbled to the bed, falling into it with a tangle of limbs.

Mikey rolled on top of her, his body pushing her into the mattress, his hand exploring her curves, when he noticed she stopped moving. Stopped kissing. Mikey pulled back, looking down at Shay and finding her eyes as round as saucers.

"Are ye all right, lass?"

Shay nodded, breathing quickly as she struggled with the words she needed to say. "I'm fine." She pulled him down, kissing him so hard it hurt.

Her movements were stiff and disjointed. Something wasn't right. Rolling off her, she clung tight, but Mikey shook his head. "Nay. Not until ye tell me what's wrong."

Shay sighed, her head falling back to the small pillow. "God, I hate this!" she exclaimed, the tears in her eyes like a knife in his gut. "Even after what they have done, they still have a hold on me. I know it's you on top of me, but when I feel it, all I see is them…"

Mikey covered his eyes with a hand, resting his head next to hers as bile rose in his throat. Gods, he was so glad those feckers were dead.

"Are you mad?" It came out soft, hurt even.

He let his hand fall, turning his head to her. "Of course not."

"You…" Shay's face tensed, pained. "You're not repulsed by me? By what…"

"Lass…" he exhaled and turned onto his side to cup her cheek. "I found ye. I know what they did. Ye don't have to explain a damned thing to me, because I already know. I only want to make ye comfortable. And, well, to kill them again. But alas, I cannot."

She gave a watery chuckle, turning on her side so they faced each other. "I would like to help with that."

"Done."

Their smiles didn't quite reach their eyes. A few moments passed, content with studying each other, when Shay opened her mouth, hesitated, and closed it again.

"What?" Mikey inquired, quirking a brow.

"Maybe we could try something."

Now, both his brows lifted, intrigued. "And what would me lass like to try? I hear I can be very accommodating." Shay gave him a mock glare and punched him in the shoulder.

"Feck!" He laughed. She had a fist on her.

"I…" She shook her head, clearly aggravated with herself. Her following words came out in a rush. "I want to try on top. They—I think it would get me out of my head. Being in control."

The declaration hung between them as concern and thrumming excitement coursed through him.

"And," he paused, not sure how to present this, "do ye know how—I mean, do ye need me to show—"

"I've been with other men, asshole!" she said, her eyes widening. "Did you..." She gasped, covering her mouth in a giddy realization. "Did you think I was a virgin before..." She waved a hand around.

Mikey's mouth opened, but he couldn't find the words to express his feelings. He had thought she... He rubbed his hands over his face in frustration. Why the feck was he jealous? He had no right, not when he'd been with plenty of women. Mikey felt a little tug on his wrists, and he let her pull his hands down.

"I'm going to kill 'em," he announced.

"Kill who? The men I slept with?"

"Aye," he growled.

Shay only smiled, pushing him to his back as she straddled his waist, pulling her shift up her thighs.

Mikey swallowed, taking in the sight of her on top of him. *Bloody hell.* Shay undid her corset, pulling it off before lifting the bottom of her shift, her gaze searing into him, watching his reaction. Raising onto her knees, she removed her remaining clothes and bared herself to him.

Gods.

He groaned, letting his head fall back, hands skimming up her soft thighs. "Is this okay?" he asked. She was shaking.

"I—" She frowned. "It still..."

His brows furrowed, seeing how much she hurt, even if she wanted this. Needed it.

"What are you doing?" she asked when he leaned over the bed, holding onto Shay so he didn't roll her off. He grabbed his pants and jiggled the belt out of the loops.

He presented it to her like a gift. "Show me what ye got, dimples."

Shay grabbed the leather, holding it with a confused expression. "Do you want me to whip you?"

"Gods no." He laughed and raised his wrists to the small bed frame. "Tie me up."

Her eyes widened, flicking between him, the belt, and the metal frame.

When she didn't decide, he asked, "It's worse when I touch ye. Correct?"

She nodded, eyes glistening with unshed tears.

"Then don't let me touch ye. Take control."

"But..." She studied him, twisting the belt in her fists. "Don't you like control?"

"Aye."

"Don't you want to touch me?"

"Aye."

Shay made a disgusted noise, whipping his bare chest with the belt lightly. Mikey jolted with the sting. If he wasn't already hard for her, he sure as hell was now. She grabbed one of his hands and put it to her bare breast, fitting in his palm perfectly. "Get your feel now, handsome. You have one minute to explore my body before you're mine."

That order shouldn't have excited him as much as it did, but the gods feckin' strike him, he was ready. Mikey's hands glided up her thighs and to her hips, reaching behind her to grip her ass. Feck, he wanted to do that for so long. A rumble burst from his chest as he sat forward, taking one of her breasts into his mouth. The shock on her face registered at the same time the sweet milk coated his tongue. Both their eyes grew big. He forgot about *that*. Gods, how could he forget she was nursing? Although—he took another pull—it didn't bother him as much as he thought it would. He had never done it with a woman before and found that if he tried, it'd be with her.

Shay's face scrunched. "I should have warned you."

The mixture of embarrassment and revulsion warring on her features settled his resolve. Michael pulled back, licking his lips before moving to her next breast. He was rewarded with the relaxing of her body, her embarrassment falling away to wonder.

"It—" She paused, hands wrapped in his dark hair as she pulled him closer. Was she aware of the action? Was the discomfort more than she let on? "It doesn't repulse you?" she asked.

"Nothin' about ye repulses me, dimples."

Shay sighed, satisfaction glazing her features as her head fell back, long dark curls tickling his thighs. "That feels so much better," she admitted.

And he could feel it, too, the softening of her breasts as he drank the milk. Gods, a woman's body was remarkable. "Don't tell the boys, aye?" Michael grinned impishly.

Shay laughed. "We won't make this a thing."

A thing. For that, they'd have to be doing this again. Mikey found that excited him immeasurably. He raised a brow and leaned back, pushing his hardness into her center.

Shay gasped, shaking in his arms. "Thirty more seconds," she said, voice strained.

His hands gently skimmed up her back, across her shoulder blades, and back to her breasts, gripping each one, kneading them until she moaned through her fright, the pleasure too much.

"Ten seconds."

His hands fell to her ass again and captured her mouth with his, kissing her like the world was burning around them. Their tongues danced to a brutal beat, and their bodies writhed, ready for what was to come.

Shay pushed him back and whipped him again.

"Feck," he growled. "I think ye like that too much, lass."

She only let out a wee evil chuckle and tied him to the bed.

It was then that Mikey realized he would do anything for this woman. And that scared the ever-livin'-shite out of him.

CHAPTER TWENTY-TWO

Shaylah

S hay looked down at one of the most handsome, scariest, brutal men she'd ever been with. The scars and tattoos adorning his body were a testament to his battles and the wrongs he committed. And yet, Michael saved her. Pulled her out of that horrible place, killed her assaulters, and checked on her even when he could easily have forgotten her.

And it didn't sicken him. Didn't make him avert his eyes in shame and disgust like it did to Hiram. He didn't even balk at the milk in her breasts. That alone impressed Shay. There were a lot of man-children who would have revolted and pushed her away in disgust. Michael still looked at her like a woman, a beautiful woman that a man could desire and take care of. Pursue without pushing. Trusting her to do what is needed to heal.

Looking at the marks, she realized they were more than just scars. They were symbols of his unyielding determination and sheer willpower to overcome any obstacle that came his way. These marks were a testament to his strength and resilience. Michael was her savior, and she'd gladly get on her knees to worship him.

She tightened the belt and smiled when he winced.

"Ye are a—"

Her finger smooshed his lips together so he couldn't say anything. "Shhh," she whispered, trying not to laugh. "Just take it." Shay squealed when he nipped her finger and bucked, throwing her off-kilter. She caught herself on his chest and froze, staring into his icy blues. "Thank you." It came out on a breath.

"I haven't done anythin', dimples."

"You're doing everything," she whispered, leaning back to grip him, and watched his eyes darken. She swallowed, feeling his thickness, unsure if this would hurt for the first time after...

"We don't have to do this," he said, snapping her out of her own head.

Shay only bit her lip, positioned herself over him, and slammed down before he could say anything else. They both yelled out, groaning with the tightness of it.

"Bloody hell," he groaned. "I should've known."

"Known what?" she gasped, rolling her hips slowly.

Every muscle on his body was taut, his arms straining against his binding as his body coiled tighter. Shay knew he wanted to touch her but didn't care enough to free him. He gave her the power, the lead, and it was gloriously everything she needed. Shay smoothed her hands up his scarred stomach, smiling at how his abs twitched before coming to rest on his chest. She leaned into him and lifted her hips just enough to slam down again, moving them up and down at an increasing speed that had him cursing in Irish.

God, I love when he talks like that.

"That ye'd be just as wild as me in bed," he admitted through clenched teeth.

Shay gave him a wicked smile. "But you thought I was a virgin before..." She stiffened at the memory that bombarded her mind and tormented her body but concentrated on the man before her and the control. Straightening, she touched her breasts as she rolled over Michael. She loved the way he watched her hands, how her body moved. He really was gorgeous, and she felt just as magnificent while using his body. Using it the way they used hers.

Except she wasn't anything like those assholes, and neither was Michael.

It was just them and their equal desire for one another. Shay had lusted for him for months, and she'd be damned if she didn't take full advantage. She began to move with a reckless, angry passion, pushing her body and his to the limit.

"Feckin' hell, woman." He growled through clenched teeth, his body pulling in on itself as his head lifted, watching where their bodies met, her hips moving at a tantalizing speed that threatened nothing but ecstasy.

Shay leaned forward, kissing him roughly, ruthlessly, more than she ever did with a man. Her hand slid up his chest almost of its own volition and wrapped around his neck as she still moved over him. Michael's eyes found hers, sparking with desire. His smirk seemed to say, "Do your worst."

She squeezed tighter and arched her back, letting her head fall back as she rode him. "Yes," she gasped, feeling the tension coil within her. "Yes, Michael." Her thighs clenched, rolling her hips in an entirely different movement, making them both groan. The rumble vibrated beneath her hand, and she let go, looking down to find his face red, deep gasps filling his expanding chest.

"Don't ye feckin' stop," he warned fiercely. Shay smiled, swinging her leg over him so he slid out of her. "What—" he began angrily, but she was already facing the door, her leg back over him. *So fucking bossy*. Shay smirked to herself as she lowered herself onto him and was rewarded with an Irish curse. She may not be able to see his face, but she was told men loved seeing her from this position.

She lifted her ass up and down with increasing speed, holding onto the bed in delight as Michael's legs bent. "Holy hell," he gasped, sounding absolutely wrecked. That knowledge had her moving faster, knowing she could do that to him. "Ye aren't like any other lass I've—"

Shay stopped, sitting back, so he sunk all the way to the base, her ass resting on his hips as he groaned. "Excuse me?" she asked in what she hoped was an air of authority. "Did you just mention another woman while you're currently inside of me?"

"Aye, dimples." He jolted, and she knew he must be pulling at his bindings but didn't turn around to check. "And I fecked them right good." Shay gasped, turning to look at him without breaking their connection to find him smirking. "Most the time, three of them at once."

Heat pooled in her, and she had to switch positions to see his face again. Shay began to move slowly, her throat thick with desire and shame as she asked, "Is that what you want now?"

"Is that what ye want?" He quirked a brow.

"Explain what you did."

"Explain?"

"In detail." A flush covered her whole body. Holy shit, this turned her on.

He must have seen the change in her because something flashed in his gaze. "Untie me."

"But—"

"Do ye trust me?"

"Yes." It came out quiet, and she began to loosen the belt, her hands shaking.

His hands felt from the binding, and he rose so quickly that she squealed. Michael placed her on the bed and stuck his head out the door, mumbling something incoherent to someone. He closed the door again and faced her in all of his naked glory, his large member still standing at attention.

Shay thought her heart would pound out of her chest, her whole body shaking. Except this was a pleasant reaction, she realized. Out of nervousness, not fear.

"Have ye ever been with a woman?" he asked, smirking as she shook her head.

Though this excited her, she needed to know his intentions. "Are you going to screw her in front of me?"

"Is that what would do it for ye?"

"I—" She shook her head as jealousy overwhelmed her. "I don't know."

Michael stalked closer, setting her thundering heart into a full sprint. "I thought it would do ye good to have some womanly affection as I made love to ye, dimples."

They both froze, eyes connecting with growing shock. Did Michael just—

A knock on the door broke the tension as they turned toward it. Shay grabbed a sheet, covering her nakedness just before a small blonde girl entered. Lord, how *young* was she?

"Shaylah..." Her name rolling through his deep voice made her shiver, "This here is Alma. She is one of me main girls." He guided her to the bed, face smooth of emotion.

"Nice to meet ye," Alma smiled sweetly, utterly undaunted by Michael's nudity as she scanned Shay's face. Shay wasn't sure what she found, but the girl seemed to want to comfort her. "Mikey does take good care of us girls."

"I bet." Shay frowned at Michael, irritated. The bastard only smiled, eyes glinting.

"You..." she hesitated. She needed to know the answer before she could continue with this madness. "You aren't here against your will, are you?"

Alma frowned but shook her head. "Not anymore." She paused with a sadness that made Shay's skin crawl with dread, but the girl gave a reassuring smile as if she was calming Shay's own fears. What had this girl been through? "It's me home now."

"And your..." She looked at her youthful face. If anyone hurt this girl, she'd kill them herself. "You're of age?"

"Aye, ma'am. Me family wanted to marry me off, but times were hard, and we needed money." She shrugged, giving a smile that didn't reach her eyes. "No one wants a poor Irish lass."

Shay stared at her, shocked. "How long ago was this?"

"Oh..." Alma looked up at Michael questioningly. "Not quite a year since Michael took me virginity."

"What?" Shay shouted, startling the girl. Michael only raised his eyes to the ceiling.

"Oh, he was the most considerate." Alma smiled, patting Shay on the shoulder. "Took a few times before he could fully—"

"Alma," Michael cut in. "She doesn't..."

"It's okay," Shay said, face flaming. He had already shared so much with this girl. How was she going to compete? Was he into virgins? She swallowed, heart racing with nervousness.

"Alma is also Keena's lover," Michael added.

"Oh!" Shay looked between them with wide eyes. "That dark-haired woman downstairs?"

"Aye." Alma grinned wistfully.

How did these two women feel about them being with men? Then again...

She pointed a finger at both of them. "Do all three of you...?"

"Aye." The girl looked up at Michael in admiration and maybe a bit of something else that had Shay bristling. She may be with Keena, but she also liked Michael a little too much.

"I thought..." Michael began, reaching down to loosen Alma's corset. Shay swallowed, watching how gentle he was with her. "That Alma could take care of ye while I'm with ye."

Shay's head whipped to him. "You're not going to fuck her?"

"Do ye want me to?" Michael asked it like it didn't matter either way. Shay pulled the sheet to her throat, not knowing what she wanted. His blue eyes met hers as Alma's clothes fell from her thin body. Her skin was the creamiest white, splattered with freckles, and a natural blush bloomed on her cheekbones as she was exposed before Shay. Shay's eyes glided down her body, the slight mounds of her breasts, the soft flare of her petite hips. Michael bent Alma over, holding onto her tinny waist as he dared Shay to protest.

She bit her lip but didn't tell him to stop. He should have his fun. He lost so much control with her, and with Alma, he could burn some of that frustration. If Alma was okay with being bare in front of her, then she sure as hell wasn't going to hide under a damn sheet. Shay let the fabric drop and squeezed her significantly fuller breasts. Michael looked like he was about to push Alma to the side to get to Shay. That knowledge had Shay's body humming in satisfaction. *Mine*, she thought. He *was* hers, damn it, and she wanted to see him lose it deep inside this other woman, knowing that she meant nothing to him. Knowing Michael was staring at her.

"Yours," he answered, startling her. She must have said it out loud.

Shay bit her lip to hold back her smile and nodded for him to continue.

Michael cursed violently as he slammed into Alma, making her scream so loudly that Shay paused. His body moved at a brutal pace, muscles bunching and uncoiling in such force that he had to pick the girl up to get better use of her body.

"Oh, dadai," Alma screamed, "Yes!"

Shay lowered her hand to her center, moving her fingers faster, unable to resist until it was too much. She jolted forward and crawled toward them, Michael didn't stop his brutal pace, and his eyes still focused entirely on Shay.

She cradled Alma's face, features twisted in desire as Shay's man—*hers* God-damnit—fucked her senseless. She pulled Alma's blonde hair roughly and swallowed her scream as she covered her mouth with her own.

"Feck," Michael groaned.

Shay reached up and cupped Alma's tiny breasts in her hand. She had never touched a woman like this before, but it…Oh, Shay found she liked it quite a lot. "Out of her," Shay demanded before she could think it through. "Go behind me."

"Oh, he gives the orders," Alma began, but Michael had already dropped her down, a smirk on his face as he did what he was told.

'You listen to me now," Shay snapped, pulling the startled girl onto the bed. "If you don't like something, tell me." Shay paused, taking in her sweet features, pale complexion, and the way the soft blue of her eyes screamed innocence. "Otherwise, you do what you're told."

"Yes, ma'am." Michael and Alma said simultaneously, making Shay grin in satisfaction.

She pulled Alma to her, kissing her roughly as she explored the girl's slim figure. Alma didn't have Shay's curves, height, or strength. She wouldn't even think about how vastly different they were, yet she didn't feel self-conscious. Michael stopped coming to Alma when his feelings for Shay changed. And, to her astonishment, Shay found she rather liked doing this with him. She enjoyed doing this with *Alma*. The girl was submissive in every way, whereas Michael and Shay constantly fought for dominance.

A thrill of excitement electrified her every nerve as she lay Alma down, her dark curls fanning the girl's face, and kissed her. Shay ran her hands over Alma's thin stomach, the wave of ribs as the girl arched her back—the perfect position for Shay to grab her tiny breast. Kneeling above Alma, Shay positioned her ass upward for Michael.

"Take me," Shay's voice cracked, "while I play with her."

"Gods damn it, woman. I think ye were made for me." His voice was rougher than she had ever heard, his hands shaking as they grabbed her waist. "Do I have to be gentle? I mean—"

"Fuck me, Michael."

Still, Michael entered her so slowly it made her teeth grit. "Fuck me like you fuck your whores," she growled.

He mumbled something so quiet she questioned it, but it sounded awfully like not being one of his whores. The thought warmed her from within. Not from passion, but a feeling that she didn't want to decipher. Not yet. She couldn't—

Michael shoved into her, making each of them curse and Alma giggle. Shay's mouth fell open in desire. The girl—woman, she amended—was cute. She could see why Michael had taken an interest in her. But Shay's eyes closed when Michael picked up the pace, squeezing her waist as his thighs slapped against hers. God, he was divine.

"Shit," Shay groaned.

"That's it, baby," Michael growled. "Ye're doin' so good. Ye're takin' me so well."

Shay warmed under the praise. She needed this for so long to feel something other than pain and despair. Shay needed a man to show and remind her that she still could feel pleasure. She reached back, holding onto his hip, needing to touch the man waking her up again. A firm grip covered it, his fingers weaving within hers.

Shay opened her eyes, finding desire in Alma's gaze. "Tell me," Shay demanded, holding onto the girl as Michael railed into her. "Will Keena be jealous?"

Shay gasped, Michael hitting that special spot within her, her pussy clenching in sweet pain. Alma began to kneed Shay's breasts, pinching her nipples. Shay groaned, letting her head drop. Through the loud smack of Michael's hips slapping against her ass, she heard Alma say, "She often is, miss."

"And does it bother you?"

Alma hesitated. "I quite like both sexes."

"Oh? And do you like me?" Shay lifted her head, holding onto Alma's shoulder while she watched her blue eyes darken. It sent an unexpected thrill through Shay. "Do you want to think about her while I touch you?"

Alma bit her lip and wavered but shook her head. "I want to touch ye," she admitted. "Think about ye, not Keena."

"Good girl." Shay smiled as she wedged her arm between them and thrust her fingers into Alma.

Alma gasped, her pretty lips parting as she watched Shay's fingers work inside of her. Shay didn't miss the way Alma's eyes traveled across Shay's ass to where she and Michael were connected. "Can I?" Alma asked.

"Yes," Shay gasped on a particularly hard thrust from Michael, not sure what Alma was asking but wanting it nonetheless.

Alma grabbed Shay's ass, spreading it for Michael to shove in more.

"Thatta girl," Michael growled. "Just like I taught ye." He rubbed Shay's back and bent over her to say something into her ear while feeling up Alma. "I'm going to play with your ass now. Any objections?"

"No," she croaked, her heart in her throat. It was already so much, but she wanted it. Wanted Michael to use her for his own pleasure. "Do it."

"Are ye—"

"Fuck me, Michael!"

He shoved a thick finger in her ass while he continued to fuck her pussy. "Gods, ye're still so tight. I can't wait to get me dick in this part of ye." Michael worked another finger into her asshole, twisting his fingers downward. That, with the angle of his cock... She gasped, rolling her hips for more friction. She was so close. She just needed...

Shay opened her eyes and told Alma, "I need you."

The girl knew what she needed.

The tension rose, her pussy clenching around Michael until he groaned, the bed creaking—threatening to collapse—as they all moved in tandem. A hot wave rolled through Shay, making her call out, screaming so loudly they undoubtedly had to hear her downstairs. She hadn't realized she'd still been working Alma, and the girl called out, too. An orgasm rolled through them simultaneously.

Michael pulled out of her so fast that she barely recognized his absence before his dick was so far up her ass she grunted in pain, stilling as he pounded in her.

Alma reached up and kissed her deeply. "Ye are doin' so good. He loves ye so much." Shay's body softened in wonder, allowing Michael to curse, fully sheathing himself within her. "I can tell. He never looked at us like he's lookin' at ye right now."

Michael reached over Shay, wrapping his hand around Alma's face and squeezing her cheeks. "Ye talk when I say," he growled at her, a clear warning lacking kindness. Shay shivered. This was the way he was with his men, and she knew he was pissed at Alma's announcement. She knew she shouldn't think it, should be concerned, but she couldn't deny how unbelievably hot it was.

"I think she needs to be punished. Don't ye, mo ghrá?"

"What does that mean?" Shay gasped, still filled with him.

"Don't ye worry about it and tell me what ye think."

"Yes. I want to do it."

Alma's eyes widened, flicking between them. "I'm sorry—"

"I said shut your gob," he snapped. "And do what ye are told."

"Yes, sir."

Michael slowly pulled out of Shay, making her grunt at the loss of him. He bent down and picked up the belt, handing it to her. She took it with shaking hands, biting her lip as she turned to Alma.

"Bend over," Shay said.

"Miss—"

"Only two," Shay reassured her. "And I'll do it."

Alma's cheeks were a deep red, her body visibly shaking as she turned around. Her butt was surprisingly round for how small she was. Shay ran a hand over it, making Alma clench right before Shay raised her hand and spanked her. Alma squealed, hands squeezing the sheet tightly.

The heat of Michael's body pressed against hers as he wrapped his thick arms around her stomach, his chin on her shoulder. "Ye're a goddess, ye know that?" he asked Shay.

Oh, she was starting to believe that, and it was all because of this magnificent, fierce man. "Are you going to worship me?" she asked.

"Every feckin' day from here on out, mo ghrá." His lips fell on her cheek as she rubbed the sting out of Alma's ass.

"How are you?" she asked the whore.

"I—" A pause and a nod. "I'm ready for ye're punishment, miss."

"Good girl."

Shay tightened the belt, lifted her hand, and whipped it across Alma's ass. The girl called out, body flinching as a red line formed across her cheeks. But Shay knew she held back and that it was only superficial. Still, it made her want to try every naughty thing with the whore. This was a power she never experienced before, and she wasn't ready to let go. She leaned forward, rubbing the sting before sliding her fingers into Alma.

"You're so wet." Shay's voice was tight to her own ears. Alma liked the pain and punishment, which alone was enough to make Shay lose herself. She pumped into the girl as Michael leaned over, entering his thumb into Alma's ass. They set up a relentless pace when she felt Michael position behind her, sliding into her as Alma's hips moved with their hands.

"Oh, yes," Shay moaned. "God, yes."

"Am I your god, mo ghrá?"

"Yes, Michael. Oh, God! Yes!"

"Feck, yes." He pumped into her so hard, jolting her forward, so she lost her balance, and he had to hold her up, losing control as she admitted everything that she had kept hidden for so many months. "And ye are me goddess."

They moved together. All three lost in desire. Alma began to clench around them when Shay said, "Stop. You don't get to feel that. Not yet."

"Yes, miss."

Shay pushed Alma's face into the mattress and took a moment to admire the view while she enjoyed the slow pump of Michael's enormous cock inside of her. Shay had Alma stay like that as her head fell back onto Michael's chest. "Thank you," she told him.

He slammed into her harder, and she grunted.

"For what?" he asked.

"This. Her."

"Ye like her?" he asked, skimming his hand up her stomach and breast. "I like these."

Shay laughed and closed her eyes, content with his slow ministrations. "I think she was the bridge to what I needed. And I think," she paused, reminiscing about all the times she thought women attractive but not really considered what it meant, "I think I always wanted to explore this part of my sexuality but never took the chance. So, thank you."

Michael ran his tongue up her neck and bit lightly. "I'll fuck women with ye whenever ye want, dimples."

"So generous of you," she whispered as she moved both his hands to her breasts and squeezed tightly, guiding his hands to do what she wanted.

She watched Alma stay in the same position, squeezing the sheet as she waited for the next hit. Shay took pity on her and picked up the belt. "One more."

"Yes, miss."

"One question," Shay said, grabbing the girl's hair and pulling it back to get a good look in her blue eyes. She saw some apprehension but no fear. Good. "You know he's mine, correct?"

"Of course, miss."

"And I'll fucking ruin you if you get in between us."

"Gods-damn it," Michael muttered, running his hands over her body, making her muscles twitch across her stomach. "I feckin' love ye. I don't feckin' care anymore. Ye're mine. I'm keepin' ye."

The fact that he could admit it and for everyone to hear was the strongest declaration that Shay could hope for.

Shay smiled wickedly, pulled her arm back sharply, and whipped Alma harder than the last time. Alma's body tightened, and she grunted. Elated and filled with so much adrenaline she was shaking, Shay dropped the belt, spun around to face Michael, and kissed him deeply. "I love you too."

Michael picked her up and placed her on the bed next to Alma and shoved in so viciously that Shay's whole body curled in on itself. She groaned at the intrusion, moaned at the fullness of it, and squeezed her legs around him, using her feet to shove him in harder.

"Yes," she gasped.

Shay reached for Alma and brought the girl's mouth to hers. It was different kissing a woman, softer. There was no bristly beard or harsh jaw. She felt Michael reach over to the girl, feeling her up as he pounded into Shay.

"Mine," Shay growled.

"Yours," he rumbled.

"Make her come. I want to watch."

Michael pulled back, brows scrunching quizzically. "Ye want me inside her?"

Shay nodded. "On top of me."

They guided Alma on top of Shay as Michael entered from behind. Alma's pouty red mouth parted on a gasp, blue eyes wide as she held onto Shay.

"This is your reward," Shay said, running her hand over the girl's face.

Alma nodded. "Thank ye, miss."

Michael was on his knees, holding onto Alma's waist—his big hands nearly circling the tiny thing—as he drove into her, his hips moving at a remarkable speed. "So feckin' tight," he gasped, eyes still on Shay. "I don't think I have much longer." His eyes crinkled with worry, restraint at holding off.

Shay reached between them, working her fingers so the girl could get off and get the hell out. Alma screamed, clenching around Michael as he grunted, but Shay pushed him off Alma and moved her to the side.

"Thank you," Shay said, "but kindly get out."

She was vaguely aware of Alma gathering her clothes and leaving the room as Michael crawled over her. She made a mental note to talk to Alma before she went home. Shay didn't want Alma to think she had any hard feelings. Had she gone too far? Shay had a moment of doubt, her stomach turning sour at the thought. She'd find Alma and get the feel of how she felt, apologize if needed. But, with the way Michael was looking at her like that—as if she was the only woman who existed, like he wanted to devour her every moment of every day—it was easy to push the thoughts of the whore to the side.

"So," Shay said, suddenly nervous again. Her stomach did a little flip as his weight pressed into her. "Alone again."

Michael cradled her in his arms and kissed her. His mouth was soft but imploring, filled with passion, but lacking the brutality of earlier. Shay raised into him, wanting—needing—to be closer. To have him inside her. Her breasts pushed against his chest, finally, skin-to-skin, as her hands roamed over his back. After a few minutes, she guided his cock to her center, and he slid in slowly. They both moaned low and long, taking their time with one another now that the fear and heat of the night cooled.

"Did you mean it?" she asked.

His hands cupped her face, and he pulled back. "Are ye crying, lass?"

She swatted his hands away from the stupid, happy tears coating her face and asked him again.

"Aye, I meant it. I love ye. Love ye like I never loved another in me life. I find meself thinking about ye constantly. Worrying if ye are all right. If your babe is okay. I worry for ye both, lass. And I don't know how to feckin' process that." His forehead fell to hers, gently rocking back and forth as he admitted everything she needed to hear. "This world isn't meant for me to have ye. But at the same time, every plan I conceive is with ye in mind. Do ye know how feckin' annoyin' that is?"

She grinned, cradling his face as he moved inside her. His eyes were so somber that Shay knew there was hope for him.

"I know I shouldn't love ye, gods damn it. I'm no good for ye."

"Shut up," she whispered and kissed him. "I love you too."

Michael moved so slowly that it was almost painful. And yet, it was so glorious that she wrapped her legs around his and cherished the divine torture. They stared into each other's eyes, the slow push and pull building up a low, burning heat inside her core.

"Don't stop," she gasped.

"Never," he said into her neck, his body tensing, his muscled ass clenching as he forced himself deeper. He lifted her hips, angling them slightly so that he hit a spot that sent a flood of desire through her.

"Oh," she moaned. "Yes, Michael." The pressure built stronger, tighter, and all-consuming. Shay's body went rigid, and Michael pulled back to watch, knowing she was about to explode.

"Feckin' beautiful," he crooned. "Such a good girl. Show me how much ye love me cock."

The coil within her shattered at his praise, ricocheting through her body and shooting through her limbs. She screamed, feeling him pick up his pace, grunting with his own near orgasm as her body twitched around him. Michael began to pull away, back arching, but she clung to him and used her feet to shove him deeper.

"I need you, Michael," she gasped. "I need you inside of me."

Michael grunted that bottomless, guttural grunt men did when they lost control. And his hips stilled, seated so far inside of her that she could feel the heat of his release. "Feck," Michael cursed incoherently, somehow shoving in more so she could feel the tip of him meet the end of her.

"Yes," she said, her head falling back.

Michael captured her mouth, sweeping his tongue over hers leisurely.

They stayed like that for some time, wrapped in one another. Shay felt content in her own body for the first time in months, and Michael plotted all the ways he could keep her.

Neither worrying about the actual threat at hand.

CHAPTER TWENTY-THREE

Emilia

SEPTEMBER 1862

The day after Bull Run, I found myself in a field hospital, trying not to step on the soldiers waiting for assistance. So many were lying head to foot, covering the entire tent and out into the field. I held my hand over my nose and mouth, unsuccessfully trying to block out the stench of festering wounds.

The previous day, when Thomas and I came to the edge of the woods after escaping Barton, we found General Stevens had been shot through the head, immediately falling from his horse. Our orders were to withdraw. The battle had turned into a blind panic as the ambulances deserted their wounded, escaping the danger rather than gathering patients. Dead men were everywhere as moans rumbled through the field. Thomas stopped to help a man whose leg had been shot. It took some time, but we helped him make it to safety. The same couldn't be said for many others. Thousands were left on the battlefield, severely wounded and crying out. They would have to wait for help. If help ever came. It would be days before some of them would see an ambulance.

Now, the groans of pain and the screams of those amid amputation pierced my ears. I still couldn't believe how lucky I'd been to come out of this battle whole and unscathed.

The guilt ate at me as I looked into their contorted faces, so filled with pain when I was blessedly okay with nothing but a bump on the head. Thomas followed me, seemingly unfazed by it all except for the occasional clench of his jaw and flare of his nostrils when confronted with a terrible smell. After some time searching, I noticed his hands opening and closing into fists. Our men lying helpless bothered him a great deal.

Finally, we found another assistant surgeon, who had already questioned two others and a nurse. "Excuse me, Doctor..." I started.

"Rood." His heavy brows caved in like angry caterpillars over his round glasses as he scanned the paperwork. "If you'll excuse me, but I must—"

"I'm sorry to disturb ye," I cut him off. "But I'm looking for me friend. I was told he—"

"I apologize, but I have a lot of patients to attend to."

Just then, another scream, slightly muffled from being in another tent, pierced the air. Dr. Rood's face hardened, ready to jump back into it.

"His name is George Hall." Thomas stepped forward, drawing the doctor's attention to his intimidating figure. "It would mean a great deal if ye helped us out."

The doctor sighed and straightened his glasses, taking great care to ignore Thomas. "Well? I may have a few moments..."

I described Hall, explaining he may have a sketchbook he always carried.

Rood cleared his throat uncomfortably. "Right this way." He weaved his way through the men while talking over his shoulder to me. "He had taken a Minnie ball to his arm. I assured him the arm needn't be amputated, much to his relief. It was then he told me of his profession and needing his dominant hand to paint." The doctor side-eyed Thomas, probably wondering if this information would placate him. "That's why I remember him. I'm relieved to say that it went through without hitting the humerus. The wound should recover with full use of the arm."

"Humerus?" Thomas asked.

"The bone in the upper arm," I answered without thinking, earning me a shocked glance from the doctor and a subtle flush from Thomas. I mentally kicked myself for making him uncomfortable. It didn't help that the doctor now studied me more closely. I shrugged. "Heard a doctor explain it about another patient."

He nodded, visibly relieved that my knowledge was easily explained. "Right. Well, we're almost there." We were in the last row of the tent. The men here were not as severely wounded, some sitting up and playing cards with their good arms or wounded legs stretched out to the side. "Is this the man you described?"

Hall was lucky enough to get a small cot instead of the floor while a young nurse checked his bandage. He said something to her that made her smile. When he spotted us, his head dropped back in relief.

"Eamonn! Thank the Lord above, ye're all right. O'Connor." He nodded to Thomas and actually smiled. "This is Miss Wilson. She happens to be one of the best nurses around."

I watched in amusement as the nurse's cheeks pinkened at the compliment.

"Call me Loretta," she said, smiling sweetly as she pushed away a stray strand of her mousy brown hair. She had a plain face that was quickly transformed when her natural kindness seeped through. Hall must have also seen it, because he couldn't take his eyes off her.

"Nurse Wilson," Doctor Rood interrupted, his face angry. "A word?"

We watched them walk away, but it was impossible not to hear their conversation.

"Your job is to treat the patients," Doctor Rood lectured. "Not to find yourself a husband."

"Sir—"

"You will take better care not to flirt with the men, or I will replace you. Do you understand?"

Loretta looked mortified as she stared at her hands crossed over her simple gray dress. "Yes, sir."

"Good." The doctor turned to leave but stopped by us. "I am sorry for that. I don't know what they were thinking hiring these women for a man's job."

I was about to take a step forward and give him a piece of my mind when Thomas grabbed my arm. I glared at the doctor, but he didn't seem to notice as he left.

Loretta was finishing up Hall's bandage, her face beat red.

"The doctor said ye are going to be okay," I said, standing there awkwardly, unsure what to do with myself.

"I hope ye didn't spend too long searching for me." His eyes flicked between Thomas and me, looking like he had something to say.

"Not too long," I said at the same time Thomas said, "All damn morning."

Hall laughed and Loretta managed a small smile. She finished checking the bandage and moved on to the next patient.

"Wait," I said, drawing her to the side. "Don't let that doctor get to you. Eventually, women will be doctors. That jerk doesn't know what he's talking about."

Loretta's cheeks reddened and her eyes grew round, but she still gave a soft chuckle. "I'm not quite sure about that." She smiled at me and nervously played with her hair. "But it is sweet of you to think of me."

"Just don't listen to him," I told her. "Ye are doing an excellent job. Women are capable of far more than what men think."

"You speak as if you fully believe that."

"I do." I smiled.

She ran her hand over her neck and stared at me from under her lashes.

Shocked, I realized she was flirting with me, and I reared back. "Yeah, well," I said gruffly. The little flirt was just told not to flirt with the men, and here she was, doing the crime for which she was scolded. Thomas tried to hide a grin as Hall looked between us, bewildered. "I just didn't want ye to think ye're not doing a good job. These doctors can be a little harsh on the women here."

"That means a lot. Thank you."

She bid me a good day and left to make her rounds. I, on the other hand, stood frozen and reluctant to go near the boys.

"I think she likes ye," Thomas said, face beaming with amusement.

"Nay." I glared at him. "I think she has a thing for Hall here."

Hall's face reddened as he sat up, mumbling something under his breath.

We made some small talk until it was time to depart. Our regiment was due to move out to Washington, and Thomas and I needed to join them. When I turned to leave, Hall grabbed my arm.

"Wait a moment," he said, rummaging in his book. "I don't know when I'll see ye again, but ye should have this."

I unfolded the paper and froze. It was a charcoal drawing of me sitting on a log as we ate dinner one night, staring up at Thomas while he talked to someone else not in the picture. The way I stared is what terrified me. Hall captured my love so perfectly that it couldn't be mistaken. I hadn't realized I stared at him so openly in public. I'd have to be more careful.

Thomas took in a sharp breath behind me.

"It's—" I began but didn't know what else to say. "Thank ye."

"Many don't look at the small details, but it's me job," he said with a shrug. "I thought ye might want it?"

I looked into his eyes, wondering if I should be worried. "Hall—"

"I've known for some time. Your secret is safe with me. I am correct in me assumptions about... about that and about ye both?" He looked at Thomas, then back to me, and I nodded. An uneasy feeling built within me, not knowing if it was better or worse than the truth. Did Hall think we were male lovers? Or did he guess the truth about my gender? Neither would be accepted in this time, and I wasn't sure which punishment would be worse.

"Hall—" I started.

"Ye aren't really cousins, are ye?" I gave a weak grin and shook my head. "To be honest, ye kept saving our arses out there. As good as any man in the field, if not better." He raised his brows, and I felt he understood the truth of it. I sighed with relief. "We truly don't know how much we're missin' by keepin' our women back at home. It's an honor to know ye." He held out his good hand and shook mine.

"Thanks, Hall. For being so understanding." I leaned close, unsure why I wanted him to hear my authentic voice. "Mick knew at the end, too. I did everything I could. I'm so sorry that I couldn't bring him back."

Hall's face saddened, but he squeezed my hand reassuringly. "That isn't on ye, lass. Ye did what ye could, and he knew it as well. Don't dwell on the past."

I folded the paper back up and slid it into the inside pocket of my jacket. It was my only photo of us, and I knew I would look at it frequently.

We walked out of the large tent, and I inhaled a lungful of clean air. At least cleaner than the tent. The smell of gunpowder still carried over on the breeze from the battlefield. I wrinkled my nose, unsure which was better—the stench of the dirty, injured men or the rotten smell of sulfur.

"I thought after ye found him, ye might look a little better."

"What do you mean?" I looked up at Thomas, surprised. Men came and went from the tent, but no one was paying attention to us.

"With Barton gone and Hall found, I thought a little weight may be lifted off your shoulders. But that's not the case?" His green eyes traversed my face, causing heat to spread through my body as I realized his mind was elsewhere.

"Don't do that," I said, thinking of the picture. We'd have to be more careful.

"Do what?"

"Look at me like that in public."

Mischief danced in his eyes as he studied me. "And when should I look at ye like this?" He laughed when I glared at him. "When am I going to get ye alone again, gypsy?"

My whole body flushed. Thomas was distracting, but unless he was actually going to undress me here and now, there wasn't much chance of improving my mood.

"Probably not anytime soon, unfortunately." I sighed, suddenly feeling the exhaustion of the battle crash onto me again, and let my head fall back. The little rest I'd gotten through the night wasn't enough. "I think I need some more sleep."

"Aye, that would help." He said it with such gravity that I laughed.

"How can you even think about that right now?" I wondered, amazed he could even think straight after everything we'd been through.

"Maybe I liked the way she was looking at ye. Maybe we could reenact that night in Madam Nora's—"

He barked out a laugh when I punched his arm, my face flaming red at his mention of our first time together. I may have listened a little too closely to the couple in the next room and one thing led to another. The thing was—No, I wouldn't let my mind go there. Even if I did think Loretta was pretty. I'd be keeping Thomas to myself. I sighed and faced the other way. How did he throw my thoughts into such disarray so casually?

"You're insufferable," I said, not voicing my naughty thoughts.

With a long sigh, his humor vanished. "I could use a little distraction, I guess."

I let my hand graze his in a silent reassurance as he steered me away from the wounded, but the feeling of unease followed me, and I was too exhausted to figure it out.

The Union wearily marched back to Washington lines. Without Boudreaux's men breathing down my neck, I could move around camp without fear. The weight seemed to drop off my shoulders, and I found even Thomas's mood lightened now that neither of us had to look over our shoulders. I hadn't realized how much they had impacted my every day, and it was an absolute relief that I only had to focus on my disguise. Though, that was enough in itself.

We left camp at Meridian Hill, following McClellan to Fox's Gap, where we received heavy fire. Later in the month, the Battle of Antietam raged on, where we met the Confederates near a farm and attacked with bayonets, driving their forces back to the edge of the town. Still, we had to retreat to Antietam Creek when the left flank of the 9th Corps had to withdraw troops to avoid being overwhelmed. General Lee returned to Virginia, leaving us with fifty-four fallen comrades. Thomas and I made it out with only minor injuries.

It wasn't until the fall, when we were recuperating at Nolan's Ferry, that I received word from Shay. We had just finished our company's morning drill—our new commanding officer, Colonel Richard Byrnes, had made sure to bust our asses, putting the unruly officers in line and bringing order among the soldiers by drilling each company in the morning and all together in the afternoon, in addition to a full inspection of our daily dress parade—when a shipment of letters came.

I bounced on my toes, waiting for my turn to look through the mail, until I saw my name scrawled on the front of one. I snatched it from the pile and threw a thank you over my shoulder as I searched for Thomas.

The air was cool, a slight reprieve from the scorching summer, promising the impending arrival of winter's icy grip. I found Thomas sitting in front of one of the tents, the canvas flapping gently in the breeze. Sullivan and Byrnes—who unfortunately had the same last name as our new commander—were with him. Their chatter mingled with the distant sounds of the camp, as they tossed a ball back and forth with another soldier who often rallied the others to play some baseball. I always declined, cringing when they caught the ball without gloves.

My smile fell when I saw how serious they were, and I slid the letter into my pocket, sitting down next to Thomas to hear the conversation. The letter could wait.

Sullivan leaned in. "New recruits are coming."

"Good," Thomas said, resting his elbows on his knees, unbothered.

"Word is they aren't Irish. The bastard is letting any goddamn man into our ranks now."

Thomas shrugged. "Ye have to see that the man is doing good." He said it casually, but Thomas always stood out from his people. He may have shared the hotheaded temper and love for a good fight, but he always considered all variables and never dismissed someone just because they were different from him.

Usually. About a week back, I had to stop Thomas from a fight with a man in our unit who was rallying the others against command. Thomas quickly halted the rebellion, and I made sure we had left the riot before facing any consequences and whatever godforsaken punishment they chose to dole out.

I couldn't have him punished for another's unruly behavior.

Byrnes huffed from his place on the ground, one arm draped over a bent knee, his eyes on a blade of grass in his hand. "That's nothing compared to what is happening in other companies." His tone was full of contempt. "They found a woman dressed as a man. Only found out when she received a musket ball to the shoulder." He shook his head as my blood shot through my veins like sharded ice.

"What happened to her?" I asked, sharing a glance with Thomas.

"They sent her packing. I hear she's not the only one, though."

"She's not?" Thomas asked warily.

"Heard another had a baby while on picket duty." Sullivan shook his head incredulously. "The men bloody helped."

Thomas ran a hand through his hair, suddenly looking anxious. I leaned in to whisper to him. "I've got a letter from home."

Thomas stood swiftly, ready to remove himself from the conversation, and jerked his head to the side for us to take a walk.

"Just think." Sullivan started, already laughing. "Our Thomas could've had a tent companion." Thomas stiffened but kept walking. "When ye finished your drills, ye could drill something else."

Thomas flipped him off, and raucous laughter erupted behind us. I walked faster, not wanting to show how much that unnerved me.

"Well," I said, trying and failing at flippancy, "they have that wrong. No drilling here."

Thomas's face was a mask of indifference. "What does the letter say?"

"I was waiting for you. It's from Shay."

I pulled the letter out and began to read it out loud.

"My dearest Eamonn." I smiled, clearly hearing her sarcasm, and my heart squeezed a bit. I missed her so much. She spewed her thoughts on the page as she did in real life.

"Do you remember when blacks could serve in the war?" she went on, her handwriting hurried. "I feel it's about damn time. I can feel the clock ticking down the minutes. Hiram has been getting antsy, swearing this way and that about wanting to do more. Do you remember the movie *Glory*? I want to tell him so badly about it. That there will be a whole regiment for blacks to join, and he can have the chance. And yet, I'm afraid. I already worry about you guys, and I just know I'll worry about him too."

"*Glory*?"

I explained to Thomas that the 54th Massachusetts Regiment would be the first African-American regiment.

"Ye know what will befall them?" he asked, voice strained.

"I suppose they will have the same struggles as us. Though—" I paused, thinking. "They will have to work harder for their rights. And their pay. Their commanding officer will be a good man. He'll help."

Thomas shook his head, struggling to believe my insight.

I went back to the letter, and my head reared back. "Why wouldn't she tell me this first?" I snapped.

Thomas quirked his brow, waiting for an explanation.

"They know who Boudreaux is. He's been working with Michael without Michael's knowledge. Michael stalked one of his men and questioned him. The man died of 'natural causes'." They eyed one another. "What if he gets caught?"

"He won't," Thomas said, though there was worry in his eyes that I didn't like. "Mikey is good at what he does."

"There's more." I swallowed a lump in my throat and pushed on through the sickness building in my stomach. "He warned Michael that his employer's property needs to be untarnished, untouched, and if I am to be sullied, he would kill the people I love one by one."

I felt the blood drain from my face, my eyes round as I watched Thomas's sullen expression turn to one of fury.

"He will do no such thing," Thomas snapped. "Me brother will slaughter him before that." The fact that Michael was watching over Shay was my only relief. If he was with her, then she would be safe.

We stopped near a cluster of trees that concealed us from the other men. Thomas clutched his hair as if to prevent himself from exploding.

"Maybe I should just give myself to him."

God, I don't want to. The idea terrified me, but I'd do it to protect my loved ones.

Thomas spun on me so fast I didn't have time to react, fisting my shirt so that we were nose to nose. "Ye will never say anything like that again. Ye will never belong to another human being. Ye control your own fate and will die before I see ye in the hands of another person who doesn't deserve ye. Do ye understand?"

My head bobbed, unable to choke anything out past the tears streaming down my face.

He let go, spinning away to pace.

"What are we going to do?" I said, voice small.

Thomas straightened. "We fight."

"But—"

"We'll figure it out. But until we have our answers, we trust Mikey to protect those at home. Boudreaux can't have word about his men yet. And we keep fighting until he is in the ground."

Thomas's gaze pierced my soul, and I felt the truth down to my core.

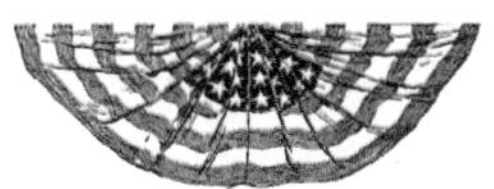

The next evening, Thomas found me a few miles down the river as I watched the sun start to dip over the horizon, singing an old song from my childhood. How he found me, I wasn't sure. I just knew I needed to be away from the men and have time to be myself. A woman without a disguise.

Shay's letter had kept me up through the night, and I was wrought thin.

Branches broke behind me, alerting me of his presence, but I didn't swing around. Instead, I stood there, detached.

"I haven't heard ye sing in ages," he said, standing beside me. I'd stopped singing when I knew I wasn't alone. I had been content with the crickets and frogs being my only audience.

"Since I joined."

"What was that song?"

Relief flooded me. I didn't want to talk about what I had to give up to fight this war.

I smiled, thinking of the song from the movie Mulan. I felt out of place, and the similarities between her and me were uncanny. "Just a song from when I was a kid."

"It sounded sad."

I shrugged but agreed. Hiding yourself from the world, wearing a mask so people couldn't see who you truly were, was irrevocably lonely. I missed myself. For the first time, I wanted to return to who I was, but I knew I couldn't. I changed in so many ways over the last year, and I knew, I *felt*, it was for the better. I was better. Stronger. I may have missed the old me, but the new me wasn't all that bad.

It'd be nice to be a woman again, though.

"Mikey will handle him until we return," Thomas promised. "He will have his men watch over Shay."

"I know."

"Then what is it?"

Boudreaux legally had every right to me. My mind. My body. Hell, he probably signed a contract for my soul as well. But what bothered me the most was that he planned to break my body and use it for his own will. I couldn't let that happen.

I began to take off my uniform while Thomas silently watched, and waded into the calm river, hissing as I let the cold water shock the nerves out of my system. I stopped when the water swelled over my hips.

I tried not to think about how my weight loss shrank my curves. The curves Thomas admitted to loving.

My only warning was a soft rustle behind me and the faint splash of Thomas walking through the water. I didn't turn around but focused on the soft orange and pink sky. I felt the warmth of him before he slowly put his arms around me, pulling me against his enormous chest. I shivered.

"Cold?" Thomas asked, voice raspy in my ear.

"Not anymore."

I felt his smile as he trailed his lips down my neck, sending a fresh wave of tingles through me.

"It's crazy how this world can still be so beautiful with all the shit going on around us," I said. "How can something lovely come from so much bad?"

His fingers trailed up my sides, and I trembled. "I was thinking the same thing about ye," he admitted.

I elbowed him playfully, unable to ignore how much I affected him as his body pressed against mine. I gasped, and my breath quickened as butterflies erupted in my abdomen. "Thomas—" I started, but his fingers began to graze down my stomach, and all thoughts escaped my mind.

I turned in his arms and let my hands trail up his broad chest, the dark hair curling under my wet fingers, and cupped them around the back of his head, weaving my fingers in his dark hair. His green eyes blazed, the pupils flung open as he took me in, but it didn't soften the crease of worry between them.

"My body isn't his," I breathed, and Thomas's muscles tightened, shielding me from the world. "I won't let him take that from me."

"I won't let him," he growled, his fingers squeezing my hips.

"I know. That's why—" I paused, but quickly continued before I lost my nerve. I wasn't sure what I'd do if he refused me again. "That's why I want it to be yours. Now."

My breath caught as Thomas's lips tightened, his brows furrowed, and I began to prepare myself for the rejection. I was about to pull away but froze when his eyes drifted to my mouth.

My whole body caught fire. Every nerve hummed within me as I waited for his next move.

My heart nearly exploded in my chest when his face lowered slowly, and his soft lips brushed mine. Our breaths intermingled as our eyes seared into one another's. Thomas' fingers trailed down my spine, causing delicious ripples through my body. In one quick motion, he hoisted me up, making me gasp as he carried me to the edge of the river and laid me on a soft blanket of leaves. Hovering above me, Thomas gazed at my body until all my insecurities roared to the surface.

"Probably not as pretty as the others..." I drifted off when his eyes flicked to mine.

"Ye are the most beautiful creature my eyes ever beheld."

I snorted, unladylike, and looked away.

Thomas grabbed my chin, forcing me to look at him. "I mean it," he said. "I never want to look at another. Ye are it for me, gypsy."

His fingers trailed lazily across my breasts and down my stomach, my skin quaking with each graze until they dipped between my legs, causing my back to bow off the ground. He growled in my ear, his teeth roaming over my body as his hand had me panting.

"Thomas, stop," I gasped, the pressure intensifying, building until I couldn't hold on anymore.

It was too soon.

I needed—

"I'm going to—"

His hand-picked up the pace.

Oh, God. Please.

I couldn't decide if I wanted him to stop or keep going.

Keep going. Oh—My whole body pulled tight like stings of a bow. I gasped, unable to hold off anymore. There was no time for choices.

There was no time—

I shattered on a loud cry, convulsing around his fingers, moaning my pleasure, until I was a puddle of mush. Slowly, I opened my eyes to find raw hunger consuming him as he watched his hand torment me again.

"I need you," I begged, pulling him over me.

Thomas hooked one hand behind my knee, pulling my leg around his waist. I panted, feeling him at my entrance. I rotated my hips, encouraging him.

"Are ye sure?" he asked, desire and restraint warring in the green depths of his eyes. "There is no going back from this."

"There's nothing I want more."

He pushed in slowly, oh so tormentingly slow, never breaking eye contact. *This. This is why I waited.* The muscles in his jaw clenched, his body shaking with restraint. My pulse quickened at the pressure, quaking with the invasion, as warmth flowed from my chest, down my limbs, and to every part of my body. *Oh, God. Oh, my God, it hurts.* I grabbed his arms in reverence even as the pain made me gasp, my body bending to his will. I loved that he was tearing me apart, breaking me like no other man had. That I saved myself for this brutal, indestructible man and he chose *me.*

He's the only one that can make me feel this. The only one worthy.

Thomas inhaled sharply, adjusting my hips for a better fit.

Oh—I clung to him, tensing against the sharp ache.

"Do ye need me to stop?" he asked, pulling back just enough to look worriedly into my eyes.

"God, no. Please." I wrapped my arms around his neck and pulled him back to me, willing him to continue. "Please, Thomas."

He grunted, rolling his hips softly so that each glorious inch of him sank in. With one more slight thrust, I cried out as he took everything that I wanted to give him.

"Feckin' hell, gypsy," he gasped, his pace increasing as he began to lose the little restraint he had. "Ye feel so good."

My mouth popped open, trying to be silent as I wanted to scream. I watched his glorious body move over me, my legs up around his hips, my feet bouncing with each thrust, the way his muscles glistened in the setting sun, and his face scrunched in desire. My head fell back as I listened to his body smack against mine. It was then I started to relish the pain. I ran my fingers through his thick beard, liking how roguish it made him look.

My own personal beast, ravishing me in the woods.

"Thomas," I gasped. "God, Thomas. Don't stop." I wanted to tell him just how much I liked it and how wildly attractive he was, but I couldn't seem to get any more words out.

Thomas raised on his arms, staring down at my body, at where we were joined, and truly began to fuck me, making it so my body had no choice but to yield to him.

"Feck, gypsy. Ye are beautiful." He grunted, shoving into me harder, and I moaned. Lifting my hips, he picked up the pace, making me scream with each thrust, the tension building within me. Heat seared through my core, my muscles contracting tightly.

It was at that moment that I knew he'd break me completely. Because it was the moment my mind, body, and soul were completely his, and his mine. He lowered his mouth to my breast, and I whimpered.

Thomas pulled me upward and into his lap as he continued to move in me. *Oh—Oh, yes. Please.*

I draped my arms around his neck as we stared at each other and began to move with him, rewarding me with pure ecstasy crossing Thomas' features. Lowering my mouth to his, I bit his lower lip, causing a feral growl to erupt from his chest.

He flipped me over onto my stomach and pulled my hips upward, entering me from behind. I moaned so loud it rumbled through my entire body.

"Please, Thomas. Don't stop!"

"Not feckin' likely," he growled through his teeth.

I gasped, holding on to leaves or whatever I could find for purchase as he railed into me, and I became utterly undone by this glorious feeling. His strong hand pinned my shoulder to the ground as the other held my hips in place.

"Thomas," I gasped. He must have felt how close I was because he picked up his delectable, brutal pace, slamming into me until I saw stars. My body tightened around him, causing him to curse as my core squeezed painfully, and I had to bite his arm to keep from screaming.

"Feck!" he shouted. And with one more thrust, my orgasm erupted around him, quaking with pleasure as he convulsed into me. I let out a series of incoherent moans, unable to control any part of my body.

Thomas' arms found their way under my chest until his hands wrapped over my shoulders, his body pinning mine to the ground as he pumped roughly into me, finishing himself off. The sounds coming from his throat, rumbling from his chest, were so animalistic that they sent another wave of desire through me. *God, how can this ferocious man be mine?*

I whimpered, rotating my hips with his gentle thrusts. Thomas's muscles loosened slowly, and he rolled over to his side, pulling me with him so my back was pressed against his chest. His hands slid up and down my curves in a tantalizing caress.

"That was—" he began.

"Great," I finished.

He chuckled, pulling me closer. "I never experienced anything like it," he admitted.

"Never?" That was hard to believe.

"No."

"Not even with... her?" I almost choked on the question. Nessa had disappeared shortly after the Second Battle of Bull Run when she must have gotten word about Barton's demise. I felt more relief than I cared to admit now that I didn't have to worry about her advances towards Thomas, though I occasionally wondered where she disappeared. Was Nessa planning something? Or was she afraid of something—or someone—else?

His hand cupped my cheek, gently pulling my face to meet his gaze. "I never loved a woman before ye, Emilia. What we just did—" He shook his head, at a loss for words. "Ye gave me something no one else can have."

"I'm sorry if I did anything wrong," I said meekly. I hated myself then for being self-conscious and inexperienced. Clearly, this man needed a woman to ravage him, and I wasn't sure I did that. Though *I* felt utterly destroyed.

Thomas placed a gentle kiss on my lips. "Ye gave me everything, gypsy." He pressed his lips to my ear, making me shiver as he whispered, "I like that no man had ye. Call me selfish, but I want to teach ye everything. And I want to hear every noise no other man will hear from ye." His fingertips trailed up my side before grabbing my breast. I moaned, pushing into his touch. I couldn't believe that I already wanted more, even with how sore I was. "It was great," he continued. "And I plan to do it again as many times ye let me."

I bit my lip, finding my body already moving against his. "I'd like that."

He stilled my hips, pressing against me so I couldn't move. "Though I want to," he admitted, "Ye will regret it tomorrow. Ye need to heal, lass."

I twirled in his embrace, slightly surprised that the arrogant, beastly man allowed it and kissed him deeply. "I don't think so. I think it'll be rather worth it."

A deep chuckle rumbled through him, tingling my breasts pressed against his flesh.

I moaned, moving into him.

Thomas cursed and rolled onto his back, his body ready for me, and instructed me to get on. I lowered onto him slowly, wincing at the pain while rejoicing at the connection.

It was then Thomas taught me how to ride him. How to move the way he liked. And all the dirty things he wanted to call me as I learned all the ways I could move on top of him, my breasts bouncing with the movement and making him curse.

Thomas grunted his release as I screamed, curving over him in pure ecstasy.

After that, we watched the sun set into a soft, golden hue until even the edges of the fall leaves turned gold and shone off the still water. I couldn't have imagined a more beautiful scene for that moment.

"I love you so much it scares me," I whispered. Losing Thomas at the end of this whole journey, whether through the ravages of war or time travel, filled me with an overwhelming sense of fear.

I stared at the bracelet he made, unable to meet his gaze. It was the only thing on my body other than Thomas.

He pulled me closer, placing a kiss on my shoulder. "I didn't know what love was until I met ye. Not truly. Ye made me feel everything I hid inside for so many years. Ye opened me eyes, gypsy, and I will spend the rest of my life thanking ye for that."

As if to drive his point home, he lowered himself and made soft, sweet love to me until the sun disappeared over the horizon, and we lost ourselves in one another under the cover of the moon.

CHAPTER TWENTY-FOUR

Thomas

December 1862

Thomas watched as a few of the boys, and Emilia downed some Applejack brandy they had found in a raid, distracting themselves from the winter's biting cold and the next day's battle.

Their company spent the fall finally joining Meagher's Irish Brigade, becoming the "Fourth Irish Regiment." With it, the winter stormed in strong, sending Emilia into Thomas's shelter tent for warmth nearly every night. They told themselves it was to keep from freezing, but they almost always ended up embraced in one another's arms. Clothes were still on, only bearing what was necessary as their hands covered their mouths to keep the camp from hearing their quiet love-making. It was usually quick and with little foreplay, but there were some nights they could take their time when the temperature didn't threaten to kill them, and Thomas could teach Emilia just what she could do with that fine body. *Christ*, what he could do with her in a warm bed and some damn privacy. He didn't dare think about it long.

Come November, the other men began to feel the effects of the cold, propelling them to start building log houses for each company. Thomas was thankful for the warmth of those buildings, but not as much as he missed Emilia in his arms. Maybe it was God's way of keeping their relationship from discovery.

His relief didn't last long. When December came, they were called to help Major General Burnside—the Union's new commander—to push the secesh back toward Richmond. They left their new shelters behind and made their way to Fredericksburg.

They camped on the edge of the Rappahannock River, having spent days building bridges to get to the Confederate forces stationed on the other side, just outside of Fredericksburg, as the rebels shot at them through the thinning fog. Men fell and were replaced by others until the bridges were finished. Their screams as they tumbled to their demise would haunt him for weeks to come.

Some men of the 7th Michigan steeled themselves to take boats across, all the while being shot at as they made it to the other side. Those who had survived stormed into Fredericksburg and began to drive the Confederates out of town. The destruction of the city could be heard from miles away. Houses and stores alike were reduced to rubble. The Union soldiers didn't take long to loot everything they could easily carry.

The next morning, they found themselves waiting to cross the river into Fredericksburg. Thomas pulled his coat tighter against the cold night, mildly amused as Emilia stumbled to him. It was a nice distraction from the wound-ed men and preparations for battle.

"*We are the boys who take delight, in smashing Limerick lamps at night,*" she sang. The band had started it up when they walked through the camp earlier in the day, and the boys kept singing it. It seemed the alcohol had taken away her singing inhibitions. Thomas pulled the bottle out of her hand.

"Hey!" Emilia exclaimed.

"Ye had enough," he scolded, leaning in to whisper, "And your disguise is slipping. No more drink."

To his relief, she straightened and tried to sober up. She hadn't lost herself to alcohol since the night she met her father. It spoke volumes of her nerves, though he wasn't sure why this battle bothered her more than the others. Maybe it was what they had done earlier in the week...

Thomas lifted the bottle to his lips and drank deeply, his heart soaring at the memory—the shock, how he had never experienced such a sense of wholeness. It had been reckless, crazy, and impossible. But they'd done it.

"I hear a doctor and his wife stayed in their home in that blasted city," Sullivan said, pulling Thomas out of the memory. "He helped the wounded on both sides. Can ye believe that? A rebel helping our men. And staying when the world was crumbling around them. He's got balls, I gotta admit that."

"Their house wasn't destroyed?" Thomas asked.

Sullivan shook his head. "When our boys went to investigate, some fiery lass came out wielding a rifle. When they didn't back down, she shot into the air." Sullivan took another swig, a smile plain on his face. "Guess they didn't think it was worth contendin' her."

"Never underestimate a woman." Thomas leaned back and shut his eyes. "There's no stopping 'em when they fight for something they believe in."

"Oh, aye?" Sullivan laughed. "Ye've been actin' strange. Ye've only been with that red-headed spit-fire once, and ye say things like that. It's almost like—" Sullivan stopped, and Thomas cracked his eye open to find his friend with his mouth half open. "Do ye have a woman, Tommy?" Sullivan quickly shook his head, as if ridding himself of the absurdity of it, and laughed. "Forget I asked."

"What's so funny if he did?" Emilia asked, thankfully in her fake accent.

Thomas stiffened, suddenly wanting to leave.

"Ye serious?" Sullivan leaned in to slap a hand onto Thomas's shoulder. "Being his cousin, ye must know our Tommy boy likes his women. He wouldn't do something as stupid as tying himself to a lass. Besides, Tommy is too busy fighting the good fight to bother with women." He jabbed an elbow into Thomas's side. "Other than for a little rumble in the sheets, that is."

Emilia snorted. "Oh, really?" She turned to Thomas with raised brows.

"I'm surprised he didn't tell ye how much he abhorred marriage." Sullivan went on, oblivious to the amusement dancing in Emilia's eyes.

"Enough," Thomas growled before Emilia said something in her intoxication.

"Relax, boyo. We're just havin' some good fun," Sullivan said, slapping a hand on Thomas's back.

Thomas couldn't figure out why it bothered him, but he had the sudden urge to tell Sullivan the truth. Well, maybe not the whole truth, but surely some of it. "I have a woman," he admitted, feeling Emilia's attention zero in on him. "Back home. As long as she'll have me, she's it for me."

Sullivan's mouth opened and closed comically, reminding Thomas of a fish. "Why didn't ye tell me?"

"Didn't want to hear ye gripe about it for ages."

The smile on Emilia's face was worth it. He should have told the men ages ago.

The night wore on, and though Emilia had begun to sober up, a paleness about her troubled him as she retired, complaining her stomach hurt. Thomas's own stomach tightened with worry. Was she unwell? Or should he have asked her permission to tell Sullivan? He hadn't mentioned her name, but maybe... No. He shook his head. She seemed happy about it at the time. Something else had to be bothering her.

Thomas watched Emilia disappear into the tent, wishing he could read her mind.

"Eamonn can't handle the drink, can he?" Sullivan grinned. "I caught him hurling his guts out the other day. Ye probably should keep him away from the stuff."

Thomas's head snapped to his friend. "What did ye say?"

"He vomited behind some bushes. I walked up on him. Said he had a stomach bug. He didn't mention it to ye?"

Thomas's gaze returned to the tent, wanting to peel the layers back until he received an answer. "No, he didn't."

Sullivan grunted, turning to another man, already bored with the conversation.

Thomas stared at the tent for a long time. Emilia said she hadn't bled for months before they laid with one another—a lack of nutrition and excessive exercise could do that to a woman, she said. Emilia couldn't have a babe in her. Besides, she would have told him.

Unless she didn't know?

Impossible. Thomas blinked, eyes feeling like sandpaper, and downed the rest of the bottle. He waited for the rest of the men to slowly disappear until he made his way to her tent. She was nestled in her blanket, only her nose poking out into the cold when he lied down and pulled her close. Emilia sighed contentedly, her body relaxing in his arms as his hand caressed her flat stomach.

A part of him wished they weren't in the war—somewhere safe, in a home they had made together as a babe grew within her. It was a wistful dream but one he had longed for quite some time now. He hadn't told her that, not wanting to distract or hear that she might not desire it. Knowing that what they were fighting for far exceeded their personal desires, he could confine that wish in his mind for now.

And yet, he couldn't stop himself from wishing this war would end, and she would stay.

Sleep evaded Thomas until the dawn of battle.

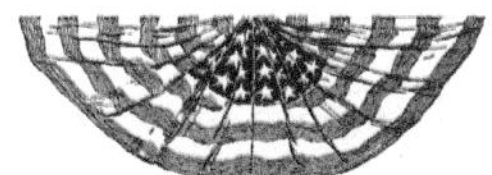

The Irish Brigade had crossed the river, sprigs of green boxwood in their caps to represent their unit. Walking through Fredericksburg, Thomas tried not to feel anything for these people. They were the ones who'd seceded. They wanted this war. So why did the broken storefronts and shattered homes have such an effect on him? Why did his gut clench at the sight of their furniture and belongings littering the streets? For just a moment, he wished he could be as callous as his brother.

Wounded men lay in the streets, waiting for medical attention or maybe a place in one of the houses. The surgeons were already working on men, blood soaking the front of them and up to the elbows of their shirtsleeves. A woman stood on the porch of a two-story house, pulling her shawl tighter as she watched them walk by, ignoring the men who came and went from the home. Thomas's eyes met hers; the hardness in their dark depths sent a jolt through him—an awareness that can only be shared between kindred spirits.

A surgeon had walked up behind her, coated in blood but wearing ordinary clothes rather than the blue uniform of the Union surgeons, and familiarly bent down to say something into her ear. Thomas wondered if it was the secesh doctor Sullivan had been talking about the previous night. Was she the fiery woman with the rifle? With a slender build and caramel ringlets framing her angular face, she didn't look like it. But the look in her eye told him she wasn't a lass to be messed with. A jolt of respect for her must have shown on his face, surprising them both.

He looked away. Without a word, Thomas knew she was a woman just as fierce as Emilia.

The city dwindled out behind them, and they walked through the trees, crossing wooden planks to get to the other side of a creek. Thomas's hands tightened on the rifle as Meagher—in his sharp green jacket embroidered with silver stars and black knots on his shoulders—put them in the middle of the brigade, their green flag billowing in the cold breeze as they waited to join the battle.

Emilia made a strangled noise when she saw the carnage in front of them. Up the hill, bodies piled up, blown apart by canisters and mutilated by bullets. Her arm pressed to Thomas's—she shook so severely that she had trouble holding still.

"If something happens to me," he said quietly, "ye save yourself."

She looked up at him, shock widening her brown eyes. "Thomas—"

"Do ye understand me?" he snapped. "Hide under the bodies, run—do whatever ye must to survive. But. Do. Not. Falter." He let each word fall like an anvil, praying their force would drive her to safety even if he could not. "Promise me."

She nodded, facing straight with tears in her eyes.

"Promise me!" he growled, making her flinch.

"I promise." Her shaking stopped, and it scared him more than when she was frightened. "But you have to promise to do the same."

He shook his head. "I cannot. There is no life without ye in it."

"Then I guess I'll do whatever it takes as well."

Thomas's jaw hardened as he bit back his protests. He knew there was no arguing about it.

They watched the Confederates shoot over their stone wall, dropping federal men all across the hill. It felt like an eternity, and yet, it was all too soon when the Irish Brigade was called to march forward. They advanced as bullets whizzed past them, almost as loud as the blood ringing in Thomas's ears.

Men began to go down in waves before them, slowing their progression up the already dangerous hill. They prepared their rifles, counting each step to load them, *one—two—three*. Closer, they could see the Confederates as more men fell. *Seven, eight, nine—shoot!* The recoil of the rifle shook through his body. Whether he hit one of them, he didn't know.

More steps. Reload. Shoot.

A loud boom pierced Thomas's eardrums and rocked him on his heels, throwing the men around him in different directions. Thomas's knee hit the ground as his hand grabbed Emilia's arm, hauling them up.

A bloody massacre, Thomas seethed.

She shouted at him, but he could only see her mouth moving before she pulled him to the side, away from the line of fire—if that was even possible. Bullets and shrapnel seemed to come from every direction. They crouched down, using the piles of bodies for cover.

Still, the 28th Massachusetts pushed on, past other units, and faced the enemy head-on. The Confederates hid behind their stonewall, shooting over it with little delay. More men started dropping around them as Thomas's heart thundered in his chest. Emilia pushed on, ashen but determined.

"Blaze away and stand it, boys!" Major James Cavanaugh shot ahead.

The men pushed on, using what they could to hide while sending off another round of fire. They carried forward against all odds. Fifty yards away from the wall, Major Cavanaugh was shot in the thigh.

Another loud boom exploded next to Thomas, throwing him to the side and on top of Emilia as the man next to him and the men behind started screaming. A leg was by Thomas, its owner lying somewhere in the mass of other bodies.

Holy shite. That could have been us.

"This way," Thomas yelled, but Emilia was still stumbling forward, no doubt as deaf as him. *Feck.* Another volley of shots rang out, and Thomas grabbed her arm, pulling her down.

A man with a hole through his forehead stared at Thomas vacantly. Thomas sent up a silent prayer for the fallen soldier as he rolled him on his side, propping him up as a shield for him and Emilia to hide behind until they could cover more ground.

His heart pounded as he looked her over, but he found no wounds. "Are ye all right?" he screamed, but she only nodded, reading his lips.

It seemed like hours—maybe it was—when Meagher came barreling in on a horse. "Two lines, men!" He straightened their ranks. "Load and fire at will!"

Smoke hung over the field like a morbid blanket covering the fallen in their eternal rest. The stench of gunpowder coated his nostrils as his feet slid on the wet grass, drenched with blood. It took everything for Thomas to stand in those lines as his instincts screamed for him to break formation. They should be taking cover somewhere Emilia wasn't in the line of fire. Picking the Confederates off from a better vantage point, not sending themselves to be slaughtered.

The men over the hill called out in accents familiar from home. They were picking off their own Irishmen, damn it. They survived the famine and the voyage over to a new land only to stand on opposite sides and kill each other. *Feckin' hell.*

A shell exploded, and chaos ensued. Men yelled that Meagher was hit somewhere on the field ahead; he was thrown off his horse and shot in the leg. As he was carried away, Thomas pulled Emilia farther to the side. They stumbled to a slope, hoping not to be hit by any projectiles.

There was a small brick house on the slope, men already using it as cover. If they could get there, they might have some respite before returning to the fight. Emilia pointed in a different direction where other men piled up wooden fence posts from rebels picket posts. The distance was closer, but Thomas didn't like the odds of staying behind it. They would be trapped.

Thomas shook his head. "The house," he yelled. "Better odds."

Emilia swallowed but pushed on. They left others behind them who chose to openly shoot at the rebels until they ran out of ammunition or perished. While running in a half crouch, a blast exploded behind them, sending grass, soil, and body parts all around.

"Fall back!"

The plea rolled through the ranks, but to do so could be more dangerous than finding a different position. Thomas looked to Emilia. *It's too risky.* Maybe if it was just him, but in no way would he put her in more danger.

Screw the bloody command.

"We can't," she said, voicing his thoughts. "Let's go to the house."

Thomas scanned the wall, watching the enemy pop over it to take down more of his men. Rage boiled inside of him, and he took another shot that went straight through a man's chest. He toppled over the wall.

Emilia tugged Thomas's sleeve, pleading for him to move out of the line of fire. They crouched, running as fast as they could with so many bodies in their way.

Thomas looked at the wall to find a cannon turning their way.

"Get down!" Thomas screamed, throwing himself to the ground.

For a split second, his cap blocked his vision, and he struggled to push it back, impeded by the rifle and men lying around him. To his horror, Emilia wasn't by him, and as he looked up, he found her several yards away, turning in search of him. Their eyes locked, and she must have seen the terror on his face because her eyes widened in reciprocated fear.

Time slowed as he took in every detail of her beautiful face. His arms lifted him off the ground without his knowledge, and as he took a step toward her, an explosion rang out, sending him flying backward in a cloud of smoke and debris.

CHAPTER TWENTY-FIVE

Thomas

Ringing. A buzzing like a thousand bees went off in his head.

Thomas coughed, smoke filling his lungs as he rolled over. Eyes burning, he tried to blink through the gunpowder. He pushed himself up only to stumble forward, barely catching himself before propelling himself onward. The sounds of battle were muted only under the piercing ringing in his ears.

How long had he been unconscious? He blinked again, his eyes still foggy as he searched the hill and tripped over a severed arm. He stumbled but pushed forward.

"Emilia!" he screamed, voice hoarse and distorted to his ears.

Thomas began to roll the bodies over. A face missing the lower half of the jaw sent him reeling back. He didn't care that they were still shooting at him or that the blood soaked into the knees of his pants and up to his wrists.

Men were still using bodies as cover, too afraid to get up. They tugged on his sleeves, but he ignored them, unable to hear their pleas. He reached a depression where a cannon tore it apart. Crawling across it, he froze, his heart dropping. *Jesus, Mary, and Joseph. Please. Please let her live.*

There was so much blood smeared across her face, but the slope of her nose and the slight angled cheekbones were undeniable. Thomas prayed to see her eyes light up for him again. For her mouth to tilt upward in a smile.

Chest tight with terror, he reached her, his hands anxiously looking for any injuries. Her hair was matted, her cap gone, and her jacket was torn to shreds, exposing part of a breast. Thomas pulled away from her to see the damage done to her body. It looked like shrapnel had penetrated her right side, tearing through her shoulder and breast. He lifted the bottom of her shirt and saw jagged, albeit minor, wounds along her stomach.

Thomas quickly tried to cover her back up, not wanting to expose her to any man who might be paying attention. He pulled Emilia toward his chest, cradling her head in his hand to find blood seeping through her hair as well. Thomas inhaled sharply, squeezing tighter as if he could heal her with his desperation.

"Wake up, gypsy," he prayed, beginning to rock as if it would somehow help. *Please, Father, if ye ever do anything for me, let it be to save her. I beg of ye.* Thomas had seen enough death in his life but experienced nothing like this. "Ye can't leave me now."

He had enough clarity to draw her arm to him. His fingers fumbled at first but found a pulse. Faint, but a pulse.

Thomas finally exhaled and took in his surroundings. The enemy wasn't letting up. They were closer to the brick house, but he would have to run while carrying Emilia. He took another deep breath. There was no clear path. Bodies were in heaps across the field. He would have to navigate around them without getting shot.

With a growl of frustration, Thomas picked Emilia in one smooth heave and began running, head bent over her, using his body to protect her. Thomas ran through the fallen, focused solely on his mission to get to safety.

A musket ball grazed his arm but didn't puncture it. He bared his teeth and kept going when another ball pierced his shoulder. He roared, cursing the rebels in every language he knew, but didn't falter. There was no stopping him when it came to Emilia. Not when they were so close.

He bounded over the last body and reached the clearing leading up to the house. Thomas rounded the back and nearly collapsed.

"Tommy?" a familiar voice called out. Thomas ignored it as he set Emilia down gently, rechecking her pulse. She was still breathing. Thomas slid down the bricks, resting his head back as he tried to regain energy.

"Ye've been hit." Sullivan appeared in front of him, his hands checking Thomas's shoulder.

"I'm fine," Thomas mumbled, unsuccessfully pushing Sullivan away.

"Ye aren't," he hissed, pushing Thomas forward. "It looks like it went through the back. Ye are damn lucky. Who would ye risk your life—" He turned towards the body on the ground. "Is that—" Sullivan paused, getting a better look at Emilia, understanding crossed his features. "Oh, Tommy. What have ye done?"

"Don't tell the others. They can't know." Thomas' hand tightened on the dagger at his belt. He didn't want to kill his friend, but he would do it to save Emilia.

"Are ye telling me Eamonn is—" he paused, taking off his jacket.

"What are ye doing?" Thomas tried to push himself up.

"Sit down, ye damn fool." Sullivan looked around, and finding no one paying attention to them, took Emilia's coat off and replaced it with his. "That should do for now."

Thomas let go of the dagger, relief and a wave of exhaustion overcoming him. "What of ye?"

"I'll be fine."

Thomas tried to shrug out of his. "Take mine."

"No. Tell me why, Tommy. Is she even your cousin? I should have known by your half-assed story."

"Emilia." Thomas watched her take another breath, and he sighed. It was a small reassurance, but a welcome one. "That's her name. It is her own story to tell. She's changed me." Thomas shook his head as a weight of fear pressed down on him. "If she dies, I don't know if I'll survive it."

"She's the lass ye were talking about?"

"Aye."

They both stared at Emilia, watching her chest rise and fall.

"Ye have to take her to a doctor," Sullivan admitted reluctantly. "There'll be consequences, Tommy. But without medical care, I don't know how long..."

"I know."

Sullivan took in Thomas's tense jaw and closed fists and turned back to Emilia, thinking. "I have an idea."

Thomas raised a brow for him to explain.

"It's probably unwise, but I don't see any other choice."

"I've done a lot of stupid things in me life. Spit it out, Sullivan."

"Ye could try to take her to that physician in town. If ye can make it there without dying, that is."

Thomas sat straight and did his best to ignore the pain in his shoulder.

That might work. It'll be damn hard, but if I can get Emilia out without exposing her...

"Ye are a damn genius."

Sullivan sat back on his heels and ran a hand down his face, mumbling in Irish about a crazy bastard. "Listen. Ye stay close to the pickets and head back the way the others retreated. I will do me best to cover your back."

Thomas went to Emilia, already going over the plan in his head. He turned back to Sullivan. "Thank ye. I'll forever be indebted to ye."

"If ye survive—" Sullivan tried to smile, but it came out strained "—I'll take ye up on that. Now go."

Before Thomas could say anything else, Sullivan grabbed his rifle and went around the side of the house, positioning himself between the enemy and his friend.

Thomas hoisted Emilia up, careful not to jostle her head, and gritted his teeth against the sharp pain tearing through his shoulder. Without a glance back, fully trusting Sullivan to have his back, he ran along the fence line as fast as he could.

Less bodies littered the perimeter; still, Thomas had to navigate around some, wasting precious time. Shots still rang out across the field, cannons booming in the distance. He had no way of knowing if Sullivan was one of the men shooting, only that no bullet tore through his flesh. For that, he was grateful. He sent out a silent thank you to God for his protection and Sullivan's help.

Thomas bounded down the creek, crossed the planks as fast as his legs could take him, and kept running well past the battle. Emilia's shallow breaths propelled him to move faster. She hadn't opened her eyes yet, and that scared the hell out of him.

He finally reached the edge of the city. Horse-drawn ambulances rumbled along the streets, carrying dozens of wounded, taken to doctors who might not get to them in time.

"Oi! You there!" someone yelled. Thomas's head snapped to the short man, quickly deciding he wasn't a threat. Still, he turned a corner, going down another street that wasn't teaming with soldiers.

He jogged, holding Emilia's head to him so as not to hurt her more. His breaths seesawed in and out of his lungs as he scanned the large houses and storefronts. If he remembered correctly, the house he was looking for was just a few streets farther.

The clip of a horse's hooves sounded behind him, and he ducked behind one of the houses, using a large wood pile for cover. They might not look suspicious, but he didn't want to take the chance of someone guiding him to the wrong hospital. Besides, it was a good time to give himself a break. Thomas kept a firm hold of Emilia and used the crouched position to transfer some of her weight to his legs.

The threat passed, and Thomas straightened even when his body screamed to stop. Still, he made it to the white, modest, two-story house without any more obstacles. If he went around the front, he knew he would find the large porch the woman had stood upon. Thomas paused, looking around the side of the house. No one was in sight, but Thomas wouldn't take the chance of being spotted and went up the back steps instead.

His knuckles skimmed the oak before stopping at the last second, not wanting to draw attention to himself. Thomas shuffled Emilia farther into his arms and tried the knob.

The door swung open on silent hinges, opening up to a vestibule. Voices carried back from the front parlors. Immediately through the doorframe to Thomas's left, a set of servant stairs led up to the second story and, just past that, the kitchen. Straight ahead was a long hallway that held more stairs for the family and now any soldier and doctor on the premises. The wounded lay on any flat surface and space of floor that didn't prevent the surgeons from walking.

"These men have been through enough, don't you say?" a distant male voice startled Thomas out of his quick inspection. "The general is sending these men to be butchered."

Thomas peered into the kitchen and found a woman working there. With her back towards him, he wondered if she was a slave or servant and watched as hot steam from the pots billowed around her dark hair. He didn't wait for her to turn around and went immediately up the back stairs, trying his best not to step on any loose floorboards—a remarkable feat under both of their weight.

Set Emilia somewhere safe. Find the doctor. Talk to him so no one can overhear. It felt like a constant chant in Thomas' mind, his mission consuming every part of his existence.

If someone Thomas knew or a surgeon who worked for the Twenty-Eighth learned of this, it would wreak havoc on Emilia's reputation and quite possibly send her to prison—a fate Thomas wouldn't tempt.

Thomas knew of only one surgeon who dared to assist both Union and Confederate soldiers, a man—Thomas assumed—whose allegiance was to his profession rather than any political cause. He was their only hope and would either help a female soldier in need or be persuaded...forcefully.

The second story led to a small bath. To his right was a nursery, empty of children and replaced with soldiers lying in all positions. God, the smell of the festering wounds and unwashed men nearly knocked him on his arse. Missing limbs and bullet wounds plagued them. One man looked at him with one eye, half of his face covered in linen as blood started to soak through where his other had been.

Thomas turned left into one of the bed chambers, following the floral carpet that he imagined must have been magnificent before the trample of soldier's boots soiled the vibrant colors. Even so, he had never been in a house so grand.

Thomas ignored the resentment forming in the pit of his stomach and set Emilia on the soft bed, not caring that her clothes would soil the comforter. Other men filled the room, but it looked like they tried to spare the bed.

The faint click of a pistol made Thomas freeze.

"How did you get in here?" a woman asked in a harsh southern drawl.

Thomas raised his hands. "Turn around slowly."

He turned to see the same woman from the porch that morning, but now her narrowed eyes and pinched mouth were filled with mistrust aimed at him. She scrutinized Thomas with a quiet fortitude that told him she wouldn't take any shite.

"Please," Thomas pleaded, doing his best to look innocent as he assessed whether or not he could get to her without being shot. It looked like it was the only weapon on her person, but surely enough to stop him. "I must ask ye a favor. Is your husband the physician?"

"Why haven't you gone to your surgeons? They have been bringing your men to John, and I didn't see them bring you in." Her eyes narrowed. "Are you stealing these poor soldier's possessions?"

"What?" Thomas recoiled, insulted. "No. They can't know I'm here."

Her eyes—the most magnificent shade of caramel and so much like Hiram's that Thomas felt a pang of melancholy—scanned over him, stopping on his shoulder covered in blood. He didn't know what she saw, but her demeanor didn't soften.

"Most of it isn't mine," he admitted.

"What?" Her eyes returned to his, startled.

"The blood. It's from the others. Only me shoulder is hurt."

"Is that why you came here? Surely, an honest approach would have been easier than sneaking about."

"No." Thomas swallowed, gauging whether he could trust her or not. She gripped the pistol tighter, but it didn't stop him from seeing her hands shake. "I came for her." Thomas took a step to the side and guided a hand to Emilia on the bed.

"Her?" The woman's brows lowered in confusion, looking at Emilia's broken body. Curious, she lowered the pistol and went to the bed. The woman's small demeanor surprised Thomas, her feisty disposition tricked the mind into thinking she was bigger. Gently moving Emilia's jacket to the side, she gasped, and let the jacket fall closed.

"The reason I can't go to our surgeons, ma'am," Thomas said quietly, aware that some men were watching the scene. The others were conveniently unconscious or delirious. "Do ye think your husband could help her?"

The woman gently pushed Emilia's hair off her forehead as a mother would. "How did this happen?"

"She's a soldier, ma'am. Goes by the name Eamonn. She's me—" He swallowed, rethinking what he was about to say "—the lass who owns me heart. I would gladly switch places with her if it were at all possible. I'm afraid it was me fault she was injured. I should've grabbed her when I saw the cannon. I did every other time..." he drifted off and took a steadying breath, realizing he was rambling. "Please," he begged. He told himself long ago that he'd never beg for anything again, but the words fell quickly from his lips now. "Save her. They can't know she's not a man. I don't know what they'd do to her."

When she looked up at him, he was shocked to find tears filling her eyes. She seemed so formidable...

It only lasted a moment, so fast that he thought he'd imagined it, when she straightened her shoulders and asked him his name and where he was from. She nodded at his answer and began grabbing clean linen stored in one of the drawers to wrap around Emilia's wounds.

"I am Miriam Ward," she said as she worked. "I'm afraid of her losing too much blood. You were right in coming here. I believe John will help, but it cannot be here. He'll need to assess her wounds to see if it's even worth—" She stopped, seeing the devastation on his face, and began lining Emilia's torso again. "I'll go get him." She assessed the wounds once more, apparently satisfied they weren't soaking through the linen. "Please, sit down. Try to look like you belong in this room."

That should be easy, Thomas thought. He was half in the grave as it was. His whole body shuddered as if groaning its protests as he lowered himself to the ground.

Emilia wasn't bleeding out, but she hadn't woken up yet, which troubled him. Though he took comfort that her breaths were consistent, albeit shallow.

Thomas did his best to look like a patient, yet he couldn't keep his fingers from weaving through Emilia's. In some way, he hoped she knew he was there, holding her to this world.

He squeezed Emilia's hand tighter. What was taking so long?

"C'mon, gypsy," he whispered, not wanting the others to hear. "Ye have to wake up."

She didn't move. Not one flutter that told him she had heard. Her skin was so pale.

Heaven above, save her.

Thomas rested a hand on her head to reassure himself that she hadn't already grown cold. "I should have talked ye out of this. Ye fought bravely, but I can't help but think I should've had ye go home anyway. Ye are just so goddamn stubborn." He sighed, frustrated. "I guess ye are like me in that way."

A man lying on the floor caught his eye, and Thomas froze. They stared at each other momentarily, and Thomas reached for his knife. The man shook his head. "Can I pray for ye?" His voice came out raw and weak as if he'd lost his voice out on the battlefield.

Thomas noticed that the man's arm was missing but otherwise intact. Mud obscured his features, hiding his identity and age. "Ye should save your prayers for yourself," Thomas said, his head falling back against the wall as the rest of his energy left him. "But I thank ye."

"Then for her?" The man jerked his chin towards Emilia. "If ye are honest, she fought valiantly for us. I wouldn't feel right if I didn't at least try."

Thomas nodded, and the man began to pray. A calm fell over the room as the conscious men listened. They needed more of this to drown out the chaos around them.

The only warning was a set of footsteps in the hall, and the man fell silent. Indiscernible whispers outside the door, the only noise besides the cries of pain downstairs. Thomas rested his head against the wall but couldn't bring himself to take his hand away.

A thin man came through the room, drying his hands on a towel as if he just washed them. Miriam took quick steps right behind him. The doctor's kind brown eyes instantly landed on Emilia. Thomas stood quickly.

"Mr. O'Connor," Miriam said softly, stepping back from his tall figure, though her husband was only a few inches shorter than himself. "This is my husband, John."

John immediately began looking at Emilia's wounds as he talked. "I would shake your hand, sir, but I'd rather not dirty them again." He looked up quickly, aware of the offense. "I didn't mean—"

"It's fine," Thomas said gruffly. Emilia had taught him about sterilization and infection and made sure to remind him to clean his wounds, even when the doctors didn't see it as a necessity. It impressed him that this doctor took precautions, allowing Thomas to breathe a little easier. "Just save her."

Thomas never felt so helpless as he watched the doctor clean her wounds. He found a large piece of shrapnel in her side that he was able to remove. If it was just a mere inch to the right, it would have pierced her large intestine, increasing her chances of infection. That was the worst of it along her abdomen, the others going no further than the flesh.

"To be honest, I'm more concerned about this injury here," John admitted, probing the back of Emilia's head.

"Why?" Thomas asked, searching Emilia's face. "It's small. Shouldn't it heal quickly?"

The doctor sighed and straightened. "I'm more worried about what happened to her brain. If she doesn't wake soon—"

"She'll wake," Thomas growled, stepping towards him.

Miriam placed a small hand on Thomas's arm. He glowered at the doctor but waited for him to finish.

"She might wake, but I won't know the damage until then. She has been unconscious for how long now?" When Thomas told him a few hours, the doctor's face tightened. "We'll assess the situation *when* she wakes. In the meantime, I'd like to close up the wounds."

"Maybe we should do it at home, John," Miriam whispered, glancing at the few men watching them.

"If ye think it's best, doctor," the man who had prayed on the floor spoke up. "Ye should do it here. I don't mean to interfere." His eyes flicked between the doctor and his wife. "I just don't want to see the lass injured even more. We'll keep quiet. Won't we, boys?"

The others muttered their agreeance.

"Good," John said and started digging in his bag. "Let's just pray that I finish before one of your surgeons walks in."

"Is that clean?" Thomas asked when he saw the needle the doctor pulled out. He didn't know if he believed in germs, but what Emilia had told him about sterilization made sense in its own way. Healthy men fell sick all the time after injuries. He didn't want to take the chance with her and told the doctor as much.

Once Thomas painstakingly ensured every instrument was clean, he allowed John to treat her. The doctor didn't seem the least bit annoyed by Thomas's insistence and listened to everything Thomas told him with interest and respect. Something the army surgeons often lacked, in Thomas's opinion.

After arguing and nearly threatening to shoot Thomas himself, Miriam persuaded him to allow her to treat his shoulder as long as he could stay by Emilia. When she was done stitching him up and wrapping a sling to support his arm, Miriam brought a carriage around the back. Apparently, this wasn't their house, and they thought it would be safer to keep Emilia there.

Miriam came up the stairs, winded but with a healthy flush of exertion in her cheeks just as the doctor finished with Emilia. It looked as if his wife was actually enjoying this. Her eyes gleamed with a newfound determination that had been absent before. *Is the lass a bit unhinged?*

"John, why don't you ensure the surgeons stay occupied downstairs. I will go with Mr. O'Connor here." Thomas raised his brows at her commands, wondering if her husband was used to it.

The doctor looked ready to refuse, but to his credit, he considered it and agreed. John turned towards Thomas. "I trust you'll ensure no harm comes to my wife?"

"Aye, sir." Thomas held his hand out, and John took it firmly. "I can't thank ye enough for all ye've done."

"I'll be there as soon as I finish my work here. Do your best to keep her head protected. As it is, I would rather not move her."

Miriam stepped forward. "We can't have them finding her."

John sighed, looking at his wife with exasperation but so much love that it made Thomas shift on his feet uncomfortably. Something told Thomas that this happened often. "Yes, dear. I understand the threat. I was merely speaking my professional opinion."

She patted John's arm and gave him a sweet smile before turning to Thomas. "Let's get goin' before the rooster crows."

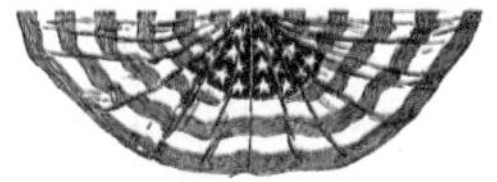

Thomas watched the light from the lantern flicker across Emilia's face when the front door closed and voices echoed through the floorboards. Thomas looked up, surprised to find that night had fallen around them. He belatedly remembered Miriam leaving a lantern earlier but was so absorbed in his worries that he didn't mind it.

Their carriage ride went without a hitch, though every jostle made him tense up and hold Emilia so that her head didn't receive any impact. They made it across town to a brick house that had not received the damage many others had. A dark-skinned man answered the door with a rifle. He must have been defending the house against looters. Unlike so many others, it would have explained why their home was intact.

The man stepped to the side as an older, heavy-set slave guided them. Her dark eyes rounded at the sight of Emilia in Thomas's arms, though she went into motion without question. Thomas watched Miriam treat her as an equal, and his eyes narrowed.

What was this southern woman playing at? And the doctor, treating the enemy as their own. There was something off about these people. They were the direct opposite of how he imagined Southerners. The few he had met often treated his friends with disrespect and cruel intentions, bred in a society of hatred and ill contempt. And yet, Miriam and John made him question what he thought, or rather that not all Southerners shared the same beliefs and prejudices. That, maybe, not all of them were bad. Just like he didn't always share the same biases as his people. It was enlightening to see, and it rocked Thomas onto his heels.

Miriam guided him to a room on the second floor, where a bed had been readied. She eyed Thomas. "I will need you to leave the room," she said, holding a sponge and bucket.

Thomas refused, holding his ground.

"It is quite indecent—"

"I know her body more than the lass knows it herself," Thomas snapped, earning a glare from Miriam. "She is as much mine as I am hers," he continued. "I will not leave her now." He reached for the sponge, and Miriam relented, helping him remove Emilia's uniform before cleaning Emilia. Together, they removed as much dirt and blood as they could before gently wrestling a nightgown on her.

Through it all, Emilia slept, eyes moving under her lids as if searching for something.

Look at me, gypsy, he thought, his whole body screaming for her to open her damn eyes. After a few moments of waiting, a loud sigh escaped him. For a moment, he believed he could will her to wake, that what they had could somehow magically fix her.

Feckin' hell.

He should've known anyone who came close to him would get hurt. He'd told her as much, yet he selfishly kept the lass and allowed himself to be happy. To love. And now look what happened. *Hold on, gypsy. For the love of God, just…hold on.*

Now, hours later, the hushed voices had Thomas pushing himself out of the rocker and creeping to the door. He cracked it and placed his ear closer to better hear.

"She can't stay here, Miriam." The doctor's voice was strained. "She's a federal soldier and a woman no less. She'll have to go back to her own people."

"Don't tell me you're suddenly rooting for the other side."

"Of course not. But the reality is we *are* living in the South, and if they were to come here—"

"We agreed to move here under the agreement that we'd try to do more. We freed slaves; we provided a safe house for anyone seeking freedom. You wanted it as much as I did. Now, this woman needs help, and you're a physician. Let her recover here, and we'll send her on her way."

"It's not so easy."

"You didn't turn me away."

"That's different." His tone took on a wary edge.

"What? She's not a whore?"

Thomas's eyes widened. What was the woman implying? He suddenly felt as if he should stop listening.

"She is most definitely colored," Miriam continued, "though not as noticeably as the negresses, I must admit. How is that any different from me? My light skin is the only reason we were able to marry. We moved to four states before settling down somewhere they wouldn't recognize me. I'm not asking you to marry the woman, for God's sake. Her case should be simple compared to what we've been through. Pray tell me the difference between her and me?"

Thomas's mind raced with all of this information. Miriam was an African? Thomas had met light-skinned Africans, but she had fooled him completely. What she accomplished was more than impressive. It was extraordinary. He suddenly wanted to tell Hiram, knowing this would interest his friend.

"Keep your voice down," John muttered. It was evident in his tone that he had resigned. "You are my wife, Miriam. That is the difference."

"I wasn't then. I was just a sixteen-year-old runaway who had a bad abortion at the brothel. You didn't turn me away then. You took me in. Healed me."

"A better man would have set you free."

"Free?" A loud bang, like a hand hitting the table, caused Thomas to stiffen. "I was already damn well free. You treated me as a lady for the first time in my life. It took years for you to marry me. I will not apologize for falling in love with you, John. If you think that—"

"You know that is not what I meant!" He growled. "You know I married you out of love and not necessity. You would do more than I ever could without you." A short pause. "We will keep her until she's well enough to leave; then, she'll be on the first train north."

"Thank you."

He sighed. "Did I even have a choice?"

Footsteps on the stairs sent Thomas back into his chair. He didn't care about their business as long as it didn't interfere with Emilia's treatment. However, if things went badly, it could be valuable information, and it was in his best interest if they didn't know that he had overheard.

He pondered whether he could destroy these people's lives for Emilia's sake and how much it would weigh on his conscience before quickly dismissing the idea. Thomas already knew he would do it even if it meant destroying his soul when the door suddenly swung open.

"Has she woken?" Miriam asked, clasping her hands before her as she entered the room and gazed at Emilia. Thomas shook his head. Miram's face pinched with worry before she schooled her features, but Thomas saw it nonetheless. "You'll be taking her uniform," she said. "I can't have them finding it here."

"Pardon me?" Thomas growled, leaning forward. "And where will I be going?"

"You can't stay here." Miriam looked aghast. "You must know that."

"I'm not leaving until I know she's all right." Thomas stood abruptly, causing Miriam to stumble back.

"What is the meaning of this?" the doctor asked, his long form coming through the open door.

Thomas repeated himself.

The husband and wife exchanged a look that communicated beyond words. Nodding, the doctor turned towards Thomas again.

"I can assure you I'll do whatever is in my power to help—" The doctor stopped when he realized he didn't know his patient's name.

"Emilia." The harshness in Thomas's tone made John pale. Had he not considered asking her name when he tended to her earlier? Or was she just another body to fix?

"Right. I'll make sure Emilia will come out of this."

Thomas closed the distance between them, slamming the doctor into the wall as he gripped his shirt with his good arm, ignoring the throb of pain in his shoulder. How could he trust this man if he didn't have the common courtesy to know her name? And to leave her here without protection...

How can I let her wake with only strangers to console her? What type of man would that make me? I cannot *abandon her.* His stomach twisted at the betrayal. *What might she think? Feel?*

"I am not leaving." Thomas said each word through his teeth. To the doctor's credit, he stayed steady without raising his hands against Thomas.

They both ignored Miriam's protests.

John's brown eyes softened with understanding. "It is safer for her if you left," he said quietly as if talking to a rabid animal.

Maybe he was.

Thomas's hands shook with fury. The only thing stopping him from killing the man was that he was the only one who could heal her.

"If they find you here," John went on, "not only will my family be at risk of harboring a Union soldier, but two. One of them is female, no less. I would rather not face imprisonment. And I am sure you don't want them to discover Emilia's identity. It would be easier to explain her presence if she were alone."

Thomas stared at him, willing himself to calm down. There was truth behind his words. He damn well knew it. But how could he abandon the woman he loved? Especially without knowing she was well. Thomas looked at Emilia, his heart-shattering in his chest. If she just woke up, he could speak to her. Tell her why he had to go.

Sensing his resolve weakening, Miriam stepped closer and laid a comforting hand on his arm. "I will treat her as my own. Make sure no harm comes to her. Please." Her smile was melancholy as she gently squeezed his arm.

With the slip of her fingers, the fiery rope binding Thomas to his fury loosened. He sighed and withdrew his hands from the doctor.

John straightened his shirt, muttering to himself.

"Does she have any family I can send her to when she's healed? I—" Miriam paused, brown eyes scrutinizing him. "I have connections that can get a letter across Union lines. Is there anything they need to know?"

Thomas began to shake his head when an idea had him straightening. He let his head fall as his gut twisted with what he was about to do.

"Are ye able to write two letters?" he asked. "I will only need ye to send one, though." When her brows lowered in confusion, heat raced up his neck. "I can send the second."

She studied his face, and her shoulders straightened. Thomas prepared himself for pity but was only met with resolution. He had a feeling she may understand more than most. It was against the law for a slave to read or write. If she knew how then her husband may have taught her. A new respect for the doctor formed, though reluctantly.

"Of course," she said, going to the door. "Ruth," she called. "Fetch me a quill and paper, please." She turned to face him once more, sweeping a hand towards Emilia as she explained, "I figured you would want to stay in here. In case she wakes."

Thomas's shoulders sank in relief even as he felt sick with what was to come. "Thank ye," he said, watching Ruth put the supplies on the desk, avoiding his gaze as she quickly left the room. Miriam struggled to sit at the small desk with her billowing dress.

The doctor re-examined Emilia, but she still didn't stir.

"What would you like the first to say?" Miriam drew Thomas's attention back to her.

Thomas felt the doctor's eyes on him, as he kept his gaze on Emilia. Her lashes fluttered across her cheek, and his heart stuttered. He wished she'd wake up to stop him from making this possibly colossal mistake. To talk him into going about it another way. But she didn't, and he knew this had to be done for her safety.

With a painful sigh rattling out of him, Thomas began to give the details of the letter that would seal their fate.

CHAPTER TWENTY-SIX

Michael & Shaylah

DECEMBER 1862

"Why are ye sellin' it?" Mikey asked, scanning the room of filled crates.

The man worried his hat in his hands, seeming to sink into his skin. He was thin and short, but wiry enough that Mikey knew he still had some strength. "Times are hard, as I'm sure you're aware." He ran a hand through his white hair, looking everywhere but Mikey. "I can't afford to keep it."

Mikey nodded, his grin spreading even when hearing the man's sad tale. "I'll take it."

The owner looked up, a mixture of shock and hope warring with each other. It seemed hope won when he smiled back, shaking Mikey's hand.

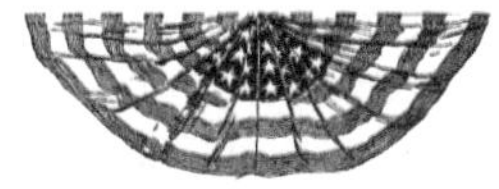

"What the hell are ye goin' to do with it?" Hughie asked.

Mikey swung the keys around his finger, smiling to himself. "Patience," was all he said as they rounded the corner, heading toward the warehouse by the docks. He waited a few days after returning to Boston before telling the boys the good news. Mikey wanted it official so as not to make himself look a fool.

Henry snorted and spit to the side. "Why do ye even want it when ye're here in the city?"

Mikey rolled his eyes to the cloudy December sky. These men were like family, but feck were they simple-minded. Could they really not think beyond today?

"The war isn't goin' to be forever, and I have plans. Don't ye worry. Leave it to me, and it'll be good at the right time."

A cold wind blew off the ocean, and Mikey had to pull his new coat tighter. It was feckin' pleasant not to have to worry about money now. The deal with Boudreaux set him up in ways he'd never imagined. If only the southern arsehole didn't plan to kill everyone close to the gypsy. What they could accomplish together would land him damn near the top.

Too bad he had to kill the fecker before he could make another deal.

Mikey sighed.

"What else do ye plan to buy with the sugar?" Henry asked, wiping his nose from the chill. It was a bloody cold day, and few dared to venture to the docks. Other than the occasional dockworker and passerby, they were alone.

"We're goin' to invest, boyos."

Hughie and Henry looked at him as if he'd grown two heads. They reached the warehouse, and Mikey flipped to the correct key.

"I have to get a shipment out to Sandy for now," he said, the cold of the latch biting into his fingers as he unlocked the large door. "We need to get the rest sold within…" The door rattled upward, and his words trailed off as they stared in horror.

"Feckin' hell," Henry said.

Hughie swore under his breath.

Mikey said nothing as he stared at the empty warehouse. The barrels of sugar—gone. Instead, blood dripped to the floor off the mutilated body of the boy he had trail Boudreaux.

His body swung with the ocean breeze, the large hook piercing his chest and a note hanging off it in an unknown language.

Se tout pou mwen nan fen an.

Mikey's fist hit the wall.

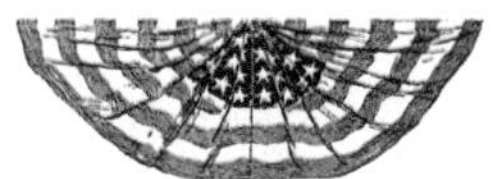

"What's wrong?" Shay asked, finding Michael pale and grumpy as all hell after Mira guided him up to the room, a look of disapproval on her face.

It had been a week since Shay saw Michael last. She would have gone to find him if he hadn't sent her a note explaining he'd be out of town. Where he'd gone was beyond her. And the fact that he didn't care enough to come to her himself had her prickly with irritation.

Shay studied Michael as they sat at the table. How he ran his rough fingers over his face and hair. He really did look like shit. Well, as bad as Michael could look.

"This isn't how I had this planned," he admitted.

"What planned?"

Libby took a few wobbly steps in his direction, and Michael froze. Shay had to bite back a smile at the apprehension written all over him. The man could kill without hesitation, but a baby coming in his direction made him lock up in fright. Libby's legs wobbled, and Michael leaned in the chair to catch her.

"Feckin' hell," he gasped, pulling her off the ground and into his lap. "Were ye just goin' to let her fall like that?"

Shay's eyes widened, and she smiled, her heart swelling in adoration. "She would have been fine. She has to learn."

"What if she hurt herself?"

Shay laughed, and Michael glared while holding Libby safely to his chest. Weren't people harder in these times? Why was he being so silly? "Michael..." she said, grinning as she noticed him grip her child tighter. "Are you worried about Libby?"

Michael scoffed, turning his glare to Libby. She giggled and grabbed his nose in her tiny fist.

"Dada!" Libby cooed, and it was as if the air sucked out of the room, time standing still. Shay felt the blood rush out of her face, a jolt of fear shooting through her. Libby had said 'mama' before, but never had she called Michael anything.

"I'm sure she meant—" Shay began.

"Dada," Libby said again, squeezing Michael's cheeks between her chubby hands.

Shay covered her mouth with a shaking hand, watching Michael's serious face as his blue eyes stared into her child's hazel gaze, perfectly still except for the increased expanse of his chest. He reached up and brushed Libby's caramel curls out of her face. She could have sworn there was a tremble to his hand. Shay waited, unsure whether to intervene or watch whatever was happening between the man she loved and her daughter conceived by his enemies.

Libby leaned in, kissed the end of Michael's nose with one of her open-mouthed kisses, and giggled, squirming her way out of his lap and onto the floor, unaware of the tumult she had inflicted upon the adults.

Michael sat there, watching Libby take a few shaky steps to Shay.

"She doesn't understand," Shay said, lifting Libby and giving her a carrot from the plate on the table.

"Has she..." he started, voice rough, for some reason making tears spring to her eyes. "Has she called H—" he cleared his throat "—anyone else that?"

Shay shook her head, praising the heavens that Libby hadn't, and frankly, quite shocked that it took this long. George lived there with them, though he was at work most of the time, and Hiram frequented the bakery, coming to pick up Evaline and visit the Wilson's. It was a miracle that Libby hadn't at least called one of the men dada.

Until now.

"I'm sorry," Shay said softly, keeping her eyes on Libby, unable to look at Michael.

"For what?"

She waved a hand between them. "This is awkward. I'll explain it to her..."

"No," the word came out loud and harsh, startling Shay into looking at him. "I mean..." His gaze drifted to Libby, and his throat bobbed as he swallowed. "Do what ye think is best." He shook his head, rubbing a hand over his face. "It is not me place."

Shay rolled her lips over her teeth, considering. "Do you want it to be your place?" she asked hesitantly, her heart seeming to drop from her chest entirely. It must have gone to wherever her stomach fled.

His blue eyes found hers. "What are ye saying, lass?"

"What are *you* saying?" she shot back, hiding her face behind Libby's back, the anxiety of the moment making her want to disappear. Shay knew what she wanted, but not knowing what he thought was excruciating.

The sound of a chair scraping against floorboards as Michael stood had Shay curling into her daughter more. Libby was unphased by the whole situation. Shay sensed him squat by them but kept her eyes closed.

"It doesn't bother ye if..." Though his finger was soft against her cheek, she still jumped in surprise, her eyes popping open to find him watching her warily. Michael's thumb brushed her lips, his gaze blazing a trail as if he wanted to taste her. Heat bloomed within Shay, temporarily muting her fears. "Would it bother ye if—I mean, would it be so bad if she—For feck's sake," he cursed. "Would it be wise for us to pretend?"

Shay leaned into his hand. "I think it would have to be real," she said, eyes darting around his face for a reaction.

"Real?"

Shay nodded. "If we allowed her to call you that, it would have to be real. You would have to accept her as..." She swallowed, the tears she'd been holding back finally tumbling down her cheeks. "As your own."

Michael stared at her thoughtfully for a moment before turning to Libby. He ran a calloused finger over Libby's chubby arm, staring at her daughter like she held the world. Shay's throat constricted. This was too much... She never meant to fall this deeply for him, to have her child get attached to anyone when they were supposed to leave when Emilia returned.

She wasn't made to stay in this time, damn it.

"Michael—" Her voice broke at the same time Libby blew a raspberry at him, spraying him with tiny, orange shards of carrot. Shay gasped, and Michael's mouth dropped open. His loud laughter pierced the shock, making Shay jump before a smile started growing, a laugh bubbling out of her, too.

Libby giggled, spitting more of the goo everywhere, causing them all to laugh harder. Shay went to cover her mouth, but Michael had already swept the girl up, throwing her into the air before catching her. Libby laughed in delight, eyes sparkling with happiness as she stared at the man who captured her heart as much as her mama's.

"Iníon mo chroí," Michael said, spinning Libby around. Shay didn't know what it meant, but she could *feel* the heaviness behind the words. The claiming. He dipped her down low, bending her backward in a dance, grinning at her giggles. He looked up through his lashes, his eyes searing into Shay and making her weak with desire. "I've somethin' I want to show ye."

Shay's heart expanded, filling her with more joy than ever before. There was a time not so long ago when she thought she'd never be happy again.

But this was damn near perfect.

CHAPTER TWENTY-SEVEN

Emilia

DECEMBER 1862

A bright golden light caused me to flinch from the window, sending pain through my skull that had me gasping. My hand shot up to find a bandage wrapped around my head. My hands gently ran over it only to find short hair, making my heart surge into my throat.

What the hell?

"How are you feeling, dear?" a woman asked quietly, startling me into a near scream.

Where am I?

The room was unfamiliar. Floral wallpaper flowed down the walls beneath dark wood. Beyond the beautiful four-poster bed, a large mahogany dresser sat across from me. All of it was well-kept despite being outdated.

The woman stood from a rocker and leaned over the bed. Had she been watching me sleep? A feeling of unease had me shifting away.

"Where am I?" I asked aloud, taking in her unusual clothing, the unlit lantern on the table by the bed, and the fire burning inside the grate. My brow fell when I realized it was the only source of heat.

The lady paused as she leaned in, capturing my attention again, her curls bouncing around her face. "Fredericksburg. Do you not remember?"

I frowned. "Where is that exactly?"

A look of alarm blossomed across her features, accelerating my heartbeat. *What the hell is going on?*

"Virginia," she said, straightening and smoothing her hands down a blue dress. "Let me fetch my husband, John. He's the physician taking care of you."

I swallowed a lump forming in my throat. "What happened to me?" I asked, but she was already out of the room.

A wiry man rushed in wearing equally antiquated clothes, his wife on his heels. "Miriam says you are suffering some memory loss."

"What happened to me?" I asked again. I tried to push myself up and gasped, falling back down. My side felt like it was tearing in half.

"You were hit with shrapnel during the battle. It tore through your side. Luckily, it missed your organs, but I'm afraid you might be experiencing some amnesia after hitting your head."

Shrapnel? Had these people lost their minds?

"What battle?" I hissed. Either these people were insane, or I was going through some mental break. "A battle in Boston?"

"You're in the South, dear." She grabbed my hand in reassurance. "Virginia. Remember? In the heart of the war."

"What war?" I snarled frustratedly and covered my face with my hands. What the hell was I doing in Virginia?

"What is the last thing you remember?" the doctor asked, checking my pulse so I had to lower my hand.

I paused, thinking. "I was in my attic in Boston. Looking through some old family heirlooms." I shook my head. I couldn't remember anything after that. He exchanged a look with his wife.

"How many fingers am I holding up?" John asked.

"Three."

"What year is it?"

"2024," I said hesitantly, gaging their reactions, though I wasn't sure why. The lady blanched.

"Why? What year is it?" I asked, suddenly fearing I might have been out longer than I thought. Was I in a coma for years?

"1862."

I laughed, beginning to shake my head, and winced. "Right. And next, you will tell me we're in the middle of the Civil War."

The doctor's hand tightened on my wrist, and my eyes flicked to him.

"A fellow soldier brought you here," he said. "You were fighting in the Union army."

"I'm a woman." I glared, indulging them a bit. "Isn't that against your rules?"

"That's why he brought you to us," she said, eyeing her husband.

"Who brought me?" A prickling sensation on the edge of my brain told me that this man might have all the answers. But for the life of me, I didn't know *why*.

Something flickered behind Miriam's eyes. "Just a soldier, dear."

"Did he say how he knew me?" I asked, feeling slightly sick to my stomach. A hollowness carved out the center of me.

They exchanged another look. Miriam leaned in and grabbed my hand.

"Just someone you fought alongside," she said quietly.

"Is he still here?" I pushed. "Maybe he can help with my memories." And whatever hellscape I landed in.

"He left just after sunset," the doctor explained. "He needed to return to his regiment to not draw suspicion to your disappearance."

I sank into the mattress, feeling defeated. He had to risk a whole fucking lot to save someone he just 'fought alongside.' Besides, I didn't fight in a damn war. This was too much. "I need to call my parents. Can I use your phone?"

"A letter has already been sent to the man of your house."

Man of my house? "A letter?"

"Yes," Miriam hesitated. "The soldier who brought you here sent it home. We agreed to send you there after you healed some. Though we didn't anticipate your memory loss."

"I worried about it." The doctor shook his head, clearly dismayed.

Panic swelled within me, and I balled my fists into the sheets. They might be crazy, but there was no question that I was injured with pieces of my memory missing.

"Will I get my memory back?" I asked, voice small even to my own ears.

"It's hard to say," he replied, face grave as he sat in the rocker beside the bed. "It could return within the hour or a month out." His pause had the hairs on my arms standing. "Or possibly not all."

My face crumpled, spurring Miriam to say more. "But Mister O'Connor has already been notified of your condition." I let out a deep, relieving sigh. My father would know what to do. "Maybe, with your family, you'll regain some of the memories you lost."

I settled back, relieved I was finally able to grasp some normalcy in this mess. Exhaustion fell over me, weighing me down like a heavy blanket, and my eyes drifted closed.

"Sleep," Miriam said, pulling the blankets to my chin. "We'll discuss more when you are well-rested."

I woke to an older, heavy-set woman in servant's clothing placing a food tray down. Her brown eyes widened when she saw I was awake.

"Miss Moretti," she exclaimed, her dark features brightening with relief. "How are you feelin'?"

"Moretti?" My brows lowered. "My name's O'Connor. Emilia O'Connor."

The deep lines in her dark face crinkled in confusion. "I'm so sorry." She hesitated, shaking her head. "I must have been mistaken." Unease settled into me at her bewilderment. The names didn't even come close.

She straightened the room around me, drawing my attention to the food platter again. My stomach rumbled with hunger. She was too polite to say something, but I could tell by her slight smile that she had heard. Besides, I had a more pressing matter to tend to.

"Here, honey." She helped me sit up, and I hissed in pain. "You must be starving'."

"Actually..." I made a face and told her I needed to use the restroom. With much panting and a few choice curses, she helped me up enough to relieve myself.

"There now." The poor woman patted the blanket back over me after helping me through that travesty. I was propped against the headboard, catching my breath, wishing I could succumb to the forever sleep, when she placed a food tray on my lap.

I tried not to grimace at the sludgy mess in the bowl. *But hey, at least my bladder is blessedly empty.* Ah, the little things.

"Porridge," she explained the slop. "Supplies seem to be runnin' low here in the South."

I nodded, stealing a glance at her from the corner of my eye. If we were in the South, was she a slave? Not that I believed I went back in time, but if I went with their story...

"What's your name?" I asked instead, hesitantly picking up the spoon.

She looked surprised that I asked. "Ruth."

"Nice to meet you, Ruth."

"I wish it was under better circumstances, dear."

I brought the food to my mouth and failed to hide my cringe this time.

Ruth crossed her hands over her ample stomach as her eyes seared into me. It looked like she was going to make sure I ate each bite.

"Honey." She hesitated after I basically inhaled half of the porridge. I looked up, feeling like I had eaten worse food, but couldn't remember when. "This may seem strange," she continued, "but has anyone told you you have a shine about you?"

I shook my head, wincing with the pain as something stirred somewhere deep within my mind, but for the life of me, I—couldn't—fucking—remember. I squinted, trying to recall what it was, like a fleeting thought on the edge of your brain that, if you just thought hard enough, you might remember. I sighed, closing my eyes when it didn't come to me. "Maybe," I said, disheartened.

I opened my eyes to find her face soft as she watched me struggle.

"I shouldn't be troublin' you with my silliness." Ruth waved it off. "Here, let me help." She poured some tea into a cup. "I'm sorry we don't have any coffee."

"Oh, I love tea," I admitted.

Ruth shook her head. "Those Irishmen have been influencing you?" Her voice was light with a bit of laughter, but it only confused me more.

"Irishmen?" I asked, feeling a tug in my chest.

"Oh, yes. You served in the Irish Regiment. Strange for a girl like you." She eyed my bronzed skin and dark hair. "But if they are like the man who brought you—" She gave me a look that told me he was handsome.

A flush spread over me. "Actually, my family drank a lot of tea." I paused, considering. The words came out before I could stop myself. "What did he look like?"

Ruth's eyes twinkled, clearly smitten with the man who was undoubtedly younger than her sixty-something years. "Hair as black as a crow." She looked at the wall as if imagining him before her, and I felt a smile tug on my lips. "Eyes as green as a field. And taller than the good doctor here."

With her description, my smile melted as a pit of despair grew in my stomach. It ate away at me as I tried to picture the man, but for some reason, I could only think of the picture hanging in my parent's pub of the brothers who had opened it. I had only looked at it earlier that day, but damn, it felt like ages had passed since I was there. And that thought was just as ridiculous as these people thinking we were in the middle of the Civil War.

I let out a heavy breath and gave her a sad smile. "Sounds like I was one lucky girl," I said.

"We were sorry to see him go. He sure went through a great deal—"

"A word, Ruth," Miriam said in the doorway, making us both jump.

"Of course, Miss Ward."

My brows fell as I watched the two women convene in the hall. I may have felt that mere hours had passed, but my wounds and thin body told otherwise. Was there truth to the story that they told me? Had I been gone for months? If not longer... And what was all this about a damned war? All of it seemed to be insanity. A part of me believed that I was still sleeping and that I would wake from this crazy mess and all would be normal. Or maybe I'd be in a kooky asylum and tied to a bed.

My eyes drifted closed again as I fought to stay awake. To figure this out and determine what I should do. But what my mind kept drifting to, no matter how hard I concentrated on the facts presented to me, was the soldier who brought me to these people. And I wondered what type of man would risk it all for a woman he barely knew.

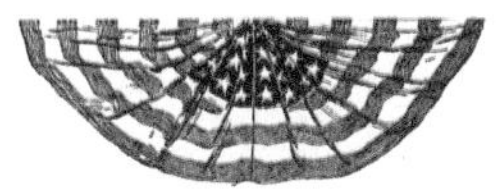

A few days had passed when I found myself sitting up in bed, Miriam talking about the exodus of soldiers. The town was emptying, and she wondered how soon the residents would return to find their homes and businesses in disrepair.

"There is something you should know," she said to me, an uneasy expression on her face. "The soldier who brought you insisted that you were in some kind of danger. He was to send another letter home in a few weeks." She waited, eyes heavy with indecision.

"Is something wrong?" I asked, feeling a heavy weight on my chest, sensing that she wasn't telling me something.

"In the second letter, he will notify your family that Thomas had passed the same time you went missing." She kept pausing, trying to gauge my reactions. Thomas. My father had an ancestor named Thomas. Would he have lived around this time? I squinted, thinking. No, that was ridiculous. I was not in 1862.

I am losing my mind.

Miriam continued when I was still lost in my insanity. "With recent circumstances and with us not knowing how long you will be in town, I thought you should know the contents of the letter so as not to be blind-sided later." It all came out in a rush, as if she'd burn up with the knowledge and had to purge herself of it.

I stared at her blankly. I knew no one by that name, and I wouldn't dwell on it further. "Am I supposed to know who that is?" Even as I said it, my gut twisted, though I had no clue as to why.

Miriam's breath came out in a rush, and she began to busy herself. "Yes, but I wouldn't worry yourself over it. All will be explained with time."

I let it go, not wanting to push it, even as my heart pounded with confusion. Clearly, it was someone I met recently. Otherwise, I would remember him. But how close could I have possibly become acquainted with him in such a short time?

CHAPTER TWENTY-EIGHT

Thomas

T homas had made it through the city without any notice. He deposited Emilia's uniform outside one of the houses with patients, hoping they would think it from a fallen soldier. He had slipped her rosary around her neck before he left, whispering in her ear of his love. Begging her to forgive him.

His heart tore again when he had to leave her uniform in that dirty alley. She should have been by his side.

A vision of Emilia smiling blind-sided Thomas, and had him stumbling back, retreating down the street before he could think more of it.

A heavy fog blanketed the streets as the grey sky darkened with the promise of night. Men gathered around their regiment's colors, trying to make some sense out of all of the chaos. Thomas saw his chance to make his way back in and slipped through the crowd of soldiers.

None of his regiment was gathered, and he stood there, trying to find someone familiar in the crowd. As the time went on, Thomas's nerves began to fray. He shifted on his feet. Had none of his regiment made it?

A formidable man with a white beard and a voice that boomed over a crowd rode his way through the ranks. Thomas recognized him as General Edwin Sumner, the commander of the 2nd Corps.

The general's eyes sharpened on him. "Why are you not in formation with the rest of your company, private?"

Thomas straightened, feeling small as he looked up at Sumner on his mount.

"This is all of my company, sir." Thomas swallowed his words, trying to dislodge them from his throat, thinking of all the men he had left behind. Of Emilia's condition.

Sumner swore under his breath and nodded to Thomas, spurring his horse away.

More men who'd been along the fence trickled into town, faces worn and defeated.

That night, the rest of Thomas's company would sleep on the battlefield, looking up to a sky filled with the shimmering green of the Northern Lights, unable to return to their company until the next day.

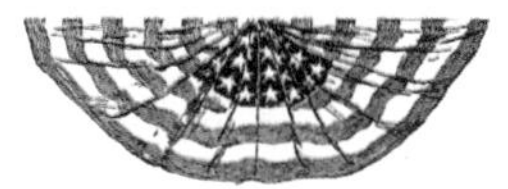

"Where have ye been?" Thomas exclaimed while awkwardly embracing Sullivan with the sling between them. Thomas felt a vague sense of relief for his friend's safety, but it was dulled mainly by the emptiness consuming him.

The Union had made it over the bridges earlier that day. They were on the other side of the river now, preparing to head back to Falmouth, and packed up to depart as other companies disassembled the bridges.

"I see ye seen the doctor," Sullivan said, ignoring Thomas's inquiry as he eyed Thomas's arm. "How's the lass?"

Thomas shook his head, unable to meet his friend's eyes. "She was still unconscious when I left her."

A deep line creased between Sullivan's brows. "What did the physician say?"

Thomas shrugged, sitting down. "He thinks she will heal but won't know more about her head until she wakes."

"Why are ye here?" Sullivan fell into a heap by Thomas.

"It's better for her if she thought I was gone."

"What are ye bloody going on about?" Sullivan snapped. "Why—"

"There are matters ye don't know of. It's best if she thought I was gone so she can continue her life. Go back home where it's safer."

Sullivan took in a sharp inhale of cold air, face contorted in disbelief. "Have ye lost your mind?"

Thomas didn't answer, unable to put everything he had lost into words. Before the battle, he told Emilia he would have no life without her. Now that it was his reality, he could only blame himself.

CHAPTER TWENTY-NINE

Emilia

Almost a week had gone by. The pounding in my head receded, but the injury to my side still made it painful to do more than get up to use the restroom. Or rather, a bedpan. *For the love of God, what I would do for a working toilet.* The thought of using the bedpan still made me cringe.

I'd just finished doing that and sat on the edge of the bed, out of breath and feeling like death. Lifting up my nightgown, I inspected my wound. A jagged line cut across my abdomen from my pelvic bone to the left rib. John said that if it had gone any deeper, I would most likely have been dead. The stitches keeping it together were gruesome, and my heart sank with the thought of the scar it would become. Maybe I could be proud of it if I remembered what had happened. Now, it was just a painful reminder of everything that had been taken from me.

I ran my hand over the small bump that started to form on my lower stomach, wondering when the swelling would go down. Sometimes, when I was still, I thought I could feel slight fluttering deep inside, and I worried that I might have some muscle damage. I dismissed the thought when it didn't hurt. Healing took time.

Miriam came in like a whirlwind, causing me to hastily drop my night-gown. She eyed me, hands on her hips.

"I think we will take a short walk today."

Ruth arrived on cue with a dress in her hands.

I looked between them, aghast. "I can't walk."

"Sure, you can." Miriam gave me a bright smile and grabbed the dress. "Doctor's orders. It would do you some good now that you healed up a bit. C'mon Ruth. Help me get this on her. Emilia should get outside for a bit."

They helped me into it until I was nearly panting. They tried to find shoes that would fit but only succeeded in boots that looked like they went through...well, like they went through a war. Miriam hesitated before informing me that they were mine, validating my suspicion. I eyed them, willing myself to remember.

Either reading the exhaustion in my posture or the concern on my face, Miriam grabbed my elbow supportively. "Let's sit down with some tea beforehand."

I smiled gratefully.

They assisted me down a hallway that branched off to a set of two stairs, each going down to the first level and steeper than what I was used to. In my condition, I would have lost my footing if it hadn't been for Miriam guiding me.

It was the first time I left the room, and my throat tightened when the antiquated aesthetic didn't differ from the rest of the house. I began to fear I might be in some horror movie where the people dress up, play a part, and murder you with a hatchet at the end. With my luck, they'd bury pieces of my body in the cellar to save for dinner later.

Heaving and hoeing, we finally reached the landing and turned down a long hallway to a dining room on the left. To my dismay, it did little to calm my trepidations. A modest table took up the center of the room. Lace curtains framed the windows, letting in a soft, welcoming light. I tried to let it calm me rather than allowing my mind to wander to crazy imaginations, like hidden saws and butcher knives hidden in one of the enormous oak China cabinets that lined the far wall. I nearly snorted at that thought. They wouldn't have cared for me this long if they wanted to murder me.

I swallowed, not wanting to consider the other possible reason for the house decor.

"Will you get us some sandwiches and tea, Ruth?" Miriam asked politely, setting the table.

"How do you and Ruth know one another?" I asked, seeing how far she would go with this act. I took a seat in one of the cushioned chairs.

"She's under my employ," she said, still focused on setting the three plates out.

"So, you pay her?"

Miriam looked up quickly, studying me.

"She's free if that's what you're implying." One of her brows raised, and I blushed. "John and I don't believe in the institution of slavery."

"That's right," Ruth said, coming in with a tray filled with tiny sandwiches and a small pot of tea. My stomach rumbled in greeting. "She picked me out of the auction herself. That day, she drew up my freedom papers, and I worked for her ever since."

"Why?" I asked before I thought better of it.

Miriam's face hardened, and something flashed in her eyes.

I grabbed her hand gently. "I didn't mean to be rude. I only wondered what changed your ways from so many others in the South."

Miriam and Ruth exchanged a look. Ruth shook her head almost imperceptibly, and Miriam sighed, seemingly resigned. She sat beside me and passed out the sandwiches while Ruth poured the tea.

"I've been through something similar," Miriam admitted. "I know what it is like to be at the mercy of another human—"

Ruth tsked, cutting her short.

"John saved me when I was younger," she continued, ignoring the eye daggers Ruth threw at her. "I was in terrible conditions, sick, and half out of my mind. He healed me. Protected me. Sa—" She cleared her throat, watching her own finger trail the grooves of the table. "Anyway. When I saw Ruth, among others, I knew I couldn't leave them. I freed as many as my money could buy and never looked back."

I sat back, feeling confused. She told the story with such conviction that I had trouble *not* believing her. We sat the rest of the meal in silence. Each of us plagued with our own thoughts, but I was pleased to see Ruth eat with us as well.

"I think that's enough for today," Miriam started, rising from her seat. She looked tired, as if whatever she'd been thinking about had worn on her. "You managed to get out of that room, at least. We'll walk on a different day."

I felt a wave of relief, already drowsy from my little activity. I stood to join Miriam and gasped as a sharp pain shot through my abdomen. I doubled over as something warm ran down my legs.

"What is it?" Miriam asked, holding my arms as she tried to support me.

I began to lift my dress, panicking, and found blood coating the inside of my thighs.

"Oh, dear," Ruth said. "These things happen."

I doubled over, another wave of pain rolling through me.

"I don't think this normal," Miriam said, lowering me back to the chair. "Ruth, get John." When Ruth hesitated, Miriam snapped, "Now."

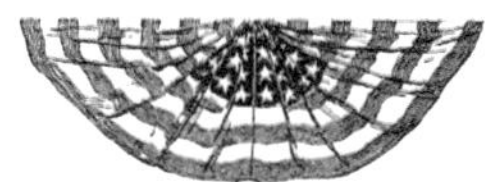

I turned my face towards the wall as John probed my lower abdomen.

"I believe we have all of it," he said softly to either Miriam or me; I wasn't sure.

"Go," she said. I kept tracing the flowers with my eye sas the doctor and his wife spoke amidst the thousand buzzing bees in my ears. "Let me talk to her alone."

The door clicked shut, and the weight shifted the bed as Miriam sat beside me. She tried to grab my hand, but I pulled it back.

"Did you know your condition?" Miriam said tentatively.

I shook my head, and tears swelled in my eyes.

"John says it looked like you were about three months into the pregnancy."

A tear fell as I stared at the rose before me. The last I remembered, I was a virgin. What happened to me between then and now? I shook my head again and closed my eyes, wanting to shut out the world.

"The father—" she started.

"Leave," I snapped, unable to bear another moment with anyone.

"Was he someone you remember? Or—"

"Leave!" I screamed, too far gone to care whether or not she was being nice. Instead, I curled into a ball, away from Miriam, away from the world, and sobbed into the pillow until my whole body shook, not caring if the rest of the house could hear me.

I lost a part of myself that I would never get back, and I couldn't even remember a damn thing about it. How I made that baby. Who with. It was all so fucked that I cried harder, feeling as if my whole world was collapsing in on itself.

What do I do? I pleaded to a God I wasn't sure cared. Tears gushed out of my eyes, the pain of it tearing me in two.

Who are you? I willed my thoughts to reach the man who did this to me. *Why aren't you with me now? Damn it. Why did you leave me? Why wasn't I enough?* I began to rock on the bed, hating—no, despising—the man who could leave a woman pregnant and injured. Then again, I wasn't even sure if he was even alive. *Why did you leave me?*

I sobbed, my whole-body convulsing with the pain tearing through me.

Why did you leave me? Why do I have to deal with this alone?

"Why?" I screamed to no one, a man I didn't know but needed nonetheless. Instead, I had a ridiculous pillow that I held tight in my arms, my throat burning with the force of my roar. "Why?"

The sobs turned silent, pulling into my body until I felt like they'd burst out of me. I coughed, choking on my own tears as I tried to pull deep, racking breaths in.

I flinched away from Miriam when she tried to comfort me. A short time later, the soft click of the door told me she left.

"Why?" I muttered. Kept muttering as I rocked myself into a dark trance, swirling flowers and tears pulling me into profound exhaustion.

I might not have remembered, but somewhere in the lost reservoirs of my mind, I mourned the loss of a child I didn't know, a man I had no recollection of giving myself to.

And I succumbed to the darkness.

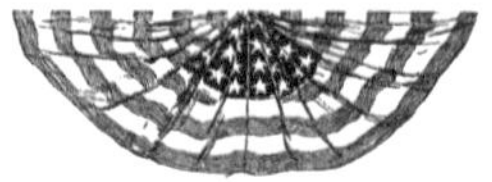

Miriam told me that it had been a girl. My mind numbed to the pain as my body tried to flare with grief. I let the detachment win.

While I refused to acknowledge their presence, John offered to dispose of the body. When receiving no reaction, Miriam insisted on burying it in the yard under the large Maple tree.

"You might change your mind," she insisted when I still hadn't moved. She knelt down by the bed. "I've been through this before. My biggest regret is that I didn't give her a proper burial. I wasn't in my right mind and…" She drifted off as I stared at the wall. Miriam rested a hand on my shoulder and sighed. "If you ever want to talk, when you're ready, I'll be here."

The windows were dark, and a lantern lit by the bed when I realized Miriam had left the room. Eyes dry, I found my hand resting over my belly, protecting my empty womb. I quickly drew it back and turned towards the wall, successfully shutting out the world.

I'd face my problems a different day.

CHAPTER THIRTY

Michael & Shaylah

The carriage rattled to a stop, pulling up to the building Mikey had bought. He shifted in the seat, unexpected nerves putting him on edge.

Shay looked at him expectantly, raising her brows. She had her hands buried in one of the blankets from under the seats and a thick shawl wrapped around her shoulders. Their breaths puffed out in white clouds; it was so bloody cold.

"We here?" she asked, giving him a cheeky smile that he could barely see in the fading daylight. It wasn't late, but the winter days were short. Michael felt the need to hurry, wanting to show her the building before it was dark.

"Aye." His voice came out rougher than he intended, and he had to clear his throat. "Wait a moment..."

Mikey descended the carriage and held his hand out, helping her down the small step. Shay smiled at him, making his chest do something odd. Why did her approval matter so much? He started to curse himself for the weakness until she looked up, and her jaw dropped.

"Oh my God!" The shock in Shay's voice made Mikey pull back to look at the building, worried that it was on fire or collapsing.

"What?" he asked, watching her draw closer, seemingly unaware of the cold or the snow she stepped in.

Shay swung around, curls fanning out around her, eyes rounded. "It was you?"

"What was me?" he growled. What was she bloody going on about? He glared at Shay, annoyed, though he wasn't sure why.

Shay wasn't fazed by his mood as she turned back to the building, running her fingers over the bricks. "You bought the pub?"

How did she feckin' know he was to turn it into a pub? She could have guessed it was already a gentleman's club, but she hit the nail too hard on the head. "Aye..." he admitted hesitantly.

Her eyes flared with what looked alarmingly like desire. If she kept looking at him like that, he'd have her—

Shay swiftly turned again, cutting off his dirty thoughts. "Take me inside..." she demanded.

"Is there somethin' ye have to tell me?" he asked.

Shay bounced on her toes, impatiently waiting for him to unlock the door. She looked worriedly toward the carriage driver.

What the hell is wrong with her?

"I'll tell you inside," she insisted.

The door swung open, and Mikey pulled down the lantern hanging on the wall and quickly lit it. Shadows fell across the tables and chairs, the light spilling halfway across the room, leaving the bar in the dark. He would have left the door open for light if it wasn't for the weather. He should have had one of the boys start a fire earlier.

Mikey felt her eyes on him as he lighted the fire, trying to get the damned thing to catch.

"They must have closed that in," she said quietly behind him. He sat back on his heels, still crouched, and waited for her to explain. She pointed to the grate and chimney. "There's no fireplace in the future."

He looked between Shay and the fire, confused. "How did ye bloody well warm the place then?" Michael paused, realizing what he'd just said. "Ye've been here before?"

Shay smiled. "This is Emilia's pub. Her family's, I should say, I was a waitress here."

Michael straightened quickly, causing Shay to stumble backward before catching herself on his jacket, the shawl slipping from her shoulders. Though he looked down on her, she didn't show the slightest bit of fear.

"What the feck are ye sayin', dimples?"

Shay bit her lip, her eyes falling to his mouth. He fixed the shawl, snaked his arms around her waist, and pulled her close, liking the way she felt pressed against him.

"I'm saying that we thought both you and Thomas bought the pub. But now I see it was you."

"Ye knew—"

"We didn't think it was right to tell you guys." She cut him off. "Emilia thought it might influence you or change time or something."

Mikey's head swirled on this bit of information. He was always the one to play into their fancies, listening to them blabber about the future without really delving into the logistics of it, but damn was it about to knock him on his ass.

Time travel... feck.

"How did ye warm the place?" he found himself asking. Shay grinned wider, wrapping her arms around his neck, and explained a modern heating system. Michael scanned the area, trying to picture what she described. "And ye thought I opened it with me brother? Why?"

"There's a picture of you and him..." Her face scrunched up.

"What?"

"Only, if you two opened it together, then..." Shay shook her head. "Never mind. You guys open it together. They have the picture in the office upstairs."

Mikey's brows rose, amazed that she knew of places he hadn't shown her yet. A sly grin spread slowly. "Did ye recognize me?"

"Not at first, obviously."

His smile fell, cursing himself for asking, until she pressed on.

"But when I saw you at the bakery, I immediately asked Millie."

Now that she mentioned it, Michael remembered them whispering together. He ran his hands up her back. "And am I what ye expected?"

"I never really thought about it. Emilia was the one always mooning over the picture." She laughed at his glare. "I think they were meant to find each other. It seems like more than just a coincidence, ya know?"

He raised a brow. "Ye believe in that sort of thing?"

"Soul mates?" How she smiled made him want to take back every evil deed he had ever committed.

Feck. He never wanted to be on the straight and narrow until this lass crashed into his life. The truth: he was already too far gone. But he thought he could try...

"Yes," she continued. "Don't you?" She batted her lashes at him flirtatiously.

He would have punished her if his chest didn't seize up, threatening to crack in half at the implication. "No," he said flatly.

Shay rolled her eyes. "Neither did Millie. I think fate has a funny way of working things out. Even with the twists and turns of life, what is meant for you will be yours."

Mikey stepped away, needing some space even as he grabbed her hand. "Let me show ye around."

The lass had lived a fanciful life before entering this century. She didn't understand what it was like to grow up in the streets, starve, and fight to survive. What it was like to be beaten down within an inch of your life. To break yourself and put it back together...only to find ye did it wrong. The pieces that were once kind and good were now hard and vicious. That ye lost a bit of your soul every goddamn time ye maimed and killed to only better your shite position in this dark world.

But that wasn't what had him pulling from her. It was the question in her eyes. What she wanted to hear him say.

Mikey guided her up the stairs, where the last owner had lived and where there would be an office in another century. He explained how he'd move there when the place was up and running. His aspirations for living a cleaner life.

"You mean it?" she asked, looking up at him with such hope that he had to avert his gaze.

"Aye." He guided her back down the stairs to the empty bar and rubbed the scars on his chest. "I about used up all me lives, I think."

Shay shook her head furiously. "Don't say that."

"It's true. Isn't—"

"Don't!" she snapped, shoving him. "Please."

The crack in Shay's voice did something to Mikey. Softened, just a fraction, the hardness within him.

Spinning her around, Mikey pressed Shay's back against the bar. "Don't worry. I shall be a businessman. Livin' a common, borin' life without any danger."

Shay rolled her eyes. Mikey's hand skimmed up her side, and he was rewarded with a shiver.

"Ye will get bored of me," he admitted, looking at her through his lashes.

She cupped his face, running her fingers through his short beard. "You are the least boring man I have ever met. I don't think we have to worry about that."

The truth of it: Mikey was tired. He'd been planning on getting out before Shay. When she crashed into his life, he took it as a sign to settle. To make a life that was worth something. A life that wouldn't be kill or be killed.

And, though he'd never admit it, he melted every time her babe looked at him. Libby may not have been Mikey's, but he was there that night. In a way, it was only ever the three of them.

If Mikey wasn't to be better for himself, he would be for his girls.

All of it—her words, his decisions—should have been a comfort. Should have settled the restlessness in his soul. Snuffed out the darkness deep within him.

And yet, it stirred. Waiting.

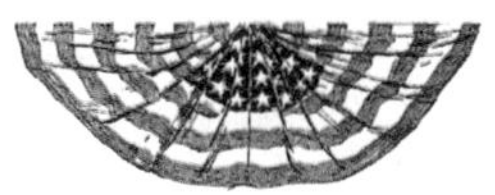

How did Michael think she could ever get bored of him? Quite frankly, it would be damn impossible. The man was like a volcano—he may be dormant, but no one forgot he could fucking explode.

Shay loved it.

Even if she wanted to believe Michael would leave the gang, she wasn't sure if he could. He liked it too much: the power and the money. He spent too long ruling his part of the city to get out now.

Still, if he meant it, if he tried to run the pub without any criminal activity, maybe she could stay. Millie was already so far in love with Thomas that Shay doubted she'd leave. Besides, who knew how long she'd serve in the war. It could still be years before she returned to Boston. In that amount of time, relationships flared, burned like a thousand fires, and died out just as quickly. Why not give Michael a chance? Why not help him open this pub?

That is if he'd want her to...

Michael's hand cupped the back of her neck, pulling her into a deep kiss that made her moan lewdly.

"Gods," he groaned into her mouth. "When ye make noises like that, I can't promise to behave."

She skimmed her nose over his, and their lips brushed. "So, don't."

A growl was her only warning before Michael lifted her up, making her squeal and laugh as he set her on the bar, her shawl tumbling behind her. They kissed for several minutes, hands exploring one another, before he pulled back.

"Move in here with me," he demanded, not really posing it as a question. Though it shouldn't have surprised Shay, Michael was used to getting what he wanted.

Still, she felt the blood drain from her face. "What?"

"You and Libby."

"But..." She looked around the room, mind spinning. "What will people say?"

"I don't give a feck what they say."

Her gaze narrowed, focusing on his cold blue eyes. She bit her lips, hiding a smile. Michael had already made up his mind; it was clear. Knowing him, he went through every pro and con about this living arrangement. She just wished they didn't *need* to worry about it. They should be able to love whoever they chose.

"And if I say yes?" she asked, raising her brows.

Something flashed deep in his gaze, and he leaned in until their breaths mingled. "Ye can do whatever it is ye like. Raise Libby. Help me with the pub. Do somethin' else. It is your choice, dimples." As he said it, his hand skimmed up her ankle to the back of her calf.

At some point, she must have raised her leg to his waist, cocooning him with her body.

Shay swallowed thickly, the heat of his hand scorching up her leg—a tantalizing contrast to the room's cold. "And if I say no?"

Michael paused, his fingers gripping the back of her thigh. "Then that is your choice as well."

"How soon will this happen?" she asked, trailing her hands down his large chest before catching on the button of his pants. She began to unfasten them, but stopped at Michael's silence. "Hm?" she asked, smiling now at the desire she saw, knowing she was distracting him.

"What?"

She unbuttoned his pants and slid her hand in, making him hiss at the chill of her fingers. "When would we move in with you?" she said, moving her hand up and down.

Michael shoved the skirt of her dress up, only exposing what was necessary to keep warm. "As soon as I fix the room above."

His warm hand enveloped hers, guiding himself into her decadently. So slowly that it was nearly torture.

"*Michael*," she gasped, his name a plea and a promise on her lips.

Michael kept his eyes on hers, still pushing in as he gripped the back of her neck, his other hand wrapping behind her knee. He had her trapped within his brutal grip, and she loved the way it made her feel. How he narrowed the world around them until she was consumed by the scorching desire between them. Michael made sure all she could see was him; all she could feel was operated by his hands. He dominated her world, and for the first time in ages, she was okay with that. She wanted it. And the security of it made up her mind.

"Yes," she moaned as he seated himself inside her.

"Yes, what?"

"Yes, we'll move in with you."

Michael's hand wove into her hair, pulling her head back so that all she could see was his blue eyes as he moved ever so slightly back out of her. She tried to wiggle, move against him, cause any type of friction that would make him pick up the damn pace.

"I can't wait to be in ye whenever I damn well please," he said. His jaw ticked, a sign of his control slipping the more she moved.

"Please, Michael," she moaned, giving the biggest puppy-dog eyes she could muster. "I need you."

Still, he moved at a torturous pace, moving in and out as if savoring each glorious inch of her. Shay wrapped her arms around his middle, trying to make him speed it up, but it only brought him closer.

She moaned, her head falling back. "Please." She gasped when his lips trailed up her neck.

"Please, what?" he asked.

For fuck's sake. Was he going to make her explain everything?

"Please fuck me."

"No." The word came out so harshly that her head whipped up, her gaze slamming into his. "I will not feck ye, Shaylah Banks. Not here. Not tonight."

It was then she realized Michael was making love to her. Not the heated kisses in the pantry or the sordid affair with the whore. This was just her and Michael becoming one in the most beautiful way.

"I will feck ye another time, in any way ye want. But for now..."

Shay cut him off with a kiss to his lips, sweeping her tongue in leisurely, tasting and exploring while their tongues danced with one another. She began to unbutton the top of her dress, needing him to touch her there. He must have sensed it, because his warm hand slipped in, cupping her breast and squeezing just enough to send warmth through her entire body.

Michael's pace quickened as they kissed, but he kept her pinned there, holding onto him as he thrusted inside her. She wrapped her limbs tightly around him, never wanting to let go, or for this moment to end.

They collided until they ignited their own heat—a flame that blazed in the deepest parts of their hearts. It smoldered in that intrinsic part that connects the heart to the soul, shielded from all but death. And even then, in the few who carry an eternal flame into the afterlife, each half of the flame waits and searches until they reunite with their twin. Yet, most only realize it when it's too late, or when the fear of losing something so pure terrifies them enough for life to pull them in different directions. Shay felt it, recognized it for what it was, and prayed that this life wouldn't take it away.

Sometimes, fate could be the cruelest dose of reality.

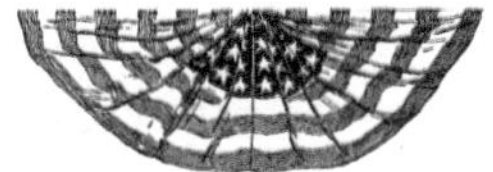

"I know it's not much..." Mikey began, looking around the dirty pub.

They sat on an old blanket they'd found upstairs and brought it down to sit in front of the fire. Shay rested her head on his shoulder while he leaned his head on top of hers and draped his arm over her knee. Mikey never felt more content than in that moment. It was everything he never knew he wanted.

He fought for more power, a higher station in life, respect. He never imagined he would want to stop clawing to the top. And here he was, content to own something that was only his, without any corruption or murder. Well, not anymore. He did what he could to get it and swore he wouldn't do it again. Not after what happened to Georgie...

"It's better than anything you could have shown me," Shay said, looking up at him, warmth in her dark eyes. "When are you going to start working on it?"

Mikey swallowed past the lump in his throat. "I plan to whenever I have free time. If I get the room cleared upstairs, I can live in it while I get everything set up." The bar and building only needed minor repairs and a new sign; the owner had sold it due to a lack of funds rather than renovation. He paused, preparing himself for what he had to say. The familiar sense of dread washed over him. "I need to tell ye somethin'."

Shay pulled back, narrowing her eyes. "Why am I getting the impression I won't like this?" She gasped, looking around at the floorboards. "There aren't dead bodies under here or anything, are there?"

"What?" he guffawed, incredulous. "Ye really think I would build an empire over the dead?" When she gave him an 'Are you serious?' look, he conceded. "No, dimples. There are no dead bodies, nor do I plan on burying any in the future."

She sighed. "While we're on this subject, I must know before I agree to move in..."

Mikey's heart lurched, and his stomach sank. "I thought ye already agreed."

"Will there be any drug deals or criminal activity? Will you give it up? Because if not…"

Mikey squeezed his hand into a fist, trying to tamp down the anger her doubt fueled, and reminded himself that it was a perfectly reasonable question. Honestly, he wasn't sure how long he'd go without letting it back into his life. But his home?

He wouldn't bring his family into it.

Tommy may have thought they kicked him out when he started making questionable choices, but the truth was, he didn't want to see little Maggie or Ma hurt. He couldn't do that to them. And he wouldn't do that to Shay or Libby either.

"Nay," he said, flexing his fingers as he willed the tension out of his body. "I bought this place to get out of that life." She just started to relax when his following words made her smile fall. "I have to tell ye. I meant to speak of it the other day." Mikey explained the missing sugar, the body, and the ominous note attached to it. Shay's composure began to crumble with each word, and she looked like she might be sick.

"You think it's him?" she asked.

"Aye," he confirmed. "It was written in his own bloody language. I had to search the city for a translator. Can't find me feckin' sugar anywhere. A whole warehouse full just up and blew across the feckin' ocean." He started swearing in Irish until he realized how much he was affecting her. Trying to control his fury, he wrapped an arm around her shoulders, pulling her tight. "It's a miracle that I already sold some and made a few investments."

"The pub being one of them?"

Mikey nodded. He was going to kill the bastard, but not before he bled him for all he was worth. Aye, the man would curse the feckin' day he came to the North. Not only did Boudreaux threaten the girls, but he killed one of Mikey's boys and gypped him out of his cut. That wouldn't stand. And Mikey would so enjoy skinning the southern arsehole who dared to insult his intelligence and manipulate their transaction.

"Why, though?" she asked.

"He must know we figured him out. Or at least suspects it."

"I just don't understand why he didn't try to take everything already? Why hasn't he tried to steal the vials? Why hire men after Millie was already enlisted?" Her voice rose with her anxiety, making him want to kill the bastard even more. "It doesn't make sense."

"Me only guess is that her disguise was good enough. That Boudreaux didn't realize where she was until it was too late. It would only take a few inquiries to find a poor Irishman willing to do dirty work for a wee bit of cash. As for the vials, I'm not sure what game the bastard is playin' at." He ran his fingers absently over her leg, thinking. Boudreaux was too cunning to leave the vials. He must be waiting, plotting, and Mikey had to be ready for whatever came their way. "I want ye to move in with me immediately," he said suddenly.

Shay turned wide eyes to him. "Here?"

"I don't like that he might be comin' for them. It's not safe for ye at the bakery anymore."

She looked around the pub apprehensively. "I'm not sure it's a place for a baby yet..."

"I'll get the room upstairs set up within a week. Then ye can move in." When Shay hesitated, he skimmed his fingers over her cheek, gently turning her face to him. "What is it, lass?"

"What changed?" she asked, not meeting his gaze. "Why are you suddenly interested in me? When I met you, you hated my people. Hated *me*."

"I never hated ye."

She scowled, and he sighed, explaining.

"Me whole life, people made it hard for me family, me people. In Ireland, it was our landlord who kicked us out. Practically starved us and sent us on a ship with no food. After we barely survived the journey, me own two sisters dyin' on that boat, they made it clear we weren't welcomed as soon as our feet hit the docks. Then, they were crammed into tiny tenements, turned away from jobs, and barred from stores. The list is feckin' long, lass. They put us in the same position as your people, and I began to see ye as competition. And if I was to compete, I sure as hell wasn't goin' to play fair."

Mikey could feel Shay studying him, but he couldn't look away from the fire, afraid of what she might see if he did.

"Now, I'm not a good a man," he held up a finger, shushing her when she began to protest. "Ye know it, I know it. And I own that. I came to terms with it long ago. But I have never allowed meself to do that to a woman. When I found ye, heard what they said to ye—me own bloody countrymen, usin' ye as if ye were nothin' but a toy. Gods, the fire of hell seared within me that night."

Mikey cursed in Irish, cursed them to the worst damnation, and hoped they feckin' burned for eternity. Shay wrapped her arms around his middle and rested her head on his chest, comforting him and shaking simultaneously.

For god's sake, he should be comforting her, not the other way around. Mikey rubbed her back, whispering reassurances in her ear that she couldn't understand but soothed her, nonetheless.

"I may have wanted to improve me lot, but deep down, I knew ye weren't to blame for me lot in this life. So, no, dimples. I never hated ye. I hated them. Hated meself. Hated what we'd become."

The silence grew heavy. Had he overstepped? Slipped and said something he shouldn't have? Unable to bear it anymore, Mikey opened his mouth to apologize, only for the words to freeze in his chest when the lass's gaze locked with his.

"Thank you," she said, reaching up to run her hand through his short beard, eyes soft and filled with unshed tears. "For telling me. I know it wasn't easy."

Mikey didn't think he could articulate, let alone decipher, what he felt then. And frankly, he was feckin' tired of talking about feelings. Instead, he guided Shay onto her back and lowered himself onto her, delighting in how her body responded to his.

"Enough about feelings, dimples."

She smiled. "Shut up and kiss me."

Gods, she's perfect.

Their lips brushed, the tips of his calloused fingers trailing her still-open bodice, causing her to shiver.

Mikey planned to elicit some of her best whimpers when the door slammed open.

Shay screamed. Mikey was up on his feet, his revolver drawn and aimed at whoever the hell wasn't even through the door yet. He was vaguely aware of Shay scrambling upward and buttoning her dress as he blocked her from—

"What the feck are ye doin' here?" Mikey snapped. Henry would be the godsdamn-death of him.

"I'm sorry, boss." Henry's gaze bounced between the two, taking in Michael's ruffled state. "Ye told me if it was important…" Henry sighed. "He's feckin' gone."

"Who?" Mikey growled, not wanting to hear who he suspected. Henry's gaze darted to Shay, and Mikey realized she was decent, standing by his side. "Whatever ye got to say, ye can say in front of her," he snapped.

Henry nodded stiffly. "Boudreaux. We went to all of his usual spots. The man up and left. Talked to a few men, and none of them know a thing."

Mikey cursed, kicking the closest chair to him and sending it flying across the room.

"Probably not good for business," Shay mumbled while going to retrieve the chair.

Michael waited, hands on his hips, breaths coming out heavy as he tried to calm himself.

Her little quip made him want to bend her over and spank her. Shay straightened the chair and glanced at him under her lashes with a little look that told him she knew exactly what he'd been thinking. Mikey ran his teeth over his bottom lip, trying to keep himself from smiling. *This woman will be the death of me.*

"What do ye want us to do?" Henry's voice redirected Mikey's thoughts, and the seriousness of the situation came crashing back down.

Sighing, he ran a hand over his face. "Ye put a few boys at the back of the bakery, one inside." He lifted a finger when Shay opened her mouth to protest. "Ye don't get a feckin' say. I'm not havin' the man come for ye. It's only until we find him or we move into here." Mikey turned back to Henry. "Tell the boys to keep an eye out at me parent's as well. I'm not takin' any chances." Henry nodded. "Get the rest of the boys and tell them to meet me at Nora's tonight."

Mikey turned to Shay when Henry left. "I'm sorry, lass."

"It's not your fault."

"This wasn't how I wanted this to go." Mikey ran his hand through his hair as she made her way over to him.

"How did you want this to go?" She smiled cheekily. "I seem to remember you already told me about the pub, and then you proceeded to defile the bar."

Mikey did smile then, pulling her close so he could wrap his arms around her waist. "I wanted your every memory of that bar to be replaced by what I did to ye and the sounds I wrung from ye."

Shay laughed. "Well, it worked. I don't think I'll be able to look at it the same." He began to back her up to the bar again. "What are you doing?"

In response, he twirled her around and bent her face first over the bar while he lifted her skirts. "I want ye to look at it now." Shay gripped the counter like a good lass as he unbuttoned his pants. Running a hand over her perfect, round ass, he slapped it, causing her to jump and squeal. Mikey leaned over to whisper in her ear. "That's for your little wisecrack earlier."

"Are you punishing me, Mr. O'Connor?"

Another spank, and Mikey thrust in, making the sweetest groan escape her lips.

"Rewarding ye, dimples," he breathed, gripping her hips roughly. "Now, hold on tight."

"Yes," she gasped.

"Yes, what?"

"Yes, sir."

CHAPTER THIRTY-ONE

Emilia

My fingers twiddled with the small braided bracelet on my wrist as we sat by the fire. It had been there when I had woken from my injury, but I didn't give it much thought. It wasn't until recently that I wondered where it had come from and why I didn't want to take it off. Important to me in a way I couldn't quite place.

It was a quiet evening. Miriam crocheted a blanket, John had a book, and I sat there, lost in my thoughts, as my tea went cold. What I thought of, I couldn't recall. I tended to let my mind wander, neither focusing on one thing for long, nor paying attention to what happened around me.

And yet, a knock on the door had my fingers stilling on the frayed ends of the bracelet.

"Are we expecting anyone, John?" Miriam asked.

John's brows crumpled. "Christmas is tomorrow. Do you think—"

How had Christmas come already? I had been walking around the house in a haze for days, focused only on my anguish. Now that I looked around, I wondered how I overlooked the whisps of greenery and the golden hue of candles flickering against the walls. There was no tree, but Miriam had decorated as much as she could during the war.

War. Civil War. All of it still numbed my mind.

The knock came louder, making me flinch. For some reason, I was startled by loud noises and everyday occurrences. They shouldn't scare me, but I couldn't seem to react normally, even if I wasn't sure why.

Isaiah—the butler and valet, or whatever the hell job the Wards needed—grabbed the rifle by the door. An action that seemed a bit dramatic to me, but I guess a war was a good enough excuse. Despite being an elderly man with a gentle, round face framed by a head of white hair, the determined expression on his broad, furrowed brow conveyed an apparent willingness to protect the household. I had to give him that. I may have been struggling with my new reality, but not even that could stop my respect for Isaiah from growing at that moment.

"Wait," Miriam started. The valet paused, holding the door handle while Miriam turned towards her husband. "You don't think it is Charles?"

"Surely not. He didn't send word..."

I watched them stare at each other, feeling a sense of dread as the color leached from her face.

"Ma'am?" Isaiah asked in a deep, rich voice.

"Who's Charles?" I found my voice, startling them. They all turned toward me. I couldn't blame them. I hadn't spoken since the day I had lost the baby.

"My brother," John said, standing up when another knock resounded on the door.

"Am I to assume no one is home?" a baritone voice rumbled.

Miriam's face hardened. "Do not let him in."

"We can't leave him in the cold, Miriam," John said with a look of irritation. "He made the trip."

I raised my brows, the mixed reactions giving me whiplash.

"Come," Miriam snapped, grabbing my arm and pulling me towards a nervous Ruth. "Charles owns a plantation. Hundreds of slaves are under his care, though he's lost some since the war."

"Oh," I said, at a loss for words. Why was it necessary to tell me that at that moment?

Though I disagreed with the ownership of slaves—if I even believed we were in the damn nineteenth century—I didn't quite understand why Miriam was so upset. Charle's was family, and she must be used to how he operated. Even if she opposed slavery, her reaction seemed more out of fright than anger. Why did she have to fear her brother-in-law? And why did her husband seem oblivious to it?

Hearing the door open, I looked over my shoulder to find a tall man with dark hair that stopped me in my tracks. My breath stalled in my chest as I stared. He removed his hat, and I let the breath out in a whoosh, unsure what it was about him. Charle's dark eyes found mine, breaking me out of the trance.

Miriam pulled me around the corner towards the kitchen, cutting off my view of the handsome man. "I would rather you not be around him," she told me over her shoulder. "But there's nothing we can do about it now."

"Is there anything I can do, Missis?" Ruth asked, twisting her hands.

Miriam shook her head, letting go of my arm as she began to pace. "He's not known for his kindness, Emilia. Though I haven't seen him in the act, I wouldn't trust him around you."

A sense of fear shot through me, and I belatedly realized that it had been the first real emotion since the loss of my baby.

God, my baby. *I had a baby.*

I tried to straighten, even though the pain shot through my abdomen. "Does he hurt women?" I asked, eyes flicking between Miriam and Ruth.

Miriam shook her head. "I just heard rumors on the plantation. He is a perfect gentleman in society."

My brows lowered. "Then why are *you* afraid of him?"

Miriam and Ruth exchanged a look. What was I missing?

"Where has your lovely wife gone?" Charles could be heard in the other room.

Miriam turned towards Ruth. "Take her on upstairs. Stay the night with her. Do not leave her side."

"Is this really necessary?" I asked, my skin prickling in apprehension. *Who is this guy to scare them so much?*

The look on Miriam's face stopped me from pushing. She nodded to Ruth, who had taken me by the waist and elbow to help me up the stairs as I hobbled as fast as my injured body could.

When in the room, Ruth locked the door as I went to my belongings.

"What are you doing?" she asked.

I rummaged through the trunk at the end of the bed, wondering what I was looking for. There wasn't much left behind. Pushing a few things aside that must have been Miriam's, my fingers grazed a wicked dagger. I lifted it, causing Ruth to gasp as my hand gripped the black leather of the hilt with a familiarity I didn't understand. I momentarily caught her gaze before diving back in and pulling out the leather strap I assumed went with it. I didn't question how I knew what to do but let my body lead me. I lifted my skirt and secured the strap around my lower leg. If it were put on my thigh, I would have difficulty getting to it.

"Miss Emilia," Ruth said breathlessly. "Surely—"

"I'm not taking any chances." I stood quickly and swayed on my feet, suddenly lightheaded as pain shot through my side. Ruth caught my arm and guided me over to the bed. I sat down, my breath heaving in and out.

"I don't know what you expect to be doing in your condition, but you should be in bed."

"Maybe for just a little while," I admitted, lying back.

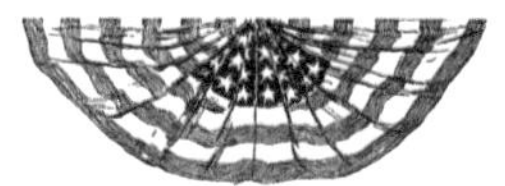

The room was dark when I woke, and the fire burned low. Soft breathing drew my attention to the rocking chair, where I found Ruth sleeping, her ample bosom rising up and down with her soft breathing. She must have taken Miriam's warning to heart. That thought scared me more than the actual encounter with the man.

Was it rude for Miriam not to introduce Charles to me? A part of me wondered. On one hand, she genuinely seemed worried about him, so I understood why she would want to avoid the encounter. On the other hand, we couldn't expect him to never run into me, considering I was living with them for the foreseeable future. Unless she planned to hide me in the bedroom, I would inevitably have to meet the man. Or did he just make a call?

That had me sitting up. It must have been the case. He most likely had gone already, and all of the fuss was for nothing.

I pushed myself out of bed, gritting my teeth against the pain. I had fallen asleep early, and though it was still night, I felt good enough not to spend hours in the room.

I walked to the door as quietly as I could through the pain. Eyeing Ruth, I left the room with a low click of the door. I froze, waiting. When it remained silent, I descended the stairs, gripping the railing to keep upright. The pain in my side was still excruciating, and though I had no visible injury to my leg, pain shot through my hip and knee with each step. I must have twisted or jarred it when I received the other injuries.

I took down one of the lanterns and lit it, thankful that I'd been paying attention this last week. Everyone else still slept, and this was the first time I helped myself to the kitchen, fumbling through the drawers until I found what I needed.

While waiting for my tea to steep, I grabbed the counter, letting my head fall. It didn't take much to exhaust me. *Damn it. When will I be better?*

The air shifted next to me, and I froze, sensing someone. I opened my eyes, and my heart nearly leaped out of my chest at seeing Charles leaning against the counter, watching me. It took all my willpower not to react.

"Trouble sleeping?" he asked before taking a sip of brandy. I watched it press to his lips and how his whiskered throat bobbed as the liquor went down.

I swallowed and tore my eyes away, flushing. Everything about the man screamed danger, but he was undeniably attractive. His darker complexion—several shades darker than his brother's—told of days in the sun, and though he wasn't taller than average, his broader shoulders and tapered waist screamed strength. Charles was a man of generous means, and the way he bore himself showed it.

He raised his hand, and I flinched, cursing myself for showing fear. His hand hesitated before gently pushing a short strand of hair off my forehead. A breath rattled out of me.

"You are a lovely one, aren't ya, darlin'?" Charles asked, his southern drawl making me cringe.

I usually didn't mind, but the way it seemed to crawl over me as he said each word was like a caress I didn't want. I couldn't help but compare it to his brother's accent, which was more refined, as if he spent hours trying to take the southern out of it.

His hand fell to his side as his dark eyes took me in. "John said ya were caught in the crossfires." He squinted at me as if he didn't quite believe it. "That must have been mighty frightening for a woman."

I shrugged, returned to my tea, and spooned some sugar. "I'm sure it was."

"It's a shame ya couldn't keep that beautiful, dark hair of yours."

Self-consciously, my hand brushed across my short locks that didn't quite meet my chin. My smile was shaky as I looked at him. "It was quite a surprise."

"Ya mean ya didn't know?"

I shook my head and told him how I'd lost my memory.

"My, my," he stated. "The lady is full of surprises."

"That's me," I mumbled, returning to my tea. Suddenly, I was exhausted, and all I wanted to do was return to my bedroom.

"I hope ya don't mind my askin'…" I tried to hold back a sigh as I turned to him and cocked my head. "What is a woman like yourself doin' without family?"

Anger flared within me without knowing why. Where *was* my family? How did I get to Virginia? The whole situation was ridiculous and left me confused and angry. "They are in the North," I said, knowing it was true. Even if I was in a different century. His brows creased as he stared at me in confusion. "I don't know exactly," I admitted.

"Ya didn't have time to evacuate?"

I almost let out a growl of frustration. How did he expect me to know if I had no memory?

"Look," I started, lifting my tea but immediately put it back down when my hand shook. "I don't remember. I don't know why I'm in the South. I don't know why my family isn't with me. I am to return to them as soon as I am better."

Charles sat back on his heels. "I see I upset ya. That was not my intention." When I didn't respond, he continued, "My deepest apologies."

I shrugged and leaned against the counter. Much to my dismay, my eyes roamed his body, unable to keep myself from looking. My heart rate accelerated. The man was quite attractive and built but refined, giving off an air of superiority and dominance that I craved in a man. And it didn't help that he showed interest in me. The way *his* eyes trailed my body earlier was particularly sinful and had me nearly panting, just remembering it.

Even so, I was in no condition to have a liaison with the man, but what would a little intrigue hurt? I'd been so numb for so long that I wanted to feel *anything* at this point. When I found his eyes, I blushed at the smirk on his face.

"What do you do?" I found myself asking.

His smile turned wicked, and I found myself regretting my question. "Well, I work with tobacco, my dear. We harvest wheat, but tobacco is where the money is, I dare say."

Charles began numbering his slaves and the work they did. The way he talked about them, like animals rather than humans, had my stomach turning.

"But enough about business." His lips twitched in half a grin. "Too much of that goes over a lady's head. Pardon me. I get lost in my work sometimes. All very boring and lonesome work without a lady of the house." His gaze found mine over his glass as he took another sip. It took everything in me not to blush again as heat flooded my system. "I'm afraid I haven't asked your name," he continued. "My manners have fled upon seeing ya at such a late hour."

He offered his hand. I hesitated, staring at it as if it would bite me. After a moment, I shook it. My eyes widened when he lifted it to his mouth, pressing his brandy-coated lips to it. My breath caught, and his eyes fell to my breasts, noticing them still. I suddenly wished my dress was higher cut. He did very little to hide that he was undressing me with his eyes.

"Emilia O'Connor," I said a little too breathlessly for my liking.

"Well, Miss O'Connor. It'll be a pleasure getting to know ya." He threw back the rest of his brandy and pushed himself away from the counter. "I'll leave ya to your tea."

"Goodnight," I muttered, already turning away from him, not trusting that I wouldn't do something embarrassing.

He paused. "What would ya say about going around town with me?"

"What?"

"When ya are feeling a bit better," he stated, and I found I couldn't look away from his teeth grazing over his whiskers on his lower lip.

I swallowed and found his eyes again. "Why?"

"Well, you see..." He smiled as a gleam twinkled in his dark eyes, "I have a carriage going to waste, and I haven't been to town in ages. Would ya mind joining me?"

"You're going to be in town for a while?" At the rate I was healing, I wouldn't be able to ride in a carriage for another week or two, at least. And I found myself wanting to go with him.

What is wrong with me?

"Yes, ma'am," he purred, somehow close enough now that I could smell the brandy on his breath. Tingles scattered across my skin, and I found myself turning my face up to his, wanting to taste the liquor on his lips. "I shall retire here for the month."

"Well," I couldn't look away from his lips, how they curved devilishly, as if he knew exactly what effect he had on me. "I guess one ride would be all right."

My gaze flicked back up to Charle's, and damn was that a mistake. I stepped back and bumped into the counter, caged between him and it, his whole demeanor absolutely feral. My body thrummed in anticipation.

"Yes," he agreed and stepped back, putting his hands in his pockets. I bit my lip. Charles knew what he was doing to me, and I was entirely out of my element.

It was fantastic. I hadn't felt this alive in so long, and I desperately wanted to feel anything other than pain.

"I can assure ya," he continued, "a ride with me would be the most exhilarating."

"Well, then, I better not miss it." I found myself smiling seductively. I felt utterly unhinged with a newfound confidence. The flirting came to me naturally in a way I wasn't used to before the memory loss. It was thrilling and effortless. A high I had never lost myself in before.

Maybe that's why I ignored the sickening twist of my gut when I promised to go with him.

CHAPTER THIRTY-TWO

Michael & Shaylah

JANUARY 1863

"Lower on the left," Mikey hollered at the men standing on the scaffolding, the large sign carved with 'O'Connor's Pub' hanging crookedly. The men tried to straighten it, and it nearly slipped off the damn building.

"Gods-damn it," Mikey cursed under his breath as they fumbled to get ahold of it. Was it impossible to find reliable workers in this damn city?

"Here," Hughie said, flicking a letter to Mikey.

"What's this?"

"Mail."

"No shite," Mikey grumbled, heading into the pub as he inspected the address.

"A thank ye would be nice!" Hughie hollered as the door slammed closed.

He ignored his men bustling around the pub, cleaning and preparing it. Mikey wasn't sure if he wanted to get them involved in the whole business, but this was the quickest way to make it livable for Shay and the babe to move in.

Mikey tore the letter open, finding an unfamiliar scrawl with his brother's words covering it. With each line, his heart sank, and his stomach turned, feeling the blood drain from his face.

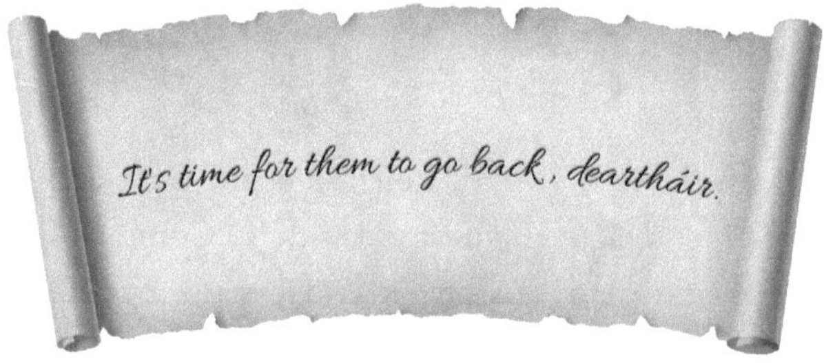

Mikey crushed the letter in hand, cursing Tommy for sending this. For deciding this now, when everything seemed to be going right for him. After he gave himself to the woman and child he loved like his own.

Feck him.

He tossed it into the fire, swearing that he never read it. Cursing the whole damned world. Every time he found happiness, it was taken from him.

Well, not this time.

The fire flickered bright yellow as it consumed the letter, turning red as the paper blackened and curled, crumbling until it was nothing but ash. At least Tommy had gotten the gypsy to safety. That was the only good thing that came out of the blasted letter. However, the condition in which his brother left her concerned him.

The door opened and closed, sending a cold draft through the room, but

Mikey didn't turn from the flames, still consumed by what Tommy wanted him to do.

"So, it's going well?" Shay asked, humor in her voice. Mikey swung around, surprised to find her with Libby on her hip.

"What are ye doin' here?" he asked sharply. She squinted, pursing her lips, and he sighed, running a hand down his face. "I'm sorry, lass. It's been a day."

"Trouble in paradise?" She smiled, and he suddenly felt lighter. Maybe they didn't have to go. If he just told her of Emilia's condition and left his brother's wishes out of it...

Mikey wrapped his arm around her waist, pulling her in for a kiss that made both girls giggle. He swung Libby from Shay's grasp and made her squeal as he tickled her sides. "I missed ye, wee one."

"Dada." Libby giggled, pulling on his cheeks. He stared at her beautiful hazel eyes and knew she had his heart as much as her ma did.

"Aye, mo leanbh."

"It's looking good," Shay stated, looking around the room before smiling at the two of them. Mikey nodded, rubbing the back of his neck. "Is something wrong?" she asked, clearly picking up on his mood.

"There's somethin' I have to tell ye," he said hesitantly, guiding her to one of the seats.

"What is it?"

Mikey set Libby down, watching her wobble on her feet while she stared at the men going in and out.

"Michael," Shay brought his attention back to her. A worry line creased her forehead, and he felt like shite making her wait.

"Me brother sent word. There's been an accident."

Shay leaned on the table and grabbed his arm in a brutal grip. "Is it Millie? Is she okay?"

"Tommy took her to a physician. A canon—" He shook his head. The lass didn't need to know the grim circumstances. "She was hit with stray fire, but intact. He had to leave her there lest they discover her identity." Shay sat back in her seat with a curse. "They're goin' to send her back when all is well," Mikey continued.

"Did he say how bad it was? Can I see the letter?"

Mikey hesitated, eyes flicking back to the fire. "I'm afraid it was ruined."

Shay sighed. "I hope she is okay. Did they say who to contact?"

Mikey shook his head. His brother blessedly left that out. Knowing Shaylah, she'd tear the world apart to get to her friend. "I don't think it's safe to relay that information, dimples." A man walked by with a big whiskey barrel, and Shay swept Libby into her lap, lost in her thoughts. "There's more." Mikey hesitated, not sure how much he wanted to say. "He thinks we should fake Emilia's death."

Shay blinked. "Because of Boudreaux?"

"Aye. But with him gone..."

"We might not have to."

Mikey sat back, feeling weighed down. They were in such a feckin' mess. "Even if he thinks her dead, he might come after—"

"Me," she cut him off.

"Aye." Christ, how could he keep her here with such danger? Unless he killed the bastard...Feckin' hell. Mikey would have to find him first. "Look, lass—"

"No." She glared daggers at him.

"Ye don't even know what I'm about to say."

"You were going to tell me to go."

Mikey sighed and signaled to Henry who swept behind the bar, whistling to get his attention. "Bring the whiskey!" Mikey called.

"You already have a stock of whiskey?" Shay asked, amused.

"Just a wee store." If he was going to keep these boys working, he needed to keep the drinks flowing.

Henry came over with two glasses and the bottle of spirits. "This good, boss?"

Mikey grunted, pushing the bottom of the bottle upward to fill his glass to the brim.

"That's enough for me," Shay said, only accepting a finger. "Thank you."

Henry cocked his brow and left, probably wondering what the hell Mikey was doing with the lass and wean that wasn't even his own. Mikey made a mental note to be transparent with his men about his relationship with Shay and the babe—that he intended to keep her—even if he couldn't announce it to the public.

That Emancipation Proclamation may have freed her people a few weeks back, but it only increased hostility between the races, and there hadn't been any real change yet in the North. Despite the celebrations when it was announced—the whole damn city rang church bells and gathered at the Music Hall to celebrate. Mikey and Shay hadn't gone, but it had been the talk of the city. People said that even Emerson and Stowe were at the hall. Mikey rolled his eyes at the fuss.

Nay, it would take time before they could make that type of announcement, though he hoped it'd be soon. Those closest to him would have to either respect his decision or get the feck out of his life. He'd handle the coppers if they dare try anything.

Mikey adjusted the glass on the table and returned his attention to his woman. "The babe is nearly weaned," he said, eyeing Libby, who tried to grab her ma's drink. A while back, Shay had told him that women in her time didn't drink alcohol while pregnant, and they limited it while nursing. An absolute crock, he thought. If he was a woman, he'd never have a wean if it meant he couldn't drink. Especially if Shay still nursed another year. "Ye can live a little, mo ghrá."

Shay cocked her head to the side. "What does that mean?" She started to smile.

For god's sake, was he blushing? He pulled on the collar of his shirt, suddenly feeling unbearably hot. He hadn't meant to say it. It just slipped out. "Don't ye worry—"

"Oh, no," she laughed, eyes dancing with mischief. "I need to hear this particular endearment."

Mikey lifted the glass, gulping down half the liquor, and savored the burn of it. His insides warmed as he already felt his muscles relaxing. He should have started drinking earlier. "My love," he translated.

"Ah," she purred, sending a thrill through him that was undeniably inappropriate with all the men in the room. Mikey paused, considering, and shook his head when he spotted Libby fumbling out of her ma's lap. Shay continued, "I love when you talk sweet to me."

Mikey looked at her over his glass and took another gulp to reinforce his self-control. If it was up to him, he'd already have her behind the bar, the men be damned. "Don't tempt me, dimples."

Shay leaned on the table, giving him ample view of her decolletage, and smirked. "Who? Me?"

Mikey leaned in, enjoying how her skin darkened with desire as she waited for his next move. "If ye aren't careful, I will have ye bent over this table and screamin' me name while all of them watch. Is that what ye want? Ye want to be punished, mo ghrá?"

Shay's breathing picked up, diverting his attention to her chest. He sucked on his bottom lip, truly considering whether he could flip her skirts up and use her in front of them. Mikey's eyes darted to Henry, wondering if he could watch Libby...

A loud bang reverberated throughout the room.

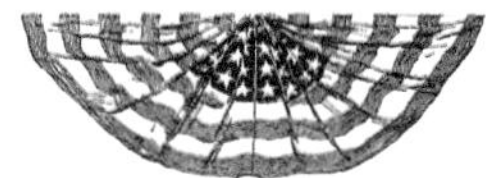

Shay yelped and swept up Libby, spinning around to the open door.

"Everyone line up!" a man in a long, blue coat and trousers busted through the door, five other police officers behind him.

"What is this?" Michael stood, infuriated.

God, he can be terrifying. She often forgot when he constantly flirted with her. Right now, she wasn't sure which was more attractive, his charm or his brutality.

"There's been word you've been selling illegally," the shaggy-haired brute of an officer declared, glaring around the room until his brown gaze snagged on her and Libby. His lip peeled back in disapproval before turning to Michael.

Michael took a step toward the officer. "What the feck ye goin' on about, Bagley? Is this what ye get into now they got rid of McGinniskin?"

"Stay the fuck there," Bagley hollered, pointing a wooden club at Michael.

Shay gasped as Michael halted, holding his hands in the air.

Oh, please, no. Not him. Not now.

The other officers swept the room, overturning the tables and sweeping objects off the surfaces with their clubs, the noise making Libby cry. Shay gripped her daughter tighter, hating these men for upsetting her.

"It's okay, honey," Shay whispered, trying and failing to soothe the child. *Michael will know what to do*, she thought, knowing it was more to reassure herself than Libby. "It's okay."

"Bagley," Michael growled. "Ye can't come in here—"

"You're disappointed you don't have your inside man?" Bagley sneered. "Well, you don't rule this city, O'Connor. Not when I'm in charge." Bagley drew closer to Michael, so close that Shay worried Michael might attack him. "Now, tell me where it is."

"I don't know what ye are feckin' talkin' about!" Michael snapped.

Bagley gestured for two of the officers to go upstairs. "On your knees," he demanded of Michael.

"Like feckin' hell—"

Bagley raised the club and Shay screamed, covering Libby's face, only to find Michael blocking the blow and his fist colliding with Bagley's face.

The three other officers stopped what they were doing, swarming and shouting at Michael.

"Don't!" Shay screamed as fear jolted through her at their raised clubs. "Please!"

Michael spun, landing a kick to one of their chests before ducking as another club came for his head. His men surged forward, ready to fight, but Michael held his hand up to stop them. Everyone froze, including the officers, on Bagley's demand.

"You Irish bastard!" Bagley spat, straightening.

"I told ye, we don't have anythin' here," Michael growled. "What the hell are ye doin'?"

"You expect me to believe an Irish gangster doesn't have a stash of his supply?"

"It's a feckin' pub," Michael said. "I don't even have the damn sign-up yet!"

Bagley gave a greasy smile that turned Shay's stomach. "We'll see about that. My source—"

"Aye," Michael snapped. "Ye said that. Care to mention your source,

Bagley? Or are ye just blowin' steam out of your arse?"

A movement out of Shay's peripheral caught her attention, and she found Hughie sneaking through the back door. She kept her eyes on the officers, not wanting to give away Hughie's location. Terror clogged her throat, and if it wasn't for Libby, she would have thrown herself in front of Michael, begging them to listen.

"Shut up that damn child, woman," Bagley growled, pointing the club at her. She shrank back, covering Libby with arms right before Michael's fist sent Bagley flying backward. The other men rushed forward.

All hell broke loose. Shouts and blows rang through the room. Shay backed up, putting distance between herself and the brawl. There wasn't much, as in weapons that she could use against them. The only thing she saw was the fire poker, and it was behind the mass of men currently beating each other.

"Stop!" Michael yelled over the noise. Not surprisingly, no one listened to his command. Hughie unsheathed a knife, and Michael had to slam into him, knocking his friend to the side to stop him from gutting one of the officers. "Ye will not kill any of these officers. Not in me business."

"Everyone, halt!" Bagley said, panting as he wiped blood from his nose. "Just hold on one fucking minute. Just calm down. Men on your knees."

"That didn't go well the first time." Michael's eyes flashed, but his gaze landed on Shay and Libby, and he stiffened. His throat bobbed as he seemed to deflate, raising his hands. "Do ye give your word to not cause more trouble?"

Bagley pointed his club at Michael again. "Get on your knees, and we'll continue our search. If there's nothing, we'll get out of your hair."

They stared each other down, weighing each other's words. Time dragged slowly as Shay held her breath, nothing but Libby's crying ringing out through the room. Just when she thought Bagley would snap, that Michael would tear into him, Michael nodded and started to get on his knees.

"Mikey," Hughie exclaimed. "Ye can't—"

"Get on your feckin' knees, Hugh." Michael glared at him before turning to meet Henry's gaze, then those of the other three Shay didn't know. Each man fell to their knees, Hughie standing defiantly until even he succumbed to the situation.

"Could this be it, sir?" A young, pimpled face, blonde officer held up several vases up to Bagley. Christ, was he even a man yet?

"Is there anything in them?" The boy held them up to the fire and shook his head when finding them empty. Shay's stomach turned. "No bother, anyway," Bagley continued. "They're too big. Keep searching!"

"What in the bloody hell are ye even lookin' for?" Michael asked, his hands still behind his head.

"Mouth shut!" Bagley growled, standing over Michael while the others ransacked the pub. Bagley turned to Shay. "Get her out of here."

"No," Shay snapped, her voice harsh even to her ears. A gruff, heavy-set officer stepped toward her. "Come near me, and you'll lose some parts you don't want to live without." She quirked a brow and glanced down pointedly.

"You bitch—" he growled, coming at her, but she ducked around the table, moving swifter than him. A loud thump directed her attention to Michael, who struggled on the floor as three men tried to tie his hands behind his back.

"If ye feckin' touch her, ye're dead, Read," Michael growled, blood running out of his mouth. Someone must have hit him in the face. Dread swarmed her system at the sight. It was her fault he was hurt. If she just kept her mouth shut...

Read paused, dark, beady eyes still on Shay.

"I'll make ye regret the day ye were born." Michael spat blood on the floor as they roughly lifted him onto his knees, his hands finally tied. Read paled even though Michael was restrained. "I will hunt down everyone you love—"

"Michael," Shay cried, eyes huge as she covered Libby's ears. She turned back to Read. "If I comply, will you leave him alone?"

"Bring her here," Bagley sighed as if she was a mere inconvenience.

Read held out his hand, his gaze still hard as she approached him. She tried not to wince as his meaty fingers bruised her arm. He jerked her through the pub until they were by Bagley, who had two of the officers search Michael and his men, relieving them of their guns and knives.

Read pulled Shay to him. "Anything on your person?" he asked her.

"No."

"We'll see about that." His sneer had bile rising to her throat. *Not again.*

Read kicked her feet apart and searched her ankles, sliding his hands up her calves, going up her bare legs even though he could have done it above her skirts.

"Get your hands—" Bagley punched Michael in the gut, making his breath gust out.

Read knelt down, circling his cold hands around the back of her thighs, skimming upward indecently high. Shay gritted her teeth and stared at the fire, refusing to show any reaction. His grip tightened on her backside painfully before coming around, brushing across her front and making her jolt.

"Hurry up, Read," Bagley growled, still holding Michael, who looked like he would kill them all.

Read stood, fumbling around her waist. "She's got a corset on. Think anything is hidden in there?"

"Leave it," Bagley snapped. "Finish your search."

Sweat beaded on Read's brow, his ruddy cheeks turning down in a frown. Shay glared at him, waiting for what he'd do next. He shoved his hand down her shirt. "Don't have anything hidden in there, do you?" Read said it so only she could hear and squeezed her breast before sweeping between the two and cupping the other one. He eyed Libby, his lip curling in disgust. "Do you even know who the father is, whore?" He pulled back and called one of the other officers. "Take the kid."

"What? No!"

"No harm will come of the child," Bagley stated.

The other officer pulled a screaming Libby from Shay's arms, the little girl's fingers woven in her mother's hair, making her wince as it was pulled out. Shay saw red, wanting to tear the man apart, but before she could do anything, Read spun her around and bent her forward so forcibly that her hands slammed against the nearest table. *Damn you*, she seethed. The bastard continued to check her back roughly but kept to the outside of her clothes as Michael cursed at him, trying to break out of Bagley's hold.

Shay looked at Michael, hoping he could read her as well as she expected. *Please, don't make this worse. I can't lose you.*

Michael saw it because he stopped thrashing, though his breaths still heaved as he turned a glare onto Read, which could make any man roll over in his grave.

Read ignored him and leaned over her. "Should stay in your own part of the city," he whispered, pressing his weight onto her.

Like hell, I will. She would have fought back if it hadn't been for Michael trying to clean up his life. They didn't need any more trouble. She'd deal with the pig and get this whole misunderstanding over with.

Read pulled her off the table and shoved Shay to her knees by Michael.

"Are ye okay, mo ghrá? Did he hurt ye? I—"

"I'm fine," she hissed, not wanting anyone to overhear. The officers continued to wreck the place, searching for whatever tipped them off.

Something at the back of Shay's mind nagged at her.

An officer's head popped up over the bar, a bottle of whiskey in his hand. "Only thing I can find back here, boss. Should I give it a try?"

Bagley swore at his man and told him to get back to work. Libby started to sob so bad that she was given back to Shay.

Oh, thank God. Thank you.

"Just don't try anything," Bagley said, eyeing the child.

Shay let out a breath she'd been holding, her arms cradling her daughter as she wrapped her little body around her mama. "It's okay, baby. Shh, don't cry. It's okay."

The look on Michael's face turned her stomach, and she wondered what the fate of these officers would be. It was another fifteen minutes before they thoroughly destroyed the place, and all the work Michael had put in was damaged.

Her eyes filled with angry tears as she vowed to make them suffer in every possible way. But then, a chilling thought crossed her mind—whatever Michael had in store would be a million times more brutal than she could imagine.

Good.

"There's nothing here," Read growled, shoving a chair to the side.

Bagley's sigh was heavy behind Michael. Shay glared at him. *All of this for nothing?* She knew Michael wanted to start an honest business, but what did they expect would be here?

"What about any of you?" Bagley asked.

"Nothing, sir."

Bagley pulled Michael to his feet, which she watched with a grim sort of amusement as he struggled to lift Michael's size. Michael winked at her, and she tried to hide a smile. The asshole wouldn't make it easy for the officer.

God, I love you.

"Take them to the precinct," Bagley said, gesturing for the others to be lifted to their feet. The room erupted in Irish curses and chaos.

"What the feck ye mean?" Hughie asked, anger rolling off him. "We did what ye wanted!"

"You found nothing," Michael growled.

"You started a fight," Bagley said, sneering. "Maybe a night at the station will jog your memory."

"How can I remember anything if I don't feckin' know what ye are searchin' for?"

"We'll continue our questioning there."

Shay stood, wobbling a little as she felt faint. "You can't do that! Just tell us what you want."

Bagley pointed the club at her, and Michael bared his teeth, a feral snarl escaping him.

"That is none of your concern, miss," Bagley said, aiming the club at the rest of them. "Now, the rest of you out."

Michael's eyes widened, falling on Shay. Clearly, they didn't intend to take her with them.

Michael broke free long enough to get to Shay, dragging a cursing Bagley along with him. "I don't want ye going to the jail."

"But—"

"Listen," he growled, his gaze consuming her. She fell still at the love and worry she saw in their blue depths. He continued to tell her where the money was to bail him and his men out.

"O'Connor!" Bagley snapped, attempting to pull Michael away.

"Wait one gods-damn minute," Michael snarled at him and turned back to Shay. "Have me da come. I don't want ye anywhere near that place. Normally, I'd have ye get—"

"Enough," Bagley barked, shoving Michael forward. Michael's stare turned from her to Libby, something like regret distorting his features.

But Shay knew. Usually, he would have asked Thomas to get him out. She swallowed, nodding. "We'll get you out as soon as we can!" She yelled it right before the door closed between her and those leaving.

Libby's cries turned into hiccups, her head on Shay's shoulder as she sucked her thumb while her eyes grew heavy, worn out after the altercation. Shay rubbed Libby's back and swayed, thinking of what to do next.

What a way to meet the parents.

She suddenly felt like she needed a nap as well.

CHAPTER THIRTY-THREE

Shaylah

S hay stared at the door, her stomach turning to stone as she paused, hand raised but unmoving. She'd put Libby down for a nap while Rose watched her and went straight to the O'Connor's after asking Hiram where the hell they lived.

"Want me to go with you?" he'd asked, golden eyes worried. Hiram clearly disapproved of her being with Michael, but he had enough common sense not to voice it anymore.

"No." She wrung her hands, pacing around the bakery. "Thank you, but I think I should go myself."

Hiram nodded, leaning back in the chair when Mira descended the stairs. The girl stopped, her whole demeanor brightening at the sight of him. Shay would have smiled if she wasn't so goddamn nervous. She left the two of them to flirt and figure their shit out.

It was little trouble to find the tenement. She quickly ascended the stairs attached to the back of the building up to the second story.

Shay pulled her hand back and—

"Oh!" a young girl gasped in an American accent, her hand flying to her chest as she held on to the door she just swung open. "You startled me!"

"I'm sorry," Shay said, feeling silly as she lowered her hand. "I'm looking for your parents."

The girl looked behind her and closed the door. Her face strained as she looked back at it and folded her arms over her chest. "Well, they're not present at the moment. Can I help you?"

"Oh." Shay worried her lip as she eyed the girl. She had met Maggie once, on the fourth of July, when she went to the celebration with Emilia, Thomas, and some of the others. Then, she hadn't realized how much her green eyes resembled Thomas's. The shock had Shay reeling. It was almost as if she was getting a glimpse of the man across the states with her best friend. Oh, she wished it were true. *Then Millie would be here with me now.* She brushed off the sentiment, fully aware of its impossibility. Instead, Shay focused on Maggie and how she blossomed into a beautiful young woman.

Shay held her hand out. "I'm not sure if you remember me, but I'm Shay."

Maggie eyed it hesitantly before giving a solid shake, her hand rough from days of cooking and cleaning. "I do. You nearly puked at the fair," Maggie said, eyeing her as if Shay would puke again. "I see you had the wean. What was it?"

"A girl." Shay smiled, thinking of her daughter's precious face.

Maggie nodded, giving a polite grin. "What do you need with my parents?"

Shay hesitated, looking around as if the girl's parents would materialize and save her from this predicament. The cold wind sent a chill down her spine, making her shiver.

Maybe it's a blessing in disguise.

She eyed Maggie again. She did look grown. Perhaps they could bail him out without the embarrassment of telling his parents. They would have to return before discovering their daughter was missing.

Shay straightened, making up her mind. "It's Michael."

Maggie rolled her eyes and swept back a dark strand of hair that escaped her bun. "What has my brother done now?"

Shay explained the situation and how Michael was wrongfully accused. With each truth bomb, Maggie's eyes widened in disbelief, her arms falling to her sides. "Truly?" she asked. "He's innocent? He's bought a pub?"

"Well...yes," Shay said, pausing. "He didn't tell you?"

Maggie shook her head. "Mikey tends to avoid Da." She looked back at the door as if she could see through it. "Maybe it's best we don't tell my parents."

Maggie's gaze skimmed down Shay, assessing. "Do you have any money on you?"

Shay nodded and pulled out her small handbag, already having retrieved Michael's money after dropping Libby off. "Your brother's."

"All right then." Maggie sighed. "Let me get something warmer to wear." Shay hesitated.

"What?" Maggie snapped with every bit of Michael's attitude.

Shay smiled. "Should I be taking you there without your parent's permission?"

Maggie scoffed. "I'm practically a grown woman."

Shay shrugged, unable to argue that, and truth be told, she didn't want to go alone. "Let's go."

Maggie looked surprised, but didn't say anything else. It was only a matter of moments before she had a ratty shawl wrapped around her that couldn't possibly be warm enough, and they descended the stairs.

When they reached the street, filled with wild children and carriages bumbling down the road, Maggie asked, "Did you meet Michael through Thomas?"

"Um, I—"

"If I'm honest," Maggie continued, "you don't seem like the type of woman he'd associate with." Maggie winced, turning her bright green eyes to Shay. "I'm sorry if that was rude. He just—"

"I understand," Shay said, though she had to tamp down the flare of anger, reminding herself Michael had been a different person a year back. "We are..." Shay hesitated. "Maybe you should ask him."

Maggie's dark brow rose, and Shay felt herself blush at the girl's sudden scrutiny. Maggie gasped and asked, "Is my brother courting you?" She really looked at Shay now, cocking her head in blatant curiosity. "I must admit, you're not his usual type."

"How do you know what his usual type is?" Shay asked harsher than she intended.

Maggie grinned. "Oh, I'm starting to see it now."

"See what?"

"Why he likes you."

Shay sighed, stopping on the curb to ensure no carriages ran them over. Waiting for a few to go by, she lifted her skirts to step over a pile of snow and ran across the street, the girl on her tail.

"So, what's your story?" Maggie asked.

Why hadn't she come up with a cover story? Shay should have anticipated these questions, yet here she was, fumbling with what to say like a fool.

"Come on," Maggie said, cheeks pink from the cold. She had a certain gleam about her that wasn't there when Shay first met her, and Shay wondered what it was about her home life that dulled the essence of the young woman. "Don't hold back."

They passed a few men on the street, and Shay had to repress a smile when a young man's head whipped around to get a better view of Maggie as she walked by. She didn't seem to notice.

"I—uh..."

"Is it really that hard?" Maggie's nose scrunched, and then her jaw fell, a look of shock on her face. "Jesus, Mary, and Joseph! You aren't a runaway, are you?" Her whisper was like a shot in the gut, but the girl's hand on her back was soft and reassuring.

Shay pulled from her touch. "No."

"Your parents, then?"

"Didn't anyone ever tell you it's rude to ask these questions?"

Maggie halted, looking bewildered. "No, miss."

So now she suddenly had manners? Shay rolled her eyes. "Well, it is."

"Why?"

Shay scanned the street at the people milling about, heading away from the strong wind blowing off the ocean. They were closer to the docks now, and Shay realized she had no idea how far the jail was.

How frazzled am I? She blew out her cheeks, looking up and down the street as if it held the answer.

"Are you planning on walking there?" Maggie asked as if she had read her mind. "Because that might take a while."

Shay swore under her breath, startling a surprised laugh from Maggie.

"Oh, yeah. It makes sense now."

Shay squinted suspiciously. "What does?"

"Nothing." Maggie grinned. "Know anyone who owns a carriage? I'm not sure how much my brother gave you. We might not have enough money to get there and back if we are to bail my brother out and his motley crew."

Shay cursed again, her head falling back. She grabbed everything he had, but she didn't know how much bail would be and for six men, no less. She hadn't thought this through. Only one person she knew would know where to get one.

She nodded and went back to the beginning.

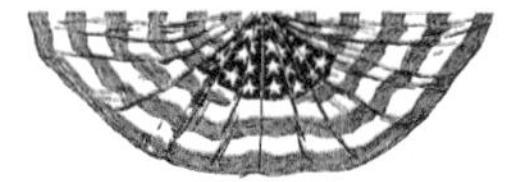

"Why didn't you tell me I needed one?" Shay asked, the carriage jolting down the street as Hiram steered. The day was cloudy, making her already gloomy mood dreary as the sun threatened to set within the hour.

They went to Hiram, knowing that his friend, Sam, owned a wagon. She would have gone to him directly, but she wasn't as acquainted with him as she was with Hiram and felt better asking for Hiram's help.

Long story short, after wasting precious time, they found Sam was out, and his carriage was in use. Which meant that the only other option would be one of a gentleman Michael had an understanding with. Apparently, the man was hooked on opium. Michael kept his supply steady as long as the man let him use his horse and wagon whenever he wanted.

Of course he does. Shay had shaken her head, though she couldn't bring herself to act surprised.

She refused to look back where Maggie now sat and fought to keep the nausea down. She hadn't been in a wagon since Michael had saved her, and the memories of that night flooded her system. Instead of dwelling on the past, she tried to focus on the task ahead. Of course, that brought on a whole set of different fears.

"I thought you were going to let his family deal with it," Hiram said, giving her a disapproving look.

She welcomed the distraction, though she didn't spare him her irritation. "I can't just leave him in there."

"Of course not!" Hiram's grip tightened, the reins creaking before he let out a large sigh that did little to release the stiffness in his shoulders. "You could've at least let his father bail him out. Instead, you brought a child."

"Excuse me!" Maggie hissed in the back. Shay wouldn't have been surprised if the girl hit him if she wasn't gripping the back of their seats. Shay kind of wished she had. "I am no longer a child, Hiram. Why don't you just fuss over Evaline and leave me out of it."

"Evaline isn't bailing a man out of jail!"

"He is my brother! And I am old enough to marry. If that isn't enough for you, you can just—just..." Maggie stuttered, her anger getting the better of her.

"Rot in hell!" Shay chimed in, giving Hiram a big grin that was met with a glare.

Maggie barked out a laugh.

"I shall tell Tommy you are corrupting—"

"Please." Shay laughed, backhanding his arm good-naturedly. "He would love us together."

"Oh!" Maggie clapped her hands. "Think of all the trouble we could get into."

"Exactly!" Shay said just to annoy Hiram. If his puckered expression was anything to go by, she succeeded.

"Besides," Maggie continued more seriously, turning around to run her hands over her skirt. "Da is in a bad way. I don't think he could get two feet, let alone across town."

Hiram cursed.

"You really shouldn't talk like that in front of a lady," Maggie scolded, and Shay had to laugh. The girl had sass, and liked teasing Hiram as much as she did.

It felt like a cold eternity until they reached the jail, but it couldn't have been more than a good half-hour, if not a bit more. Shay's stomach was in her throat as she descended the wagon, looking up at the imposing structure.

Oh, Michael.

It was a hulking, granite building with four wings built much like a cross if you laid it across the ground. She wondered where he was in all of that mess. If he was stuck with a murderer or had his own cell. Regardless, she wondered if she had to worry much. Michael was probably worse than most men in there; he just hadn't been caught yet. Well, until now...but that didn't count. He was falsely accused, and she stayed steadfast to that truth.

"My God," Maggie gasped. "He's in there?"

"He's going to be fine. We'll get him out in no time." Though Shay wasn't sure who she was trying to convince, Maggie or herself.

"I'll go bring it around back," Hiram said, leaving them to wait while he parked the carriage.

The large atrium was well-lit, with large windows spanning the walls. Even the smell wasn't atrocious, ventilated by the windows, but Shay suspected the wings with the inmates would be notably worse. Still, it wasn't as bad as she imagined, yet it didn't detract from the gloom.

There's nothing like a bit of incarceration to bring down the mood.

"How cheerful," Maggie muttered, scanning the high ceiling.

"I told you it wasn't a place for ladies," Hiram said, taking the lead to the front desk.

Maggie snorted. "We're ladies now? Really, Hiram. You must make up your mind."

Hiram gave her an exasperated look before talking to the officer at the desk.

"Want to make a bet?" Maggie leaned closer to Shay, casting a side-eye at the officer.

"What?"

"How much do you want to wage that my brother already has some of these men in his pockets?"

Shay's mouth almost fell open as she eyed the other officers milling around. Could Michael bribe them? Were they corrupt? She wouldn't put it past him. "On that, we can agree," she said.

Maggie sniffed. "No fun."

"I'm sorry, sir. Bail isn't posted—"

Shay pushed past Hiram. "Bagley said he would make bail!"

"And who are ye, ma'am?"

"Does it matter? Other than I work with Michael O'Connor. Do you want to go against my word, sir? You really want to weigh—"

"Here now," the man snapped, his beady eyes darting between them, "Are ye threatening an officer?"

"Well, n—"

"Oh, yes! She is!" Maggie said, pressing her fingertips to his desk. Shay's eyes widened in surprise. The girl had guts. "And I am Margaret O'Connor. I will contact my brother, Tommy, to see where it goes from there..."

"Who the feck is Tommy?"

Maggie's face fell, followed by a baffled expression. "O'Connor? You never heard of the O'Connor brothers?"

An older Irishman appeared around the desk a look of defeated acceptance weighing his features down. "Aye, I know of 'em. Come with me."

Maggie smirked at the guy behind the desk, who only glared back.

They were led through the atrium to the back wing, where they kept the men. The airy and open impression they first had upon entering quickly dwindled to a rising sense of claustrophobia and overpowering body odor.

Shay wrinkled her nose. "He's in there?"

"What'd ye expect?" the officer leading them asked. "A suite?"

No, actually. She just wasn't prepared to see the conditions or for the odor to be so intense.

She ignored him as they went, passing row after row of cells of men whistling and shouting obscenities.

Hiram's lip raised in disgust. "You shouldn't have come here."

"If not me, then who?"

He whirled on Shay, eyes blazing. "It's not your problem!"

Not my problem? The audacity—

Maggie stepped in between them, preventing Shay from giving Hiram his own problem.

"Hiram, please," Maggie said, voice strained and hand pressed to his chest. "Tommy would want us to help."

"Do ye want to see your man, or are ye goin' to waste me time squabblin' all day?" They turned to the officer, a look of annoyance creasing his lined, gaunt face.

Shay gestured for him to go, quickly falling in step with him. "How do you know Michael?" she asked.

His watery brown eyes slid to hers, his jaw set. "We've had some business."

Business. Jesus Christ. He *did* have some cops in his pockets. Would she ever not be surprised by what Michael was capable of?

The officer led them up a set of stairs and unclipped his ring of keys. "Ye have company, O'Connor."

Shay peered around the man's shoulder to find Michael lying on a small bed, arm over his face. Was he seriously sleeping? Her stomach flipped in either relief or annoyance. Probably both. The man had her running around town, worried shitless over him, and he was passed out without a care.

"Michael," she hollered.

His leg bent, and he slowly rose into a sitting position with the ease and grace of a panther. Michael's blue gaze found hers, blazing fury in those beautiful depths. Shay swallowed past the sudden lump lodged in her throat.

"I told ye to get me feckin' family."

Maggie stepped forward, and Michael started swearing in Irish.

"Nice to see you as well, brother," Maggie returned, raising a brow, completely unaffected by his mood.

The key clanged in the lock, and the bars slid open. Shay wished she could say she was as calm as the girl, but she suddenly wanted to relock it and run. The officer stepped out of the way for Michael to exit.

Michael prowled toward her, his jaw clenching as he took each of them in.

"I expect me cut," the officer said, but Michael focused on Shay, unwavering and all-consuming. Her breaths stopped in her chest.

Michael pulled at her dress.

"What are you—" she began, but Michael was already in the slit where she kept her change purse, pulling it out to get his money. Why did he affect her like this? He was feral and domineering, altogether reckless, a bit of an asshole, and all she could think about was how much she wanted to kiss him. *Now.*

Michael kept his eyes on her, looking as if he knew *just* what she was thinking when he handed the money to the officer.

"There should be enough for the rest of me men as well, Banwell," he said.

Shay swallowed again, attempting to clear the growing rock in her throat while her heart thundered. It didn't help when she licked her lips nervously, and Michael's eyes darkened, following the trail of her tongue. He slid the purse back into her dress, his fingers gliding across her hip, causing a shiver to jolt through her.

"Aye," Banwell said, counting the money. "That should do."

Michael nodded, his dark gaze sliding over to Hiram with a sudden fury. "And why the feck did ye let her come?"

"You think I could stop her?"

"I expect ye to not bring me woman and sister into a damned jail!"

"Your woman?" Hiram spat, golden eyes igniting. "Maybe you shouldn't bring *your* woman into this mess!"

For Lord's sake. These men. Shay wanted to wring both of their necks.

Shay slid between them with a hand to each chest. "I came because I was the only one who could get the job done." She ignored Maggie's mutterings and dug her hands into their coats when it looked like they might go to blows. "And I do whatever the hell I want," she hissed, eyeing each of them before looking at the men in the adjacent cell.

The man looked like he was ready for some popcorn to enjoy the show. She snarled and turned to Michael.

"I came because—" She glanced at Maggie, resolve straightening her shoulders, "Because Maggie was the only one there, and we are more than capable of making our own decisions. You don't have to like it, but you must accept it."

A muscle flexed in his jaw, but he didn't argue, and she would accept that win.

Shay turned to Hiram and shoved him. "And you have no say in what I do. I asked for your help, and I appreciate it more than you can imagine. But if you pull that misogynistic bullshit again, I will cut you. Do you understand?"

The two men continued to glare at one another.

"Listen," Banwell practically drawled in his Irish accent, "this isn't the time or the—" He stopped as she turned her own glare on him and muttered something under his breath.

"I believe a thank you should be involved," she practically growled at Michael. It took a few long moments for him to look at her, but when he did, the world tilted on its axis.

"Tá mé faoi chomaoin agat, mo ghrá. Anois agus go deo. Caithfidh mé mo shaol ag déanamh suas duit é." The words flowed off his lips, caressing her skin and causing her to shiver even though she didn't know their meaning. She didn't have to. The promise within them was clear enough. Michael's thumb brushed her cheek, and he turned on his heel toward Banwell.

Michael spoke with the officer as he released the rest of his men. They exited the cells with a mixture of smirks and deathly glares. Hughie's sent another chill through her that was drastically different from the one Michael's evoked.

There was something ominous about him, a darkness that seemed to emanate from his soul. Michael may have done unmentionable acts, but Hughie seemed to enjoy inflicting pain, reveling in the misery of others. She hated to think it, but it almost would have been better if Georgie lived instead. He at least had some semblance of morality.

Or a soul, she thought, unease prickling her skin.

Michael's hand rested on her back as they walked out of the jail, the other prisoners cursing them as they went.

"There is somethin' ye should know," Banwell told Michael as they neared the exit.

Michael stilled. "Aye?"

"The man that turned ye in..." Banwell shifted on his feet, "He wasn't from around here."

Shay paused, bile rising in her throat.

Michael's expression grew dark. "Did ye get a name?"

"He made sure to keep quiet, but a man with an accent like that doesn't go unnoticed," Banwell said, glancing around as if afraid someone might overhear them. "I did some diggin'."

"Diggin'?"

"Aye, I asked around. He's an old plantation owner, one of the big ones down south. I guess he has been in the North for some months now. Goes by the name Marcel Boudreaux."

Michael cursed at the same time Shay pressed a hand to her stomach. She should be used to his surprises, but the man haunted them like a damn wraith. He came after her friend, lied to Michael, stole his share, and murdered one of his men. Now, he had Michael and his men turned in under false accusations.

If Michael wasn't—well, Michael—who knew how long he'd be locked up. Would they ever escape him? Her head spun sickeningly as she tried to make sense of it all. How had she ended up in this cutthroat world?

She met Michael's steely resolve, and she knew, had known for some time now...

Marcel Pierre Boudreaux had to die.

CHAPTER THIRTY-FOUR

Emilia

February 1863

"**Y**ou will not go."

Miriam paced my room as Ruth struggled to get me into a different dress. I had filled out some in the last two weeks, and the borrowed dresses no longer fell limp on my figure, pulling a little tighter across the areas that used to be curvy. I held back a curse as I looked in the mirror, a wisp of the woman I once was. At least the bruising had gone down, and Miriam gave my hair a trim to straighten up the straggly waves that just brushed my chin. I gritted my teeth at the short length, even as Miriam pinned it back, making the length less obvious.

"I already told him I'd go," I told her, ignoring the flip in my stomach. I didn't tell her I'd been looking forward to the trip. How I imagined what we would do, and if Charles showed interest in me. "When he asked again last night, I didn't want to be rude."

"Well, why indeed?" The roll of her eyes could be felt miles away. She fussed, stopping before me with her hands on her hips. "You are clearly still healing."

"I'm nearly better," I said indignantly. I refused to move lest Miriam saw the stiffness that still plagued my abdomen.

Miriam cursed worse than any man, and I couldn't help but smile.

"This is serious," she snapped.

My face fell. "I know. It's only for a ride, Miriam. I'll be fine."

I understood she didn't trust the man. That he could very well be a despicable human being. I did.

I just couldn't get myself to care.

For the first time in my life—that I could remember—I wanted to rebel. Why not do it with a handsome man? I didn't have to like him. I could even despise every wrongdoing he committed. But I was going to feel something, damn it, and *no one* would get in my way of that. Not even Miriam's fear.

It was time to take my power back.

Miriam sighed, running her hands over her face. "Ruth, you must go with them."

My whole body deflated. I refused to think about why I didn't want her to go.

Ruth's hands paused on my corset, but quickly went back to loosely tying it to keep it from aggravating my wounds. "Of course."

Miriam nodded and left the room, only to return moments later with an olive-green bonnet in her hand, long silk ribbons hanging from it. "Wear this," she said, handing it to me. It matched my plain green dress quite well. When on, I saw why she wanted me to wear it. My short hair no longer threatened to spill down.

I took a long look in the mirror, noting the dark circles under my eyes and how my bones protruded through my skin. I bit my lip self-consciously. I'd never been conceited, but this was too much. How long had I looked like this? Did the father of my child care that I'd lost my curves? Because I sure did...

Miriam grabbed my hand, drawing my attention to her. Her caramel eyes warm with worry. "Promise me you won't be alone with him."

I swallowed and nodded, already planning on how to lose Ruth.

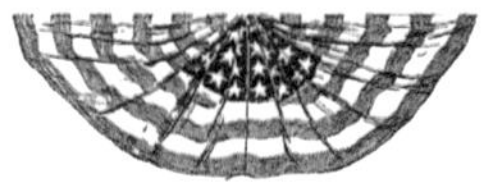

The carriage bumped down the streets of Fredericksburg, and I had to hold back a wince as it jarred my wound.

"Ya look quite lovely," Charles said, blowing smoke out of his cigar.

"Thank you." I smiled at him, pulling the blanket further up my lap. His eyes caught on the movement but didn't linger.

A gust of air blew through the cracks of the carriage. I cringed and looked to Isaiah, steering the horses from the front bench. Guilt ate at me as I watched Ruth up front with him. Both had to be freezing out there. All because Charles wanted to take me around town. Silly, if you thought about it, considering it wasn't even his town, and most of it was destroyed.

Charles had been leaning against the carriage, smoking one of his cigars as he watched Miriam help me down the front steps. He didn't offer assistance but watched me, his gaze blazing down my figure and back up.

So much for Southern decency.

The man didn't even have the manners to hide what he was doing. A dark part of me reveled in it, and I wondered for the umpteenth time exactly what I'd forgotten. Who had I become?

When Charles realized Ruth would join us, a brief flash of annoyance crossed his face so quickly that I thought I had imagined it. After that, he made sure to amplify his Southern charm.

The carriage went over another bump, sending a shot of pain through my abdomen. I held back a wince.

"I'm afraid I didn't have the manners to inquire about your injuries," he said. Clearly I hadn't hid my discomfort as well as I thought. His eyes roamed over my body, but there was no pity. Only an interest that sent my pulse into a frenzy.

"They are getting better," I admitted, taking a mental inventory of all the aches while refusing to acknowledge the one that hurt me the most.

"I knew a formidable woman such as yourself would heal nicely." He took another puff of the cigar as his dark eyes consumed me. "Though, under unusual circumstances, I dare say."

"Unusual times," I muttered, turning my attention towards the window.

"That I can agree with." A bloom of smoke fell over me, a warning of his attention. I fell still as his hand slid dangerously high up my thigh. My breath increased, a flush spreading over me as I waited for what he'd do next. I looked up and found his heated gaze on me as his large hand seemed to swallow my leg. We sat like that, each studying the other to see what they would do next. "I never met a woman like ya," he admitted.

I took a deep breath, noting how it drew his attention to my chest. I suddenly wished Ruth had tightened my stays a little more.

When I said nothing, he continued, "I must ask, have ya ever been kissed by a man?"

My chest felt like it was going to explode at the loaded question, and I turned away, bombarded by the loss of my child and the man I couldn't remember. In truth, I never *remembered* kissing a man, though I must have. So, technically, I hadn't. Right?

I looked back up at Charles, all nerves as I shook my head. He squeezed my thigh and removed his hand, studying me as he took a long pull of his cigar, a look of satisfaction sliding across his face.

I turned to the window, not wanting him to see how nervous I was or how my hands shook. A light tug on my bonnet had me gasping and my hair cascading down, framing my face in a wild frenzy.

"Lord, to hear ya make that sound again. I will think of that moment all night."

My mouth fell open at the implication and his forwardness. Were southern manners a fabrication, or was I lucky enough to meet the only ruffian out of them all?

What is wrong with me? Honestly, I didn't care as long as Charles made me feel something other than the pain and worry. And I would keep chasing that as long as possible.

Charles smirked, and my breath froze as his warm fingers trailed across my cheek, pushing my hair back so they could weave into it. "I think I would like to kiss ya now, Miss O'Connor."

I tilted my chin higher even as he tugged on my hair, pulling my head back. My tongue ran over my lips, and I was rewarded with searing heat as he tracked the movement. Charles' lips pressed against mine, and I ignored the sickening twist of my gut, the guilt I didn't understand, and let him guide me.

I opened for him, his tongue sweeping in as he pulled me closer, his hand gripping my thigh and brushing upward. I gasped, and he growled, deepening the kiss until I lost all sense of where I was. Charle's hand slid over my neck, his thumb brushing my cheek surprisingly gentle, causing butterflies to take flight in my belly and an unexpected desire to course through me.

And yet, somewhere deep down, tugging—not a memory, per se—but maybe a feeling? Guilt and aversion had me pulling back, pressing my hand to Charles' chest and gently stopping his pursuit.

"My apologies," Charles said, not looking the least bit sorry and more like a cat that got into the milk. "I was too forward." He posed it like a question, but it was apparent he didn't regret it, not with the wicked grin still on his face.

I swallowed past the lump in my throat, the nausea churning in my stomach, and forced a smile. "It's all right."

Though it felt anything but. I bit my lip, and Charles took it as a sign to brush his thumb over my mouth. He watched the movement with barely leashed longing, and I held my breath, waiting for what he'd dare to do next. Prayed he would back off, though I didn't know why. Did my mind still long for the man I'd been with? Perhaps a tiny part of me knew that I belonged to another?

The thought sent a flash of anger through me, and I found my hand brushing against Charles' as I leaned forward, brushing my mouth against his warm one. "Don't apologize," I whispered, "when I wanted it too."

"Oh." He chuckled darkly. "I'm going to enjoy this."

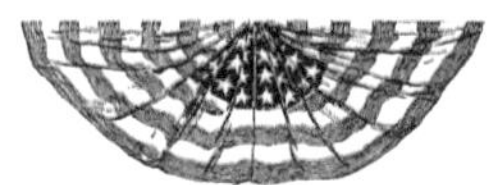

As our carriage rattled through the streets, an increasing number of bumps and jolts over piles of snow had me constantly gritting my teeth. The over-crowded streets filled with civilians and soldiers erased any desire I may have had, replacing it with anguish. All those families had lost someone in the battle or known someone who did. Their town was destroyed, and life as they knew it would forever be changed. As mine had changed.

At least I don't remember losing the father of my child, I thought bitterly.

We went around a bend, and I stifled a gasp, getting a clear view of wrecked houses and buildings teeming with doctors and nurses on their way to their next tasks, the next patient. And past the chaos, a field burned and stained with war. Tears wet my cheeks as men still hammered wooden headboards into the earth.

God, what had I forgotten? There's no way I was part of that. Is there? My hand brushed my short hair and fell to my injured abdomen. *How did I survive? I'm not a fighter. Soldier.* The tears were a steady current now, cascading down my face and neck, falling between my breasts. I refused to turn to Charles, who surprisingly kept silent, transfixed by the effects of the brutal war. Refused to let him see this weakness. No, this *grief*.

I pressed a hand to my mouth, shaking my head, refusing to believe it. Miriam had to be mistaken because if those men had died, I surely would have been in the ground with them. Nothing short of a miracle had to keep me alive, and I wondered if that miracle walked in a different field. And, for the millionth time since I'd woken all those weeks ago, I questioned why I was left behind.

CHAPTER THIRTY-FIVE

Shaylah

Shaylah

March 1863

He looked handsome in his uniform, the brass buttons and blue trousers the brightest colors Shay had ever seen on the man.

"Well, look at you," she said, even as fear overwhelmed her pride.

Her nerves made her jittery all day, but she couldn't blame it solely on Hiram's recruitment. No, she dared not think about anything else that might send her over the edge and into hysterics. Shay refrained from an eye roll.

Stop being absurd. You have never been hysteric a day in your life.

Until maybe today...

Hiram ran his hands over his uniform, looking happier than she had ever seen him. Everyone had met at the bakery. Jackson and Isaac were resplendent in their uniforms, having enlisted as well, and their three other sisters came by to say goodbye, all fussing over their brothers like mother hens as Mira cried into a handkerchief. Not only were her brothers leaving her, but the man she loved. Shay sighed. She might think the girl was silly, but she had a big heart. How could she fault her loving Hiram so much?

Shay glanced at George and Rose, radiating pride at their boys fighting for their freedom and enjoying all their children in the same room, possibly for the last time.

Shay turned away as tears pricked her eyes. *God, what if they don't make it?*

She stared out the window at the light snow blowing through the street and prayed for their safe return. Everyone she cared about was fighting in this damn war, and she didn't know what she'd do with herself if they didn't make it back. Shay knew she shouldn't, but she still couldn't help the relief she felt whenever she thought of Michael staying home.

No, you will not think about him right now.

The hysteria threatened to rise again as the image of Michael and Libby playing in the pub flashed in her mind. She'd left them only an hour before and missed them already. He took the role of a father naturally, and that thought alone settled her nerves. Who would have thought Michael O'Connor could have a soft side?

Shay snorted and looked around the room, hoping no one heard.

Hiram appeared at her side and stared out the window, his tan face serious but almost radiating off a glow, as if his triumph was seeping through his pores. "I never thought I'd see the day," he'd said.

She smiled sadly and looked up at him. "Just..." She took a deep breath. "Just be careful. Come back."

Golden eyes met hers, and his grin spread, freezing the breath in her chest. Hiram was always handsome, but he was stunning when he let go of the anger he carried with him everywhere. "Are you worried about me?"

She bumped his shoulder. "Maybe just a little bit." She spotted Mira staring at them and raised her brows. "But I think someone else will count the minutes until you return."

Hiram followed her line of sight, and his face brightened in a way she had never seen before. It was like looking at an entirely different man. Her heart crumpled while thinking about all the trials and tribulations he would endure in the next couple of years.

Please, don't let him die.

"My only regret is not marrying her sooner," he admitted, shocking Shay into silence. She grabbed his arm tightly, eyes widening in shock.

"Are you telling me you asked?"

His face fell as he glanced at Mira. "Not yet. I didn't want her waiting for me in case something happened..."

"She'll be waiting whether you ask or not. When you feel that way about someone, your heart will always wait, even when it seems impossible... Can I give you my opinion?"

Hiram shifted uncomfortably but nodded. "Haven't held back yet," he said roughly, making her smile.

"Don't wait. Don't waste one minute without her. Because that girl will wait for you for years on an unspoken promise—in here," Shay held her hand above her heart, "she already belongs to you, and she'll have to live without knowing what she meant to you. Fate can take a life away from us whether we're at war or just walking down the street. Waste no time apart, marry that girl, and soak up every blessed moment. Because waiting for a man who hasn't declared himself hers is unbearable in itself. Loving a man that gave himself to you is well worth the fear of losing him in this damn war."

Hiram's shoulders straightened, and though he didn't look at her again, Shay could swear she saw resolve in his eyes.

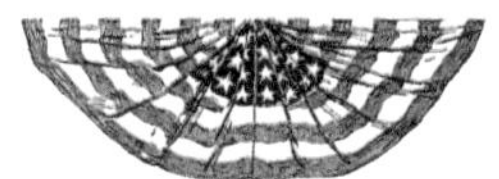

Shay waved, hoping to find a cab to take her to Charlestown. An omnibus turned down the street, and she flailed her hand manically, ready to jump in front of the damn thing to make it stop, when a loud whistle pierced the air to her right.

A man of average height with a bowler hat over his short-cropped hair was flagging down the cab. "Looked like you needed some help," he said in a Northern New England accent.

Hearing the varying accents, brogues, and lilts still surprised her. It was absolutely fascinating and not an experience she encountered as much in the twenty-first century—other than on television—so hearing the more common Bostonian inflection was still surprising.

Shay suppressed a sigh, feeling absolutely ridiculous. *This century is wild. I should have traveled abroad before traveling centuries.*

"Thank you," she said, meaning it as she descended the curb to get to the cab. The man followed close behind her, causing apprehension to skitter up her spine.

"Let me." He held his hand out to help her up the step.

She looked into his dark eyes and found them clear and kind. Slow exhale. *Not every man wants to hurt you.*

Shay accepted his help and got into the cab, while he followed suit and took another seat in the row behind her. The journey to Charlestown was uneventful, with passengers getting on and off until only a handful were left, including the man behind her.

Why is he still on? A few stops, fine. That would make sense. But ten? He could be going all the way to Charlestown, but Shay had the uneasy feeling that he was waiting for something. More like waiting for *her.* Only God knew why. She didn't dare look back.

Shay leaned forward, heart thundering in her chest, and hollered, "Stop here!" When the driver didn't stop, she hit the roof and hollered. The omnibus pulled over, the horses snorting their response as she descended the step.

The nearest alley was empty and dirty, but she flew down it, only sparing a glance to see a shadow turning off the street. Shay picked up her pace, the wind whipping the shawl around her shoulders as she turned onto the next street filled with abandoned buildings and trash.

Where are all the damn people?

The door to the nearest building wouldn't budge.

"Come on!" she hissed, slamming her shoulder into it. Pain shot through her arm, and she ran to the next, practically whimpering in relief when it swung open, and she stumbled in, shutting it quickly behind her.

Gasping, she let her eyes adjust to the dark room, finding it empty, only a crate and some loose floorboards littering the dusty space. She attempted to lock the door with shaking hands only to find it broken.

A figure walked past the cloudy window, and Shay held in a gasp, hands clamped around her mouth. The minutes dragged on as she waited, her heart pounding in her ears, half expecting him to bust through it. When no movement appeared outside the door, she shuffled backward until her back hit something hard.

Her shrill scream rent the air just before a hand clamped around it, cutting it off with a sweet scent.

Shay's vision faded to black.

CHAPTER THIRTY-SIX

Emilia

A few weeks passed since my carriage ride with Charles. Since then, I healed enough to go for walks and often went out with Miriam for fresh air or market trips. The town was still recovering from the battle and swamped with injured soldiers and the families coming back home to discover any damage done to their property and men. And yet, even with the devastation wrought throughout their streets, there was a sense of triumph and celebration.

The South had won the battle.

With each increasing day, my resentment of the people and what they fought for grew, and I struggled to interact with them. How could anyone celebrate the death of another? And though the Emancipation Proclamation went into effect on the first of the year, I saw little change. There were those still dealing in slavery, and those who were freed had to face the harsh treatment of Southerners who despised Lincoln and his *Proclamation*.

If I felt a fraction of this bitterness before I lost my memory, there would be no denying why I fought for the Union. The trade was despicable, the people were despicable, and I had no sympathy for those who were that way because that's how they were "raised." No. The thought alone had me wanting to bear arms and fight for the other side.

If I didn't have to wait for the doctor to approve of travel, I would have left this horrid state ages ago.

I spent my days drowning out the resentment, the aching loss of what I didn't remember, by sneaking heated kisses in the shadows of the house. To fill the void that was like a yawning pit in my soul—a deep longing that Charles never satisfied—while becoming increasingly familiar with the man I didn't want beyond our sordid encounters.

The loss had been eating at me particularly bad, to the point that I didn't even want to get out of bed. One more menial task would have set me off. I found myself plotting. Planning something that would distract me. So, when the house was conveniently empty except for Charles in the kitchen, I undid my dress, loving how his brown eyes darkened, his lids heavy with desire. It was intoxicating—the power I had over someone.

He stopped what he was doing as I shyly smiled, my fingers fumbling with the buttons just before we were at each other like animals. Charles shoved his hands into my hair, and I gripped his wrists, holding on as if it would save my sanity.

Our breaths came out in quick pants, and then suddenly his hands squeezed my thighs. I squealed as my ass hit the counter. Charles pushed up my skirts, his hand gliding up my bare leg, and my breath stalled, head falling back as his tongue ran up my neck.

"I've been waitin' to do this with ya for weeks," he groaned, and I moaned, my thighs squeezing his waist.

I was reckless, desperate, and falling apart like never before. Charles ran his hand down my neck and to the opening of my dress, brushing my breasts, larger now that I had put on some weight. I shivered with anticipation.

"God, just when I thought ya couldn't get any more beautiful," he muttered, gripping my breast in his firm, calloused hand.

"Yes," I gasped, pushing into his almost painful grasp. Soaking up anything that would make me forget everything I went through the last few weeks.

I took pleasure in the way he admired my body, my peeked breasts on full display and long legs wrapped around him. My legs tightened so he was flush with my center and right where I wanted him.

His mouth consumed mine, brutal and punishing, not at all in the way a man should treat a lady who supposedly was a virgin in this time. It was true Charles was no gentleman. What was even more accurate: I didn't want one.

"I should take you to a room," he said between a sweep of his tongue. My lips were going numb, and I relished in it. "Your first time will hurt, and I want to take my time with ya."

"Oh?" I asked, giving him my most innocent eyes while biting my lip.

I may not have remembered losing my virginity, but I knew far more than what Charles suspected. I gripped his shirt as he nodded, enjoying the game he didn't know we were playing. I would have never done anything like this before losing my memory, but I found I didn't give a shit anymore, even if I didn't know why. As if I was in my own type of shaded rebellion. I ran my hands over his shirt buttons and skimmed his chest with my fingertips. "What exactly would you do to me?"

Charles watched my hands work as his throat bobbed, body practically shaking in restraint. "That might not be somethin' for a lady—"

"Please," I begged. "What does a man do with a woman?"

A thud behind Charles had my eyes flitting to the back kitchen door. My heart jumped into my throat. *Is Miriam early?*

But Charles dark gaze found mine, and I froze, forgetting the noise as I watched the hunger turn feral. He shoved my skirts to my waist and ran his fingers over my center. I gasped, mouth falling open as he observed me. "Let me show ya, sugar."

Charles stuck his finger in my mouth, startling me. I sucked it before he withdrew and ran it over my center, making me jolt. Slowly, he pushed one finger into me, and my breathing increased, heaving my chest up and down for him.

"Oh," I said quietly, unable to hold back the reaction.

He undid his pants with his other hand, and I rolled my lips nervously. Charles pulled his cock out and took my hand, making me grip it tightly. He didn't give me an option, and I found I rather liked that.

"Just like that, sugar. Your hand feels so good."

He thrust into it, and I shivered. Had I done this before? It would have been great to remember so I could pull out any tricks I learned, though I suspected Charles liked that I was a virgin. So, maybe it was good that I didn't remember.

"Like this?" I asked, pumping my hand up and down.

"Such a good girl."

I warmed under his praise and smiled up at him.

"Oh, ya like that?" he asked, running his other hand through my hair and pulling my head back. He pushed a second finger into me, causing me to whimper and revel in the stretch of it, the way it filled me deliciously. He withdrew his fingers, and I pouted. Charles chuckled darkly before shoving them into my mouth, making me choke on them. My eyes flew wide, surprised by the ferocity.

"That's right, sugar. Taste yourself."

They went down my throat, and he kept them there until I gagged, my eyes watering.

"Good girl."

I pulled in deep breaths as he positioned himself in front of my center, trying to blink past the tears but finding I wanted this. Wanted him to use me. Wanted to give my body away to erase anything of the past and what I'd done.

His tip pressed against my entrance, and he pulled my hair painfully so I couldn't move or do anything but stare at his face. "This is going to hurt," he said.

I swallowed, body shaking in anticipation. "What if I don't want this?" I asked, not meaning it, but wanting his answer, nonetheless.

Charles laughed, the bitter incredulity of it causing goosebumps to erupt over my body, a prickling sensation skittering up my spine.

He wouldn't take it easy on me, even when he thought it was my first time. Fear pulsed through me, and I rejoiced in it. Basked in the danger, the utter lack of empathy for me or my desires, and silently willed him to plunder me into oblivion. "It's a little late for that."

"Please," I pleaded, holding his arms, delighting in how his features shifted while he got off on my fear. What was wrong with me? Why did I like this? Had I fallen so far that I used Charles like a drug? I had to be sick, morally aberrant, to want this when I couldn't even remember doing it before. "Please."

His fingers bit into my bare hip, indeed leaving bruises, while his other hand twisted harder in my hair, making my eyes water. "I'm goin' to show ya what a better man couldn't," he admitted with a dark and greedy tone I had never heard him use before. This had been his plan for weeks, and he thought he'd been playing me the entire time. I whimpered and gripped him tighter, playing into his sick desire.

He didn't know I'd been playing him, too, and he just fell into my trap.

"Don't," I begged, wiggling against him.

Charles only grunted, simultaneously squeezing my hip and wrenching my hair back as he shoved inside me. I screamed, relishing in the pain.

"That's right," he growled. "Take it like a good girl."

His thrusts became faster and harder, giving no time for my body to adjust. "Give me what should be your husbands. Let me use ya like the dirty little whore ya are."

"Stop," I cried, even as I pulled him closer and wrapped my legs tighter. "Don't, please!"

"Ya, little tease. Think ya can go around this house, practically askin' for it while stickin' your tongue in my mouth, and think ya won't bend over for me?" He laughed, shoving into me so hard my ass moved back several inches. I grunted. "Ya know, I think I'd rather like ya like that."

He pulled out of me, and I whimpered from the loss, though a smile bloomed on his face at his assumption of my relief. Charles yanked me off the counter, flipping me around so my hands slapped onto the counter. He wasted no time in lifting my skirts.

"What are you doing?" My voice broke from the excitement, thrilling him more.

"Hold tight while ya take it like a bitch," he ground out.

He slammed into me. I called out, fingers pressed into the wood counter as his thighs slapped against mine, taking up a steady rhythm as it rang out through the silent house.

"Ya are so tight," he groaned, pulling my hair again—a move he was obviously fond of—causing my spine to bend painfully. My wounds smarted a bit but were, thankfully, healed enough to not incapacitate me. "Lord," he continued, squeezing my ass. "This is far rounder than expected. God, woman." He let out a low rumble of a laugh. "Ya look good with me inside ya. Maybe I should try this next..." I tensed as he pressed a thumb into my ass, the intrusion unfamiliar and filling me uncomfortably. He spat, and I flinched as his spit coated me.

"What—" I started, but he had already shoved another finger into the tight hole, and I yelled, his pace excruciating. Hell, did it feel good. The pain and pleasure were a delectable mixture.

"Yes," he groaned to himself. "A good little bitch, indeed."

"Please," I said again, reaching back to grip his arm. "Please."

He pulled his fingers out of me and grabbed my face, caging my back to his chest so that I was away from the counter as he continued to pump into me. *Finally.* I slid my hand between the counter and myself and reached between my legs, beginning to rub myself without his notice.

His fingers squeezed my cheeks, pinching them together painfully. "I am in control here," he said savagely into my ear. "Ya will take it."

The slap, slap, slap of his thighs increased with my fingers, and my core began to ripple.

"Oh, ya like me inside ya?" he groaned, his pace picking up and at an impossible speed, becoming sloppy in his haste. "Say it."

"What?"

"Say it!" His hand moved to my throat, choking off my hair.

"Use me, Charles!"

"Fuck!"

A gargled moan escaped me as sharp ripples shot through my core, and I detonated, body convulsing in his arms as he shoved further, his hips firmly pressed into my ass as he spilled himself into me.

He bent over me, the sweat and juices from our brutal act leaving our flesh slick. He kept inside me as he grasped my breasts, pinching them painfully, so I whimpered.

Charles shoved off of me, and I stayed there, willing tears to fall. It wasn't hard now that the disgust of what I'd done with him overwhelmed me. I hadn't expected the guilt that weighed me down or the self-degradation. Not when the heat between us had been building for weeks. Weeks of planning and dancing around each other.

"Don't pretend like ya didn't like it," Charles muttered, the tinkle of his belt letting me know he was dressing himself, but I didn't move. His hand brushed across my bare ass, and I flinched as he drew closer to whisper into my ear, "I felt how much ya liked it, whore." He laughed deeply, and my skin prickled with apprehension. "See what man will marry ya now."

Charles reveled in taking what wasn't his and got off on inflicting pain. It didn't surprise me that he enjoyed ruining my life. Little did he know, I already lost more than he could ever take away.

His words were like a dose of cold water, washing away any regret and reminding me how much I liked this game we were playing.

I pushed off the counter, deliberately moving slowly. "But I thought..." I let the words drop off as I stared into his cold eyes.

"Thought what?" He chuckled. "That I would want to be with a girl like ya?"

Anger boiled within me, but I didn't dare show it.

"Ya will be nothin' more than a lowborn servant if anyone will have ya." His eyes raked over me, my still open dress. I crossed my arms over my chest. "Ya are a looker, though." He nodded, appraising me as if I was nothing more than a show mare. "Ya would thrive in a cathouse. I could see ya makin' plenty in a night."

The tears coated my cheeks and fell onto my arms. My body shook with anticipation. "I thought you liked me," I said, voice conveniently breaking.

"I wanted what belonged to another man. Now, I have it, and we can go our own ways."

I spat at his face.

He flinched and then backhanded me, sending me flying to the floor. "Ya filthy slut." Charles' foot barreled into my stomach, sending a blinding pain through me as I screamed and rolled to my side. I knew Charles wasn't a good man, even knew what he wanted from me tonight. I didn't anticipate him hitting me, though.

I started to crawl away, the flicker of the late afternoon sun reflecting off the floor, when the familiar creak of the front door had us pausing. I barely had time to look behind me when Charles wrenched me upward. I hissed, trying to pull my arm from his grasp.

"Fix yaself." He cursed, running his hands through his hair.

My fingers fumbled with the buttons of my dress, missing the holes and causing him to curse more. Footsteps and Miriam's voice rang through the hallway.

My hands shook to the point that I couldn't get more than two buttons closed when the kitchen door opened. Charles stepped in front of me, blocking their view.

"Ya are early," Charles said to his brother.

"What is going on here?" John's deep tone cracked through the silent room, and I looked to the floor in embarrassment. I tried to control my breathing, but I could do nothing about the flush across my skin.

"I knew we shouldn't have left her alone," Miriam cried, concern clogging her throat as she clung to her husband. "Oh, John."

The door leading from the large pantry opened, emitting an ashen Ruth. "I heard it all, Mista John," she said, dark eyes refusing to glance my way as she wrung her hands.

My stomach rolled as nausea flooded my system. God, what did she hear? Or see, for that matter...

"Mista Charles hurt that poor woman. He did."

"Ya lyin' cu—"

"Enough!" John bellowed. "Did you assault my guest?"

"No," Charles snapped, looking down at me. "Have I, Miss O'Connor?"

I bit my lip and shook my head, unable to look at John. Miriam came to me, helping button my dress.

"I heard her refuse him!" Ruth admitted. "He forced himself on poor Miss O'Connor."

My head fell in guilt at what she must have endured while watching what played out.

"Is that true?" John asked, turning to his brother.

"No." He turned to me. "Tell them it's a misunderstanding."

"I told him no," I said, turning my watery eyes to John. "He—" I swallowed. "He—"

"Ya conniving wench!" Charles tried to backhand me again, but my arm came up of its own accord and blocked him.

My eyes widened, ignoring Ruth's scream. *When did I learn how to do that?*

"What?" Charles sputtered, spittle flying out of his mouth as he grabbed me, ready to drag me away.

Miriam clung to my arm, begging her husband to stop this.

John gripped Charles's shirt, wrenching him from us. We watched them grapple with one another, crashing into pans and making the cutlery rattle. Charles seemed to give up the fight rather quickly, shoving John off and raising his hands.

"She's not worth this mess," he snapped, his dark gaze shooting daggers at me. Guess, I wasn't his little sugar anymore. "She wanted it, John."

My eyes narrowed as I imagined all the woman he used the same excuse on. I started toward him, ready to throw a fist into his face when John beat me to it.

Ruth screamed. Again. And Miriam covered her mouth as mine fell open. *Well, damn.* I wasn't expecting that. I eyed the doctor in a new light, my respect for him growing.

Charles wiped the blood from his mouth with the back of his hand, looking at his brother as if he had never seen him before. The room stilled, waiting for what he'd do. And I reminded myself he deserved this. Charles shoved past John and left the house with a crash of the front door.

Miriam and I flinched, waiting in the silence to see if he'd return.

John ran a hand over his face. "I don't know what came over him. Usually, Charles is the perfect gentlem—"

"John," Miriam stalled her husband. "I don't think Charles is the man we thought..."

He sighed, body deflating. "I think you are right. I assure you, Miss O'Connor, I will deal with him accordingly. My brother will answer for his crime. Are you..." he drifted off. "Do you need—"

"Can I just be left alone?" I asked. Miriam stiffened next to me. "I mean... I mean, can Miriam and I..."

He nodded. "Of course."

Miriam led me upstairs while Ruth followed, reminiscent of weeks ago. I blocked out that memory and refused to mourn that loss.

We entered my room, and Ruth barely had the door closed when Miriam threw her arms around me, squeezing me until I could scarcely breathe. "Thank you," she said fiercely. "I'm so sorry it went so far. But, thank you."

I squeezed her back. "Of course, Mir. I owe you everything..." I'd do it again—for her and all the women he'd hurt before.

When Mir finally told me about Charles and how he assaulted her years ago, I knew we had to bring him down or at least reveal it to John in a way that would leave no doubt about Charles's despicable actions. Miriam thought a tiny tryst might do it. A night when we were alone, so John could find Charles in the act when he returned home with Miriam. A kiss here, a no from me there. An act per se. I didn't tell her I knew it would have to be far worse, nor how far I wanted to go. Maybe it was selfish of me to want this evening with him. Though the man sickened me, I needed to know I could retake control. And if it brought down a horrid man, that was just icing on the cake.

"But what you had to endure..." she continued with a worried pinch between her brows.

I closed my eyes, ashamed of what I did. What I enjoyed. "I wanted to do this."

She pulled back, and we both turned to a wide-eyed Ruth. I'd almost forgotten she was there.

"What is this?" Ruth asked.

Mir and I may have plotted Charles's demise, but we kept everyone else out of it. My gut still twisted at what the woman saw. All the ways I let him degrade my body.

I looked at Miriam. She shook her head.

"Ruth, dear," she said to her friend. "May you go get Emilia some tea?"

Ruth stared disbelievingly when Miriam failed to explain. After a few heavy moments, she gave a curt nod and respectively left the room to help ease my ordeal.

Miriam grasped both of my hands in hers. Fury in her eyes. "Did..." She shook her head. "Did he hurt you more than what I'd seen? If I'd known he'd go so far..."

"We went as far I wanted," I admitted. "You have nothing to feel guilty over."

Her brows puckered. "Exactly how far?"

I gave her a sad smile. "I took what I wanted while accomplishing what you needed."

Slowly, she let out a breath and shook her head. "You are a stupid woman," she scolded, even as a small smile began to bloom. "A stupid, courageous woman. If not for you…"

"He put his hands on you, Mir." I cocked my head, feeling vital for the first time since I woke all those weeks ago. "We can't allow that."

"I should have—"

"No. It was as we discussed. This way, it doesn't come from you. It will not be a rift between you and John. You get to keep this secret, and Charles gets what he deserves." I thought John should know what his brother did to his wife years ago, but that was her story to tell.

She sighed, letting go of my hands. "I wouldn't go that far. Charles deserves so much worse than a scolding and eviction."

My stomach turned as the truth ate at me. Charles deserved time in jail, at the very least. I wouldn't have minded a few lashings for every woman he hurt as well.

"And even then," she continued, "he'll still abuse those girls at home."

My head fell back as I considered telling her the truth. I hoped that the Emancipation Proclamation would start to have an effect. It was an excruciatingly slow process given by a man who wasn't controlling the southern territory. But it was signed, and I hoped that those under Charles, and every other slaveholder, would be able to break from their chains.

"Maybe they won't be under his control for much longer…" I said hopefully.

Miriam gave me a disbelieving look. She looked like she was about to say something when the door swung open, letting in a flustered Ruth.

"He's leaving!" she cried, chest heaving as if she ran up the stairs.

"Charles?" Miriam asked enthusiastically. "Truly?" Her brows nearly met her hair when she turned bright eyes onto me.

"Yes, Missis!" Ruth answered. "The carriage is out front, and I heard him in his room, readying his trunk."

"That was fast," I said, unable to keep the shock out of my voice.

"Fast indeed." Miriam's grin brightened the room, and my chest tightened, glad I could give someone a shred of happiness.

After all, it was the closest I could hope to feel it myself.

CHAPTER THIRTY-SEVEN

Michael & Shay

March 1863

*N**ot again.*

If there is a god up there, Mikey would gladly make any sacrifice to bring her back safely. An animal, a human, hell, he'd even sell his own soul if it meant she was well and home with Libby. Burn himself at the stake to spare his lass this torment.

But first...Mikey was going kill every damn man who dared even look at her. They never experienced pain until an O'Connor had a hold of them.

Witha quick twist of the wrist, the cylinder spun on his Colt and slammed shut. Michael shoved it into his holster across his chest before pulling out its twin, checking it for the third time since they entered the carriage.

"We'll find her," Hughie said, a note of boredom in his tone.

Michael snapped the cylinder back into place and pierced his closest man with his deadliest glare. "Where were ye?"

Hughie didn't so much as flinch.

"She was in the bakery," Hughie explained again, slowly as if Mikey's wits leaked out of his ears. "She must have left when I went for a bite."

Mikey surged forward, shoving the barrel of the Colt under Hughie's chin. "Ye're job was to keep your sights on her."

"When did it become me job to watch over your negress?"

Mikey slammed the butt of the Colt on the top of his friend's head and felt the prick of a dagger on his throat in the next breath. *The bastard.*

Mikey should have asked Henry to watch Shay instead of Hughie. Apparently, he had more honor than his so-called best man. And to top it off, that man had a knife to his neck now. Fury, like a raging storm, ate through Mikey as all the signs of Hughie's betrayal came to mind—how he eyed the gang's leadership for years. Mikey had ignored the warnings, believing their friendship meant something. He should have known that Hughie cared for nothing other than his own desires.

They glared at each other as enemies. "If ye ever call her that again," Mikey growled through his teeth, "I will put a bullet through your head. Do ye hear me?"

"Do it," Hughie taunted. "It's like I don't even know ye anymore, Mike. The man I knew would never consort with a group of coloreds, like ye do, let alone feck one. What's wrong with ye?"

"I don't have to explain shite to ye. If ye want to cling to your ways, go right on ahead. But ye won't be doin' it with me. Ye'll be out of the gang and on your own. I won't have a man I can't trust."

"Can't trust?" Hughie pressed the dagger into Mikey's throat until it drew blood, shaking in fury. "Ye can't trust me? Ye knew the slag for a year! I've practically known ye me whole life! We ran these streets. No one gets between us. Think about it, O'Connor. Ye want to throw away years of work for some *woman*?"

That was just it. Mikey did know Hughie. He was ruthless, impulsive, and narcissistic. All traits Mikey valued in a man he often used for his dirty work. To torture answers out of men and scare others shiteless. Hughie was a walking warning, and Mikey reveled in it. Hell, he even participated in most of it. But whereas Hughie got some sick pleasure out of it, Mikey only used it as a means to an end. He didn't *want* to cut off fingers or kill someone's family member.

That was the difference between them. Mikey knew he was doing wrong. Hughie couldn't differentiate between right and wrong if it was spelled out for him.

Not that Hughie could spell for shite, either.

Mikey pushed his neck into the dagger, gritting his teeth. "I will burn the whole damn city down, gang and all, if it meant keeping her safe. *Nothin'* matters except her and the babe. And until ye can get that past your thick skull, ye're dead to me. Ye're out, Callahan."

Hatred flared in Hughie's eyes, and Mikey knew.

It only took a second.

A slight shift of the knife.

A moment of clear certainty.

Mikey pulled the trigger, spraying the inside of the carriage with his oldest friend's skull and every fecked-up piece of his brain.

Swinging the door open, Mikey tossed Hughie's body onto the street and leaned back in, straightening his coat as Henry flicked the reins and pushed the horses faster.

Hughie wouldn't have stopped until Shay was dead.

And Mikey just ensured there was one less body between him and the woman he loved.

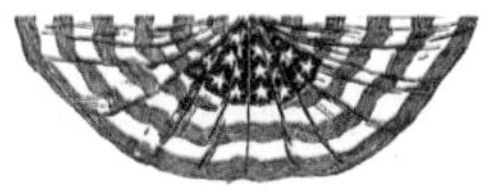

Mikey descended from the carriage and straightened his cuffs in front of the warehouse.

"What are ye goin' to tell them?" Henry's usual jovial personality was somber, and Mikey had to push down the grief trying to eat through him.

It had to be done.

"Let him be a warnin' for those who think they can question me."

Henry looked at Mikey as if he'd grown a snake for a tongue. "I know Hughie had his faults—"

Mikey whirled on him, gritting his teeth like a wild animal, and bent so they were nose to nose. "We can talk about this later. I'm only explaining this to ye now because we go way back. Hughie threatened what's mine. He'd been plannin' on takin' me position for years, always plottin' and questionin' me orders. And was a threat I could no longer ignore. If he lived, she wouldn't. His actions get people killed."

"And ye're so innocent?"

"No." *Gods, no.* "But I'm tryin' to do better. Be better."

Henry shook his head mournfully. "The lass has changed ye."

Mikey straightened. "Is that so bad?"

"Nay." Henry hesitated. "But I wonder what it means for the gang's future when ye have this newfound conscious."

Mikey scoffed. "Don't get ahead of yeself. I'm still the man I always been."

He didn't wait around to hear what Henry grumbled. Nor did he contemplate the wee voice that whispered, *Maybe he's right.* Instead, he went back to work.

They walked around the side of the warehouse to the back door. Twelve of his men filled the room, all scattered around a bloody man tied to a chair in the center.

Mikey removed his coat and rolled up his sleeves, feeling a steady calm settle in his bones, as it always did when he had a particular *job* to take care of.

"This is the driver?" Mikey asked the room.

The man started to grunt past the rag tied around his mouth and thrashed against the ropes tied around his chest. A red gash marred his dark forehead, the injury that must have knocked him out in getting here.

"If I take this off," Mikey started, "ye are not goin' to scream. Ye're goin' to answer me questions, or ye aren't goin' to like what I do to ye."

The man nodded, eyes pleading.

"Mikey…" a boy to Mikey's left piped up, then hesitated at Mikey's glare.

He was a tough kid, having lived on the streets since he was small until Mikey took him in, fed him, and put a roof over his head the last few years in exchange for errands. It wasn't until the previous year that Mikey allowed him on the more complex jobs. Apparently, seeing this part of Mikey smacked some common sense into him.

"Sir," he amended, "I've just been thinkin'. Is all of this really worth the girl? I mean—"

"Ye better choose your next words wisely." The threat in Mikey's tone had the boy cringing before stealing his nerves, his jaw raised in a way that only irritated Mikey more.

"I've just been thinking—all of us really—" He waved his hand around the room "—that the gang has lost sight of the goal."

"The goal." Each word fell like an anvil, weighing Mikey down until he burned with the embers as his fury rose to immeasurable heights. All trace of his calm vanished in the smoke. "And what is your goal?"

"Well…" James' ruddy brown eyes widened as he looked at each of the men. "You've got the pub now, and we haven't been selling as much. And the loss of all those weapons…"

Mikey's brows rose. "Have I not earned ye enough cash the last year?"

"It's not that—"

"Is this how ye all feel?" Mikey turned to the others. "Ye're questioning—"

"Where's Hugh?" another piped up.

Mikey sighed, chest tightening with the truth he had to tell them. He eyed the driver and pulled out his dagger. "I will answer your questions once I get mine."

"Mikey—"

"Get out!" Mikey yelled at his crew, completely unhinged, and slammed the dagger in between the man's thighs with a loud thud.

The driver's muffled scream rent the air as the men filed out the back door, leaving only Henry. The man's breaths increased, threatening to hyperventilate.

"Now," Mikey started, dislodging the knife, "ye will answer truthfully, or the next time, I won't miss."

His eyes widened, his head bobbling on his neck theatrically. Mikey removed the gag.

"I'll tell you whatever you want," he gasped.

"Did ye pick a lass up today?"

"I pick up a lot of women—" Mikey grabbed his finger, ready to cut it off as the man pleaded. "You'll have to be more specific! I'll tell you whatever you want! Please."

Mikey paused, thinking of the dress the lass had on when she left. He'd been playing with Libby, but nothing could keep him from noticing how the dress hugged all of her curves. Jealousy flared again when he remembered just who she was going to see.

Hiram.

If not for him, Shay would be safe in Mikey's arms right now.

"Yes," the driver admitted when Mikey described her attire. "Long curly hair?" the driver asked, eyes hopeful.

"Aye. Did anything odd happen? Where did ye drop her off?"

The driver's brows fell as he considered Mikey's question. "I dropped the lady and a man off shortly after we crossed the bridge."

"A man?" Mikey's pulse skyrocketed, threatening to break out of his chest. What was she doing with a man? Could it be one of Boudreaux's? "White?"

"No, light-skinned, but no."

"Describe him to me."

The man's appearance was nothing remarkable, although the nice suit and bowler hat stood out. As the best-dressed passenger, he looked like someone who would have his own carriage. But the driver didn't question it, not when more money was lining his pockets.

"Did he have an accent?" Mikey asked, squatting down to better see his reaction.

He shook his head. "Same as those born around here."

Mikey sat back on his heels, lost in thought. What would he want with Shay? Granted, she was beautiful, but men didn't go around kidnapping women in the middle of the day unless they wanted something. And there was one thing Shay had worth the risk.

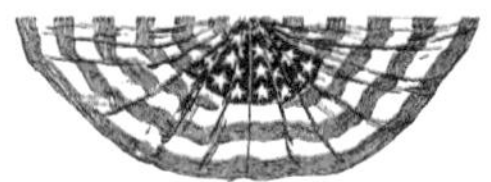

Shay pried her lids open, the effort seemingly one of the hardest things she ever had to do.

"God," she croaked. *Where am I?*

It felt like sandpaper grating over her eyeballs, like cotton filling her mouth, except...there wasn't anything actually in it. It must have been the aftereffects of whatever knocked her out.

At least she rested on something soft and surprisingly comfortable. The absurd thought had her groaning.

"Ah, you're awake," a deep voice rumbled, causing her eyes to finally open fully and her head to spin. Shay had the urge to jerk forward, only for her body to twitch sluggishly. "I thought my man may have used too much. Alas, you're awake, and we can rest assured of your well-being."

What the fuck?

Shay's head rolled to the side, blinking through her fuzzy vision, only making out a flickering fire and an oil lantern on a small table. A dark, blurry figure of a man sat in a decorative chair to the side.

"What—" Shay coughed, trying to moisten her dry mouth. "What did you do to me? Where am I?" she croaked out.

Boudreaux leaned forward, his elbows resting on his knees, rubbing thick hands together before clasping them. His thoughtful expression didn't salve the threatening panic that began to eat through the haze.

I knew he had a hand in this. Damn him. I should have been more careful.

She struggled to keep from baring her teeth at him.

"I believe you have something of mine," Boudreaux said.

"I don't understand—"

"Don't act stupid with me, woman," he snapped, leaning back in his chair and seemingly gaining composure. "But we have all the time in the world." His sweeping hands had her taking in the space, finding a modest-sized room with an armoire, dresser and mirror, a basin, and pale, all surrounding the big, four-poster bed she was currently on. It was probably the most elegant room she had been in since she arrived in the nineteenth century. Even the thick, velvet curtains screamed wealth. Their deep green was enriched by the warm fire that offset the cream and gold floral wallpaper.

A pretty prison, then.

Wincing, she sat up, finding she was alright other than the effects of whatever they'd done to her.

God, did they chloroform me? How long have I been sleeping?

"Are we still in Boston?" She had to know she was at least in the same city as Michael.

Oh, God. Libby. Tears pricked her eyes. Michael would keep her safe, but the thought of not seeing her was like a shot to the gut. She hadn't been away from her daughter for more than a few hours.

Boudreaux sighed and rested his hands on his knees to stand. "That is not information you need to indulge yourself in. Now, if ya want to answer my question, I will gladly open up. But until then, you can make yourself comfortable." He pulled out a set of keys, heading for the door.

"Wait!" Shay said, sitting up so quickly her head spun. She pushed past the nausea and dropped her legs over the edge of the bed. "Where are you going? You're not going to keep me in here!"

Boudreaux's smile turned her stomach. The grin of a man who was used to getting his every desire. "Ya better make yourself comfortable. These four walls are the only thing you'll see for the foreseeable future."

"You can't!" Shay shoved herself off the bed, but he was already through the door, the key rattling in the lock when she hit it, pounding her fists against the wood. "Let me out! You can't keep me here!" Her heart thundered in her chest, head swimming with this impossibility. Her forehead hit the door in despair.

Shit, shit, shit. What do I—Her head snapped up, a glint of hope hardening her resolve.

"He's going to find you!" she yelled, not knowing if Boudreaux heard her, but she felt he was listening to every word. "Michael is going to find you, and you're going to regret this!" Shay's throat nearly tore with the force of her yell. "He's going to kill you, you bastard!" Fists pounding the door, she laughed humorlessly. "Do you hear me? You're a fucking dead man!"

Footsteps descended the stairs, and Shay sunk to the floor, a tear sliding down her cheek.

"He's going to kill every last one of you," she whispered through her raw throat. "And I'm going to help him."

CHAPTER THIRTY-EIGHT

Emilia

MARCH 1863

"Ye need help, lass?" The deep brogue had my head whipping up and my heart accelerating unsteadily. My eyes collided with a middle-aged man, his brown gaze kind but unremarkable. My pulse slowed, and I shook off the odd reaction.

What the hell? My body had been doing that the last few weeks without explaining *why*.

Miriam placed a hand on my arm, a look of concern creasing her brow.

"No," I said, giving the man a shaky smile. "Thank you."

"If ye need anything, I'll be right over there." He pointed to the aisle where he'd organized groceries on the shelf. A feeling of warmth flooded through my system, a blanket of comfort shrouding me as I listened to him speak.

"Over here," Miriam said, guiding me to another part of the store.

A quick look around, and we bought some flour Miriam put in her bag and ordered grain to be delivered to the house. As we left, I couldn't help but pause, resting my hand on the trim, unable to tear myself from it as I glanced over my shoulder at the man. It felt as if my heart was tearing in two, but for the life of me, I couldn't figure out why.

"Emilia?" Miriam called out, already a few paces away, as if she just noticed I'd stopped.

With one last glance, I spun away and caught up to her.

"Was something the matter?" she asked as we walked down the street, turning the corner.

"No," I hesitated, thinking about what had just occurred. "I think it was his accent." I shrugged. "It just felt..." I shook my head, unable to explain the irrationality of it.

It felt like *home*, but that couldn't be right. I never been to Ireland and hadn't heard much of the accent in person. Well, other than when I'd practiced it as a child, but that atrocity couldn't be the reason for this.

Miriam's troubled glance was so quick that I almost missed it. Her pace quickened; her hands carefully bundled in her jacket.

"What?" I asked, trying to keep up with her, but I was wildly out of shape since being injured, and my breaths came out heavy. "Just say it."

She sighed. "It would make sense, considering you were in an Irish regiment. Don't you think?"

I dodged a couple rushing to a carriage and considered. I accepted that I was in a different century, even though I couldn't remember how, but enlisting in the Civil War? It was laughable. "You think I...what? Feel close to people who speak like that?"

Her features hardened, her mouth set in a tight line that told me her thoughts went in a different direction.

"Just tell me," I snapped, too irritated to be polite. Miriam and I had grown close in the last few months, and I began to think of her as a friend. Which allowed me to speak freely now. "You obviously have an opinion."

"I do..." she said, choosing her words carefully. "But it is entirely my opinion, and I don't want to say too much before you're ready."

I scoffed. "It's been months, Miriam. I'm ready."

"But John—"

"Please," I pleaded. "I need *something*."

Miriam sighed, and we stepped over a melted puddle of snow, checking both ways to cross the street toward the strip of stores. "The man you were with..."

My heart seized, constricting painfully. Did Miriam know more? What had she said his name was, again? It took me a minute, but I remembered it was Thomas. I only recalled because I felt ridiculous comparing him to the Thomas from my parent's pub.

"He was Irish," Miriam continued. "You had a strong connection with him. I mean, from what I learned of the soldier who brought you to us, the impression I received was that you cared for him." She stopped, turning to me. I held my breath as I tried to read her serious expression. "Loved him."

My heart sank as I became more suspicious that she knew far more than she had let on. But it made sense that he was Irish. If I was to believe I was in the all-Irish Regiment, then Thomas must have been as well. I should have pieced that together months ago.

"Tell me." She knew something, and she was going to tell me.

Now.

Her face softened, her eyes turning sad. "Emilia..."

"Please." I grabbed her arms, willing her to tell, even though I didn't know what I was searching for. "You've given me scraps of what I need. I can't keep going on like this."

I watched as her walls broke down, feeling triumphant.

Finally.

"Thomas, he—" Her face paled, her mouth opening like she was about to say something before snapping it shut. Odd. "I'm sorry. I just know Thomas died in the same battle you were injured." She shook her head. "I only know what little information was given to me."

I knew this. Knew that he had died, but that name did something to me. It ignited every nerve in my body as if it remembered for me.

"Thomas?" My voice cracked, going over his name over and over. If only I could just *remember*.

He was an enigma, and yet a part of me, long trapped in the vault of my own mind, beat on the door, shocks of emotion reverberating throughout the cracks and into my body without releasing the actual memory. It was disorienting, feeling so tormented for someone I couldn't even recollect.

"That's it?" I asked, unsure if I wanted there to be more or leave it as it was.

Miriam nodded gravely. I dropped my hands, letting go of her arms.

Well, now I know. That's it. It's better this way. No child, no man. I can go on as if nothing happened.

Except the scars on my body would never let me forget. They would constantly remind me of what I lost and the possibilities of what could have been.

"I'm sorry, Emilia," she said, her features contorting as if she was at war with her thoughts. "I wish—"

"Thank you," I said, nodding almost robotically. "I needed this. Really."

Weaving my arm within hers, I pulled her down the street and tried to ignore her worried glances.

"You sure you're well?" she asked.

"No," I admitted. "But I will be."

We were about to cross another street, heading toward their house, when I almost collided with a woman turning the corner of the building.

"Watch where ye—" The red-head stopped in her tracks, her annoyed expression quickly turned into shock.

"Sorry," I mumbled, pulling Miriam along.

"Don't ye take off, ye wee slag," she hissed, grabbing my arm and spinning me around.

"Excuse me?"

She looked me up and down like she had seen a ghost. The rouge on her cheeks was overdone, and I knew enough that her burgundy dress was highly revealing for that time. Not to mention gaudy. Even so, she was stunning, curvier than most of the women here, and I had a deep suspicion of where she got her money from.

"My, ye look a wee bit on the haggard," she breathed, cocking her head as her piercing green eyes met mine. The blood drained from my face.

Do I know her?

"And remarkably *alive,*" she continued her tone hardening.

I tried to shake off her iron grip to no avail. "Sorry to disappoint," I snapped, surprised by my rudeness. I would never have talked like that to someone before the accident.

"Pardon me," Miriam pitched in, planting herself between the woman and me. "Have we met before?"

The woman turned her attention to Miriam, her scowl deepening. "Me business is with the gypsy bitch."

My mouth fell open at the audacity of her. "And who the hell are you?" I asked, yanking my arm out of her grasp.

"Ye can't play stupid with me," she hissed. "First, ye steal me man, and then gone and done this to me hair." She pointed to the mass of curls. Upon closer inspection, her hair seemed pinned up to keep small strands out of her face, as if it was shorter in some spots than others.

My face scrunched. "What would I have done to your hair? And what man?" Now, *that* didn't sound like me at all.

"I think you must be mistaken—" Miriam started.

"Where's Thomas?"

My body jolted. She knew Thomas? I shared a worried glance with Miriam. Was I a homewrecker? Did I steal this woman's man and conceive a child with him? "I don't know—"

"Don't play stupid with me, bitch. Clearly, ye gave up your little act, but don't give me some shite about ye forgetting the last two years." My stomach hollowed out, and I swayed on my feet. *Two years?* "That man always followed ye around like a sad little pup." Her lip pulled up in disgust. "Ye poisoned him against me, ye did. Worked your gypsy magic—"

I laughed incredulously. Was this woman nuts?

"I hate to tell you this," I spat, "but Thomas died during the battle."

It was then I was grateful for my memory loss. To be able to dissociate myself from the pain I knew I'd feel for his death. That is, if I had any feelings for him in the first place.

I paused, considering this. I assumed I had a relationship with the man, but what if it was just a tryst? Or, heaven forbid, he assaulted me. I quickly dismissed that idea. The soldier wouldn't find it necessary to write home about his death if he didn't mean something tome.

My mind spun with the realization. He wrote home. I'd accepted that I was in a different century weeks ago, unable to ignore the difference in the world around me. So, who the fuck did he write to? My family would be in the future...

I turned my attention to Miriam. "Who did he write to?" I asked her.

Her mouth opened as her face took on a confused expression. "Who did—"

"The soldier," I clarified, ignoring the other woman who had taken on a deathly complexion. "I know he couldn't have written home. My family—" I stopped myself before admitting my time travel. She may have thought I was confused initially, but I toned down my crazy when I realized I actually might be in the past. I shook my head, not knowing how to go about this. Not when I didn't understand it myself.

"That's what he said—"

"Who said?" I asked, needing more. "What was the soldier's name?"

Miriam's face went splotchy, seemingly at a loss for words. She was always so self-assured that it took me aback. "He didn't give me a name."

"You let a soldier in with an injured woman, and you didn't ask him his name?"

"What are ye talking about?" the red-head snapped, grabbing the front of my dress. "Stop your lying."

"Listen," I snapped, shoving her hands off me, "I don't know who you are." I held up my hand when she opened her mouth. "I don't remember. I don't remember the last two years, apparently. But what I do know is that when I was injured, Thomas had died as well."

She shook her head, backing up as panic overcame her. "No," she gasped. "Ye lie. O'Connors don't die. They come out swinging!"

My heart jumped into my throat, and I clung to her arms.

"What did you say?" I asked. "What name did you say?"

Miriam placed a hand on my arm. "Come, Emilia."

"Get your hands off me, you crazy bat!" the lady hissed, pushing me away.

We were certainly getting some stares now, but I couldn't bring myself to care.

"Ye well know those brothers will make it out of whatever hell they get themselves into. If ye don't remember, then ye don't know."

"Excuse me," Miriam interrupted rather loudly, shoving between us. "I don't know what Thomas meant to you, but I am sorry for your loss."

"Then it was all for naught." She shook her head, red strands of hair falling into her face. Hysteria seemed to overwhelm her as she talked to herself. "I gave up everything. Worked for that wretched man. I'm out," she cried. "I'm finally out, and he's..." Her words trailed off as tears tracked their way down her cheeks. She began to back away. "My God, it was all for naught."

"Wait," I started, her pain raising unwanted sympathy in me. "Don't—"

"Just ye leave me be," she snapped, her green eyes cutting into me. "Ye got him, and now he's gone. Just...leave me the feck alone. Ye ruined everything!"

I pleaded for her to stay, but she was already tearing down the street, colliding with a couple as she wiped tears off her face. I stood there, feeling defeated and a little sick at what occurred.

"Is everything all right, Miriam?" an elderly voice broke me out of my daze to find Miriam reassuring an older woman in a big fur hat.

"Yes, dear. I will call on you soon," Miriam smiled reassuringly, and the lady left, side-eyeing me.

With that display, I couldn't blame her.

I waited for Miriam to say something; when she didn't, anger boiled within me. I asked her if there was anything else, and she lied. With considerable effort not to pull my lips back from my teeth, my words still came out grated with emotion. "His name was O'Connor?"

Miriam hesitated only a moment, but I saw it. "Does that mean something to you?"

"I told you my name was O'Connor," I hissed before pulling myself together.

Had I found him? My father's ancestor... *My God*. Had I gone back in time and found the only person that would be linked to me? What would possess me to look for him?

The confusion overtook me like a storm raging in my mind. My head spun, and I had to steady myself on Mir's arm.

"Yes." She hesitated before continuing, "May I be frank?"

"That would be great," I ground out, scrubbing my hands over my face so I didn't rake my nails down hers.

Miriam tugged on my arm, and I let her gently guide me to a bench before sitting us down. "We did not expect your memory loss. When the soldier left you with us before writing the letters, he didn't anticipate this predicament. I do not know how to explain this to you other than the loss of Thomas and that your only family, his brother, is waiting for you in Boston."

"He said that?" I asked, my face contorting in disbelief. "That I'd be going home to...his brother?" That seemed odd. Why would I be sent to a lover's brother? Of course, these times were different; women had less freedom. The pieces still didn't quite fit together.

She sat back, twisting her hands nervously in her lap. Why was this affecting her this way? Why would she even care, just relaying information?

"Why would I go to his brother?" I asked.

"Well," she took a fortifying breath, "he is your brother-in-law."

My body seemed to fold in on itself, a numbness suctioning all the simmering anger I had left." I was told to send a letter to Michael and Shay when you were heading home, as you have no other family."

My back hit the hardwood of the bench as nausea threatened to choke me. Michael. The brother...

"Before," I swallowed past the lump in my throat, "before you said you'd send a letter to the man of the house."

She nodded, brown eyes wide and imploring.

"Did you mean Michael O'Connor?" I didn't dare ask about Shay.

Holy hell. Had Shay gone back in time with me? And what is she still doing in Boston? Why would I enlist in a war and leave my best friend behind? The implications of it had my bones quaking in worry.

"Yes. When you told me your name was O'Connor, I thought you might have remembered something. But with your confusion still evident, we thought we shouldn't push it."

"Wait..." I sat straighter, an iron rod going through my spine, and the blood drained from my face as her words came back to me. "You said, 'brother-in-law'."

She nodded, her tight curls dancing around her face. "Yes. I was told," she swallowed, looking at me with so much sadness that I wanted to get up and leave right there, "I was told Thomas was your husband, and the closest relation would be Michael. I am so sorry, dear. I was hoping I wouldn't have to tell you. That you might remember..." She shook her head, appearing as though she was having difficulty finding the right words to say.

I'm going to puke.

This was a turmoil deeper than a one-night stand or any other fleeting encounter. The revelation of my marriage hit me like a tidal wave, leaving me gasping for air. How much had I missed? And why hadn't she told me this when I'd been asking her all those questions?

I glared at her, the tension between us crackling in the air like a live wire. I was mildly surprised she didn't catch fire with it. I'd give the lady credit, though. She grabbed my hand reassuringly, even with the ire radiating off me.

"Emilia, there's something you should know—"

For Christ's sake. I held up my other hand to cut her off. I couldn't bear one more thing. "Please," I pleaded. "Don't tell me."

"I've been debating whether I should tell you. I really think—"

"No," I snapped forcefully, pulling my hand out of hers. "Honestly, I can't." My mind returned to the photographs in my parent's pub of how Michael and Thomas opened it together. It was one vital piece of my father's history that I found fascinating, and now it returned to haunt me. Maybe I was truly insane, and I would wake up in an asylum. They would tell me I imagined all of this. That I had some psychotic breaks due to stress regarding finding my biological parents.

What a mess.

Her face fell, but I couldn't bring myself to care. There was nothing she could tell me to make this better. Thomas was dead. Michael wasn't. Shay was with him. End of story.

"If that's what you want..."

"It is."

She nodded, biting her lip. "Again, I am sorry you found out like this."

A momentary prick of irritation consumed me, but I ignored it. In an infuriating, roundabout way, Miriam had been looking out for me.

"I understand. I just..." I shook my head. "I can't talk about this anymore."

Knowing Shay was in Boston, I suddenly wanted to flee the South and run straight into my best friend's arms.

Shay will know what to do.

CHAPTER THIRTY-NINE

Thomas

MARCH 1863

The regiment endured a long winter, facing the loss of men and a decline in morale. They marched through land and war with all they could muster. At the end of the grueling "Mud March," the company was spared the worst of the storm that battered others, leaving them to trudge through sodden roads that turned into quagmires.

Ultimately, they made it to camp where they were to stay until spring. Those who remained received new clothes and boots. And with the lack of new recruits, those who stayed were promoted.

Sergeant Thomas O'Connor.

He took little joy from his new title. Nor did he find pleasure out of the few activities they had in camp. March came with a heaviness that Thomas felt in his soul. He had no way of knowing how Emilia fared, whether she made it to Boston. He would know if she traveled through time. Wouldn't he?

It'd been months since he wrote to Mikey. He couldn't trust his letters not to be read in transit, and everything he needed to ask his brother would jeopardize Emilia and himself. He had to trust Miriam got her home and that Emilia went back.

Now, the camp was transformed into a raucous celebration for St. Patrick's

Day. Men and those following the army participated in the events, coming to watch the horse race that would earn a man a five-hundred-dollar reward. Thomas watched with a dull sense of awareness.

"Take one, mate." Sullivan handed Thomas a drink, trying to pull him out of his head. But how could he focus when he should have been celebrating something else?

The crowd exploded as the horses came around the bend, charging toward the finish line.

Thomas took the drink but couldn't bring himself to care. Not when all he could think about was Emilia and how he missed another one of her birthdays. He hadn't cared about them before, the celebrating of one's birth. It just wasn't done in his family. But Emilia had cared, and they spent her last birthday together, walking by the water before eating a small cake with Shay and the others at the bakery.

It wasn't extravagant or extraordinary, but her day made it his most valuable one. All he could think of was all the years he would have lived without her.

The horses blew past them with a thunder of hooves and chunks of mud, and the crowd went wild as they called the winner.

Thomas turned, walking out of the crowd to spend the rest of the day in his tent.

CHAPTER FORTY

Emilia

MAY-JUNE 1863

The spring air blew across my face, and I closed my eyes, relishing the beautiful day for what it was.

I was going home.

Well, to Shay, and from there, we would figure out the rest. As long as I had her, everything would be all right. I was ready to leave this city and century behind. I yearned to see my parents again, my brother, and nothing would stop me from getting to them.

My memory hadn't returned like John had hoped, and he finally gave me the go-ahead, with the exception of traveling with me until I was with my family again. A reasonable condition concerning my state. I wouldn't admit it, but I was beginning to worry if I'd ever regain my memory or have any long-term effects.

"Do you have everything, Emilia?" Miriam's voice pulled my attention from the sun, and I turned to find her standing inside the back door's doorframe. I didn't miss how her eyes flickered to the small mound under the tree where fresh grass began to grow. There was no headstone or any marking for my sweet baby, but it was enough to have her here with these people. I couldn't take her where I was going, but John and Miriam would remember her.

Someone had to remember my sweet Lizzie.

I didn't know why I needed to name her Elizabeth other than it just felt *right*. When I told Miriam, she grabbed my hands, tears in her eyes, and told me it was a beautiful name. I chuckled through my tears and finally let go of the anger I'd felt all those months. I accepted it was her time and admitted I could love a child I'd never met.

My only regret was that her father did not know.

I smiled at Miriam now and nodded. "They're on top of the trunk."

I didn't have much and could carry what I had in a bag.

"Good." She took a deep breath, eyes sad, and I felt a part of me deflate. I would miss her too. "John is nearly ready. I will have Ruth pack your things."

She swung briskly back into the house, a move I learned she often did to hide her emotions. I turned back to the yard and took in the green grass, the small white picket fence, and the shed. It was a quaint little place that I grew to love. I never had much of a backyard in twenty-first-century Boston, and I found I enjoyed the slowness of the south and peaceful feel of a quiet life. Then again, maybe it all would feel slow in the nineteenth century. My last memories were of the fast-paced, high technology of the future.

I smiled and picked some fresh purple and white wildflowers along the fence line before kneeling by the grave and placing them over Lizzie.

"I'm sorry I have to go," I whispered, the breeze whipping my words around us. I pushed my hair back and placed my hands on my knees, feeling my chest squeeze. "I'm sorry you didn't get a fair chance. If I could have done things differently, I would have." I paused, letting my head fall back as I watched the wind rustle the green leaves.

Would I, though? I didn't remember what happened or what decisions I made to lead me here.

"Maybe that's not true," I admitted. "But I wish I could have done things differently to keep you with me. And for that, I am so very sorry." Warm tears flowed down my cheeks as I wondered what could have been. Of what I had to leave behind.

I sighed, placing a hand over her grave, and told her just how much I loved her and promised to see her and her father—my *husband*—again when it was my time.

I froze as a jolt of realization shot through me. Were they together already? I clutched my hands to my chest as I turned my face to the heavens, the sun on my face like a warm caress from my small family I couldn't remember, but loved, nonetheless.

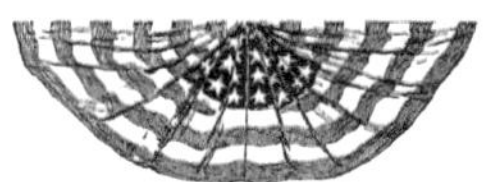

A small bag and two trunks were sitting by the front door. I turned to Miriam with a look of confusion, taking in her traveling dress and her smile.

"What is going on?" I asked, my gaze flicking between her and John, who just walked in.

"I always wanted to visit the north," Miriam said, eyes twinkling. I never saw her, so... *giddy*? It was odd seeing her break out of her typical serious demeanor. "You needed a chaperone, and I just thought," she looked to her husband, "well, this is as good of a time as any. Why let it pass me by?"

"You're going with me?" Apparently, the hit to my head made me a little dense.

Miriam pulled out three travel passes and waved them at me.

A genuine smile bloomed on my face as relief overtook the nerves eating at me for days. I wouldn't have to do this alone.

I still had people who cared about me.

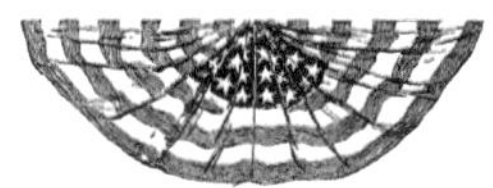

Planes, trains, and automobiles.

Someone, save me.

I wished we had a plane. It would have saved us weeks of travel, money I didn't have, and my sanity. Between the sea sickness while riding the steamboat, the over-crowded trains that we almost couldn't board—them being in high demand with the military—and that short time we had to ride in a stagecoach, I nearly threw in the towel and joined the army again just to gain passage without the hassle.

Yeah, I'm sure they have it easy. I almost snorted at the thought of it.

We almost didn't make it into Washington D.C., Miriam and John having southern accents. They were confronted with stern glares and a hostility that terrified me. It didn't take long to explain as my doctor, I needed John, and it was only natural for his wife to be with him. Apparently, it wasn't hard for them to believe I was a northerner, though they took extra care to look at my travel pass. One bristly old man looked at me over his spectacles and clicked his tongue.

"What is your ethnicity, young lady?"

I kept myself from shrugging and tried to answer him as honestly as possible. "I was born in America but adopted by an Irish couple. I don't know my true parents."

He stared at me momentarily, his ruddy, round cheeks reddening further as he studied my features. Sure, I had a tan and had darker hair than most, but damn. My cheeks started to heat at his scrutiny.

"Is this really necessary?" Miriam asked, coming to my aide. "We still have quite a way to go, and our patient shouldn't be standing this long."

His murky brown eyes slid to hers. "She seems fine to me."

"I can assure you," John cut in, "most of her injuries are hidden to the eye. As well as the injury to her head."

The old man's jowls jostled as he blustered about, tapping our passes on the table before handing them to us. "You may go."

That had been days and many train stops ago. Now, I shifted on my seat as our train whistled loudly, its engine humming with my nerves.

Old Boston flew by in a blur, unrecognizable and yet oddly familiar at the same time. It had my gut twisting, and the only thing keeping me from heaving my breakfast was knowing Shay would be waiting for me at the end of this.

God, what had she been doing for all of these months? I hadn't received word from her, though Miriam had correspondence with an O'Connor, she said it was hard enough to get the letters between the warring states. Even if I sent multiple letters, they were not guaranteed to make it to Shay.

"How are you?" Miriam asked from the seat across from me, pulling me out of my thoughts and the worries I had about Shay.

"Good," I said too quickly, causing her to smile. "A little nervous."

She nodded and glanced at John, who had his head in a paper. "It's been quite some time away. I'm sure your friend has missed you."

"It's not that." I paused, considering the best way to explain it to her. "It's the memory loss. The 'not knowing' what I've missed and what's changed in the time I forgot."

She leaned over and squeezed my hand. "We will not leave you until you feel comfortable." Her eyes were warm with sympathy, and some of my worry faded.

"Thank you."

The train slowed, sending my nerves into a fresh upheaval as Miriam sat back. I swallowed past a lump in my throat and grabbed my rosary, playing with the beads. It was the one piece of normalcy from my old life that comforted and ground me when everything else threatened to spin me out.

I turned back to Miriam. "I think you'll like her."

"If she's anything like you two," John cut in, folding his paper, "I'm sure we'll have trouble on our hands."

Miriam and I shared a smile, and I suddenly felt a pang in my chest. I would miss her when we left, and a part of me didn't want to say goodbye.

"You keep mentioning your friend," Miriam said hesitantly. "What happened to your family?"

I let out a shuddering breath and made up some tale about not seeing them these last couple of years, and how I was not even sure where they were right now. It was all true, even if I couldn't tell Miriam where they were.

Miriam nodded, twisting her hands in her lap so tightly I could see the whites of her knuckles. "I haven't seen my family since I was a child."

John looked at his wife with so much love and sympathy that my skin tightened, feeling intrusive. He squeezed her hand, and they shared a look that spoke volumes. She turned back to me.

"I tried—" her face contorted, and her throat bobbed with emotion. She cleared her throat, but I couldn't ignore the tears in her eyes, "I tried to find them later on, but they had moved. Or died." She sighed and tried to smile. "I don't think I'm making my point as clear as I thought." She gave a watery chuckle. "I don't even know why I told you all that."

I understood it, though. Speaking about a similar struggle with someone who understood was a relief. Albeit a small one.

I bit my lip and turned to look out the window at the buildings now moving slowly by the passengers waiting to get on and the families waiting for those to arrive. I wanted to respond to Miriam, to give her some reassurance, but the words failed me. I had none when my own world, my own sense of reality, was so skewed that I could barely differentiate between fact and insanity because of this ever-growing, messed-up ball of chaos that was my new life.

Thankfully, the train stopped, and I didn't have to think up a response before everyone started to disembark.

We retrieved our luggage and hailed a cab to ride to the location apparently given from the one and only letter we received from my "brother-in-law." The content was nothing more than a hastily written address—no mention of Shay or any clue as to whether he actually knew me and the sharp command to come straight to him without any stops. I found that strange, but I took comfort in John and Miriam staying with me until I located Shay.

It wasn't until we neared a familiar set of buildings that I recognized where we were. I gasped, gripping the frame of the carriage's window as I nearly pressed my face against the glass.

Tears fell down my face as the pub's sign grew more prominent the closer we got, and I had to wipe them away even as a smile bloomed on my face.

My God, it felt like coming home.

It *was* coming home, and I had to keep myself from jumping out and busting through the door.

That bitch, I laughed. No wonder Shay didn't want to leave. She'd found our place.

"Is everything alright?" Miriam asked.

"I know this place." I smiled broadly at her, and she exchanged a happy glance with John.

"That's great," he told me as the carriage pulled to a halt.

Butterflies fluttered in my stomach as I stood on the curb, the warm sun descending behind the city buildings. I gazed at the familiar door, gathering my courage to knock while waiting for John and the driver to retrieve the luggage.

"Here," Miriam said, handing me my bag.

"What do you think he's like?" I asked, nervous as all hell to meet Michael.

"Well, let's find out."

I knocked on the door and let my hand fall, bouncing on my toes impatiently.

What if he hates me? Is Shay in there right now? My face scrunched as I thought how weird it must be to stay here with him.

She must live somewhere else.

As the door swung open, my body tensed.

An imposing figure filled the doorframe, his presence dominating the space. My eyes first landed on a pair of weathered boots, then traveled up a pair of long, powerful legs, a black fitted vest, and the man's flexing forearms beneath his rolled-up cream-colored shirt. Summoning all my courage, I met his gaze, only to find my breath caught in my throat. His piercing, icy blue eyes, framed by long dark lashes, seemed to bore into my very soul.

"About damn time, gypsy," he growled in a rough Irish accent, and Miriam and I exchanged worried glances, wondering who the hell the gypsy was.

"Excuse me?" I was sure this was Michael in the pictures, but did he mistake me for someone else?

He sighed, mumbling something in Irish, and swept his arm behind him. "Why don't ye get off the street before anyone sees ye."

"Are—" I stumbled over my words, needing to make sure he was who I suspected. "We are looking for a Michael O'Connor."

"For Christ's sake, lass. They weren't lyin' about your brains bein' knocked around."

"Excuse me?" I snapped, my hackles raising. "Are you him or not?"

"Aye. Ye are in the right place. Now, get the feck in before I have to drag ye." He looked at John, who was paying the driver to take their trunks to the inn. "Who the hell is this?"

"My friends."

He started muttering in Irish again and walked away, leaving us to exchange worried glances.

"Are you sure you want to go in?" Miriam asked. "We don't—"

"Emilia?" a sweet voice called out, garnering my attention.

A young girl with hair as dark as Michael's and a set of green eyes that had my stomach sinking bounced a baby on her hip.

"Why didn't you say something?" She smacked Michael's arm and handed over the baby, sweeping over to me. It only took a second, and she threw her arms around my neck. I let out a harumph as I struggled to hold her weight, her toes barely balancing on the doorframe. "He didn't say you'd be here so soon."

"I told ye she was on her way home," Michael groused.

Home.

My eyes met his as I awkwardly patted the girl's back, unsure what to say. It was strange not remembering someone who clearly knew me well enough for this embrace, and I didn't know how to break it to her.

"Hello," I said hesitantly. I felt grateful when she pulled me inside the warm pub and grabbed my hand.

The room fell silent as a rough-looking group watched me cautiously. Apprehension skittered across my nerves, but the girl let go and turned to me with a carefree smile, paying no attention to the others.

"I'm sorry," I said, looking between her and Michael. "I—" A deep breath and another glance at the others. "It's clear you know me, but I—"

Her mouth fell into a comical 'O' with understanding. I would have laughed if I wasn't so nervous.

"My apologies. Mikey told me what happened. I'm Margaret, but most call me Maggie. Or Mags. Anyway," she said, taking a break to breathe. "I just forgot in my excitement..."

I nodded, worrying my lip. I eyed the baby, pulling the menacing man's hair without a care. "Is Shay—"

"Mama!" the baby cooed.

I staggered forward. "Did she..."

"Aye." He took me in as if waiting for a response.

"You mean, she's..."

"Shay's," he finished. "Aye. Ye met Libby when she was a wean."

A wean. I reached out with shaking hands until I realized maybe I shouldn't. "May I?"

Michael handed Libby over, Shay's *child*.

I was already in love.

"Aren't you the sweetest?" I told her, mesmerized by her beautiful hazel eyes and bouncy brown curls, and a part of my chest caved in.

I missed so much or forgot it. Either way, I lost a large part of my friend's life, and that tore another hole through me. I wasn't sure how much more I could take. But I was here now and wouldn't waste one more minute.

I grinned at the girl as she squealed in delight, smooshing my cheeks between her little hands.

"Where's Shay?" I asked while trying to keep the girl's hands from ripping out my hair. When no one responded, I looked up, and my smile slipped at their solemn expressions. "Where's Shay?" I asked more forcibly, looking between the siblings.

"That's what I needed to talk to ye about," Michael said flatly.

"I'm sorry," John said, putting his hand out for Michael to shake before introducing himself and Miriam. Maggie grabbed the babe out of my arms, leaving me bereft as my anxieties assailed my insides until I felt nothing but an empty shell.

My mind spun as Michael guided us to a table. It wasn't until Miriam called my name, giving me a look that told me she called me more than once, that I came back to myself.

"Is Shay okay?" I blurted.

Michael set out a few glasses and began to fill them with whiskey I hadn't noticed on the table.

"You already opened this place?" I asked. "But I thought it wasn't until—" I stopped, my mouth snapping shut at what I was about to reveal.

Surprisingly, Michael's sharp gaze met mine with more knowledge than I expected. I tilted my head. *Does he know?*

He straightened, setting the whiskey bottle down without breaking our connection. "Not yet, lass. Just have some unexpected but necessary guests."

I dared another glance at the group that was outright staring now. I couldn't quite place why they stood out. Maybe it was their attire? On closer inspection, the style was—

"There has been an..." Michael started, drawing my attention back to him, his strained muscles, as he motioned for us to sit before doing so himself. "Feck, lass. I don't know how to tell ye this. There's been an altercation."

I straightened in my seat, my whole-body trembling as I watched this strong man raise a shaking glass to his mouth before chugging it as easily as water.

What the hell happened?

"If I may give my professional opinion," John cleared his throat, not waiting for a response, "In her present condition, it may not be wise for Mrs. O'Connor to receive any upsetting news you are about to deliver."

I didn't miss the way Michael's eyes flared at the mention of my name. Did he not know?

"I'm fine," I said, shooting John a glare, not caring if I was rude. No one would get between me and Shay. I turned back to Michael. "Tell me."

Michael poured himself another two fingers. "Doctor, with all due respect..." He didn't bother to look up from his glass as he tilted it back and forth, watching the contents slosh along the sides. "Our girl is far more capable of handling what shite this world dishes out. In fact, it's her I need to carry out this mission."

Our girl. I wasn't sure if I was more shocked by the claim or that he needed me. What could a useless girl like me accomplish? Still, my whole body tingled at the declaration. To be a part of a group, a family. That's what I'd been missing. But who was Michael to me? To Shay? A true brother-in-law? Or just another person who wanted to use me?

I grabbed the glass and took a swig, relishing the burn down my throat. "What do I have to do? Where is she?"

"I'm not sure how much ye remember..." Blue eyes met mine before weaving me an unbelievable tale about a man who killed my mother. Who traveled across the states to find me and my vials. A man who took my friend in the search and held her captive, waiting for me to return.

"I tried to find her," Michael finished. "I swear to ye. I spent weeks looking, and I couldn't damn well find her." His fist slammed onto the table, making the whole table flinch. "I never had such trouble."

Maggie's face was solemn as she swayed with Libby.

"What makes you think I can do anything about this?" My voice rose with each panicked word I sent Michael's way. "I'm just one woman!"

"Ye are far more than just a woman."

I scoffed.

"I did what I had to. Now, we need ye to draw him out."

My face scrunched in a defiant snarl.

Michael...smiled.

I crossed my arms, completely denying what he was telling me. Of course, I wanted to save my friend. It was the delusion that he thought I could fix this that I doubted.

Michael stood, prowling around the table, before stopping behind my chair. My breaths came in and out quickly, goosebumps sprouting on my arms. *What is he—*

The chair was ripped out from underneath me. Miriam screamed, and John yelled for Michael to stop, but it was I who had a knife pressed to Michael's throat, my chest heaving as the blade dug in deeper.

Holy shit. I did that.

His smile grew into a full-out grin. "It seems all our training hasn't gone to waste."

My elation simmered as my face scrunched in confusion. He trained me?

"Oh, aye. It's nice to know ye cherished me gift."

"Gift?" His eyes fell to the dagger in my hands, and a few answers clicked into place. Michael trained me and armed me with the weapon I continuously wore as if it were an extension of myself. Just how much time had I spent with this man? My hand squeezed the handle, making the leather creak.

I'm not giving it back. I narrowed my eyes, daring him to try.

"Though," he continued, his smile dropping, "ye let yourself get soft again. Have ye not been training?"

Soft? I glowered. Yes, I gained weight, but only past the unhealthy stage. I still had a lot more filling out to do to get where I'd been before all of this.

"I was healing." I seethed.

"Ye lost muscle. How do ye expect to stand a chance against an opponent?"

I lowered the blade. "I won't be fighting anyone."

"So, ye will leave her there at his mercy?"

"How am I supposed to save her if you can't?" I waved the blade up and down his body. "There's no chance."

His jaw clenched, his nostrils flaring in anger. I took an involuntary step backward.

"Like I said," he said slowly, as if I was stupid and needed to listen to each enunciation of the words, "ye have something I don't. He wants ye. He wants what we hid. And if we present him with what he wants..."

The blood drained from my face, and Miriam slapped her hand on the table.

A trade. I can do that.

"Absolutely not!" she protested, standing with a jolt. "I did not nurse her and bring her across the states for you to throw her to the wolves!"

"I'm not saying—"

John stood slowly, with the same look as when he fought his brother. My eyes flicked between him and Michael, hoping he wouldn't try anything because, deep down, I knew Michael would destroy him without a thought. "I believe it is time we take our leave," John said, grabbing the coat he had hung on the back of his chair. "Emilia, you can stay with us until you find somewhere else."

I bit my lip, glancing at Libby in Maggie's arms. A pressure grew within me, filling me with a determination I wasn't accustomed to. Resolve settled my nerves, and I straightened.

"What do you need me to do?" I asked Michael.

"Emilia," Miriam hissed. "You can't be serious?"

"I can't—I won't leave my friend. If I can help, I will."

"It could very well mean your life," John cut in, face solemn.

"Then so be it."

Miriam and John exchanged glances, but I was too busy staring at an older man who walked into the room, his coat pushed back as his hand rested on a revolver. I froze even as my mind jolted, and looked at a face I'd repressed years ago. It shocked me how easily it came back.

"Figlia." *Daughter.* I couldn't take the time to ponder how I understood him. I gripped my skirts, crushing the fabric, the burn of tears threatening their release when he continued in Italian. "I hear you've been through a great deal."

Interesting. Only the memories of my time travel seemed to have been affected by my injury. I'd heard of such things about losing chunks of time before an accident that could be triggered back into existence with a similar event or sensory input. It hadn't happened for me, though I prayed it would soon.

If I had doubts before, they were now erased. My lost memories were solely from the last two years after searching the attic; all the others, including my early childhood recollections, were still intact. I wracked through them, what I could recall of the man before me, but only brief glimpses of his face, his smile as he stared at me and a woman...I shook my head as it began to pound. The amnesia, coupled with the repressed memories of my parents, was too much.

I'm missing so damn much.

Taking a deep breath, I failed to calm my nerves, and had to ignore the shock and frustration as I pulled myself together enough to respond. "Sì, papà."

Manfri Moretti. The name floated to the surface of my memory, shrouded by fog that kept the rest at bay, even as the language flowed off my lips.

My father didn't seem nearly as shocked as I felt. Of course, Michael must have warned him of my return. That had to be it.

His dark, peppered brows crinkled in worry. "You do not remember, but we met not long before you left for the war."

My jaw dropped, and I cast an inquiring glance at Michael. He nodded.

"And now it looks like the man who sought me out a year past, at your request, has found me again." My father spoke in English for everyone to understand.

My heart pounded in my chest as I looked at Michael, finding another nod of confirmation.

"I wouldn't have, but I saw no other choice," Michael said, his shoulders stiff as he took in the men in the room. It was then I realized why they had looked out of place. They had the Roma's flowing, colorful clothes, darker features, and varying brown and black hair.

Gypsy, Michael had called me, the sound of it an echo of something larger, more meaningful. The word had negative connotations hooked to it, but growing up not knowing where I came from, in a misconstrued sort of way, I felt like they didn't apply to me. I could almost hear the word whispered to me, like a gentle touch, transforming it from something negative to a tender endearment that left me yearning for home—even though I was unsure if I fully understood what that meant. Goosebumps covered my arms as I pondered the weight of this word and how the meaning behind it became so much more.

I shook off the feeling and focused on what they began to tell me.

Boudreaux had gone into hiding. He had found a location so discreet that not even Michael's men could hear a whisper about him. My papà had correspondents in the city who had helped Michael find my papà the first time. That's why Michael was able to find a traveling band of Roma, but couldn't find the man who had kidnapped my friend.

Michael had searched extensively in the city, but my papà expanded the search to the countryside where Boudreaux was likely to hide. Boudreaux preferred the quiet life with his slaves, which was impossible in Boston's loud and busy streets. Even more so, he would want to keep Shay away from Michael and push us out of the city, where we had the upper hand.

My papà and his team hunted for Boudreaux for months. It wasn't until a mere week before my arrival that they found Boudreaux holed up in a sprawling house several miles outside the city.

With the promise of my arrival, my papà convinced Michael to wait. Boudreaux wasn't the type of man Michael was used to dealing with, and if he had Shay, he'd use her against them if I was not there. Hell, he'd still probably use her against us, but I was who he truly wanted. And we could use *that* to *our* advantage. Even if the plan didn't work, I would sacrifice myself to the man so she wouldn't have to spend one more day in his company.

"I'm so sorry you have to deal with this now, figlia," Papa said in Italian, dark eyes pleading. "I told you before, I thought I had ended the man who killed tua madre. But I swear to you, I will help you finish him now and save your friend. It is my fault you are in this mess."

I ran my teeth over my lip, considering his words. My head still spun from meeting him, from meeting all of them, and finding out about Shay, so much so that I didn't know what to do.

I looked at Miriam, finding a crease between her brows as she studied me. She shrugged. "Do what you think is best," she said, glancing at John.

"But know we cannot be a part of this," John admitted, his gaze soft even with the firm set of his shoulders. He cared, he just wouldn't put his family in danger. I couldn't blame him.

"Okay," I told the room, letting out a breath as I did so.

It seemed this time wasn't through testing me—it had taken my baby, her father, my innocence, even the very memories of how those losses came to be.

I sure as hell wasn't about to let it have my friend, too.

CHAPTER FORTY-ONE

Shaylah

July 1863

The young servant—Kezia, Shay learned weeks ago—took the food tray, glancing pityingly at Shay. She was struck by how much Kezia's dark eyes reminded her of Emilia's. Even the long, dark hair and olive skin tone were the same, so much so that Shay had to keep herself from grabbing the girl and shaking answers out of her. Was she related? She could very well have been if Emilia's mom had escaped from this horrid man, leaving behind her family in haste for freedom.

Shay deduced that Kezia was instructed not to engage in conversation, often looking away from Shay or ignoring her altogether. Even with Shay's prodding, Kezia promptly left the room without a word every night. Hell, she only knew the girl's name because Boudreaux decided to grace her with his presence one evening and mentioned it offhandedly.

And then there was the fear radiating off the girl. Had Boudreaux done something? The slightest imagination set Shay's blood on fire.

Kezia couldn't be more than ten, yet she had the demeanor and mannerisms of someone much older. It made Shay's heart ache with fierce protectiveness toward the girl. If only she could grab Kezia, free her from the horrors that had aged her, and run somewhere safe.

Give me time, and I just might.

Shay breathed deeply, watching the girl exit the room.

One more moment.

She held her breath as she waited for the lock to click. Her body tensed, making herself sit still as she let out another slow breath. *Wait. Don't screw this up. Just...* Another breath. *Wait.*

The click came, and Shay's muscles strained, wanting to get as much done as possible. A few quiet minutes passed, and voices floated up the stairs but no steps on the second floor. All was silent.

It usually was in her part of the house.

Finally, Shay gave it enough time to deduce no threat of a visitor and jumped up, tearing off her dress and removing her corset with a deftness only accomplished with practiced patience. It had been weeks since she decided to take matters into her own hands.

Of course, she believed Michael would find her, but she wouldn't wilt in a room like some damsel in distress.

No. Shay was done with waiting. She would either break out of this house or die trying.

Once she removed it, she folded her dress as she would on any ordinary night. If someone walked in, it would look like she had readied for bed. Going to the bookshelf, she took out *A Tale of Two Cities* and flipped to the page where she hid the needle.

As soon as she felt well enough, Shay had searched the room high and low for a weapon or makeshift tool, only to find the bare necessities. They didn't even provide her with silverware, only a spoon for her meals, and they took that with the tray afterward. On the third day, she found a stray sewing needle under the bed. Someone must have dropped it before she was locked in this hellscape.

At first, she didn't know what to do with it. She ruminated on all the ways she could use it. Imagined stabbing it into Boudreaux's eye. Possibly using it as a pick, before she quickly decided even if she could figure out how to pick a lock, the little instrument needed a partner and more durability. It wasn't until the following day, when she was getting dressed that she felt the hard steel sewn into the corset.

After that, a plan began to form, and she started the tedious task of dissembling the material. However, the fabric turned out more challenging than anticipated, and she labored over the stitches, picking one at a time for hours with an insufficient tool. It took several nights working her fingers raw before removing the first rib. When she did, she stared at the long steel bar and wondered how the hell she would sharpen it.

But be damned, she was going to.

She spent each night removing the stitching on the rest of the corset before moving on to sharpening the steel, only to find every surface insufficient. When she wasn't pulling the hem, she contemplated what to do with the damn thing. Ultimately, she used the fireplace grate to bend the rib in half, rubbing it up and down the rough metal until a sharp, rugged edge formed the thin rib into a deadly weapon. It took some time, but after aching arms and a few choice curses, she smiled, pleased with her makeshift dagger.

Shay grabbed the needle and the corset and crawled into the bed, ready to finish the last rib. She hoarded the other sharp pieces of violence under the mattress like gold to a dragon. After this, Shay would keep them on her person, and plan an escape. She hated what she'd have to do with them, but if Boudreaux visited her himself...

A nervous energy at the thought of it made her hands shake, and she set the needle down, taking a deep breath before picking it back up. A half hour went by when footsteps clipped out in the hall.

Shay paused, heart pounding as she strained her ears. It sounded like it was down the hall, but... Footsteps picked up again, getting louder the closer the person came. Shay scrambled to hide the needle back in the book, shoved the corset in the sheets, and picked up the book as if she was reading it, the cool bite of the rod a reassurance as it warmed to her body heat. The footsteps stopped outside, and a jingle of keys sent a jolt of fear through her.

What does he want? He'd never come this late before. Unless it wasn't Boudreaux. *Then who can it be?* Her thoughts spun in a maze of chaotic panic.

Shay hurriedly pulled the blankets over her, wanting to conceal her lack of clothing, and waited as the doorknob twisted. She held her breath as the door swung open, revealing a dark figure just out of the lantern's light.

It paused there, as if not expecting to find her in bed already, making this situation all the worse.

At least I wasn't using the chamber pot. Now, that would have been mortifying.

"You know," she said, ignoring her thunderous heart, "you could knock."

"I do not have to knock in my own household," Boudreaux's familiar voice rumbled as he entered the room, the firelight throwing shadows over his thick, white beard.

"I wasn't aware this was your house."

He threw Shay a dark look that had her skin tightening. "You would mind your mouth if you want to be fed again, girl."

Bowing her head, she probably looked every bit the cowed woman when, in reality, she had to hide the fury blazing from within.

The chair's creak and swipe of a match told her he was settling in. She had to fight off the urge to grab the smooth rib and stab him in the neck with it. God, she spent too much time with Michael. And yet, it was nowhere near enough. He and Libby were the only reasons she was fighting so damn hard to escape.

The flare of the cigar drew her attention as they sat in silence. Shay shifted, uncomfortable with how little she had on.

"You've been reading?" he finally asked.

"Not much else to do," she said before she could stop herself, but Boudreaux just nodded, quietly studying her as he blew out a puff of smoke. Were they just going to sit here and enjoy each other's company? The absurdity of it, the anger still percolating within her, made her snap, "What do you want from me? Why keep me here, wasting your money on food?"

He raised a brow and crossed an ankle over his other knee. "Do you propose Istop feeding you then?"

"No, I just—"

"It is not your place to ask questions." Another puff of smoke. "Though, I assume you may have guessed what I want."

Shay's heart was going to bust out of her chest, her breathing intensifying. *Finally, we are getting somewhere.* "Yes," she admitted.

"Enlighten me."

"I don't know where the vials are," Shay lied. With Michael's help, she'd hidden them beneath the floorboards of Madame Nora's. Not even Keena and her...*clients* knew the vials witnessed the debauchery committed in that room.

"No, I believe you don't." He smiled then, slow and patronizing, as he watched her reaction. Goosebumps shot across her body as she tried to find some hidden meaning behind this.

"What—"

"I know you don't because I have them."

The world tilted, the entire axis thrown off as dread flooded her system, rendering her breathless. "Then why—"

Boudreaux's leg lowered, his elbows resting on his knees as his gaze was a bullet straight through her soul. "I want her."

Millie.

Unchecked fury blazed through Shay's system. "You have no right to Emilia," she snapped, her hands aching with how tightly she gripped the book.

He smiled, the look of it making her sick. "She belongs to me as much as her mother. I do not take the loss of my property lightly."

"You can't own a person!" Shay shouted, pushing the book to the side. "They're living *beings*. What makes you think—"

"Did I not purchase them? Feed them. Nurture them. They are an investment and a profitable one at that." Shay's stomach clenched as she fought the urge to stab him there and then. She would have if she had sharpened it. "When I lost the girl—"

"She was never yours," Shay hissed. "Clementina escaped your hell hole. Her daughter never even set foot on your plantation."

Boudreaux sat back. "Surely, you can't be so ignorant of our ways." His gaze skimmed her dark skin along the white of her shift, and a low, considering growl rumbled in his chest. "Yes, you would have made a pretty penny."

Shay's lip curled in revulsion. "I belong to one man, and that's only because he fought for that right."

"Ah, Michael," he purred condescendingly. "How is our man now that the majority of the North Boys had split?" When she didn't respond, too dumbstruck to string together a sentence, he continued, "Well," Boudreaux chuckled darkly, "how would you know when you won't even leave this room?" Boudreaux sneered as if she chose entrapment. "Your man's boys left him. It seemed they didn't wholeheartedly agree on your rescue. Or, would be rescue of a *colored*. It looks like without his crew, he's but a simple man."

Left? Nausea surged into her throat at the implications. What would that mean for Michael? She knew the men didn't like her, but she didn't think it was enough for them to rebel.

Shay's lip curled in a snarl, refusing to let her worry show.

"Bullshit!" She spat, the glob falling at his feet. "Michael will gut you and pin your intestines to the fucking wall."

Boudreaux laughed, infuriating her more. Shay sat up, the steel rod clenched in her hand beneath the covers.

"If you don't believe that, then you'll find it utterly shocking when I reveal Michael had killed one of his closest men."

"What?" She squinted. He was lying. He had to be because why would he tell her all this? To get a rise out of her? To twirl her up in so many lies and deceptions that she might give him some information?

Shay swallowed past the lump in her throat. Boudreaux was playing a game she wasn't sure she could understand, let alone win.

"My men found Hugh Callahan on the side of the road, a bullet through his skull," he explained, watching the emotions flitting across her face. "It looked like your Irish swine pushed him out and kept rolling. Tell me, is that a man you want warming your bed at night?" His thick brows rose, his head tilting to the side. "Or watching over your babe?"

"Don't you dare speak of my child!"

"Ah, your child. And what would you do if someone took that babe from you? Raised her as his own?"

"Are you threatening me?"

"Simply asking a question, ma chérie."

"I..." Shay hesitated, genuinely giving it thought. But what was there to think about? "I would do anything to get her back."

"Then we understand each other." He leaned forward, dark eyes glinting in the firelight as fury overtook his features. "I want my daughter. And you will give her to me, or yours will be the one to pay the price."

"Your—" Shay froze, eyes widening as she took him in. Really looked at him. Boudreaux was tan, but she assumed from years working in the southern sun.

Oh, dear God. No. It can't be. Indeed, she was mistaken. Shay scrutinized his white beard, trying to imagine it dark years ago.

Please, be wrong.

Boudreaux couldn't be Millie's father. But then, who was Manfri? Did he genuinely think he was Millie's dad? She didn't want to consider the alternative.

"I can see you fell for his lies," Boudreaux confirmed her suspicions, leaning back in the chair, the cigar clenched between his teeth.

"But...why would he lie?"

"He wanted the vials." He said it offhandedly as if she should have known ages ago.

Shay's face contorted in confusion. "You're saying... Wait." She hesitated, trying to piece it together. "Are you saying *you* had the vials this entire time?" She sneered. That, she knew to be false. Maybe this *was* all a ruse to get information out of her. "Impossible."

Boudreaux rubbed a big finger between his brows as if to ease a headache. "I see that I will need to work a little harder to convince you."

"You can't expect me to believe you had them. *We* had them."

"Or rather, you *believed* you had them," he rumbled, giving her a pointed look.

"Then why are you here?" she snapped, heart pounding. She needed to get it together, or she would say something stupid. Of course, she knew why he was here. Millie. It has always been Millie.

He took another puff of the cigar, considering her. "I want my daughter. When I arrived in Boston, I needed to ensure it was her. I had her followed and watched who she conversed with and where she went. It wasn't until Manfri and his kumpania cornered her that my suspicions were confirmed. By your reaction, I can only assume he gave you imitations of the vessels?"

Shay's mind reeled as everything she believed was turned on its head. Had they never had the means to get home? Her heart plummeted into her stomach. She didn't realize how much the option to go to the future comforted her until she no longer had it. And Manfri...what? Tricked them? For what? He didn't even stay intown with Millie.

But then Boudreaux's previous comment floated back to her.

The vials. Boudreaux had the vials—vessels—and Manfri thought he could use Millie to get them.

"Why didn't you just tell her?" Her voice was quiet, subdued. "Tell Emilia the truth?"

"She left before I had the chance." A deep sigh gusted out of him. "I had to resort to hiring low-born fools to bring her back. I couldn't take the chance of Manfri discovering my plans."

"Do you expect me to believe you are the good guy in this story?" Shay scoffed, eyeing him with disdain. "You murdered her mother! We will never trust you. You're disgusting." Her lips pulled back as if she smelled something foul. There was no way this man was decent. Even if he meant Emilia no harm, he owned slaves. *People*. She bit her lip. "Why are you even telling me this? Millie will want nothing to do with you."

Boudreaux sat there for a long moment, silent and intimidating. "First, you assume I care what she wants. The girl is mine, and I do not take kindly to those who steal my things. Second," He held up two fingers with the hand that held the cigar. "Your friend has returned, and that imbecile you call a lover called in the very man we have been avoiding the last year."

Shay gripped the sheets, keeping herself still as cold sweat covered her. Millie was back after being injured, only to be on danger's doorstep again. And Shay was locked up here, unable to do shit about it.

"And, for everyone's sanity," Boudreaux continued, "I did not kill Clementina."

Shay's gaze swung up to his. "Excuse me?"

He knocked loudly on the table, causing Shay to jump. "I thought you might not believe me without some evidence," he explained. An answering knock thudded against the door, and Shay turned her attention from Boudreaux to it, faintly aware of him telling the person to come in.

The door swung open, stealing Shay's breath straight from her chest, as a woman glided in, beautiful red skirts swaying around her, long brown hair swept up high to cascade in tumultuous waves over her shoulder. *Wow, she's gorgeous*. Dark eyes met Shay's, and before she knew it, Shay was standing and going to the woman, grabbing her hands.

"Clementina?" she asked, though there was no question she was Millie's mother.

She could see it in the shape of her face, though slightly worn with age, and the color of her eyes, a deep brown, almost the color of amber in a particular light. That was where the similarities ended. Clementina was of slighter build and more angled than Millie's curves, but Shay suspected that Millie might be the spitting image of her mother if it wasn't for Millie's nutrition growing up.

"It is a pleasure to meet you," Clementina said in a heavy, flowing French accent, glancing at Boudreaux as if waiting for his approval. Shay's stomach turned when he did just that, and Clementina turned back to Shay. "I've been told you are a friend of my daughter. No?"

"Yes, "Shay said, looking down at her shift. "I wasn't aware I'd have guests. I would have put something more..." She trailed off, brushing her hands down herself.

"Ba," Clementina blurted in an apparent dismissal. "I do not blame you."

They both looked to Boudreaux and found him assessing each woman with the intensity of a predator stalking its prey. Shay repressed the sudden chill going through her and offered Clementina a seat.

"I'm sorry," Shay said, sitting on the bed as the other two sat in the only chairs. "I don't understand. We were told that you were killed."

Clementina bit her full lip, daintily placing her small hands in her lap.

Shay could see why Boudreaux kept her—she was like a pretty, life-sized doll he could play with. The thought sickened her. That, and if the tightening of her features and shifting in her seat were anything to go by, Clementina was uncomfortable. Was she here to lie and deceive? Just because she was Millie's mom didn't mean she could trust her.

"Oui," Clementina agreed. "Marcel thought it best for Manfri not to know of my existence anymore."

"Right." Shay drew out the word before she could think better. She dared a glance at Boudreaux, but he wasn't even paying attention to her, looking at the fire as he puffed on the cigar. "And why shouldn't Manfri know of your existence?"

Clementina took a fortifying breath but didn't look up from her hands. "Manfri had tricked me," she answered, voice wavering. "At first, I think he loved me, but when he discovered the vessels, his greed killed that love." Her steely gaze met Shay's. "When Marcel found me and took me, Manfri took the only leverage he had."

"Emilia."

"Oui. I thought Manfri loved her as his own, but it became evident that the older she got, the more he knew she wasn't his. He began to resent her, and it was just another reason for him to feed into that greed."

"Then why hasn't he done anything yet? Why wait?"

"Because," Boudreaux rumbled, "he's been waiting to play his cards. A trade, the vessels for my daughter."

"You'd do that?"

"No."

Shay didn't know whether to be relieved or terrified. Millie's life outweighed everything. But they *needed* those vials to get back home—or have there assurance to be able to—and neither of these men could be trusted with them.

"What do you want with the vials?" Shay asked. "Why not just give them up?" Then she drew back, hesitating at a thought. "If the vials were fake, and you had them, then how did Manfri send Emilia through time?"

She didn't dare ask how they retained the vials to get to the nineteenth century in the first place. That was a question for the future. Somehow, someway, the vials ended up in the pub's attic in the future. Shay could only pray that that future was set and the subsequent events would not erase it.

Boudreaux grumbled incoherently in French, sounding much like profanity.

"His mère." Clementina paused at Shay's look of confusion and explained, "His, ah, what's the word?"

"Mother," Boudreaux translated.

"Ah, oui. His mother adored my Emilia and loved her as her own. I entrusted her with a vessel if she ever needed it."

"A gift that you had no right to bestow," Boudreaux snapped.

Clementina lowered her head, cowed by the intensity of his glare. It didn't matter that her people wielded the magic within the vessels. As his property, everything that belonged to her was rightfully his.

Shay had to refrain from rolling her eyes. "But if Manfri wants the vessels, why would he waste it on Emilia?"

Boudreaux sighed. "To spite me, no doubt."

"Though he knew Emilia wasn't his," Clementina explained, "Manfri raised her as his own from birth for three years. That love does not vanish overnight. And if he was not to have the vessels, then surely Marcel would not have Emilia. Manfri knew Marcel would never give up the vessels."

Shay slumped. The weight of what these people carried was almost too much to bear. Why own someone? Why not just love someone or let them go? Did greed, pride, and jealousy have to override everything? If they only loved Emilia and let Clementina go, so much pain and heartbreak could have been avoided. Now, nineteen years later, they were still dealing with the repercussions, and Shay was stuck in the crossfire.

"What do you want with me?" she asked Boudreaux.

"Our daughter will come for you."

"And what?" Shay looked at Clementina. "You'll take her against her will?"

Clementina flinched, paling. "We can convince—"

"There's no way Emilia will go with you on this green earth."

"Then," Boudreaux smiled, groaning as he pushed himself off the chair. "It is good that she will have you when we bring her back home."

The blood rushed from Shay's head, her hearing going hollow as the total weight of their intentions crashed onto her. "You—" Swallowing "—You can't keep me. I am a person. I—"

"We all belong to our master," Clementina said, face blank of any emotion. "Marcel will give you a good life."

Shay sat there, dumbstruck. She couldn't be serious. Had all these years of enslavement broken her will? Was this really the woman who escaped and crossed the country while pregnant? A whisp of the woman who had such fervor to survive.

Shay spit at Boudreaux's feet. "Over my dead body."

Before she could blink, Boudreaux backhanded Shay across the face, sending her sprawling over the bed. She put a hand to her stinging face, eyes burning from the force of it.

"You really shouldn't put yourself in these positions," Boudreaux told her, taking the cigar out of his mouth. He pointed at her mid-section. "Especially in your condition."

Shay stiffened, and Clementina gasped, blatantly staring at the small mound growing with each passing day. Her second pregnancy started to show far earlier than Libby's, but Shay's stomach was still flat when they took her. In truth, Shay planned to tell Michael the very day she was captured.

What if he never knows he will be a father? She clenched her teeth, refusing to cry. *Stop it. You're getting out of here.* We're *getting out of here.*

"You think my servants wouldn't tell me you purged at least once daily? It doesn't take a wise man to figure out your condition."

Shay sat straight, billowing her shift out so it was no longer on display. "I haven't lost the weight from my previous pregnancy," she lied. "And I haven't been feeling well. I'm not pregnant." Chin lifted, she stared him down, daring him to contradict her.

Clementina's gaze darted between them. "Is...is it yours?" she asked Boudreaux, obviously not believing Shay either. Her face crumpled. God, was the woman jealous? She couldn't want this man for herself, not after everything he'd done.

To Shay's disgust, Boudreaux grabbed Clementina's chin. "Hush, ma beauté. You're still the only woman I want in my bed."

Lying ass. You've been screwing Nessa for months.

Something flared across Clementina's face so fast that Shay thought she'd imagined it. They stared at each other for several awkward seconds until Clementina broke into a meek grin and cupped his cheek. Shay watched, completely flabbergasted by this display of affection. The man just hit her daughter's friend, for fuck's sake.

"Je suis désolé d'avoir douté de toi, mon amour. Vous savez à quel point je peux être jaloux," Clementina purred, raising on her dainty shoes to brush a kiss across his mouth. Boudreaux grasped the back of her neck, nearly encircling it with his large hand, and deepened the kiss. Shay didn't know what she wanted more—to throw up or slap some sense into Millie's mother.

When Boudreaux finally extracted his tongue from Clementina's mouth, Shay regained control of her composure and stood. "He will come for you," Shay stated. "If you keep me, a war will be on your hands."

"Looks like plenty of those are going around." He smiled. "Come, mon amour. Let's plan for our daughter's arrival. I hear she's bringing a war to our doorstep."

Clementina followed Boudreaux, pausing with a hand on the doorframe to look back at Shay with the saddest eyes she'd ever seen. Shay stared her down, unable to find solidarity with the woman who refused to fight for her daughter, if not for herself anymore.

She swept from the room, the door slamming closed with the derisive click of the lock. It wasn't until Shay skirted the table that she found something tan on the ground by the doorframe. Shay looked at the door, brow scrunching as she wondered who may have dropped it.

Paper? She began to unfold the tiny squares and went to the fire to see the sweeping script.

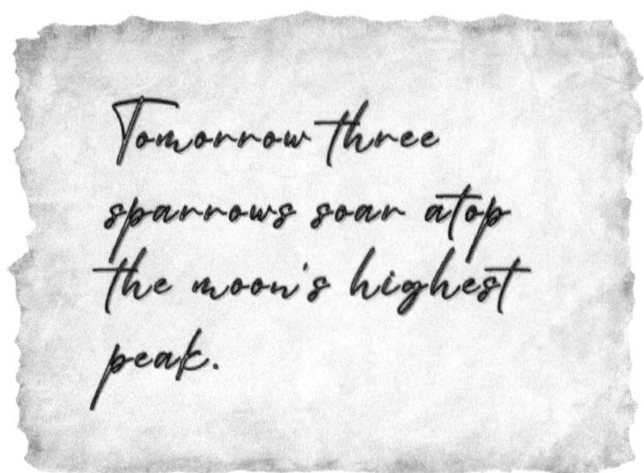

Maybe I won't need Michael to help me, after all.
Shay's heart pounded like a war drum as she tossed the note into the fire, a visual of her hope rekindling. A small smile danced on her lips while she

gathered her weapons.
Tomorrow, we fly.

CHAPTER FORTY-TWO

Thomas

July 1863 – Battle of Gettysburg

Thomas knelt on the crushed grass, staring up at the priest who had married him and Emilia between battles all those months ago. He trusted the man, having spoken to and gone to confession throughout the war. So, when Thomas asked Emilia in the middle of the night, beneath shared blankets and whispered promises, she said yes without hesitancy. His excitement remained undiminished, even as he persuaded her to trust the priest.

The next day, they met in a slight, battered tent, just the two of them and the priest. It might not have been official without the witnesses, but it was true for them and in God's eyes. They planned to do it again with family after the war.

The memory was sharp, but Thomas did not dare let himself ruminate on it, knowing it would cripple in the upcoming battle if he succumbed to the thoughts that plagued him these last few months. That would only lead to an unfortunate demise, or worse, he might get one of his men killed.

As he watched Father William Corby forgive the soldiers before the impending battle, Thomas pleaded with God to absolve him of the unholy acts he had committed. Thomas swore that he would fight for what was right and give his own life for these men if God only healed Emilia and forgave his wretched and fecked-up life. It didn't matter if Thomas was never happy again or had to struggle for the rest of his days; he'd do it gladly for her. Hell, even if Thomas' soul was already damned, he'd burn for eternity with a smile on his lips as long as it meant Emilia lived.

Let me be the man she deserved. One that she could be proud of when time has passed.

Thomas hung his head as the summer sun beat upon his neck, and the father's words carried over the crowd.

What was he thinking? He'd never be more than a common thug, destined to run the streets with nothing but his fists and the weapons he carried.

Whilst the priest still spoke, Thomas stood and left them to do what he did best.

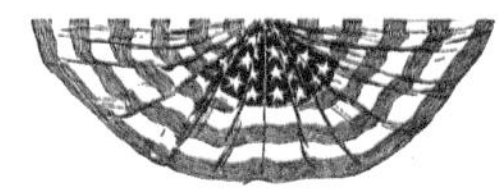

They charged into the wheatfield, soldiers on both sides fell to the ground. Blood-soaked the soil.

Thomas held his rifle ready, picking off Rebels as fast as he saw them. They had surprise on their side as they entered a forested area and overwhelmed the Confederates, where the soldiers fled or were taken prisoner.

"Well, shite," Sullivan muttered, baring his teeth in a gruesome grin made worse by the dirt coating his face. "How should we celebrate?"

The words were barely out of his friend's mouth when men started shouting from the direction of the Peach Orchard. The Confederates advanced from the right and headed straight for them. With an order from Colonel Byrnes, he and his men were to retreat through the Wheatfield.

Thomas swore and raised his rifle even as he began to withdraw, going against his instinct to save the fallen men. If he fell, he couldn't help those retreating. Thomas would be no good dead or captured, and he couldn't sacrifice good men for the sake of those already down. He would have to live with the knowledge that the fate of those men would haunt him forever.

Or, at least, that's what he told himself until he saw Sullivan's leg give out, a musket ball to the thigh. His friend stumbled but managed to lift his rifle to put down the man who'd shot him. It wasn't enough, though. The Rebels kept pursuing, and Sullivan couldn't return on one leg.

Thomas let out a stream of curses and shot as fast as he could reload. He took five men down by the time he made it to Sullivan.

"Go, ye fool," Sullivan snapped as his rifle jammed. He swung it around and slammed it into the face of a man ready to attack.

"We go together," Thomas growled, shooting his last shot. He slung the rifle over his shoulder and pulled out his pistol.

"How many shots ye have left?"

Thomas scanned the body-strewn field. "Enough."

Sullivan snorted, pulling out a wicked dagger. They would have to fight their way out.

Thomas slung Sullivan's arm over his shoulder and hoisted him upward. Sullivan muttered curses under his breath, but offered no complaints.

They made it a few paces when a bullet tore through Thomas' shoulder. He stumbled, losing hold of Sullivan as they tumbled forward. Three Confederates appeared seemingly out of nowhere.

Feckin' hell.

Sullivan slashed at the closest, taking him out at the legs before plunging it into the man's chest. Thomas shot his last bullet through the forehead of the second man. Before the man hit the ground, Thomas had his dagger ready, swinging around for the third man to find him a few yards away with a rifle pointed to his face.

Emilia's face flashed in his mind before he had time to blink.

A flock of birds burst from the trees, scattering north as the shot rang out, sealing his fate.

Forgive me.

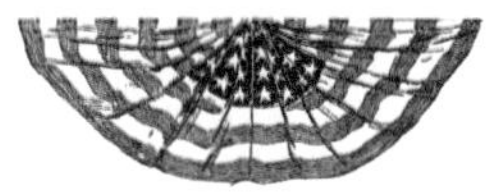

That day, nearly half of the 28th Massachusetts Regiment was either killed or taken prisoner, leaving 107 men dead or captured. The remaining soldiers withdrew to Cemetery Ridge, where they would learn of the fate of their fallen comrades.

CHAPTER FORTY-THREE

Emilia & Michael

JULY 1863

Sweat beaded on my brow as I dodged another punch, ducked, and lashed out with my weapon. Michael's legs buckled as my wooden stick hit just where I wanted, and his knees crashed to the ground with a curse on his lips. I barely had the chance to smile, before I was on my back, pinned beneath him, a gasp escaping my lips.

"Still. Too. Slow." He growled while shoving off me.

I lay in the dirty alley behind the pub, heart thundering in my chest. I still didn't have my memories, but I felt like I'd known Michael for years instead of the two short weeks he'd been training me. When we weren't training, he picked my brain, asking me questions until he was sure I had no recollection of the last two years. Then he would throw a hissy fit, storm off, and I wouldn't see him for hours.

He was like an annoying brother that I wanted to throttle most days. Others, I could spot a glimpse of how much he was hurting. How much he worried for Shay, and a part of me shriveled inside, reciprocating the helplessness of the situation.

I wanted to get Shay out just as much as he did. But we couldn't go just yet, guns blazing. Michael needed more supplies and more eyes on the house, and he used that time to train me.

"I'm trying my best," I said between breaths.

"Well, ye're best isn't good enough. Not if we are to get her tonight."

"You think I don't know that?" I shoved myself up, glaring at him. "If I can't do it now, I won't be able to later. This is what you get. It'll have to be good enough."

Michael started cursing in Irish. "Just do better," he hissed before storming back into the pub.

I was left there, dusting myself off, when I heard the back door open again. "Seriously?" I asked, still trying to pat my skirts to no avail. "I told you—"

"I wish there was a different way." My papà's voice had my head snapping up. He stood on the back step, watching me. It was still weird to see the man I'd been searching for. It felt like I began the search only months ago, but it had been *years*.

So much time I only brushed the surface of, and I found myself reserved around the man. He was a stranger, even if he had the memories I'd sought. Even if I couldn't grow a relationship out of this, I could get the answers.

And after we saved Shay tonight, rid ourselves of the man who murdered my mammina, maybe I could finally find peace with my past. We could go *home*.

I gave him a weak smile. "There's no way I'm sitting behind when I can do something to help."

Manfri's dark gaze stayed fixed on me, face unmoving, calculating. "You mistake me. I wish things hadn't turned out the way they had. The choices. Tua Madre. What you went through. All of it."

I rested my hands on my hips, pushing my shoulders out to stretch my sore back. "Nothing we can do about it now," I said honestly. "The only thing that matters is Shay." *And going home*, I stopped myself from saying. "Then we can get past all of this."

"Why haven't you used the vessels?"

My head reared back, feeling like whiplash in that change of conversation.

"I—" Hesitating, I thought about everything that had happened to me since I woke up. What could I tell him? What others had told me happened, or what they perceived as my truth? Tell him I stayed for a man? For a war that would result in the Emancipation of my mammina's people? I sighed, letting my head fall back to look at the blue sky.

"I guess I wasn't done here yet." I shrugged, not really wanting to clarify further.

He nodded. "So, you still have all of them?"

"Well," I started, returning my attention to him as I thought of where Michael hid the vials, "yeah. I didn't waste any or break them if that's what you're asking." My brows scrunched in confusion. I wouldn't be here now if I used them.

"Good," he said, nodding still. "Good."

Even hours later, I thought about the exchange and how odd he acted. My mind was consumed by a wariness that lingered like a dark cloud I couldn't shake.

I should have listened.

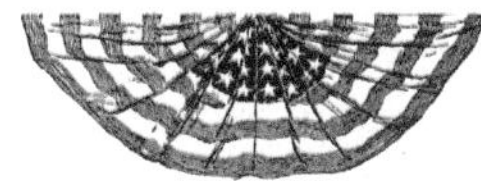

She's in there.

Mikey took in the large double-story house, the stacked porches across the front, and the land that sprawled in every direction and scoffed at the absurdity of it.

Who needs that much space? It's too damned quiet out here.

A click of his revolver centered his thoughts and narrowed his focus on the mission. Shay was in there, and they would get her out. Tonight.

The moon was high, bright enough for them to see. Dark enough for cover against unsuspecting targets.

Mikey signaled for Manfri and his men to sweep around the house, blocking all exits. They were getting in, but nobody was getting out.

He nodded to Emilia, crouched beside him, her revolver ready, and settled at the fury in her eyes, no hint of fear. War had done her good. Even if she couldn't remember it...

The thought had him nearly snorting. Mikey knew he had been hard on her, but he wanted to make sure she was ready for tonight. No mistakes could be made in saving his woman.

Gods. He never thought he would get to this point. And yet, he couldn't see it any other way.

"Ye ready?" he asked the gypsy.

With a quick nod, they crouched around the side of the house where they could quickly get to the back door, waiting for the explosives to go off in the front yard. Manfri and some of his men were surrounding the living quarters at the side property where Boudreaux's men slept. Henry and the few men who still ran with Mikey were to go around the front of the property as he and Emilia went through the back. Mikey would be damned if he let Boudreaux sneak off into the night.

The ground shuddered as a loud boom shook the windows; at the same time, the back door opened. Emilia raised her gun only for Mikey to shove it down, his heart thundering at the three dark shapes darting out the door. Two womanly shapes and one the size of a child stumbled and turned toward the commotion before sprinting at an impressive speed.

Yells came from within, loud bangs and moving furniture. They must have had a plan for when he'd inevitably arrive. But did they know about the three escaping?

Mikey cursed, taking off after the fleeing figures.

"Shaylah, gods damn it," he cursed, following the figure. She halted, and he could do nothing but collide into her, spinning so he could take the impact of the fall on his back, Shay, safely on top of him. A small scream erupted out of the child.

"Michael?" Shay croaked, eyes scouring his as her hands gripped his face, long fingers pulling through his short beard. "What are you doing here?"

What was he doing?

"Saving ye..." Mikey almost laughed. Clearly, the woman could handle herself.

"We must go," a heavily accented voice strained down to them, finally bringing Mikey back into the moment. "You know this man, oui?"

"Yes," Shay said a little breathlessly, still staring into Mikey's eyes. Gods, he missed her. She scrambled off him to stand, but it was only a matter of seconds before he had his hands on her, bringing her into a kiss that he had spent months dreaming about. The way her body felt pressed against—

Mikey reared back, hand brushing between them against the tight fabric and lack of corset. Her abdomen swelled as it did the first year he met her. A sudden, visceral rage overtook him.

"Who?" His jaw clenched so hard he could have sworn his teeth cracked. If a bloody, rotten, feckin' scum of an arsehole touched her...

His visceral thoughts eddied out when she gave him a nervous smile that crinkled her nose in a way that would be cute if he wasn't so angry.

"You."

The rage faltered as his brain tried to catch up with Shay's words. He heard her but couldn't comprehend what in the hell she was saying.

"Me?"

Shay rose on her toes to whisper into his ear. "I think it was when you bent me over the bar."

He felt her shrug, but all his focus was on his hand still roaming her belly. A baby. Gods, he never imagined he'd have one, let alone be gods-damned happy about it.

"But I could be wrong." The breathless way she said it made him want to reenact what she just conjured from his memories.

"We have to go!" The other woman snapped, surprising them both. Honestly, Mikey had forgotten she was there.

He looked at the small, beautiful woman clutching a young girl's shoulders. Each had long, dark hair and enough vibrant clothes to be spotted a mile away. "You three go." He explained to them where the carriage and a driver were waiting.

"Come with us," Shay said, brows drawn down. "I'm out. We can go."

Mikey shook his head, looking to the house, when a gunshot went off. Another followed after it mere seconds later.

"Feck!" he cursed, finding the back door open and Emilia nowhere in sight. Shouts erupted in the distance as Manfri's and Boudreaux's men met, followed by a loud commotion in the house.

Damn the lass. She never knows when to feckin' listen.

Michael turned back to Shay, a look of fear etched into deep lines between her brows.

"Emilia is in there," he explained. "We cannot let Boudreaux live. I will not have ye in danger again."

"Emilia?" The other woman gasped, clutching onto his arm. Mikey pulled back a bit, wondering if she was worth the trouble.

"We'll go with you," Shay said, already heading in that direction. Mikey grabbed her arm, swinging her back into his embrace.

"Are you saying my daughter is in there?" The woman yelled.

Mikey reared back. How many turns was this night going to take?

"She is," he responded quickly before looking down at Shay. There was no more time to waste. "Ye need to get to safety," he told her. "Your job is to keep ye and an leanbh safe."

He rubbed her stomach, marveling at what he had created, but also terrified at what the child would have to endure in this fecked-up world. But if Libby proved anything, he could love and provide for this child to the best of his abilities. Maybe it'd be a lad; they could have one of each. That thought sent a bolt of warmth through him better than the finest liquor.

Gods, I'm gettin' soft.

"Michael." Shay's voice broke as he cradled her face. This strong, beautiful woman would be the death of him one day.

"I love ye," he told her, meaning it to his deepest, darkest parts. He never meant anything more in his life. "I'll get her out of there. Now, go."

"There's something I have to tell you."

Another blast from within the house had him spinning on his heels. "Go!" he growled, already heading toward the lass's scream.

"It's not Boudreaux!" Shay yelled after him. "Manfri wants the vials! Boudreaux only wants Emilia, his daughter. They both can't be trusted!"

Feckin' hell.

Mikey kept running, though he nearly froze at the absurdity of this mess. A deep chill ran through Mikey as he realized the monster *he* had brought into their midst. No wonder it had been so easy to find the bastard.

These people were more fecked than he was.

As Mikey approached the house, he heard another scream, and tried not to think about how his brother would kill him if something happened to the gypsy. Hell, he'd never forgive himself.

As another bullet blasted through the night, Mikey prayed to a god he didn't believe in that he could make it in time.

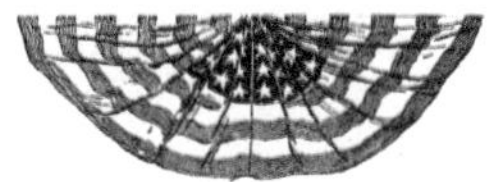

Michael took off after Shay, allowing me to breathe easier as I tackled what I had to do next.

She's safe, she's safe, she's safe. I repeated it like a mantra, and my heart raced as my second task loomed ahead:

Kill Boudreaux.

The floorboards creaked as I ascended the back porch. A flickering light from a candle shone in the kitchen, and hushed voices carried out to me. I only had moments before someone would find the open door.

A harsh French accent yelled something from the second floor, and the loud bang of a crashing door made me flinch. I kept my gun ready as I looked around the kitchen for any of Boudreaux's men. Though most weren't here yet, I knew they would be soon. I had to move fast if I was to complete this unimpeded.

The man persisted in shouting in French, and an anxious female voice responded to him. When a screech and a thud hit the floor, my nerves steeled, knowing the man hit the woman. A rumble of feet down the stairs had me lifting the revolver as I took in an older man, grizzled face distorted in a fury, his hand holding a large gun.

The man halted, his anger quickly morphing into surprise. "Emilia?"

"Don't move," I growled out as I tried to keep my hands steady, my name on his lips unnerving me more than I was prepared for. "Are you Boudreaux?"

He raised his hands, and I lifted mine higher, ready to shoot if he so much as moved toward me.

If he was Boudreaux, I had learned nothing but dreadful things about him these last few weeks—killing my mother, tormenting my people, and kidnapping my friend. The appalling list just went on.

He'll get what he bloody well deserves. The anger consumed me even as doubt crept in. *Is it really him?*

My hands shook as my palms dampened, making the gun slippery. I tried to calm myself, knowing it would be a tragedy if I made a foolish mistake.

The bastard showed me his hands in good faith. I squinted in suspicion.

"There is much you don't—"

"Are you Boudreaux?" I said louder as if he didn't hear me the first time.

"Yes."

I pulled the trigger, making him curse as he stumbled back, covering his arm where I'd hit him. "Salope!" he shouted, lifting his own gun.

I dove just in time for a bullet to hit the counter, sending splintering wood everywhere I'd been standing only seconds before. I crouched behind the cabinets, a pantry behind me, and listened for what Boudreaux would do next.

"You insolent, reckless child!"

"You killed my mother," I hissed. "You deserve every bad thing that happens to you."

"Is that what he told you?" I didn't have to look. I could hear the sneer in his words. "The web he spun to turn you against your own père?"

My heart fell as my head spun, my world off-kilter. I'd only just met my father, not having the memories from all those months ago. I barely knew Manfri, though I could have sworn I could remember my mother's smile. Manfri's laugh. I shook my head. "You can take your lies and shove them right up—"

Another bullet hit the cabinet next to me, and I screamed, ducking away from the small explosion.

I crouched down, holding my revolver ready. "Is that what you do? Try to kill your own daughter?"

"If she tries to kill me first, oui."

The audacity of this man.

I can't be his daughter. Can I? What is Manfri playing at?

My pulse pounded as I cautiously edged around the corner of the cabinet and took a quick look around. But before I could even take a shot, a large boot slammed into my hands, sending the bullet into the air and my revolver across the room.

I scrambled back, caught between the cabinets to my right, the pantry to my back, and Boudreaux pointing his gun right at me. I didn't dare glance at the open back door, where I could hear men's screams in the distance.

Jesus, what is happening out there?

I glared at Boudreaux, ignoring the distraction. "So, you kidnapped my friend to get the vials? What sort of father would do that?"

Not that I believed him. I just needed to keep him talking while my hands fumbled behind me, quietly opening a drawer, hoping to find a knife or anything worth using as a weapon. My dagger was strapped to my thigh, but I couldn't retrieve it without his notice. And as a gun was currently trained on me, I *really* didn't want to make the wrong move.

To my surprise, Boudreaux gave a degrading laugh. "I already have the vials, child. We wanted you."

My hands paused in their search, momentarily perplexed. "Me?"

"Did you believe that man would willingly surrender such rare magical properties? Hard to attain, and a myth to most. For him to have them, which he did not, he would have to be a fool to give them to you." He growled the last bit, his face contorting in disgust.

I only learned about receiving the vials last year, so this news was still fresh, making my head spin. "What would he gain by giving me false vials?"

Boudreaux spread his hands, encompassing the room. "To distract you, knowing I'd come."

"But they're fake..." I had trouble keeping up with the dramatics and began to worry my injuries caused more damage to my head than I realized. "If you knew they were real, why would they draw—"

"For you," he snapped. "I've cut my losses years ago, but your mère wouldn't *shut up*, knowing of your return."

The floor practically fell out beneath me. "My *what*?"

"Your mother," he growled, annoyed.

My hands fumbled behind me even as my head spun. "But, she's dead." My voice was as weak as the rest of me, as if the news took what little resolve I had left. "How..."

"Why the bastard lied to you is not of my concern."

"But," I tried to focus on Boudreaux even as a figure darkened the doorway. Then something hit me. "What do you mean she knew of my return?

How?"

Did they have some kind of messengers around the city?

"Her spirits revealed a return in her cards."

Tarot. My brows rose in surprise. I didn't realize my mammina practiced the craft.

"She did two other readings before she allowed herself to believe it. All three times, the same reading. Eight of Wands—swift travel. Aries—spring arrival. And Six of Cups for someone returning. When the Page of Wands fell, your mère had no doubt it was you and pestered me relentlessly until I brought her back to this damned city."

It sounded unbelievable, but who was I to argue the validity of his story when they returned to the city and found me after being gone so long? It was too fantastical to be a coincidence. And the fact that my mammina was alive—my heart swelled, and tears welled in my eyes.

"She's here?" I let the tears fall, not wanting my vision impaired by the stupid emotion. I needed to *focus*. But with my question, Boudreaux's face darkened.

"She was but seems to have vanished with that she-devil of yours."

So, that's who Shay escaped with. I grinned, letting him see the nastiness in it. The retribution. "*Good.*"

Boudreaux's large hand collided with my cheek, backhanding me to the ground as pain throbbed across my face. "They took my daughter, your sister, with them. You and your people have been nothing but a plague to me. If I don't get your mère and Kezia back, your people will pay the price."

I didn't have time to process those words when another gunshot went off, causing Boudreaux to stumble back. A hole in his shoulder to match the one I put in his arm.

"Stop!" I yelled to Michael. "He's mine."

Boudreaux kept his eyes on Michael, apparently seeing him as the more significant threat. I stood, already having removed my blade from its sheath, and crept toward the man who shared my blood but who I would never consider my *father*.

That title belonged to another O'Connor.

Wait, what? I grimaced. I couldn't think about how weird that sounded.

Michael kept his gun trained, but didn't shoot. "Ye sure, lass? I'd be more than happy to…"

I squeezed the handle of my dagger, wondering if I could really take a man's life with his back to me. Now that the chaos had ebbed, I had more time to think, and with thinking came doubts.

Could I really stab him? Do what had to be done as his blood flowed over my hands? The image had nausea burning its way up my throat, and I had to shut everything out.

Do. Not. Falter.

The words that came to mind were not my own but rather those of an Irishman I had long forgotten but wished to remember. I desperately tried to hold on to the fleeting memory but could only grasp the feeling it evoked.

I won't. I let out the breath I didn't know I'd been holding, and…

I. Did. Not. Falter.

CHAPTER FORTY-FOUR

Shaylah & Emilia

"You go," Shay told Clementina when they could see the carriage in the distance, but Clementina had already grabbed Shay's arm, stopping her in her tracks.

"Manfri's man," she hissed, clutching Kezia to her side as well.

"What?" Shay asked, confused.

"That is Manfri's man." Clementina jerked her head to the carriage, the dark-haired man illuminated by the high moon, and Shay felt all the blood drain from her face. *Michael brought Manfri here?* "We cannot go with him."

Shay cursed, pushing Clementina and Kezia toward the trees. Luckily, there had been enough cover for the man not to notice them, but Shay didn't dare take a chance for him to spot them standing there like utter fools.

"Hide in the woods," Shay told them. "We will come for you after. I have to go back."

"I go."

Shay had to grab Clementina's shoulders to stop the woman from storming back to the house. "You need to go with Kezia. I will get Emilia."

"She is my daughter."

Shay's face softened in sympathy. "So is Kezia." She looked at the girl, wide brown eyes flitting between them in worry. "She needs you more right now. I have no doubt Michael will get Emilia out, but I could never forgive myself if Manfri did something. I have to make sure that Emilia knows."

"You are with child," Clementina said, as if Shay could forget. Even now, her stomach was tight, uncomfortable, and threatening to pop.

Shay ignored the worry in Clementina's face. The fear. If she worried about herself, the babe, she wouldn't be able to make herself go back.

"Hide," she said, backing up through the underbrush. She'd skirt the tree line until reaching the house. By then, she should be out of sight of Manfri's man. "Please. Stay safe. For Emilia."

Yells and gunshots went off in the direction of the servants' quarters, and Shay took off, running as fast as her body would let her. She held her belly for more support, the weight and pull of it a concern she couldn't be distracted by.

Breaking out of the trees, she ran around the house, planning to go through the front door, praying it was unlocked. From what she could see, Manfri and his men were still by the other building, having yet to make it to the main house. Good. She didn't need more people in the chaos.

Using the railing for support, she made it up the steps and tried the door. It swung open on silent hinges, revealing the soft light of flickering candles.

Thank the stars.

Shay had never seen this part of the house. She was unconscious when they'd brought her and had been kept in the one room ever since. Only a vague recollection of the upstairs and the back of the house where she escaped gave her an idea of the layout. Not that it mattered; the voices were loud enough to easily find in the kitchen.

Son of a bitch. Her breaths came in and out in big heaves, and a painful stitch in her side had her hobbling like a ninety-year-old woman. Using the furniture as support, Shay pushed her way through the formal dining area, cursing all these months without actual exercise. She wasn't remotely close to possessing the endurance she had before.

Shay heard a loud grunt and bang of bodies clashing into cabinets before she rounded the corner to see through the doorframe into the kitchen, where Millie grappled with Boudreaux.

Millie lifted a large dagger, only for Boudreaux to block it, crushing Millie's wrist in his brutal grasp, preventing her from plunging it in his throat.

Just beyond them, Michael stood, watching, gun at the ready.

Why the hell isn't he doing anything?

Shay lurched forward, and Michael's eyes widened. He shook his head, halting Shay in her tracks. She raised her brows in a way that clearly asked him what the hell was happening.

Millie yelled, drawing their attention back to her, and found the dagger clattering to the floor.

"You impetuous child! You dare—"

Boudreaux's words cut off with a loud gurgle, his face a comic display of shock as Millie's hand pulled from his throat and blood spurted across her front. Shay jolted, hand flying to her mouth.

Oh, my God. She did it. She ended this.

A part of Shay was shocked that Emilia could do such a thing. On the other hand, she was ashamed to admit that she felt relief they wouldn't have to worry about him anymore.

A trail of blood trailed from Boudreaux's mouth as his hands fumbled with the wound, trying to staunch the flow to no avail. *God, there's so much blood.* A stumble back and a crash into a large table caused Boudreaux to sink to his knees.

Shay winced.

Face grey and eyes wide, he looked at his daughter for the last time. It was only a matter of seconds before he slumped to the floor, his lifeless eyes staring at the ceiling.

Shay jolted at Michael's harsh laugh and tore her eyes away from the dead man to give him a dubious scowl.

"I can't believe it," Michael chuckled. Actually, outright chuckled, even with Boudreaux's body still leaking blood all over the floor. He continued, almost incredulously, "Ye actually killed someone with a cutlery knife."

Shay whipped her gaze to the weapon still in Millie's hand and nearly laughed with Michael as she remembered the weapon Millie chose to practice with so long ago. It was the reason Michael gave Millie one of his daggers in the first place.

Now pale and a little unsteady, her friend only looked at him with confusion. Shay did laugh then, causing Millie's head to whip to her, mouth falling open in surprise. Shay must be in shock if she could laugh at a time like this. Either that or Michael had more of an influence on her than she realized.

"What are you doing here?" Millie asked, worry clouding the shock now.

"I told her to get to the carriage," Michael grumbled, but neither woman paid him any mind.

"I couldn't leave you," Shay told Millie.

Millie gave her a sad smile, even as she wiped the blood off her hands. "I missed you so much," she admitted, face crumpling slowly with the weight of her emotions.

Shay's heart constricted painfully as she wished to fix this for her friend. "I missed you, too."

"Hate to break up the reunion," Michael interrupted, a wry grin on his face as he took them in, "but we need to get out of here."

Shit. He's right.

"Manfri," Shay began. "We need to find—"

A loud boom rattled the windows in their frames.

Shay screamed, her heart pounding as Emilia ducked, turning on her heel toward the intruder. But Michael, Michael just stood there. Staring. Staring at Shay, eyes wide, grin vanishing into a mask of shock.

Time slowed.

Where did the noise come from? Who? We need to get out... Shay couldn't comprehend what she was seeing. Didn't understand. Why wasn't he moving? Didn't—didn't he...

Someone started screaming, the sound muffled as if in another room, while a bead of blood dripped down Michael's nose. It was then Shay's eyes focused on the hole through Michael's forehead, and she realized it had been her who'd been screaming, her body reacting before her mind could catch up.

God, no. Please no. Please. Oh God, oh God. Oh my God.

Michael's knees hit the floor with an impact that stole the scream from her throat. His crumpled form revealing Manfri behind him, pistol still raised.

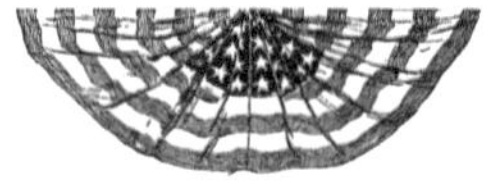

The screams were a sort of devastation I had never heard, and prayed I'd never hear again. The pain and despair tore through my soul like an open wound. The sound unbearable. Gut-wrenching. The type of pain that someone couldn't recover from, and if they did, would never be the same again.

I squatted there, frozen by the sight of the man before us. My father—or rather the man I had thought was my father—holding the gun that just killed my best friend's lover, the man who had taught me how to survive in this century, and possibly the only connection I had to my own lost lover.

Everything in me stilled, and with it, a rage hotter than a thousand suns ignited.

Shay rushed over to Michael, her screams turning to heart-wrenching sobs. Her body heaving as she held onto him, gripping his clothes as if she could shake him awake.

"What did you do?" I asked Manfri, rising to my full height and hiding my trembling hands in my skirt.

"He was working with the enemy," he told me. "He wanted the vials for himself."

I fought the urge to look at the body, at my friend crying into his chest. I knew Michael would get the vials only for Shay and me.

"Was anything you ever told me true?"

The expression of innocence on his face disappeared quickly, leaving behind a stern glare.

"Where are they?" he growled, raising the gun. How many fathers would turn on me today? It was pathetic, really, these men who claimed me as their daughter. They could all rot for all I cared.

"I don't know," I answered honestly. "I assume Boudreaux has—" I looked at his body on the floor and corrected without feeling, "had them. Why don't you ask him?"

He nodded, lowering the gun. "We can find them together, then."

I scoffed. "I'm not doing shit with you."

"Listen, figlia."

"Don't call me that," I hissed. "You lost the right to call me that almost twenty years ago when you started caring more about the vials than your own daughter."

"His spawn," he spat. "I was constantly reminded of what he had done to tua madre. I couldn't let him walk away with *everything*."

"Everything?" I yelled. "You had me! But I wasn't what you really wanted, was I? He had your woman and your precious vials. I was just an inconvenience and revolting reminder of all the ways you failed."

"Sì!" he screamed it so loud I flinched. "I couldn't look at you without seeing him take her from us. It was better that I sent you away."

"Hm," I grunted, understanding why he did it even though it hurt. "I guess you should have made sure I stayed there. Tell me, did you ever think of trading me for them?"

The hurt I saw flit across his features was real, but the guilt was worse.

"I wasn't going to let that man have anything else. At the time, I thought your mammina dead. I would retrieve the vials another way."

"But you never succeeded." I sneered. "You failed and lost everything." The wrath contorting his face told me all I needed to know.

It only took a fleeting, desperate moment for me to become the nightmare I once sought to destroy. After all, I had once promised to love a monster. Why deny the one inside me?

I raised Boudreaux's gun that I'd hidden in my skirts and shot Manfri in the chest right before a slight hand came from behind him, dwarfed by Michael's dagger sliding along his neck for the finishing strike.

The second man I had considered a father figure fell to the floor, revealing a woman with decades of ferocity. I struggled to breathe as I gazed at her, her dark hair cascading down in waves and eyes blazing with vengeance. It took me only a heartbeat to recognize her face. The shock was overwhelming, disbelief flooding my senses. I couldn't believe what I was seeing. Happiness, despair, wonder—all of it sent me to my knees.

"Mammina?"

"Oui, ma fille. I've been searching for you."

CHAPTER FORTY-FIVE

Shaylah & Emilia

July 1863

The rain dripped down Shay's face and soaked through her clothes, but she didn't notice. Couldn't feel the biting cold as they lowered the coffin into the ground. A matching headstone next to it for the two brothers.

The letter had come in the mail of Thomas' death at the Battle of Gettysburg. But she couldn't bring herself to feel it. To feel anything. Knew that her friend had to be hurting as much as her, standing by her side with Libby swaying in her arms, oblivious of what happened to the only father she'd ever known. Shay couldn't bring herself to think of it. To make herself care about anything, actually.

She was hollow. An empty vessel, shipwrecked and sinking to the bottom of the deepest ocean.

She vaguely knew that Boudreaux's and Manfri's men killed each other. The ones who didn't die quickly fled when they found both their leaders slain. Shay only knew this because Henry was the lone man able to take them home. The only one of Michael's who stayed by him in the end.

After everything Michael had done for them, none came to the funeral. She would have hunted each one of them down, dragged them here if she could make herself *feel*.

Nothing mattered anyway.

Nothing matters.

The soft thud of dirt hitting the wood buried the love she once knew. Buried the part of herself that came alive all those months ago.

It doesn't matter.

A loud keening cut off the Priest's words, and Joney tried to dive into the graves of her sons. It didn't matter if they never found Thomas's body. In fact, it was worse because she couldn't put her son to rest. Not really.

It was the same for the two girls she had to throw over the ship all those years ago, meeting a watery grave. Surviving four of her late children was a fate no parent should have to endure. And one that Joney had to do alone while her husband stood there in a stupor, face blank of emotion, as he watched the holes slowly fill.

Shay dimly wondered if she looked like that. A statue. Feeling and showing nothing. Bereft in the sea of mourners.

Why did you leave me?

Maggie grabbed her mother, easily holding her back now that she was the same size as Joney. Her green eyes blazed with a strength Shay didn't feel, even as her features contorted in pain.

When did she grow up? Shay couldn't remember when the girl became a woman, plainly destined for greatness.

For what her brothers desired but could not attain.

There it is. The sharp bite of pain she'd been missing. Indomitable as it was fleeting, it blew away on the storm's wind. There were some sorrows a person couldn't recover from, and Shay didn't have the strength to endure it now.

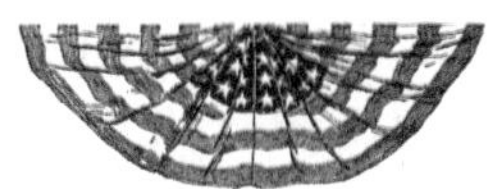

I stared at the headstones while whispering futile reassurances to Libby. I had known Thomas had died already, but I couldn't bring myself to explain it to Shay. She had been detached since Michael's death, and I wasn't even sure I could break through the haze she had succumbed to.

I snuck another glance at her and found no tears. It was like she had no more since the night Michael was killed. As if with his loss, she had lost herself—the very essence of her gone. In fact, I couldn't get any emotion out of her, and it scared the hell out of me.

"It's okay, sweetheart," I muttered while patting Libby's back.

"Mama," she wailed, reaching her small arms out to Shay, who did not seem to hear her.

I winced as Joney let out another blood-curdling wail, and I pulled Libby closer, wishing to shield her from this.

"Give me l'enfant. Oui?" Clementina reached for Libby with the calmness of one who had faced such calamity and grew accustomed to it. My heart pulled for my mammina and the life she bore.

I looked to Shay, a question forming on my lips when I realized I would have to decide. My friend wasn't there. Not really.

I nodded to Clementina, handing a wailing Libby over to her, and watched them walk far enough away from the funeral. A soft singing of a language I'd forgotten carried over to us through the rain, and Libby's cries ceased.

My hand grasped my friend's, squeezing lightly to remind her I was there. My heart thundered in my chest as her cold hand stayed limp in my own. But I held on, determined to bring her out of this. It didn't have to be today. Just...eventually.

Thomas.

The name drifted past my lips, daring to remember. I wondered how it sounded when I called out to him. Did I whisper it when we made love? Or did I scream it out in waves of ecstasy? I might never remember and never get the chance to do it again.

Several minutes passed, my body pulling apart in every different direction, shattering all over again for those I had lost, before a slight squeeze on my hand stilled my rising panic and the despair threatening to eat me alive.

A firm grip held my own.

We'll overcome this together.

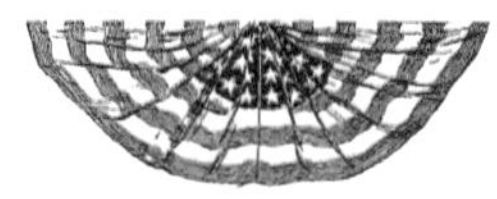

"I wish you wouldn't go," Maggie said as she wrapped a towel over the tea kettle handle.

A week had passed since the funerals, and I dragged Shay to visit the O'Connor women to see how they were faring. It was only fair since she dragged me to Rose and George's to say goodbye to their family that morning, though I couldn't recall the time I'd spent with them.

"I know you don't remember," Maggie continued as if she read my thoughts, "but I've grown to think of you both as sisters."

A pang in my chest had me staring at my hands, clasped around the empty mug. "I know," I said. "We will miss you. But we aren't meant to be here."

Not anymore. Not now that the brothers were gone, and we had the accurate vials to take us back to our own time. If my suspicions were correct, and I fully believed they were, the passage of time should be the same going back. Talking with my mammina, and even Manfri the weeks I had been with him, eighteen years had passed in both the twenty-first century and the nineteenth.

I talked with Clementina after Boudreaux's death. She admitted to not wanting to be responsible for the time-traveling vessels and was relieved to pass them on to us, having no desire to use them herself. No, the danger they posed in the wrong hands was too great. As for other vials, she was uncertain of their existence but wished no others would be made.

My mammina left the decision to stay or leave up to us, a blessing we treasured. It wasn't a difficult choice to make. Shay and I agreed that she needed to be home with her family in a century when Libby could thrive and where Shay could give birth in a hospital. I could tell the thought of having another baby here scared her more than she let on. As for me, though my mammina was here, I could already tell she was getting restless. The emancipation and Boudreaux's death meant most of her family was free. I suspected that she would soon search for them. That was an undertaking I didn't care to share.

No, the family I'd grown up with was back in the twenty-first century, and I needed to return to them. I had finally found the closure I sought, a sense of finality in my journey. And, honestly, I missed them so damn much.

Maggie came over to the table, pouring us some tea. Shay thanked her, seeming to break away some of the shell she had hardened around herself now that she was around Michael's sister. It took several days for Shay to start talking again. Before we came here, she told me what she and Maggie did to get Michael out of prison and what a spitfire the girl was.

The girl's gaze found mine, and my breath caught, fixated on the sharp green as her upturned eyes transfixed me to the spot, almost—almost like—my brow furrowed, trying to recall what I had seen, how it seemed to instill a sense of tranquility through my soul. One quick glance and my entire being filled with a forgotten but marvelous feeling I knew I had experienced.

Like coming home after a long journey.

Home. I had known it for a time. If I could just...

I shook my head and turned my gaze to my hands, disassociating from the moment. From eyes that I—

Maggie's laughter sent shockwaves through my system, and I had to blink back tears.

What is wrong with me?

She gestured with her hands, telling a story of Michael stealing some bread when he was a kid and how Mr. McCusker chased him down the street with a rolling pin. To my surprise, Shay smiled, face beginning to glow again as she held her growing belly and laughed. Actually laughed. I laughed too, even as a part of me twisted painfully, jealousy and guilt that I couldn't do this for her. I hadn't known Michael long enough and forgot the months I'd spent with him. But I couldn't let it bother me. Not when Shay started to break out of her shell.

As I listened to them talk, my negative feelings receded as relief flooded in. And hope. Hope for healing and a better future. We'd get through this.

We had to.

"My brothers were better for knowing you two." I looked up and realized Maggie was talking to me, smiling sadly. "They would never admit it, but I saw change in them."

"Good change, I hope," I said, making them laugh.

The door opened behind me, letting in a windswept Joney, a bundle of meat and bread in her hands. "Emilia," she said, looking stunned to see me before finding Shay. "Shay. What brings ye here?" Then, as if realizing how that sounded, she quickly added, "Not that we don't love your company."

Shay and I shared a look before directing our attention to her. I thought I'd have to speak to the woman whom I only met at the funeral when, to my surprise, Shay spoke first, "We thought we would say goodbye."

A beat of silence. "Ye're leavin'?"

"We are."

Joney and Maggie exchanged a look. She sighed and set the food on the table. "I am sorry to hear that, dear. Though I understand."

We spent the rest of the morning talking about the brothers who had changed our lives. Joney recounted the trouble they got into as boys and how they grew into the men they became. A deep sadness ran within her, but she gave a watery smile, not letting their deaths overshadow their lives. And a piece of me settled, the restlessness within my soul stilled, and I knew I had found what I had come for two years ago.

We stood, and the two of them hugged us, tears still in their eyes even as they gave us bright smiles.

"Thank you," I said, squeezing Joney tighter.

"Whatever for, dear?"

"Letting us into your family." My throat constricted painfully. "For raising those boys who did everything to help us. We wouldn't be here today if it wasn't for them." Hot tears tracked their way down my cheeks to her shoulder. "Thank you."

Her whole body shook with silent sobs as she held onto me, speaking a language I didn't understand. I clung tight, desperate to decipher the meaning, as a shudder ran through me. There was something about the feeling behind the words I couldn't explain. Heavier than a goodbye.

If I could just—

Joney stepped back, cupping my face as she smiled sadly.

"What does that mean?" I croaked past the tears.

She shook her head and pulled my head down, kissing my brow. "Ye are meant for so much. Don't let anything hold ye back. Not anymore."

My gaze darted between each of her eyes, confusion clouding my understanding, knowing her answer and the original response were not the same.

What isn't she telling me? Hold me back?

"But—"

"We'll miss you," Maggie said, taking Joney's place. Each woman embraced us warmly, and we soon made our way out the door, feeling the warmth of their farewell lingering.

Shay passed me, squeezing my hand to pull me out the door when I over-stepped, catching my skirts on a small table and bumped my hip against it, sending papers to the ground.

"I'm so sorry," I mumbled, feeling the heat of embarrassment rising in my cheeks as I bent down to pick up the fallen letters.

I paused.

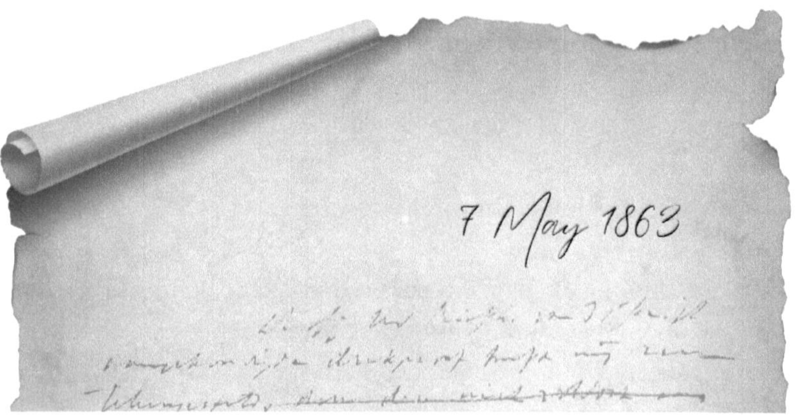

My gaze narrowed, scanning the document only moments before shouts could be heard from outside.

"What is that?" Shay asked, eyes wide, holding her stomach. I stood up, the letters forgotten as I placed them on the table and turned to Maggie and Joney.

"I'm going to go check it out," I told them. "You stay here."

"I'll go with you," Shay said, already opening the door.

"Well, I'm not staying," Maggie declared, throwing a shawl over her shoulders. And before I knew it, all three women were coming with me down the stairs.

"What do you think it could be?" Maggie asked when we rounded the corner of the tenements and emerged on the street. A large crowd grew on the

North End, a hostile one at that. Men and women gathered around, scream-ing something unintelligible, as they surrounded the front of a building.

"What's going on?" I asked a man to my left, pushing closer to the chaos.

"There's to be a draft," he snapped, turning back to the crowd, where I saw two men in the middle. "First draft in the damn nation. I didn't come all the way across the ocean to die in a war that I didn't want."

My stomach turned, worry lacing my nerves as I stared at the men around me. I may have fought, but I chose to do so. What would it be like to fight for a cause you didn't believe in? Or leave family behind that needed you?

I turned to Shay. The lightness of our visit had softened her grief, but this predicament stole that relief and replaced it with trepidation. Anger and desperation hung in the air, thick and suffocating.

"They're the draft agents," she said, pointing to the two haggard men being heckled in the center.

I shook my head. "We should go. This could go badly."

We already dealt with so much. I can't do this. Just the thought of rioting had my stomach turning uncomfortably and a cold sweat covering my body.

Shay readily agreed and turned to the two women with us. "You should go back. You can do nothing to stop this, and you are exempt from what is to come." She had to yell over the shouts and guide Joney and Maggie to a less crowded sidewalk. "Please. Go home. Millie and I are leaving as well."

Joney nodded, but Maggie looked like she wanted to argue.

"We cannot allow them to take our men," Maggie snapped, face contorted in outrage. "I don't care what you say, Mama, I'm staying."

Joney pursed her lips, considering her daughter. After a brief moment, she turned back to Shay. "We will stay. Ye go."

With a few more long hugs, we left the O'Connor women to partake in a fight that was no longer ours. Instead, we searched for a carriage to take us back to Charlestown, where my mammina, Kezia, and Libby waited.

Only, there were no carriages on the street for hire. In the hope of finding one on the next block, we made our way around. The noise grew louder with each step, as if we weren't leaving the mob behind us and heading straight for it.

"Do you think there's more?" Shay asked, holding her belly for support. I needed to get her to a seat. *I shouldn't have brought us here. I'm not prepared for this century. I may have been once, but this is too much. All of this is too much.*

I shook my head, not knowing myself. "I hope not."

We reached Prince Street to find hundreds of people surrounding the Cooper Street Armory.

"What in the hell?"

Men had dug bricks out of the ground and threw them through the armory's windows. A crash and glass shattering created another wave of uproar. *My God.* Screams, curses, and fists flew. Down the street, a smattering of uniforms fell in line—the militia had been sent to dispel the rioters. Shots rang out, and I swept myself around Shay, prepared to take the shots to my back to keep my pregnant friend safe.

"Millie," she whispered in my ear. "It's okay. I think they were blank cartridges."

I looked to find no injuries in the crowd. A woman pushed past us, a child in her arms as she yelled, "I dare ye to shoot now, ye bastards!"

I stared at her in horror as I grabbed Shay's hand and dragged her away from the crowd. "We need to go somewhere else. We can't—"

The crowd surged around us, moving like a tumultuous ocean, pushing, pulling, tearing us apart. I lost Shay in the chaos, my hand torn from hers as they surged me away.

"Shay!" I yelled, trying to see over the heads of so many people. "Shay!"

Not again. The thought invaded my mind, my body, my very soul. Shaking me in ways I didn't understand.

"Cowards!" people screamed at the soldiers as others tried to break into the doors of the armory.

There had to be at least five hundred people here, if not a thousand—primarily immigrants, and all rioting against the draft that would send their men to the battlefield. Too many of them had already died. Women struggled to take care of their families while finding a way to put food on the table; all the while, the war skyrocketed the prices.

This damned war needed to end, or these families would find themselves in graves alongside their men.

A loud bang rang out. I threw myself to the ground, knowing the sound of a cannon like my own name. Debris rained down. And the screams. My God, the *screams*. My whole body shook with them.

Not again, not again, not again.

The panic, the familiar smell of the powder, the gore on the street. It was too much. I couldn't focus, couldn't breathe.

Flashes. So many flashes left me disoriented, stumbling with the influx of them.

And yet, there was one thing I knew for sure. That I kept repeating, or else it'd get lost in the muddle of my head.

I needed to find Shay.

If something happened to her—I shook my head. I couldn't let myself think and consider it. Shay was all right. She had to be. I would overturn this whole damn century before I let anyone else die.

Shoving people out of the way, ignoring those panicking and even the injured, I stopped for no one.

Not anymore.

Men picked up friends and family. Women screamed with crying babies in their arms. The militia yelled and directed others off the street as the police took others in.

I screamed Shay's name again, turning in a full circle when I caught sight of long, curly hair. Skirting around a woman and passing a man with lacerations up his arm and through his jaw, I stumbled sideways, staring at the familiar wounds as I propelled myself toward where I thought I saw Shay.

A few more minutes of chaos until I found her, twisting and turning among everyone in search of me.

I saw her yell over the crowd when she spotted me but could not hear over the screams. I waved like a fool and made my way to her.

"Are you okay?" I asked, looking her over. She looked disheveled, a little dirty, and was holding her belly, but all right.

"Yes, you?"

I nodded, barely registering her inquiry as I pulled her away. "Let's go."

We hurried down an alley, desperate to escape the chaos behind us. It would take us several hours to find a carriage and a way back to Charlestown when it should have been only thirty minutes. During that time, I was too preoccupied with over-worrying about Shay's safety to even begin ruminating on what I recalled.

As we crossed the bridge, I stared at the river's rushing water and started to piece together the flashes the cannon resurfaced—everything that had happened—and what it meant for the future.

Squeezing my fists to still their shaking, I let the fury consume me.

CHAPTER FORTY-SIX

Shaylah

1863 ~ Charlestown, Massachusetts

Shay took a last look around the pub, trying to absorb everything from the beginning. Michael had built this. Well, he did not precisely build it, but purchased and started the business for his family. She wondered if the picture of him and Thomas opening the pub would be gone when she returned. *It has to be.* Tears welled in her eyes. *It was our fault. If we never came, those boys would still be alive.* The weight of her guilt was crushing, and she almost staggered back with the impact of it.

The O'Connors had been there almost daily, picking up where their son left off. To know how much Michael had changed, tried to be better, made his death all the worse for them. Not that they hadn't grieved before, but to know what type of man he had become without realizing it, without acknowledging it, and telling him how proud they were. That was something they couldn't get back, and she knew it crushed Joney inexplicably.

Shay sighed, tears falling as she grabbed Libby.

"You remember what to do?" Millie asked her.

Clementina and Kezia were off to the side, seemingly giving them privacy while they prepared. The girl had grown on Shay when they were in that house. She would miss Millie's little sister. It was too bad that Millie wouldn't get to know her more.

Shay nodded. "I don't know how I could forget that experience." She arched a brow. "Dead ancestors all over me and all."

Millie smiled weakly. "I—" She swallowed. "I may not remember everything that happened here, but I know I couldn't have done any of it without you."

Shay's face contorted. "You went above and beyond for me, Mill. You were willing to die for me. I'll spend the rest of my life making it up to you."

Something changed in her friend's expression, an emotion Shay couldn't quite place. She grabbed Millie's hand, squeezing lightly. "I love you," she said.

Tears lined Millie's eyes as well. "I love you, too."

Libby leaned over and pulled Millie's hair, making them laugh as she yanked so hard that Millie's head jerked to the side.

"You, devil," Millie laughed, trying to pry the girl's tiny hand open. When she was free of Libby's death grip, she tickled the girl until she broke into giggles.

"Okay," Millie said, looking around the room. "I think it's time."

Clementina and Kezia came over, embracing each of them tightly. "I wish we had more," Clementina said, the emotion in her voice making it harder to understand her deep accent. "But I understand you must go where you belong. Oui?"

Shay hugged Libby tighter, wishing she could visit them and the others she'd become close with whenever she wanted. But they weren't merely moving. They would have to stay in the twenty-first century where they belonged, and there was no going back.

Millie grabbed Libby so Shay could put on the rosary and retrieve the vials. Kissing noises and giggles filled the room, and suddenly, Shay felt thankful for them. She had had enough misery for a lifetime. It was fitting they left on a good note.

Millie was playing with Libby's curls and straightening her dress when Shay looked up, ready for her daughter and this miserable journey to end.

"Okay." Millie sighed, handing Libby over.

Shay knew Mill wouldn't admit it, but there was a sadness in her friend's eyes, a tension along her shoulders. She was going to miss this time.

"Show me how to do this," Millie continued, meeting her gaze. "You go first."

"It's simple, really." Even if it was difficult, Clementina could probably show her if Millie had questions. Still, Shay went over the steps and gave a sad smile. "We'll see you on the other side," she said, upending the bottle and sprinkling it over her and Libby.

She gazed at the three women as the world tilted. Their exotic beauty struck her with wonder and affection, each distinct yet equally bewitching. She knew she'd have loved the other two as much as Millie if given time.

Shay was struck by a profound realization when she saw the expression on her friend's face. The emotions she read there tore at her heart, plunging her into darkness as time seemed to shred her soul.

CHAPTER FORTY-SEVEN

Emilia

2 Years Later ~ Charlestown, Massachusetts

I turned my face to the sun, letting its warmth soothe my sore muscles as
I took a break from working in the pub all day. A soft breeze picked up,
cooling my hot skin.

I took a deep breath, looked at the familiar buildings around me, and
smiled. A cacophony of everyday life flourished as people went about their
day. A young boy laughed, dark hair flopping over his forehead as he ran
around, and my heart constricted.

At that moment, I could see the old and new city weaving together. And I
missed it. It had been two years, and I still missed the city that I would never
see again. The life that I had to leave behind.

God, I missed him so much. When my memories returned, I had trouble
differentiating between the lies, deceptions, and the truth. Even now, I don't
quite understand it all. For a time, I couldn't see past the rage, the bitter
resentment I felt about how it all turned out. If I hadn't lost my memory,
if Thomas stayed with me instead of going back into battle, if Michael just
told us sooner about Boudreaux, about what he'd been planning all those
months, things might have ended differently.

He might still be alive.

I sighed, stretching my arms in the air as I turned to go back into the pub.

I had no more anger, only a yawning emptiness I could never entirely fill. I mostly ignored it by more work and bitter denial.

A rumble of wheels, a hushed conversation, and a door slammed. I continued inside, ignoring the pedestrians on the street as I opened the door. I barely made it in when I was suddenly hit with overwhelming emotion, making me trip on the step before catching myself on the doorframe.

What the hell?

I stood there, frozen, trying to figure out what my body told me. The skin prickled across my back, and my breath stalled in my chest as all my thoughts seemingly emptied out of my head.

I spun around as my heart soared. Confusion flooded my system, my body reacting before my mind could decipher the meaning. It was as if—I shook my head. It couldn't be.

The heat spreading within my body told me otherwise.

A driver went by, the light rumble of the wheels drawing my attention across the street.

My world narrowed until it felt like a raging storm within me, swirling and morphing into something that mere words couldn't explain. It was like my body had come alive for the first time in years, awakening sensations I had long forgotten. Like flowers bursting forth from the ground in the spring, and an eagle soaring over a mountaintop, the tumultuous power of a waterfall just before the plunge. Beautiful, all-consuming, and terrifying.

Green eyes found mine, searing my soul and settling something within me.

Thomas.

My breath came out in a whoosh.

He removed his cap from his head, the navy blue worn and faded from years of battle, revealing his mass of dark hair flopping across his forehead. It was longer than I've ever seen it. I scanned his body, looking for any signs of injury.

Intact. He was intact. Thomas was okay.

The soft clop of the horse's hooves faded as we stared at one another.

He survived the war. Made it to the end.

Those two years I waited, all those months I spent fuming at his deception. How could he let me believe he was dead? I had my suspicions when I found the letters at the O'Connors.

Then, when the cannon went off, and my memories flooded my system, I was so *angry*. Furious that he could lead me to believe he was dead just so I could go back to the twenty-first century.

To his credit, he had been MIA for some time. They had reported his death, only to find him in a field hospital with a bullet to the shoulder. Knowing how it was in war, I wasn't surprised.

I knew I couldn't tell Shay what I'd planned. Not when I knew she'd choose to stay. My deception ate away at me for the whole first year until I wrote her a letter explaining why I had to stay. I had hoped that she would discover it in the attic with the others and find it in her heart to forgive me over time.

God, I missed her so much.

Thomas stepped off the curb, and I held my breath, frozen as we soaked each other in. He was thinner than I remembered, worn, and more lines creased his face, giving him a more mature, rugged appearance. Before, I didn't think he could get any more handsome. Damn, was I wrong. Even so, I couldn't ignore the tension and the devastation written on his features after surviving what he had.

I wanted to tell him that I loved him, hated him for lying, and yet loved him nevertheless. I wanted to scream it from the building and claim him in front of everyone, but I couldn't admit it just yet. I would love Thomas anyway, any time, any form that I could take him.

I nervously trailed my hands down my dress—a bright Romani style that I'd taken to wearing—and wondered what he thought of me. I'd gained the weight I'd lost, and my hair grew. I refrained from touching the bangles and earrings my mammina gave me before she left. Instead, I straightened, letting him take in my new appearance. By the darkening of his eyes, I guessed he liked it.

My heart fluttered as he stepped onto the curb, taking me in. I thought it would race and imagined I'd run into his arms, but it wasn't like that. It wasn't a rush of excitement or a burst of affection.

Peace.

After two years, an inexplicable sense of calm washed over me, leaving me finally settled after being lost for so long.

"Ye're still here," he said, looking torn between angry and hopeful. Good, after what he pulled, I wanted to play.

"And you're still alive." I bit my lip, trying to keep myself from climbing him.

It had been two years since he had thought I had left, and he could have lost interest or found another woman. That nearly tore me apart every night as I wondered what he was up to.

"Ye don't look as surprised as me," he said, the column of his throat bobbing.

After I recovered my memories, I told Joney not to tell Thomas I'd stayed. He needed to focus on the war, not worry about me. It was then that Joney told me what Sullivan had done, how he picked up a rifle from a fallen soldier and shot a Confederate before he could kill Thomas. The reality that he almost died, that they *thought* he was dead long enough for a letter to be sent home, still turned my stomach. The fear that it had been so close to being true, that Thomas could have been lost, was a feeling I couldn't shake.

If Sullivan wasn't there... I couldn't let myself think of it.

Now, Thomas chuckled, the deep rumble erupting butterflies in my belly and warmth through my limbs. "Ye never do what ye are told. Do ye?"

I shrugged, feeling a smile begin to tug on my lips. "I learned from the best."

"Oh, aye? And who is that?" he asked with a hint of jealousy, feeling the situation out. "A new man in your life?"

Oh yes, definitely jealous.

"You." I smiled. Thomas squinted at me in suspicion as I stepped toward him. "I missed you."

His eyes softened, studying me as if I were a ghost, and he wasn't sure he could believe it. I suppose, with the way things went, maybe I was. Slowly, he reached out, brushing his fingers over my cheek and through my hair, marveling at the dark strands that shone in the sun. I leaned into his touch, not caring who saw us.

Thomas let his hand draw a path down my neck and arm, sending ripples of goosebumps across my flesh before he grabbed my hand, interweaving his fingers with mine. He lifted our hands so that they hovered in front of us. "Ye still wear it." He eyed the bracelet that he'd made me when we were married.

"Yes." My heart thundered in my chest.

His green eyes met mine, searching and absolutely ravenous. "Have ye been faithful, wife?"

My gaze shot to his, and my stomach dropped when I thought of Charles and what I did to help Miriam. I'd spent two years preparing what to say to Thomas and couldn't think of one that would make a difference at this moment. If I remembered Thomas before it happened, I never would have...

My emotions must have been warring on my face because his grip tightened, and his jaw clenched before his whole body relaxed. "Worry not, lass. Your actions were your own. It is what I wanted."

"Thomas, my memory—"

He smiled crookedly, and his gaze sharpened and consumed me wholly. But the knot in his throat bobbed, and I knew it was something we'd need to work through.

"Ye are mine, either way." The glint in his gaze made my body flush with desire. Yeah, we'd work through it later.

I stepped closer, so close I could smell the warmth of the sun on his uniform and the underlying scent of man. I gripped his jacket and pulled him flush to me. "Okay." I swallowed past the lump in my throat and gave a mischievous grin. "So, tell me, what woman will I have to kill, husband?"

Thomas dragged his teeth over the short beard under his lip and considered me. "I thought ye gone."

I ran my hands up his chest and behind his neck, ignoring the twist and drop of my stomach. "I don't blame you. Just give me a name, and I'll take care of her." I pulled his face to mine, breathing him in. I couldn't look away from his lips. *Mine.* My fingers trailed along his neck and across his cheek until they traced a path over his mouth.

"I haven't been with a woman since ye, gypsy."

My eyes shot to his. "Truly?"

"Aye. I told ye I'd never want another woman again. I suppose it's time to buy ye a proper ring."

My heart swelled in my chest.

We stared for several heartbeats until I surged onto my toes and collided my lips onto his. It started out slow, sensual, sending shockwaves to my fingertips. As it deepened, heat blossomed in my belly, making my knees weak so that the only thing holding me upright was his arm around my waist while his other hand gripped my hair, bending my head back for better access. My hands glided down his arms, over his muscular chest, up to his face, every part of him that I could touch in public.

The kiss felt like an eternity, yet it left me yearning for more, wishing I could do it forever. Well, I guess I could now that Thomas was back with me.

I smiled, and he pulled back, breathing hard as he leaned his forehead against mine. "I thought I wouldn't ever get the chance to do that to ye again."

"Mm," I agreed, mind still fuzzy. "I can think of something else we haven't done in a while."

His deep laugh rumbled through my chest as he shook his head. "I should've known."

"Known what?" I mumbled, running my fingers through his rough whiskers.

"That ye would come back to me."

I leaned in and whispered into his ear, "Not even time could keep me away from you."

I had the privilege of witnessing Thomas' eyes transition from a soft moss green to a lush Irish field. Wrapping my arms around his neck, I promised to never let him go again. "I saw one of the letters you sent your mom," I said. "I didn't have my memories back yet, but I learned enough about you since my injury." I explained to him everything that happened since regaining my memory. "I almost left with Shay, but I looked at the date and knew I couldn't go. I chose to stay at the last minute, knowing Shay wouldn't return home if she knew what I planned. I couldn't leave knowing there was a chance you'd make it out of there." My face fell. "How could you let me think you died?"

He had the decency to look guilty. "I thought it was best for ye. Being in your own time."

"This is my time."

We stared at each other as he considered that, and I watched his features soften as he heard the truth in it. I gave a small smile. "Your mom told you about the pub, then?" I asked.

"Aye," he said, eyeing the building behind me. I knew Joney sent a letter about Michael's death and the pub he left them, but I wasn't sure how much he knew about it. I wondered, not for the first time, if the pictures changed in the future. Thomas took on a sad, thoughtful expression. "He really turned around. Didn't he?"

I looked back at the pub and nodded. "Yeah," I agreed, wishing Michael could be here now to see it flourish.

We'd finished it in '63, and it had grown popular this past year. Michael really could have made something out of it. I refused to wonder about Shay's baby, whether it was a girl or a boy. What kind of dad Michael would be.

I missed my friends.

"He saved me," I admitted. "Well, he helped me with Shay in the end. With Boudreaux. He never gave up." I gripped my chest, wishing I could stop the ache inside.

Thomas cupped my face and smiled sadly, unshed tears lining his eyes. "I rather regret the time I lost with him."

"He loved you."

"I know."

Thomas let his forehead drop to mine, and we stood there, letting the world pass us by as we allowed ourselves this moment. Eventually, Thomas pulled back and gave me a soft kiss.

"The boys will be home soon, I expect," he said, changing the subject.

I smiled then, knowing Hiram and Jackson were expected to be discharged from the 54th Regiment within the next few months. Though, it still pained me to think about Isaac and Sam, who both died at Fort Wagner in '63.

"Yes, I'm sure Mira will be excited to see her husband again." I waggled my brows, making us both laugh.

"I can't believe I missed it," he said.

I shrugged. "He missed ours, too."

"True." Thomas sighed and turned to the building. He grabbed my hand, giving it a light squeeze. "Show me," he said, jutting his chin to O'Connor's Pub.

I grinned, excited for him to see all the work we'd put into it. "I think you'll like it."

I started to pull him to the door when he jerked me to a stop.

"What?" I gasped, my heart accelerating.

Is it too much? Maybe he doesn't want to see it. My worries must have shown on my face because his softened. Thomas enveloped me in his arms, his embrace firm and comforting. He pressed his face against my neck, eliciting a surprised squeal from me.

"I love ye, me gypsy," he murmured in my ear, sending shivers down my spine. "I couldn't bear another moment without telling ye."

I brushed my lips against his, my smile wide and blazing against his. "I love you too, O'Connor."

It was there that I found where I belonged—not in a time or a place, but in Thomas's arms.

Thomas O'Connor was my home. And I was his.

Where we belonged.

Epilogue

Present Day ~ Charlestown, MA

The long string of the apron fumbled through Shay's fingers as she tied it around her waist, readying for her shift at the pub when a loud thud and suspicious mumbling of children broke out.

"What are you guys doing?" Shay yelled to the four kids in the dining area.

She cursed under her breath, hoping they didn't break anything. Millie's brother, Sean, was in the back finishing up some inventory before taking the kids home. The doors would be open to customers in a few minutes.

Sean had taken his new role as pub owner from his parents and often found himself working longer hours. Shay helped him in any way she could around her usual evening shift.

They both loved it, even if for wholly different reasons. However, the one they shared was the most important: it connected them to those they lost.

Emilia.

Michael.

Shay's chest tightened, her heart giving a familiar sore throb.

Time didn't always heal. Not fully.

"Not getting into trouble, I hope," she said loud enough for them to hear but to be ignored, no less.

Shay sighed even as a grin tugged at the corner of her lips.

She found them sitting at the few tables under the wall of old pictures, one off the wall and in her daughter's hands.

Her smile slipped.

"Tell me the story now, Mama," Michaela said. Her daughter never asked and always demanded, but Shay kept the details of the past to a minimum.

Shay looked at the photo of Emilia and Thomas standing in front of the pub with their three kids. The pictures showed up the day she returned, and she knew her friend had chosen to stay behind.

It hurt knowing Millie decided to stay without telling her. Shay realized it the moment she looked at her, Clementina, and Kezia, and there was nothing she could do to stop time. She'd already poured the vial over her and Libby. She was infuriated with Millie for a while, but how could she stay angry once she saw the picture? Not when her friend had her chance at love. She couldn't deny anyone that, not after losing Michael.

Since then, she had been just sad. Even now, looking at the picture, it was bittersweet. A tiny smirk curved Thomas' lips as if he was trying not to smile. Emilia leaned down, holding the youngest boy still. The kids looked particularly rowdy. Shay smiled, thinking they must have gotten it from Thomas. The photo perfectly captured her friend's face, joy radiating off it as her dark hair was pulled back in soft waves. The little boy tugged on her arm, and the older two—a girl and boy—looked on at the photographer.

Shay didn't know if the photographer couldn't take a better one, if it was too expensive for another shot, or if they chose this one to capture the essence of their family, but it was real.

It made Shay inexplicably happy that Millie found her place.

The photo of Michael and Thomas opening the pub had vanished. She wished she had it. Even now, tears welled in Shay's eyes, but they didn't fall. She'd have to keep the memory of his face confined within the recesses of her mind.

The pub was the last gift Michael had given them. It still constricted her throat with a mixture of happiness and grief. She was happy that Michael finally turned his life around but incredibly sad that he couldn't live out his dream with her, with their daughters.

Shay ruffled Michaela's brown curls and stared into pale blue eyes that she got from her daddy. What was the harm in telling her a little bit?

"That is your Auntie Milia," Shay said, rubbing her thumb over her daughter's cheek, thinking of how much Kaylah reminded her of Michael. "She helped run this pub a long, long time ago. It used to be a boarding house upstairs where they would help new immigrants get on their feet and assimilate."

"Who are immigrants, and why can't they get on their feet?" Michaela scrunched up her nose in confusion. She was only eight but full of curiosity. More times than not, it led her into trouble, which was another thing she inherited from her daddy.

Shay sighed, shook her head, amused, and gently pulled the picture out of her daughter's hands. She hung it back on the wall as she explained. "They helped people who came from far away and gave them a place to stay in until they could find another home to live in."

"Oh." Kayla dragged out the word so long that Shay was unsure if the girl understood. "Why don't we see her anymore?"

"Ugh, Kayla," Libby scoffed in annoyance. "You know we left her behind."

Shay frowned, seeing Sean watching the exchange from the doorway. He went to her, grabbed her hand, and slowly rubbed her new engagement ring in soothing motions.

"Your mama did not leave my sister," Sean explained. "Millie chose to stay with Thomas because she loved him."

Shay looked up at Sean and smiled gratefully.

It had been eight years since she returned. It had been hard at first, getting on her feet with two babies to take care of by herself. And then, when Sean's wife had passed, he was left wholly devastated, running the pub and taking care of his twins. They leaned on each other for a few years before deciding to try dating. It was one of the best decisions Shay had ever made. She couldn't stop grinning when she thought about Sean confessing his childhood crush on her.

Life took some unexpected turns, but they all led back to each other.

"Dad," Gracie mumbled in her pre-teen angst as she checked her nails. "You're so gross."

"What can I say? I'm a sucker for love," Sean said, leaning in to kiss his fiancée.

The kids let out a collective groan.

"I miss her," Liam said, still staring at the picture. He was particularly close to his aunt Milia and still talked about her consistently. After the photographs had shown up, there was nothing she could do but explain to Sean and his family their journey to the past. Emilia's letters had done the rest.

"But why does it look so old?" Michaela asked, inspecting the photo. "And why is she wearing those weird clothes?"

Shay laughed and squeezed her daughter's shoulders. "It was a different time, sweetie."

"You mean my daddy's time? You said he was from a special time."

"Yes." Shay smiled sadly.

A day didn't go by that she didn't think of Michael and the time they shared together. Their love burned so intensely, no matter how brief, that it would smolder deep in her soul until her last breath. An ache throbbed in her chest.

"I promise to explain it to you when you're older. Just know she was—is my best friend and your Uncle Sean's sister."

"Adopted sister," Gracie muttered. "Technically, she would be his great, great, great grandma or something."

Shay paused, looking back at the picture. She never thought of it like that before. The blood drained from her head as she realized Sean wouldn't be here right now if they had never gone back in time. Maybe—maybe they were always supposed to be there. At least, it would make sense for Millie to stay; she was born in that century.

A slight grin blossomed on her face.

"Eww," Libby said. "That's so weird."

"I don't get it," Michaela said, shrugging out of her mother's grip with indignation. "Can we go play?"

"Just for a bit," Shay said, but her daughters were already thundering up the stairs. "Just don't get into anything you shouldn't! You're leaving soon!"

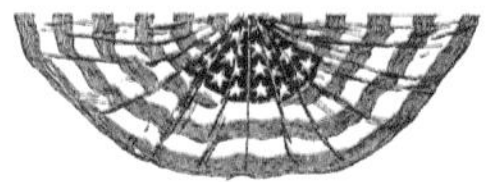

The girls reached the top steps when Libby turned to Michaela, ignoring her mother's warning. "Wanna see something cool?" she asked.

"Sure! What is it?"

"You'll see." Libby led her sister to the front room containing the attic door. She climbed onto the desk and pulled the string to lower the steps.

"It looks scary," Michaela whispered, but excitement drove her to follow her sister into the darkness instead of fear.

Libby turned on the flashlight she had grabbed from the desk and guided her sister to the other side of the attic. The beam of light landed on a large chest, illuminating years' worth of dust.

"This has all the stuff from where Auntie Milia is," Libby explained. She lifted the top up and sneezed, sending dust flying everywhere. "We wore this." She held up a rosary, its twin lying in the trunk. She pointed to the last vial, not daring to pick it up. "Then poured that on our head."

"Wow." Michaela sighed in delight and reached for the vial.

"Don't touch it!" Libby screamed, making Michaela jump back. "Those are so dangerous. Mama would kill you."

"Then it just takes you there?" Michaela asked.

Libby nodded, lifting an old flag and different papers.

"Mama cried when she read one of these. She said Auntie Milia explained to her why she had to stay." Libby shrugged.

"It's no fair you all got to meet her, and I didn't." Michaela crossed her arms in frustration.

"I don't even really remember her," Libby admitted, putting everything back. "She was nice, I guess."

"Well, I'm going to go see her one day."

"Don't be stupid." Libby rolled her eyes. "C'mon, let's go before Mama finds out I showed you."

Michaela slowly followed her sister down the stairs, thinking it wasn't all that stupid.

After all, her daddy was from that time, so why wasn't she?

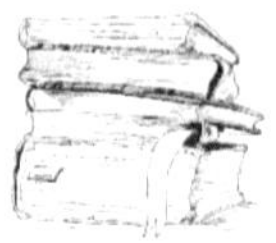

Translations

1. An leanbh – The baby

2. Aye, mo leanbh – Yes, my child.

3. Cuil, mo ghrá. Faigh an chinniúint atá tuillte agat. Beidh mé leat i gcónaí. Más rud é nach bhfuil sa saol seo, ansin an chéad cheann eile. Gheobhaidh m'anam mise i gcónaí - Fly, my love. Find the destiny you deserve. I will always be with you. If not in this lifetime, then the next. My soul will always find yours.

4. Dia cabhrú liom. Tá tú ar buile, a bhean - God help me. You are mad, lady

5. Femme – Woman

6. Figlia – Daughter

7. Grá – love

8. Iníon mo chroí – Daughter of my heart

9. Je suis désolé d'avoir douté de toi, mon amour. Vous savez à quel point je peux être jaloux - I'm sorry for doubting you, my love. You

know how jealous I can be.

10. Kumpania – A group or band of Roma

11. L'enfant. Oui? – The child. Yes?

12. Mère – Mother

13. Mo ghrá – My love.

14. Oui – Yes

15. Oui, ma fille – Yes, my girl.

16. Salope – You, bitch.

17. Se tout pou mwen nan fen an – It's all for me in the end

18. Siúcra. – Sugar

19. Sono tuo – I'm yours

20. Sucre – Sugar

21. Tá mé faoi chomaoin agat, mo ghrá. Anois agus go deo. Caithfidh mé mo shaol ag déanamh suas duit é. - I am indebted to you, my love. Now and forever. I will spend my life making it up to you.

22. Tá tú ag dul a aiféala an lá a rinne Dia tú - You are going to regret the day God made you.

23. Tá grá agam duit – I love you

24. Ti voglio bene anch'io – I love you too

25. Tua madre – Your mother

The author translated these to the best of her ability. However, she is not fluent in either language and apologizes for any mistakes.

<h1 style="text-align:center">Author's Note</h1>

Cultures

As an American with deep roots in Ireland, the story of the 28th Massachusetts Regiment resonated deeply with me when I learned about it in college. It would be several years before I set out to learn more about the Irish regiment for the creation of this series.

In historical fiction, we must research, travel (when we can), and gather input and insight from others, especially when dealing with other cultures. I have visited Boston several times, and it is one of my favorite places. It was exciting to see the North End (Little Italy) today compared to the Irish streets of the 19th century!

My book portrays various cultures and people, hoping to reflect the world's diversity. I wanted to acknowledge the prejudices of this heavily conflicted time, with characters who fought against them or struggled to understand why change was needed. And in doing so, as their understanding of the topic grew, so did their character growth.

I have strived to represent each culture with the utmost respect, and I sincerely hope that I have succeeded. If not, I am always open to input and seek to learn more with each book.

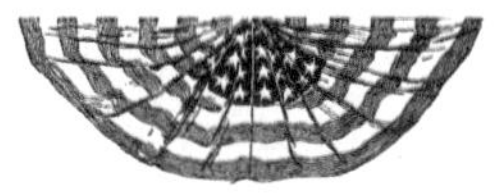

Real People, Places, & Events

Possible spoilers! Wait to read until you finished the book.

Naturally, I wanted to create characters to join Emilia and Thomas on their journey and into battle, but I wanted to make them historically accurate (with some exceptions). To do so, I researched the 28th Massachusetts Regiment and the men who joined in December 1861, particularly in Company C.

I must note that the following men were likely heroes. They did not try to capture, befriend, or fall in love with a fellow female soldier (that I know of). Out of respect for these men, we should consider them heroes and not the villains of my story.

- Barton - Henry Barton, a laborer from Braintree, was wounded and missing in several battles, but he did not perish at the hands of an enraged Irishman, as in *The War Between Us*, and was mustered out on 17 October 1864.

- Brennan, Captain John H. was in charge of Company C until he was severely injured on 17 September 1862. He resigned and was discharged in March 1863.

- Currivan - Wiliam Currivan, a bootmaker from East Stoughton, was wounded and missing in the same battle as Barton, The Second Battle of Bull Run. However, he had been discharged several months later for his wounds and would rejoin a different regiment.

- Corby, Father William – Served as a Priest for the 28th Massachusetts Regiment and prayed over the soldiers. However, he did not marry Emilia and Thomas!

- Driscoll- Jeremiah Driscoll, a laborer in Boston, was wounded in Fredericksburg and discharged several months later.

- Hall—I wanted to capture George W. Hall in his most authentic form, and I imagined he would have been as much as I described him in the story! A painter from Boston, he was wounded at Chantilly on 1 September 1862 and discharged that December, the exact dates as described in the book.

- Mick - John McNamee, a stonecutter in Boston, had been wounded and made prisoner at James Island, South Carolina. Mick died as a Prisoner of War a month later in Charleston, S.C. I continue to imagine Emilia fighting for him and mourning his loss at his unfortunate demise. I hope he had someone to care for him in real life as he did in this book.

* Sullivan - Dennis Sullivan, a laborer in Boston, would have stayed by Thomas's side until he was discharged for disability on 12 April 1864.

Names of officers and more can be found here:

—. n.d. *Regimental Roster.* Accessed 2024. https://28thmass.org/Com pyC/CompC.htm.

The Cameron Highlanders of the 79th New York Emilia remarks upon did fight along Company C, as did the other regiments mentioned throughout the battles. I had painstakingly researched each battle and their layouts, where the regiments would be placed, where they would eventually fight, and whether they would impact the 28th Massachusetts. Though I had taken artistic liberties with Thomas and Emilia, the battles, including the weather, were accurately described to the best of my abilities. If a report said it rained or the sun was scorching, I ensured Emilia and Thomas experienced every bit of the reality.

Chapter 28: I want to note that soldiers did indeed see the Northern Lights on the battlefield in Fredericksburg, Virginia. I couldn't pass up that remarkable detail.

Also, in Chapter 28, after Thomas leaves Emilia wounded with John and Miriam, he encounters General Edwin Sumner, the commander of the 2nd Corps, who asks where the rest of Thomas' company is. This, in fact, happened! Though with an unnamed soldier. It worked so perfectly with my story that I had to make that soldier Thomas.

Source: Infantry, 28th Massachusetts Volunteer. n.d. *Regimental History:*

1862. Accessed 2024. https://www.28thmass.org/history3.htm#:~:text=When%20Gen.%20Edwin%20Sumner%2C%20commander%20of%20the%202nd,soldier%20replied%3A%20%22This%20is%20all%20my%20company%2C%20sir.%22

Chapter 42: "Nearly half of the 28th Massachusetts Regiment was either killed or taken prisoner, leaving 107 men dead or captured."

Source: —. n.d. *Regimental History: 1863.* Accessed 2024. https://28thmass.org/history5.htm.

Chapter 45: The Draft Riots of 1863 did occur. However, the riot on Prince Street in the North End occurred in the morning, while the Cooper Street Armory happened later in the afternoon, and not at the same time as in my story. This worked best for the plot and showed the real reactions of the people, the targeted draft agents, and the conflict that ultimately led to the loss of lives.

Acknowledgements

I want to thank everyone who listened to me talk about this series for the last three years. I hope it was so much that you now feel like you live in 19th-century Boston, a setting that holds a special place in my heart and the story! Don't run into any gangs while you're there. Well, if you do, ask for an O'Connor...

Thank you to everyone who has taken the time to read it, judge it, and tear it apart! I'm just kidding. Thank you all for reading my baby. I wouldn't have been able to do this without your input, any review you gave, and (of course) your interest.

ARC readers! I can't express how unbelievably happy I am that you showed interest in my work! It makes my little heart swell. My life would be more challenging if you weren't here to help propel my book into the world.

I want to thank my father for listening to my rant about derailing trains, whether it was believable, and for your suggestions after reading it! Also, thank you for the input on the fighting scenes. I hope I did well with them!

Thanks to my mother, who provided me with day-by-day updates while reading. I hope I didn't traumatize you! Your involvement and endless support mean the world to me.

I want to thank my family, especially each of my grandmas, for always asking about my writing, whether I'm done yet, and encouraging me to keep going. I tried to warn you! Again, I'm sure there was some trauma in there. We can discuss it at the next family gathering. (Ha)

My husband is privileged to be my sounding board for every minor inconvenience. Thank you for looking mildly interested in my plot holes and formatting woes. I will continue to plague you with each book I write. Mwah!

Shelby, Kelley, Katie, and Michelle, I can always count on you to keep my TikTok and Instagram views up! Your support means the world to me! Shelby, my murder guru, I hope I did well by you. I only plan on getting more gruesome and elaborate from here. Be ready! And Michelle, I told you not to worry, IT would happen! Was it enough? ;)

Hailie Camarillo, my brilliant editor, I'm deeply grateful for your enthusiasm in taking on my second book. I especially appreciate your willingness to return to the 19th century!

And to you, dear readers, I owe a debt of gratitude. Your interest in the voices and places in my head has made them more tangible. They may exist if we all know them, and we can keep them alive together. With your help, I hope Emilia, Thomas, Michael, and Shay will continue to flicker through time as their story is shared and passed around.

And maybe a wee bit more time travel will be needed in the future. Or shall we say, "A lass in the past?"

Aye, I think so.

About Author

Tara Nolan was born and raised sandwiched between The Great Lakes, where she has dwelled in the Mitten state ever since. She occupies a house with her three gremlins, a husband she has known since the first grade, and their various creatures. She can be found drinking coffee, reading, listening to the wind in the trees, or looking for possible fae traps that will send her into a different realm!

Now that Tara has finished the *Fearless Sons of Erin and the Time-Traveller Series*, she plans to focus on the book that started her journey, *When Darkness Calls*. It will be the first book in the fantasy romance *Fallen Kingdoms Trilogy*. And now that you have read *The War Between Us* be sure to look out for Kayla's journey and where (or to whom!) she might go! Be sure to let Tara know if you want to join the ride.

You can interact with Tara on Facebook, TikTok, and Instagram @author.taranolan or her website authortaranolan.com.

Sláinte!

Possible Trigger Warnings

This series contains dark elements throughout the story. A list of some triggers has been provided for you to make the best decision for your mental health: violence, death, murder, explicit romance, birth, gore/brutality, miscarriage, war/PTSD, and off-page SA talked about from book one.

Proceed with caution and enjoy the ride!